Trudi Pacter, a former I
chronicling the lives of t
years. She is the highly a
Kiss and Tell, *Screen Kiss*
is married to Baronet Sir

By the same author

Kiss and Tell
Screen Kisses
The Sleeping Partner

TRUDI PACTER

Living Doll

Grafton
An Imprint of HarperCollins*Publishers*

Grafton
An Imprint of HarperCollins*Publishers*
77–85 Fulham Palace Road,
Hammersmith, London W6 8JB

Special overseas edition 1992
9 8 7 6 5 4 3 2 1

First published in Great Britain by
HarperCollins*Publishers* 1992

Copyright © Trudi Pacter 1992

The Author asserts the moral right to
be identified as the author of this work

ISBN 0 586 21187 X

Set in Sabon

Printed in Great Britain by
HarperCollinsManufacturing Glasgow

All rights reserved. No part of this publication may be reproduced, stored in a retrieval system, or transmitted, in any form or by any means, electronic, mechanical, photocopying, recording or otherwise, without the prior permission of the publishers.

This book is sold subject to the condition that it shall not, by way of trade or otherwise, be lent, re-sold, hired out or otherwise circulated without the publisher's prior consent in any form of binding or cover other than that in which it is published and without a similar condition including this condition being imposed on the subsequent purchaser.

To Nigel, my husband

1

Essex and London, 1963

Liz knew she didn't stand a chance of winning. Not a chance in hell. Not with Rita Morton in the line-up. Rita Morton and Sally Phillips.

It was odd because she'd always looked down on them. At school she could run faster, read faster, get higher marks in anything they went in for. But now that coming top really mattered, Sally and Rita were streets ahead of her.

Rita, Sally and Liz – the sexiest girls at Westcliffe High. Sally and Rita, fair and freckled. Liz, their best friend and competitor, dark and sly like an Italian street urchin. The three girls had been inseparable since the first year. Now they were all studying for their 'A' levels and thinking of the world beyond school. Rita and Sally knew they would get married sooner or later, so they planned on being secretaries until that happened. Liz wanted something better: she wanted to be a film star, or a top model on the pages of *Vogue*. She didn't put herself down for secretarial school. Instead she just dreamed and drifted and hoped that something would turn up. And it did.

The Southend Pier Beauty Contest announced itself on the 'Entertainments' pages of the local paper. It wasn't like any of the other line-ups, for the judges weren't looking for a professional beauty queen. They wanted a different kind of contestant. Someone younger, thinner, less experienced. The first prize wasn't the usual ten pounds and a night on the town either. The first prize was a modelling course at the Lucie Clayton School, with the added incentive of earning a place on the agents' books.

It was exactly what Liz was looking for – her chance to make something of herself. Her friends could tap their typewriters in Southend-on-Sea for the rest of time as far as she was concerned. They could meet Mr Right and have a dozen children, but that wasn't for her. Liz wanted to get shot of this town. No matter how well she did at school, she was going nowhere here. Her future lay in London in the big time and the bright lights. Lucie Clayton was her first stop. Lucie Clayton of Bond Street. Only now, she cursed, she wouldn't be going there after all, because she had told Rita and Sally about it, and they wanted a crack at the contest too.

Liz surveyed herself mournfully in the broken mirror that stood in the hallway of her mother's boarding house. If those two hadn't decided to go in for it, she thought, I could have won. I've got the legs to be a model. She tilted her face up. I've got the profile for it, too. And the hair. With something like despair she ran her hands down her chest. The only thing I haven't got, she acknowledged with a sick feeling of misery, is a bosom. She thought of Sally and Rita. Two years ago they had buds just like her, then they started to grow and she didn't. Now they both wore bras all the time, not just for games. Liz was the odd one out. She knew she was twice as pretty as the other two. She was taller and better made and if the contest hadn't come up she wouldn't have worried at all. But now she felt her whole life was in danger of being ruined because of the bust she didn't have. She sighed and went up to her room to change. Maybe some plan would come to her by the time she got to the coffee bar. Some way to get round her deficiencies. Whatever else Liz Enfield was, she wasn't a quitter.

The Studio in the backstreets behind the seafront was the unofficial headquarters of Liz's gang. They would meet there most nights to drink espresso coffee and ogle the boys. If they were in the mood they would encourage them. And if the boys were good looking enough, they could be persuaded to part with their telephone numbers. But no serious dating ever took place at the Studio. It was strictly a meeting place. Liz and her friends might still be in school but even then they knew better than to sully their own doorsteps.

When Liz arrived it was nine thirty and the place was starting to fill up. She had to struggle to get down the steep staircase to the basement and the fug from the cigarettes was so thick she could hardly see across the tables to where her friends sat. The girls had got there before her and they had already been spotted by a group of boys in motorcycle jackets sitting at the adjoining table. Liz noticed the guy on the edge of the group had a gold cigarette lighter. What a shame, she thought as she approached the table, that the ugly, pathetic ones always had the solid gold Ronson. Why couldn't the dreamboats have the spare cash? She sat down in the empty seat next to the sad little runt. This wasn't going to be her evening.

By midnight she knew her instincts had been spot-on. Rita and Sally had bagged the talent before she got there and they weren't letting go for a moment. With something approaching despair, Liz watched her friends in action. They had both pulled out all the stops tonight. She guessed they had been to the hairdresser and the same hairdresser too, for their beehives were combed and lacquered in identical shapes. Their bosoms looked the same too. Large and substantial Beauty Queens' bosoms. The boy with the gold Ronson began to speak to her. Normally she would have ignored him, but she was low and any attention was better than nothing, so she let herself be drawn into conversation. He introduced himself as James and said he was studying to go to university. Liz started to yawn. This was all she needed. A skinny little wimp who wanted to talk about higher education. She made to get up, then the wimp said something that caught her attention. He mentioned the name of his father. Liz sat down hard. The little twerp was only Tony Waller's son. She glanced around the table to see if any of the others had heard, but they were far too busy flirting. Liz moved her chair closer to the weedy looking boy and went to work. Tony Waller was the local councillor who was judging the beauty contest. On his nod one of the contestants would walk away with the crown and the modelling course at Lucie Clayton. Liz knew for certain now that that contestant was going to be her. All she had to do was convince Tony Waller. She would make his son like her so much that he took her home to meet his father.

In a matter of days Liz had James convinced that something very special had happened. Within a week he was in love with her, and the moment that happened, Liz turned the screws.

'I'm a respectable girl,' she told him, 'from an old-fashioned family. I think I should meet your parents.'

If James had known how much Liz had stretched the truth, she would never have met Tony Waller, but she took care not to reveal much about her background. She never took James home, for if she had, he would have known her family was anything but respectable.

Her father, Ernie Enfield, sold used cars in Romford. That was the best thing that could be said about him. His other habits, the ones he was well known for, didn't bear inspection. Ernie was a reprobate, a rotten apple. Right from the time she was a little girl, Liz never knew when she was going to see him. When he went off with other women he neglected his family. When the affairs fizzled out, he came home to nurse his wounds, recharge his batteries and spoil his daughter rotten. Liz would fall for it every time, adoring him until he left again to go away on another of his adventures.

The last time was the worst time of all. When Ernie left, he left part of himself behind. Three weeks after he took off, Liz's mother discovered she was pregnant. Ernie didn't come back for a year after that and when he did, he found he had a son. Ernie was so appalled by this extra, unexpected responsibility, that he began divorce proceedings on the spot. That was four years ago and neither Liz nor her mother had seen hide nor hair of him since.

It took Liz a long time to get over her father. In the beginning she blamed herself for his defection. If only she had been better, more obedient. If she hadn't complained that Ernie was never there, things might have been different. For six months she cried herself to sleep every night over her father. Finally when her baby brother caught scarlet fever and she and her mother took turns to nurse him round the clock, she saw the truth. Ernie had deserted them, not because they were bad, but because he was. Her father was a weak, wicked man, incapable of true emotion. She wondered if any other kind existed.

Liz was fourteen when men first started to notice her. She wasn't curvy or rounded like her school-friends, but there was something bold about her. Her lips were very red and her hair was very black and she had a way of carrying herself that made people turn round and stare.

She lost her virginity to the local vicar's son just before her fifteenth birthday. He respected her feelings even less than her father did. The moment it was all over he asked if she had been careful.

'What do you mean, careful?' Liz asked.

'Did you do something to stop having a baby? Did you take precautions?'

'No,' she protested, 'I thought you did that.'

The boy looked at her with distaste.

'I don't have to,' he told her. 'I'm not the one who gets lumbered if anything goes wrong.'

Liz stayed awake every night and worried until she got her period and when she knew she was in the clear, she went out and bought herself a packet of condoms. After that, she never went anywhere without them.

Liz didn't have sex with James. She didn't need him enough for that. All she wanted of him was to meet his father and she did, quite easily, once she'd mentioned it.

At her suggestion James had taken her round to supper at the family's semi-detached home by the golf course. The moment he told her where he lived Liz was impressed. Only rich people could afford houses in that part of town. Everyone knew they cost a fortune.

Liz took special care of herself that night. All the girls in her year were wearing false eyelashes – it was a kind of craze among the upper fifth. Little strips of black fronds that looked like spiders' legs. Liz stuck them above her own lashes and they made her eyes look bigger and somehow more mysterious. I'm a born model, she told herself, inspecting the finished result. Mr Waller is bound to notice the second he sets eyes on me.

Tony Waller didn't look at Liz's eyes when he met her that night. He didn't look at her sheath dress either the way she had expected him to, but then James's father wasn't in the least bit like she imagined him. The man she had in her mind was plump and florid, a wheezy old windbag in an old-fashioned suit. Tony Waller wasn't old at all. He didn't even look like a councillor. On the contrary, he reminded her of Paul Newman. He's not bad, Liz thought. Almost worth going to work on.

They were very comfortable, the Wallers – they even had fitted carpets. It was the first thing Liz noticed, the powder-blue fitted carpets. It made her think of the tatty old mats in her mother's parlour, and she felt ashamed. James cut in on her thoughts.

'Mother said will you have a slice of breast, or do you prefer the dark meat?'

Liz eyed the plump juicy bird. For her the best part of the chicken was the leg, because you got more of it. She hesitated: if she asked for a leg she would appear greedy, and she was here for a reason. She wanted to impress Tony Waller, to prove that she was charming and deserved to win the Southend Pier Beauty Contest. She asked for some white meat and was rewarded with a minute portion on the side of her plate. Never mind, she thought, I'll fill up on bread when I get home tonight.

Tony Waller fixed his eyes on her. 'What are you interested in?' he asked directly.

Liz cleared her throat. It was now or never.

'What I really want to do,' she said firmly, 'is to model. That's why I'm going in for the contest at the pier next week. The first prize is a course at Lucie Clayton.' She reddened and looked at Tony Waller. 'But you know that already. I mean, you are the main judge.'

James looked surprised. 'You didn't say anything about going in for that. Why didn't you tell me?'

Liz cast her eyes down to the plate in front of her.

'I was embarrassed,' she said. 'What if you didn't think I was pretty enough?'

'But I do think you're pretty. You're the prettiest girl I ever took out.'

The words came out of James all at once; and the councillor looked at his son sharply.

'You should go beyond the surface, lad,' he said. 'Sometimes character is more important than looks.'

There was an awkward silence after that, and when the conversation went back to normal, the contest wasn't mentioned again. Liz felt weighted down with misery. She'd wasted nearly two weeks of her time on boring little James Waller. She'd got to meet his father, and just when she was in sight of the finishing post, everything fell apart. Tony Waller, it turned out, didn't approve of beauty, or beauty contests come to that. He was probably only judging it because his name came up on a list.

Somehow Liz got through the rest of the evening. At last it was half past ten and James's father offered to run her home in his car. She accepted gratefully. Anything to get the evening over with.

James fetched her coat and as she was putting it on, the councillor turned to his son once more.

'There's no point in you coming along as well. Liz doesn't live a million miles away.'

Now she felt really wretched. I didn't meet with his approval, she thought. I can tell he doesn't want James to see me again. Then she set her face. Sod James, she decided.

I only went out with him because of his father. If he doesn't want to help me, it's good riddance to the lot of them.

Liz was silent on the way home, not because she

didn't know what to say, but because she couldn't be bothered to make the effort any more.

Suddenly Tony Waller turned to her.

'Where did you get hold of that dress?' he asked.

'What's it to you?' Liz snapped rudely.

'Nothing. I just thought it was very attractive.'

Liz felt irritated. What was this pompous man doing patronizing her?

'I thought you weren't interested in appearances,' she shot back. 'Isn't character more your thing?'

Tony Waller slowed down the car. 'I'm sorry if I upset you back there. I didn't mean to.'

'What did you mean to do?' Liz asked.

Her companion considered for a moment. 'I meant to stop my son making a fool of himself. He's completely besotted with you, you know. He talks about nothing else, and you've only known each other for five minutes.'

Here it comes, Liz thought. The big talking to from the heavy father.

Any minute now he'll demand that I stop seeing James. She turned round in her seat so that she faced him.

'If you're going to tell me what a bad influence I am you can save your breath. I've got better things to do than lead little boys astray.'

There was a silence while he pulled the car over to the side of the road.

'What about their fathers?' he asked quietly.

Liz still didn't get it. 'What do you mean, what about their fathers?' She looked at the expression in his eyes and the penny finally dropped. So that's what it was all about. The remark about her dress and why he didn't want James along on the drive home. He fancied her himself.

Liz had been waiting for a chance like this all along.

Now it had come, she was at her wits' end to know what to do about it. She had been used to boys of her own age. Boys like James who she could twist around her little finger. But an older man. A powerful man like a councillor. The prospect terrified her.

Her fear must have been obvious, for Waller didn't make any move to come closer to her. He fished in his pocket for a pack of cigarettes and passed one across.

'Help yourself,' he said. 'You look as though you could do with one.'

It was a small gesture, but it made Liz feel grown-up and some of her confidence began to return.

'Aren't you taking a bit of a risk,' she said baldly, 'in your position.'

He stared at her across the dark interior of the car and for a moment Liz felt cut off from the rest of the world, as if the only two people who existed were herself and this man.

'Life is full of risks,' Waller said softly. 'You risk your future the day after tomorrow when you go in for that contest.'

He let his voice trail off and Liz suddenly realized what was required of her.

'Suppose you tell me how I could cut down that risk,' she said.

Waller didn't answer. He slid across the seat until his face was on a level with hers. Then he kissed her. It was like no other kiss Liz had ever experienced. The boys who she'd known had been rough, hungry and unsubtle. This man was in no hurry. Despite herself she was roused. He put his arms around her waist and before she knew it the back of her dress was undone and his hands were sliding up to her breasts. Alarm bells sounded at the back of her mind. I shouldn't be doing this, she thought. Not this quickly. Not this easily. But her body was coming alive under his touch, and before she knew it, his tongue was in her mouth and he was pressing down on top of her. I'm finished, Liz thought. Nothing can save me now.

At that instant the whole of the interior of the car lit up. Tony Waller let go of her and sat up in his seat.

Liz fumbled wildly for her dress, suddenly conscious that she was almost naked. Good God, she thought, it's the police. We'll be had up for indecency. Visions of a major scandal flashed through her mind. The councillor and the schoolgirl. She could see the headlines now. Then she looked up and she realized there was no-one there.

'There's no need to jump out of your skin,' said Tony kindly. 'It was only another car coming down the road. He must have caught us in his headlights.'

Liz had had enough. This man was old enough to be her father and had nearly succeeded in having his way with her. What for? Once he had used her, he didn't have to promise her anything, he didn't even have to give her the time of day.

'I should go home,' she said firmly. 'It's very late.'

Her companion lit a fresh cigarette and started the engine.

'Will I see you again?' It was a loaded question, but he asked it as lightly as he knew how.

Liz kept her eyes on the road ahead of her. 'I don't know,' she said. 'I'll think about it.'

'How long will you think about it,' Waller pressed.

He wanted her now. Badly wanted her, and he didn't bother to disguise his need. It was then that Liz finally saw the chance she was waiting for.

'The Beauty Contest,' she said, 'is the day after tomorrow. I'll think about it till then.'

Waller looked tense.

'What happens when you've finished turning it over in your mind?'

Liz turned round to him then, fixing him with her widest stare.

'We celebrate me winning, of course. What else did you think I'd say?'

2

On the morning of the contest, Liz packed a case with everything she was going to need. She knew she would be spending the night away from home, so she prepared herself. Her sensible underwear and her silly underwear went in, followed by fresh tights, a change of clothes and all her make-up.

For the contest itself she packed the strapless swimsuit her father had bought for her four years ago, before he left. Then, almost as an afterthought, she tucked in her prize possession. Her false fall of hair. She knew it wouldn't make any difference whether or not she wore it. Liz wasn't going to win this competition on her looks. But the hairpiece gave her comfort. She felt confident with all that extra hair falling around her shoulders, and she had to look as if she had made some kind of effort with herself. She might be cheating to win this modelling course, but she didn't want to be seen doing it.

Miss Southend Pier, true to its name, was held in the Variety Theatre at the pier's end. During the season a succession of seedy comedians and ventriloquist acts paraded across the stage, then, once a month, it was the turn of the Beauty Queens.

A communal changing-room was set up at the back, and it was here that Liz ran into her two best friends, Sally and Rita. In different circumstances the sight of them would have made her nervous, for they were at their most competitive. It was almost as if they knew they had the edge on her, and they were intent on rubbing her nose in it.

Sally looked her up and down. 'The judges disqualify anyone who uses padding,' she said caustically, 'so what are you going to do about yourself?'

Liz fought down the urge to hit her.

'Not a lot,' she replied sweetly. 'Some men I know look for more in a girl than just prettiness. They go for character.'

Both her friends laughed at that one.

'Don't be daft,' said Rita. 'What goes on this afternoon is all about looks. It's a Beauty Contest we're talking about. None of the judges care about what you're like underneath.'

Liz fished around in her suitcase for her precious fall of hair.

'I wouldn't be so sure,' she said.

It was getting on for four o'clock and most of the contestants had gathered in the changing-room. They were a mixed bunch, and there were even one or two professional models.

How different they look from the rest of us, thought Liz. They're the only ones here who know what they're doing. She was right, for the models wasted no time on small talk. Instead they went to work on themselves. There were three of them and each girl seemed to have a set routine: the dark one with short frosted hair started with her body, stripping everything off and oiling every inch of her skin with baby lotion; the bleached blonde who arrived five minutes after did exactly the same, and the other more natural-looking blonde concentrated on her face. In the space of an hour, they were all laced into their swimsuits and ready to go.

Liz looked at them and sighed. They seemed so perfect, like dolls wrapped in cellophane in a shop window, waiting for someone to come and pick them out. Only today nobody was going to choose them.

She cast her eyes around the other contestants and she was surprised at how many pretty girls lived in the down-at-heel seaside town. It doesn't seem fair, she thought. They all came here today thinking they had a real chance to go on a modelling course. To make their names. For a moment Liz felt a pang of real regret for the fate of these unknown sisters of hers. Then she put the feeling aside. Life wasn't fair, she knew that already, just as she knew she could never make it so. All Liz could do was to play the cards that had been dealt to her and if that meant pushing a few people out of her way, she supposed God would forgive her.

There was a knock on the door of the changing room and a man came in.

'I'm your host for this afternoon,' he announced. 'In five minutes exactly I will be calling you all on to the stage.'

Liz shivered slightly. This was the part of the show she was least looking forward to. No matter what the outcome was, she resented being picked over by an audience of curious strangers. She knew it was what happened in Beauty Contests, but she didn't have to like it. She thought about the evening ahead of her. She wasn't going to like that either.

The compere went out of the door and on to the stage, and from somewhere far away Liz heard the band strike up. Then they were on. One by one the girls filed through the door, until it was her turn. Liz took one last look in the mirror, then kissed goodbye to her reflection. When I next see you, she thought, your whole life will have changed.

The moment Liz came out on to the stage she was blinded by the lights. Then she realized she hadn't got a clue what she was going to do. She had been so confident of winning she hadn't bothered to find out how to go through the motions. She made her way over to the compere who was clutching a microphone and staring out into the audience.

'What do you want me to do?' she hissed through clenched teeth.

The man looked at her in astonishment. He knew models were dim, but this girl took the biscuit. The notice on the changing-room wall informed them all to make one circuit of the stage. Hadn't she seen the others practising all afternoon? He sighed and leaned in close to her.

'Put on your best smile, dear, and trot round in front of the audience. Once will do nicely.'

He shook his head as she set off. She doesn't have a hope, he thought. She hasn't even got much of a figure.

Liz looked ahead of her and focused on the audience. Somewhere down there Tony Waller would be sitting. Tony Waller and her mother. It was the thought of her mother that pulled her up sharply. Liz wanted to look good for her, to make her proud she had a daughter pretty enough to show herself in a competition.

She pulled her shoulders back and thrust her nose in the air. Suddenly, from nowhere, she had a feeling of incredible control. She was in command of herself, of her body, and because of that she was in command of the audience. Like a queen Liz smiled out over a sea of faces and sensed them smiling in return. Then as if she had been born to it, she began to stalk around the stage. Liz knew she had no bosom, yet she carried herself as if she did. All the time she was walking, she believed she was the Beauty Queen to end all Beauty Queens. When she took her place in the line-up there was a round of thunderous applause.

Liz smiled inwardly. Who knows, she thought, I might even win this contest on merit.

At a signal from the show's compere all the girls filed off. Forty minutes later they were called back in front of the audience. The judging panel had made its final selection, the compere was ready to announce the winner.

Liz went cold. The judging panel, the man had said. She heard it clearly enough. There was not one judge, there were several of them. Tony Waller didn't call the shots after all. Why hadn't she checked? She saw her future disappearing in front of her. There would be no Lucie Clayton modelling course, no picture on the front cover of *Vogue*, no fame or fortune. Liz rubbed the tears out of her eyes with the back of her hand and wondered how soon she could get off the stage when she heard her name being called.

She looked up to see everyone staring at her. What had she done wrong now she wondered. Was there some instruction she had ignored?

The compere walked up to her and took hold of her wrist.

'Pay attention, you silly cow,' he muttered. 'You've just won the first prize.'

Without further ceremony he dragged her to the centre of the stage where Tony Waller was standing. He was wearing his dark suit and holding a tinsel crown. Liz had never seen a man look more nervous.

The same feeling that she'd had earlier in front of the audience came back to her, and she smiled.

'Aren't you going to congratulate me, Tony darling,' she said softly.

Before he could reply, Liz leaned forward and kissed him on both cheeks. The audience went wild, clapping and whistling and shouting for her to do another circuit of the stage. The councillor handed her a square, flat package wrapped in gold foil.

'You'll find the details of your modelling course inside that,' he told her. Then he cleared his throat. 'When all this is over,' he whispered, 'I thought we might have dinner – just the two of us at a restaurant in town.'

Here it comes, Liz thought. Payment for services rendered.

'Which restaurant?' she asked.

Waller lowered his voice.

'Actually it's not a restaurant. It's more of a roadhouse. Do you know The Lawns outside Billericay?'

Liz nodded.

'I'll meet you there at seven thirty. Take a taxi – I'll pay the other end.'

The clapping was dying down and out of the corner of her eye Liz saw the compere signalling at her to do one last circuit.

Liz straightened up again and pushed her mane of false hair back over her shoulders. Then before she faced her audience she gave Tony Waller one last glance.

'See you at seven thirty,' she said.

It took Liz ten minutes to find herself a taxi. The driver picked up her case and put it in the boot.

'If we get a move on,' he told her, 'we'll get to the railway station in time to make the seven twenty.'

Liz began to tell him she wasn't going there. Then something stopped her. What if she did get the seven twenty? She could take it all the way up to Fenchurch Street and stay with her aunt in Whitechapel. Then, first thing in the morning, she could enrol at Lucie Clayton.

The idea began to appeal to her. She had changed her life that day by winning the contest, tomorrow she could start her new future in earnest. She thought about Tony Waller. He would be sitting waiting for her at the roadhouse. There would be a room booked upstairs in a bogus name and he would expect her to go there with him after supper. It was at that moment that Liz knew she couldn't go through with it. She jumped into the back of the cab and told the driver to step on it. The councillor would be furious of course, but what could he do? He couldn't make her give the prize back. Not without telling the world the reason why, and he wouldn't want to do that. No, Councillor Waller was well and truly backed into a corner.

Liz caught the train with minutes to spare, and as she watched the flats of Canvey Island flash past her through the window she reflected on the men who had betrayed her: her father, the vicar's son who nearly got her pregnant, the lovers of her girlhood. There wasn't one of them she would miss. Then for the last time she thought once more of Tony Waller. He was the one man who hadn't let her down. The one man who had come through for her. For a moment she felt guilty, but only for a moment. In the battle of the sexes, she decided, there will always be a winner and a loser. From now on, I know which one I'm going to be.

3

Since before Vanessa could remember her mother had always known what was best for her. At school, when all the other children wore jeans and rompers, Vanessa was kitted out in velvet dresses and clean white socks. If the socks were dirty when she came home – and they often were – her mother would frown and click her tongue.

When she was old enough to go to Queensgate it was the same story. The things she was going to wear each morning were picked out for her the night before, and if Vanessa hadn't put them on properly, or if she had used her own judgement and worn a different blouse or added a belt, she would be sent back to her room and ordered to put things right.

She grew up both loving and hating her mother. Most of all she grew up needing her approval, so when the Honourable Sybil Grenville decided her daughter would become a great ballerina, Vanessa did everything she could to comply. No-one worked harder than she did at her classes. Hours after everyone else had gone home she was still there practising at the barre, trying to be perfect.

In time, she was perfect. At the end of term when the school put on 'Swan Lake', Vanessa was chosen for the lead role, and she was so good in it that all the other parents were convinced she would end up in the Royal Ballet. She would have done, except for one thing – nature was against her.

Vanessa began to grow when she was fourteen,

shooting up out of the neat pleated skirts and tailored suits her mother always liked her to wear. One day she was a child, tiny and delicate and perfect; the next, an awkward teenager with pimples and swelling breasts. At seventeen she became a woman, tall and slender with butterscotch-coloured hair which she wore long, and eyes so pale and so huge that she looked almost myopic.

She became uncontrollably moody. In the past, when she was a child, she had always done what she was told. Now she rebelled. She threw out all the clothes her mother had chosen for her and went and bought boots and thick woollen tights which she wore with mini-skirts. That year all her friends were changing shape and the bold girls, the girls with mothers who didn't nag, gloried in their new figures.

Suddenly Vanessa wanted to be like the others. What was wrong with having hips and a waist and a pair of legs that curved? After she asked herself that question, she put it to her mother. Sybil, as always, had an answer for her.

'You'll lose your chance of being a ballerina,' she said. 'Giselle never had a thirty-eight-inch bust measurement.'

Actually, Vanessa's bust measurement never grew beyond thirty-four. It was her height that disqualified her. By the time she was seventeen she had shot up to five foot nine, and the chances of joining the Royal Ballet corps dwindled away to nothing. She thought about going to university, but her father scuppered that plan. Charles Grenville disapproved of clever women. His wife, Sybil, had gone to Oxford when she was younger and it hadn't done her any good. In his opinion, she would have been a great deal less bossy if she'd stayed at home. That was what he suggested Vanessa should do.

Vanessa wasn't interested. She didn't want to learn how to arrange flowers to please a future husband. In fact, she didn't want a husband at all. Her mother had filled her with ambition to make something of herself.

If she couldn't be a ballerina, she'd be famous doing something else. But what?

The front page of *Vogue* provided the answer. On it was a picture of Fiona Campbell-Walter. It wasn't the usual model-girl pose – all pouting lips and false eyelashes. Instead, Fiona looked every inch the grand lady: from her ears were suspended diamond earrings in the shape of chandeliers; her neck was circled with even more diamonds, and her face was pale and powdered to perfection.

That's who I want to be, Vanessa decided. Even mother couldn't disapprove of that. All the same she didn't tell her mother her plans but started to apply for vacancies on the quiet. She made a list of all the top English couturiers, then she rang round and asked if they were taking on any new models. Digby Morton, Victor Steibel and Hardy Amies turned her down flat. Norman Hartnell asked her to come in for an interview.

For her first interview as a model, Vanessa pulled out all the stops. She twisted her long butterscotch-coloured hair up into a french pleat, she wore her highest heels and she put on a new knitted dress that ended half way up her thighs. As an afterthought she added a felt hat with a huge brim, and a pair of dark glasses. When she walked up the grand staircase of the salon in Bruton Street, Vanessa felt like a cross between Garbo and Marlene Dietrich and was delighted to see her feelings about herself communicated as the chief vendeuse greeted her like an old friend.

'Am I pleased to see you,' she said taking her by the arm. 'You're just the girl I'm looking for.'

Before she could ask her why, Vanessa was shown into a crowded changing-room. On all sides of her there were racks of clothes. Along one wall there was a long mirror where two other girls were in the process of doing their make-up. Ignoring them, the vendeuse shepherded Vanessa over to a rack of suits and day dresses and, grabbing a black suit off the rail, held it up against her.

'That looks as if it's going to fit you,' she said. 'Why don't you get into it?'

Vanessa did as she was told, climbing first into the skirt, then the blouse. The clothes fitted her like nothing she had had on her body before. Vanessa was used to good things. Her mother had taken her to Jaeger and the young fashion room at Harrods, but this suit skimmed her hips and curved into her waist as if it belonged to her, as if the man who constructed it had put it together with her in mind.

The vendeuse looked Vanessa up and down then told her to walk the length of the changing-room.

'I want to see how it moves,' she said.

Vanessa strode past the racks of clothes, and as she did a change came over her. She was wearing a priceless suit. A suit made for a princess.

She put her shoulders back and her head up and the fabric rearranged itself around her contours. For an instant, Vanessa became someone else, she became the princess the suit was intended for. When she reached the end of the changing-room, she pirouetted round on the balls of her feet, the way she had been taught at ballet school and made her way back to the vendeuse. The woman rewarded her with an approving smile.

'I like it,' she said. 'Now I want you to do the same walk for Mr Hartnell.'

She took a heavy cape off the rack and threw it over Vanessa's shoulders, fastening it in the front. Then she pointed towards an archway at the end of the room.

'He's through there,' the vendeuse said. 'Show him how you wear his clothes.'

Vanessa put her head up and walked through the archway and on to the catwalk beyond it. When she was half way down the ramp she saw the audience. They were sitting beneath her feet on rows and rows of tiny gilt chairs. Why didn't anyone tell me I was doing a show? she panicked. I thought this was an audition.

She felt the urge to run, to cover her face with her hands and flee the crowded room. But she didn't. She just kept on walking, and when she got to the end of the catwalk she repeated the pirouette she had turned in the changing-room. Half way round she felt the fabric of the cape puff out round her body and swing as she changed direction. It's moving with me, she marvelled. This suit understands what I'm trying to do. As she came back through the archway, she felt better. At least she hadn't made a total fool of herself.

The vendeuse caught her as she came off the stage, pushing her to one side as the next model went into her walk.

Vanessa looked at the older woman and realized something was wrong.

'Why didn't you take the cape off?' the vendeuse hissed. 'Didn't they teach you anything at Hardy Amies?'

'But I haven't come from Hardy Amies,' Vanessa spluttered. 'Who did you think I was?'

The woman looked startled.

'Why, Lulu Carter of course. Cherry Marshall told me this afternoon you were coming straight on from

Hardy's show. It was a bit of a rush, but we were desperate, so we said yes.'

Vanessa began to understand.

'You thought I was someone else,' she said. 'You thought I was a real model.'

The vendeuse grabbed hold of one of the racks to steady herself.

'Don't tell me you're not a real model.'

'Of course I'm not,' she shouted. 'I've never done this before in my life.'

The woman passed a hand over her brow, then straightened up.

'I should throw you out here and now,' she said, 'but we're in the middle of a show, so we're going to have to make the best of it.'

She took a beaded evening dress off the rail nearest to her and handed it over to Vanessa.

'Put this on, and do exactly as I tell you to do – and make it snappy, there's only three minutes between each change.'

Vanessa had no idea how she got through the next half hour, but somehow she muddled through. The third time she went out on to the catwalk she ventured a look at the audience. What she saw surprised her. The people who were watching her were all women – women who looked exactly like her mother. They were all wearing hats and the sort of tailored clothes she went in for. They even looked her over like her mother did.

For some reason Vanessa didn't understand she felt reassured. The next time she walked on to the catwalk she tried sucking in her cheeks and looking haughty. It worked like a charm. She could almost feel the waves of approval coming up from the women in the audience. They like me, she thought, they like looking at me in these clothes.

The last change was the wedding dress, and to her surprise the vendeuse picked her to show it.

'Why don't you put it on one of the others,' Vanessa asked. 'I don't have the experience for this.'

The grey-haired woman didn't mince her words.

'If it fitted the others, I'd be only too pleased, but it doesn't, so you'll have to improvise.'

The last time Vanessa went in front of the audience something inside her snapped. This is my one big chance and I've blown it, she told herself. Norman Hartnell will never let me in here again. Nor will anyone else. The knowledge, instead of defeating her, somehow liberated her. It put a bounce in her step and a smile on her face. She started to flirt with the audience, fluffing her hair out as she turned, and at her final exit she treated everyone to a saucy wink.

Then she stumbled through the archway and into the changing-room, throwing herself onto the nearest chair.

'This is one bride,' she announced to no-one in particular, 'who is never going to walk off into the sunset.'

'Do you want to bet?'

Vanessa looked up and saw a tall silver-haired man standing in front of her. He was wearing a carnation in the button-hole of his morning coat, and he reminded her of a benevolent uncle. A rich benevolent uncle. He extended one perfectly manicured hand.

'I'm Norman Hartnell,' he said. 'I don't think we've met.'

Vanessa wanted to pinch herself. This can't be happening to me, she thought. This can't be Norman Hartnell. It was, and he didn't want to throw her out, he wanted to employ her.

'That little performance with the wedding dress was charming,' he told her. 'It was young and a bit skittish, but that's the way brides are meant to be.'

'What about the rest of it?' Vanessa asked.

The couturier looked thoughtful.

'When you weren't looking scared to death, you were actually quite good. You need to learn the ropes of course, but the girls here will show you what to do.'

After that the vendeuse took over. Vanessa was to join the salon as a trainee. Hartnell had half a dozen full time models whose job it was to show the collection to buyers and customers. During the season there were three shows a day, and at the beginning Vanessa's time was taken up looking after the other girls.

She made them coffee and laid out the accessories before a show, and when the girls were showing the clothes, Vanessa helped to dress them as well. Gradually, she became familiar with the routines of the salon and a whole new world opened out in front of her.

At first it showed itself to her in tantalizing glimpses. The other models would talk about the parties they had been invited to.

'Ghastly late night,' they would say putting cold compresses on their eyes. 'Went and drank far too much champagne. Vanessa, you couldn't get me some more coffee could you? There's a love.'

And Vanessa would go off and brew up another percolator taking care to come back as quickly as she could so as not to miss any of the gossip. They all seemed to go to places with glamorous sounding names – Les 'A', Annabel's, the Saddle Room. The girls Vanessa had grown up with had been secretive about their boyfriends. The teenage kisses, the fumblings in the back row of the cinema were things they only talked about in whispers, as if any moment an angry parent would overhear one of them. The models at Norman Hartnell were a whole different story.

They talked about their love affairs from early morning to late at night, and they didn't care who heard them. One of them was going out with a man who owned racehorses and quite often he would fly her over to Paris for the weekend. Another was dotty about an American millionaire. The loveliest of them all, a sultry brunette called Annegrette, was keeping company with a married man who was so famous and so rich that he was regularly seen in the society columns.

Vanessa's favourite time of the day was just after the shows when the girls were unwinding. It was then that they really let their hair down and went into detail. Vanessa had very little idea of what went on between men and women. When she had asked her mother about it, she had pressed her lips into a disapproving line and told Vanessa she'd find out everything she wanted to know on her wedding night.

'But that won't happen for years,' she had protested. Vanessa's mother refused to be drawn. What her daughter didn't know couldn't hurt her, or influence her, or corrupt her.

The models at Norman Hartnell didn't give a damn about corruption. They were all four or five years older than Vanessa and none of them was a virgin. More to the point, none of them wanted to be a virgin. Their sex lives kept them going. What else was there to live for if you weren't in love?

Vanessa longed to be just like them. She took to daydreaming in her spare moments, and in her fantasies she was being swept off her feet by a

European prince – a dashing, wicked European prince who bought her caviar and oysters out of season and ravished her in his suite at the Ritz.

In her dreams, Vanessa was always deflowered in the Ritz because it was the only grand hotel she had ever been to. A cousin of hers had been married there and Vanessa had managed to get a glimpse of the suite where she was staying on her wedding night.

In the end though, her daydreams, however exotic, didn't satisfy her. Vanessa yearned for the real thing, a proper man who she could see and touch and feel. If he wasn't a prince she was content to settle for the next best thing.

Vanessa got her chance a month after she started at the couturiers. The chief vendeuse had allowed her to appear in some of the shows and because she was actually modelling the clothes, the other girls started to accept her as one of them. It was as if she had grown up overnight. They no longer saw her as a dogsbody, a coffee machine. She was a woman, too. With the friendship came the invitations to parties.

Julian Boulting came into Vanessa's life at a lunch party in San Frediano's. A group of the models liked to meet there on Saturdays when they were all in town, and in their wake they brought an entourage of designers, photographers and men in the advertising game.

None of them was to be taken seriously, the girls insisted. The real men, the men they were busy getting their hooks in to, were down on their country estates over the weekend. The escorts who came to the Italian trattoria were strictly there to fill in time.

Vanessa was flattered to be asked along. So far she had been like a fish out of water at the drinks parties they had invited her to, for she hadn't known anyone, and no-one had made any time for her. This party she vowed would be different. This time, even if she had to get drunk, she would get over the shyness and break into the enchanted circle.

The group met at twelve thirty in the tiny bar at the top of the crowded white-tiled restaurant. Right from the start it was the same as all the other parties. Everyone knew everyone else. They all kissed and hugged and whispered secrets into one another's ears. I hate this, Vanessa thought. These people make me feel like a baby girl. I'm eighteen years old, she wanted to shout. I'm much more grown-up than I look if you'd only give me a chance. The men in their faded blue jeans only seemed to be interested in talking to each other. Vanessa turned round to the bartender and asked for another Campari and lemonade. The drink arrived three minutes later, but as she went to pick it up somebody got there before her. A member of her party had pushed his way in front of her and was bearing her drink away with him. Vanessa grabbed hold of the hem of his black leather jacket and pulled.

'Excuse me,' she said politely, 'but that drink belongs to me.'

The man turned round and stared at Vanessa and she saw how big he was, and how fierce. He probably plays scrum forward for his rugger team, she thought. But there was no going back.

'Hand it over,' she said, 'and next time get your own drink.'

The big man began to smile and Vanessa noticed he had surprisingly blue eyes. They were the only thing about him that wasn't threatening. The eyes and his voice.

'Don't lose your hair,' he said softly. 'I don't go around stealing from pretty girls.'

He leaned across her and ordered another Campari. Her drink he placed on the bar. Miserably, Vanessa stared at the floor. My one conversation, she brooded, and I had to blow it by being rude.

'What's eating you,' asked the soft, mellow voice. 'I gave you your drink.'

He was still there, and even though his Campari had arrived, he showed no signs of going. With an effort, Vanessa smiled.

'I'm not all that good at parties,' she apologized. 'I can't seem to get in the swing of things.'

'That's probably because you don't push yourself. I saw you last week at Annegrette's. You were all bundled up in a corner looking sorry for yourself. None of us dared to come up and say hello in case your mother had died or something.'

This time Vanessa's smile came of its own accord.

'If my mother had died,' she said, 'I'd have been celebrating.'

'The mouse roars,' the man laughed approvingly. 'Come and roar at some of the others. Or at least wiggle your ears.'

He put an arm round her shoulders and drew her into the circle. It was like being chosen to play netball for the school team. One minute you were on the outside shivering in your gymbags, the next you were part of something. You were warm and you were included and people wanted to listen to what you had to say.

Vanessa realized that nothing had changed since her school days. These terrifyingly smart young men in their weekend blazers and tweed jackets weren't frightening at all when you got to know them. Or the girls. The girls were just like the models she worked with. Vanessa found herself relaxing and joining in with their gossip. She knew most of the people they were talking about. If she didn't know them, she had read about them and by the time they went and sat down she felt she almost belonged.

Julian, the man who had come to Vanessa's rescue, sat himself beside her and her heart lifted. She liked him better than the others because he had found her interesting when nobody else had noticed. She decided to find out more about him.

He told her he was in the music business, something to do with arrangement and recording. Vanessa remembered what the other girls had told her – none of the men you meet here are important, they don't have any clout or any money. Vanessa wanted to prove them all wrong. It became vital to her that this dark man sitting beside her was worth her attention.

'Are you rich?' she blurted out.

Vanessa went bright red and felt like a fool, yet her question didn't seem to bother him. He took a forkful of spaghetti, twirled it round his spoon and regarded her thoughtfully.

'What difference would it make if I was?' he asked.

Now what could she tell him? It all seemed like so much nonsense.

'It wouldn't make any difference at all,' Vanessa told him firmly. 'I'd like you whatever you were.'

In the old days she would have considered herself forward saying that, but she had drunk more than her usual quota of Campari and she was feeling no pain.

Julian filled up her glass several more times and Vanessa became animated. She wanted to know all sorts of things about her companion – where he lived, why he was here today, who his friends were. Every time she asked anything, he diverted her with questions of his own and stupid jokes. In the end she gave up. The afternoon had taken on a momentum of its own. It was like a huge tide taking her in a new direction and because she didn't want to be left behind she went with it.

After lunch everyone went off to a flat in Earls Court. It was at the top of four flights of stairs and she was so unsteady on her feet that Julian had to help her keep her balance. It didn't bother her. For the first time in her life, Vanessa was at the centre of things. These people, the crowd who had allowed her to join them, were in touch with what was happening now. They didn't have time for the yesterday world of her parents with its rules and rigid structure and prim little morals. Her new friends invented their own universe, made it up as they went along. More than anything Vanessa wanted to be a part of it.

The first thing she noticed about the flat was how dark it was. The walls were painted black and the only illumination came from candles stuck in glass bottles. Vanessa was surprised at the shabbiness of everything: sagging sofas and armchairs that were losing their stuffing were spaced all around the room; ashtrays covering every available surface were full of yesterday's cigarette butts.

She sat on one of the big sofas next to Julian who had put his arm round her, and in that moment she stopped worrying. Julian was her saviour, the man who had drawn her into the dance. Nothing bad could happen as long as he was there.

She leant her head back and closed her eyes and sighed a sigh of pure happiness. This was the biggest adventure of her life and it was only just beginning.

Someone had turned the music on and it made her sit up and take notice. It was urgent and somehow indecent. It made her think of sex, and that excited her. Before now, that kind of thing had been something for other people, something the girls talked about after a show. Now, sitting here with Julian, she knew it was real and it could happen to her. He must have seen the effect the music was having for he put his hand on the back of her neck and started to play with the tops of her shoulders, massaging them and softening the muscles under the skin.

Vanessa smelt incense then, or at least she thought it was incense until she saw one of the girls had lit a joint and was passing it round. When it came to her turn she shook her head and passed it to Julian.

'I don't smoke,' she said. 'Not even cigarettes. It makes me cough.'

Julian smiled at her – the intimate, jokey smile he had used when he picked her up in the restaurant.

'This won't make you cough,' he told her. 'Try it and you'll see.'

Because she wanted to please him, Vanessa took the joint between her forefinger and thumb the way the others did and puffed on it. A stream of acrid smoke filled her mouth making her splutter and gag. Julian took the reefer out of her hand.

'You're doing it wrong,' he said. 'Here, I'll take a drag and you can watch.'

He inhaled deeply, pulling the smoke through his teeth and as it went into his lungs, the look of concentration on his face intensified. Then he passed the butt over to her again.

'Your turn,' he said.

This time Vanessa was more successful. She actually got the smoke past her mouth and kept it down. It tasted horrible. Worse than anything she had ever experienced, but Julian looked so pleased, so approving that she couldn't tell him how much she hated it.

She went through the same routine twice more when the joint came round, then she started to fly. The music that she had found so disturbing suddenly seemed to make complete sense to her. It was lust, and living, and experience all rolled into one. Why hadn't she seen it? She must have been blind. Blind and deaf.

Julian whispered in her ear.

'I want to fuck you,' he said. 'I want to take all your clothes off and ravage you.'

Vanessa didn't know why but it seemed terribly funny that this nice warm man should want to do something so brutal. She started to giggle.

'Will I like it?' she asked weakly.

He stood up then and grabbed her hands, pulling her to her feet.

'You'll love it,' he assured her.

They half-walked, half-stumbled down the corridor outside until they came to a room.

It was a barn of a place, dark like the other room they had been in, but this room had a bed in it. Vanessa saw the bed was only half made, as if its owner had got up in a hurry that morning. She began to worry.

'Does anyone know we're here?' she asked. 'I mean, will they mind?'

Julian smiled and closed the door behind them. Then he turned the key in the lock.

'Nobody minds what they can't see,' he said.

Then they were on the bed. Vanessa had no idea how they got there so quickly. There seemed to be great gaps in her memory. One minute she was kissing Julian and he was stroking her hair, the next she was lying on her back with her dress all undone down the front. She supposed she should tell him to stop joking around. She didn't go in for this sort of thing – well, she hadn't so far and she was sure it was wrong. But she felt so comfortable lying there, so natural.

Julian started to stroke her skin with the tips of his

fingers. Every time he did it Vanessa felt all tingly and soft inside. Then he undid her bra, touching her breasts, and she felt the beginnings of desire. It was like a huge knot inside her, growing and swelling until her whole body came open. Again, there was a gap in her memory, a blank space, for when Vanessa opened her eyes again she had no clothes on at all and nor had Julian. He was doing something to her now, something with his fingers. They seemed to be lodged in the crevice between her legs and they were stroking her now until they found the place that made her come alive.

As it happened the whole world exploded in a wild mixture of feelings and sensation. She felt as if she had turned into gold, molten gold and her whole body was running over the coverlet, disappearing through the floorboards.

In the distance she could hear Julian's voice.

'Come back little girl,' he crooned. 'Don't pass out on me. We haven't got to the action yet.'

With an effort, Vanessa brought herself back to earth and she saw Julian now crouched over her, parting her legs. Then she saw what he was going to do and for a moment she felt alarm. Then she relaxed and sighed. He's not going to hurt me, she thought.

But he did. His cock was nothing like his fingers. It ripped and tore away at her insides. Searing through her. Making her bleed. After it was over he looked at her and the blood that covered the inside of her thighs.

'Christ,' he said. 'You never told me you were a virgin.'

4

The 'Head Girl' at Lucie Clayton looked to Liz as if she had a poker up her arse. The students called her the 'Head Girl' because she made them feel as if they were all back in kindergarten.

'Stand up straight,' she would instruct them. 'Tuck your tummy in and *gliiiide*.' This last word she would pronounce like a dying swan. They would all fall about trying to look like they were dead serious, when really they were hysterical inside with laughter.

The girl's name was Janelle, and Liz was introduced to her on her first day at the agency. When she arrived, it took her rather a long time to explain who she was and why she was there. And at first nobody believed her.

'We don't have Beauty Queens at Lucie Clayton,' a fat woman with a plummy voice informed her. 'This is a model agency.'

But Liz wasn't going to be deterred. She'd promised her body for this chance. She would have promised her mother's body if it had meant escaping from Southend, and she certainly wasn't going to take any nonsense from some fat cow behind a typewriter.

The woman finally got the message, and summoned Janelle.

Liz disliked her on sight. She was tall and blonde and so middle class, you could cut her accent with a knife.

'So you're the girl who won a place with us,' she

observed. 'You don't really want to be a model, do you?'

For a moment Liz lost confidence. It wasn't Janelle's remark that did it, it was the way she looked her over, as if she wasn't good enough. But I am good enough, Liz told herself. I'm nearly five foot seven. No-one could call me fat. If my face is good enough to win a beauty contest, then it's good enough for this lot. She stood her ground.

'I want to be a model,' she said firmly, 'and I'm going to be a model.'

There was something about the way Liz said it, that stopped the teacher in her tracks. In this kind of case she would usually try to give the girl a refund – she didn't want a silly beauty queen in the school, disrupting all the other pupils. But this girl wasn't going to take no for an answer.

'Calm down,' Janelle said, pressing her lips into a thin line, 'and let me take a good look at you.'

She examined Liz from all angles, taking note of her height and her thick black hair. Then she showed her through to a long carpeted room with a catwalk in the middle and told her to walk along it. This Liz did with such confidence that the blonde woman shook her head in regret.

'If you were an inch or so taller,' she said, 'you'd make a wonderful mannequin. I could place you tomorrow. But it isn't to be.'

The first real prickle of alarm started at the base of Liz's spine.

'What do you mean, it isn't to be?' she protested. 'You mean you won't let me go on the course after all.'

The teacher motioned her to come off the catwalk and over to where she stood.

'I didn't say you couldn't go on the course,' she

said reasonably. 'I simply said you couldn't be a showroom model. You're too tiny. But there are other possibilities.'

'Like what?'

Janelle thought carefully about what she was going to say next. The obvious solution for this girl was to go onto the photographic side. Her figure was dead right for it and her cheekbones would show up beautifully, but there was something wrong about her. This girl was certainly lovely, she couldn't argue with that, yet she didn't have the right look for today. She was too common, too ordinary. None of the top fashion photographers would look at her.

I should tell her to go home, and stop wasting her time, she thought. Then she remembered the determination in the dark girl's eyes when she tried to talk her out of the course before. I'll take her on, she decided, but with certain provisos.

Janelle turned to Liz.

'The career I have in mind for you,' she said, 'isn't really on the fashion side at all – not the high fashion side at any rate. I can see you being photographed for a mail order catalogue for instance. You'd look good on knitting patterns too, and if the right product comes along, the advertising agencies could be interested in you.' She gave Liz a hard stare. 'Would that be acceptable?'

Liz returned her look with a certain venom.

'Not really,' she replied, 'but it will do for a start.'

The first two weeks of the course were murder. Now she knew she wouldn't be showing clothes, Liz didn't bother to pay attention to the classes. The only times she really concentrated were when Janelle demonstrated the different ways to do a make-up. Liz knew she would need that expertise if she was to go in front of the cameras.

During the other lessons she caused mayhem with the rest of the class. There were twelve of them, all fresh out of school, all looking for a bit of life. Liz teamed up with the wildest of the bunch, a manufacturer's daughter from Kingston. Her name was Carole and like Liz she didn't care too much about learning anything. Her father had showrooms in Great Titchfield Street and she knew she could walk straight into a job modelling cut-price fashion the minute the course was over.

The two girls decided to take London by storm. After the classes they would go and have a coffee in the Swiss Chalet on the corner of Bond Street. There they would draw up plans for the evening ahead, then Liz would go back to her aunt in Whitechapel and Carole would return to her parents in order to prepare themselves.

If Janelle could have seen them, she would not have approved, for they hardly looked like the young ladies she was attempting to turn out. Both of them sported mini-skirts as high as they dared get away with. Liz favoured matching knickers. Carole went for dark wool tights. They both went in for false hair, false nails, and false eyelashes.

'Anybody who gets us into bed,' observed Liz on one of their nights out, 'is going to be in for a big surprise.'

Nobody even raised an eyebrow. The boys who haunted the clubs they went to were used to women who came apart in their hands. As long as they didn't come apart in any other direction. What they were after were one night stands, not emotional commitment. And that suited Liz perfectly. She had come to London to have fun and make her name. And she was on the way to doing both.

Only she didn't tell her mother about the fun. If

there was one thing that bothered her, it was walking out on her mother in order to have a better life somewhere else. Liz knew she had to, of course, just as she knew she couldn't take her mother with her, but she didn't have to rub it in. So when she rang home she pretended life was one long, dull, hard slog from early morning till late at night. She sent a little money out of her wage packet every week and with the money came a promise.

'When I start getting famous, I'll earn enough to keep you in style.'

She meant it too. Liz was so convinced she would be inundated with work the moment her photographs were in circulation that she decided to get her own flat. She and Carole were joining up together with a little help from Carole's father. They chose a pad in Old Church Street, just off the King's Road – right in the centre of all the photographers' studios. The flat had a long reception room complete with parquet floor and windows all down one wall.

The moment the money comes rolling in I can give little cocktail parties here, thought Liz. Only it didn't. Janelle had been right in her predictions! Liz wasn't fashion material at all. Her face might have launched a thousand knitting patterns, but *Vogue* and *Harper's Bazaar* left her strictly alone.

Liz began to worry. She had to be lacking in something to be overlooked like this, so she started to ask around.

Carole couldn't see anything wrong with her. 'You've got long hair, long legs and big eyes,' she reasoned, 'what more could you want?'

'Terry Donovan to notice me,' Liz replied.

She enquired further afield. Barry Brogan was the next to be put under the microscope.

'Why do I only do this kind of work?' she demanded. 'Why isn't somebody taking my picture for *Vogue*?'

'Because you're too ordinary,' Barry said abruptly. He never minced words with models. If they decided to put themselves on the meat market, then they had to take the knocks.

Liz was furious. 'What do you mean, ordinary?' she demanded. 'Men don't think I'm run-of-the-mill.'

'That's because they're looking for a tart for the night,' Barry told her. 'Anyone pretty would do, but I'm not talking about pretty. I'm talking about unusual, knock-em-dead looks. I'm sorry darling, but with the best will in the world you haven't got those.'

Liz got up from where she was sitting and heaved her bag onto her shoulder.

'We'll see about that,' she retorted.

She decided to change her image. At Lucie Clayton she had been taught to use a bright lipstick, something with colour and definition.

Now she was thinking for herself she realized it was all wrong. Mannequins went in for corals and reds so that the punters could see them from the catwalk. Jean Shrimpton and Tania Mallet hardly used any colour on their lips at all. Liz redesigned her face, whitening the skin and emphasizing her cheekbones. When she had finished she turned her attention to the rest of her body.

She was too fat, she decided. Among her friends she didn't look fat, but there was a difference between shapely and skinny, and she had learned by now that the camera put on five pounds. She went on a drastic diet.

There was a man in Harley Street who doled out pills and injections and guaranteed a stone off in two weeks. Liz went to see him and he put her on a regime of tinned grapefruit and grilled meat. She forced it down her throat three times a day, even at breakfast, and before every meal she swallowed a pill. The results were instantaneous. In the first two days she dropped five pounds. She also started to feel lightheaded, but she persevered. At the end of two weeks she looked half starved, but she was starting to look interesting. Then she had her hair cut. With the rest of her rent money she paid a visit to Vidal Sassoon and walked out of the salon with a dramatic Cleopatra bob that swung just clear of her shoulders. Every time Liz moved, it moved. It was the cut that changed her. Before she had been a King's Road dolly, decorative, sexy and totally forgettable. Now she had style. Not every man would find her his cup of tea, she knew that, but no man would dare ignore her.

She had her photographs taken again, then she personally delivered a set of them to all the top fashion boys. She hoped they shared the revised opinion she had of herself.

After three weeks Liz realized she had been wrong. The gamble she had taken had backfired on her. Not only did none of the top photographers get in touch, but her regulars backed off. She looked too exotic now for knitting patterns and they gave her sessions to other models. After a month Liz had had enough. She decided to quit modelling altogether. I'll try something else, go into sales, she thought. At least it will pay the rent while I think about what to do with the rest of my life.

Then the phone rang. It was Lucie Clayton telling her Sandy Boyd wanted her for a fashion shoot. Liz began to breathe again. Sandy Boyd, she thought. Now that was more like it.

5

From the mid-1960s a handful of top photographers hogged the fashion pages of the glossy magazines. Donovan, Duffy, Bailey, Parkinson, Avedon, Snowdon, Lichfield and Boyd. Of all of them, Boyd was the quirkiest. None of his models was ever photographed smiling; most of them looked like acrobats or contortionists, so obscure were some of his poses. Yet he made the clothes look more than just clothes. To Boyd a skirt wasn't a skirt, it was an expression, a comment. His peers called him an intellectual to his face, and an eccentric behind his back.

Sandy gloried in the controversy that surrounded him. He had fought long and hard for his place in the sun. Longer and harder than any of his rivals because he didn't have the good fortune to have been born a cockney or an Irishman from the wrong side of the tracks.

On really bad days Sandy would dwell on his disadvantages. He was the second son of a civil servant who worked in the Treasury. That wouldn't have been so bad if he could have disguised the fact, but his looks were against him. In an age where craggy pock-marked faces were all the rage, Sandy looked like a romantic lead from a 1930s film. He was tall, dark and slightly foppish. It was hard to get people to take him seriously.

Sandy completed five years' apprenticeship with Norman Parkinson where he was trodden on by a succession of assistants. However, the great photographer spotted his talent and gave him his chance. *Honey* magazine wanted a fashion spread that Parks simply didn't have the time to deliver so he suggested his dogsbody Sandy Boyd did it in his place. He gave the magazine his solemn promise that if the pictures weren't up to scratch, he would re-shoot them himself.

Parks never did get to keep his promise. The spread was the first of many Sandy was to do for the teen magazines. After a while, he got bored with straight fashion. It was too simple, too unsophisticated. He also realized that if he was to develop his talent he would have to leave Parkinson's studio.

He set up on his own at the beginning of the sixties with a loan from his father and an understanding bank manager. He needed understanding for he nearly went broke several times before the glossies would accept his style.

Then *Vogue* discovered him and in the space of six months he went from being a nonentity to one of the faces of the era. After that he moved from his shabby little darkroom in Notting Hill to a grand town house in Holland Park where the whole of one floor had been converted into a studio. It was here that he did all his fashion work, his portrait work and his still lifes, and it was here that Liz showed up on the dot of ten thirty for her breakthrough assignment.

Sandy was relieved when he saw her. He had booked two models for the session, and the other girl had been a disappointment. The pictures her agency had sent in had shown a gorgeous creature with long, red shiny hair and huge pale eyes. Yet when she turned up she looked nothing like them. She had been crying, and her whole face was puffed up.

Then Liz walked in. Sandy sighed. A gift from heaven, he thought, and you don't know it yet.

Sandy showed Liz through to the models' room and told her to change into a black PVC trouser suit.

Liz did as she was told, then she looked the other model over and fought down a feeling of resentment. Ever since she had come to London she had been up against this kind of bitch. Her eyes took in the translucent blue eyes, the fragile bones, the tilt of her chin. She's got top drawer stamped all over her, Liz thought.

'I haven't seen you around the circuit,' said Liz conversationally. 'Which photographers do you normally work with?'

'None of them,' said the girl, tugging at her thick, tawny hair. 'I was full time at Norman Hartnell till the season ended ten days ago.'

Liz nodded. I thought so, she said to herself. She's some bloody deb slumming it till she finds a rich sucker to marry her.

'It didn't take you long to find something,' she observed acidly, 'but then you do have the right look.'

'Do you think so?' The girl sounded genuinely surprised, and Liz looked sharply at her.

'Don't play the innocent with me,' she snapped, 'I'd like to bet most of the top fashion boys in this town are queuing to snap those loopy upper-class looks of yours. You're all the rage, or haven't you noticed?'

Liz hadn't meant to sound so tough, but there was something languid about this over-indulged creature, something that made you want to kick her in the teeth.

Without warning the girl burst into tears and suddenly Liz felt shabby. She hurried over to where the girl was sitting.

'I didn't mean to bite your head off,' she apologized. 'I'm sorry.'

But there was no stopping her. Vanessa had been teetering on the edge of tears since early in the morning when she got the result of the pregnancy test. All it took was one sharp push to send her over. This bossy, common model had been the one to deliver it.

'Leave me alone,' she sobbed. 'I can't cope any more.' She grabbed a handful of tissues and blew hard into them, wiping off most of her face in the process.

Now Liz was really alarmed. If she went on like this, the girl would be in no state to do the session. The whole job would be blown and Liz would be right back where she started. She decided to go into action. Pulling the tearful girl into a sitting position, she slapped her. The blow was hard enough to shock her, but not so rough that it would leave a mark. The girl stared at her.

'What did you do that for?'

'To bring you back to the present. Whatever it is that's eating you, it's got nothing to do with what's happening now, and that's something we've both got to get through.'

Vanessa threw her handful of soggy tissues across the room.

'Get through it yourself,' she said. 'I'm finished for today.'

But Liz wasn't taking no for an answer. 'That's what you think,' she said. With practised skill she dipped into a pot of cold cream and started smearing it over the other model's face. Then before the girl could protest again she had wiped it off neatly and was dabbing under her eyes and across her cheeks with astringent lotion.

'If I use a really thick pan-cake on you and follow it up with green powder, no-one will know you've been crying.'

For a moment, the girl stopped thinking about her sorrows.

'You don't have to help me,' she said. 'All the clothes are the same size. Why don't you talk Sandy into doing the whole session with you?'

Liz was tempted. It was an easy option and it would give her the limelight she needed, but there was something about the girl sitting in front of her that stopped her. It was obvious that she had been let down badly. If Liz jumped on the bandwagon and took advantage of that fact, she would be just as guilty as the person who had hurt her. Liz was sure it was a man. I must be getting soft, she thought as she searched in her hold-all for the green dusting-powder, but I can't let her destroy herself. Not on my account.

When Liz asked herself afterwards how they got through the session, she put the whole thing down to Sandy. It was as if he knew the tawny-haired girl was in trouble, and he compensated for her lack of spark by doing all the work for her. He shot her from curious angles, focusing on her legs and the fall of her hair. He had arranged the lights so that her face was bleached into a blur and all that could be made out were the elegant lines of her body.

With Liz, Sandy was less generous. He wanted her to give something of herself to the camera, so he cast a spell on her. She had been working with photographers for two years now, and she thought she knew everything. Now she realized she was an amateur.

Liz had never lost herself in what she was doing. She thought that as long as she was in control the photographs would have some meaning. Now she realized she had been wrong. If there was to be a message in the clothes she was wearing, it was not her message, or even the designer's message. The pictures only really worked when the photographer played the tune.

Liz worked with Sandy Boyd for four hours at a stretch and when she was in front of the camera her concentration was absolute.

She became an extension of Boyd's personality, and after a while she didn't have to listen to the directions he was giving. An instinct she didn't know she had picked up exactly what he wanted. Her face, her arms, her legs, her feelings flowed into patterns she had never known before, and for the first time in her life Liz was at peace with herself.

When it was over she felt as if she was coming out of a trance. She took her time changing back into her own things. With a pang she realized she was reluctant to leave this experience behind her. I wonder whether Sandy Boyd will ask me to model for him again, she thought.

The other model broke into her reverie.

'I want to say thanks for getting me through the session,' she said. 'No-one else would have done that.'

'Nonsense,' replied Liz. 'If I'd been in trouble I would have expected a helping hand.'

There was a sudden silence.

'How did you know I was in trouble?' the girl said quietly.

Liz paused, measuring her words. 'I didn't,' she said, 'why, are you?'

The other girl looked as if she was about to fall apart all over again. Then she shook herself.

'I got the results of a pregnancy test this morning. It was positive. There's no doubt about it.'

Liz knew she should walk out there and then and leave this loser to sort things out for herself. It wasn't her fault she was pregnant. Anyway she didn't need anyone else's problems. While she was hesitating Sandy Boyd popped his head round the door.

'Do either of you want to come to the pub? We could all do with a drink after that session.'

Vanessa mumbled something about having to get home, but Liz stood to attention. This is it, she thought. Drinks with the great photographer, a chance to talk him into using me again. Then she looked at the other model. Her shoulders were set in a line of despair and in her eyes there was a look of such misery, that Liz caught her breath. I can't leave her, she thought. She might top herself. She turned to the photographer.

'I'll take a raincheck on the drink,' she said. 'My friend here needs seeing home.'

6

As soon as Liz heard the girl's story she made up her mind to get rid of her. She was a wimp. A snivelling wimp who didn't have the guts to stand up to some guy who'd picked her up in a restaurant and filled her full of dope. It wasn't the dope that got Liz all worked up – everyone smoked these days – everyone young who went to parties anyhow. What really infuriated her was the girl's attitude towards men.

'You must have known where it was going to end,' Liz accused Vanessa, who was slumped on the sofa in the middle of her flat drinking coffee. 'Why didn't you do something before it was too late?'

Vanessa peered at her from under her butterscotch-coloured fringe.

'What should I have done?' she demanded. 'Cried rape? Nobody would have taken a blind bit of notice.'

Liz sighed. This spoilt little deb was really getting on her nerves.

'I wasn't talking about making a protest,' she said. 'I was talking about looking after yourself, taking precautions. You didn't have to get pregnant you know.'

Vanessa started to cry. It wasn't the angry sobbing and heaving of shoulders that Liz and her friends went in for. What happened to this girl was more of a slow dissolving – she folded in on herself as if her last reserves of strength had finally deserted her.

Liz looked at her and suddenly her contempt was

replaced by pity. She's just like my mother, she thought, putting all her faith into a man. Letting him get away with murder, then when the worst happens, all she can do is sit here in a pool of misery and think it was her own fault. She looked at the tangle of limbs and long hair that made up Vanessa. You're hopeless, she thought. You and my mother and all the women like you.

'Have you thought about finding this man?' Liz asked. 'He might just do the decent thing if you push him.'

The girl widened her eyes. 'Don't be silly,' she said. 'I didn't like him for seducing me, so I'm hardly going to spend the rest of my life with him just because of a baby.'

Liz hadn't expected such spirit, or such a show of independence. Despite herself, she was curious.

'But I thought that's what you were cut up about. I mean being loved and left.'

Vanessa looked indignant. 'I was hardly loved,' she said. 'I got picked up at a party and royally laid. We're not talking about "Gone With The Wind", you know. I don't suppose I'd even recognize the man if I bumped into him in the street.'

There was something honest about the way Vanessa said it. Honest and painfully naive.

Liz grinned. 'You'd better not repeat that story to your parents.' Vanessa's earlier indignation was swiftly replaced by anguish.

'Don't talk about my parents,' she said weakly. 'If they knew what I'd been up to they'd kill me.'

It turned out she lived in one of those winding little streets behind Harrods. It was all terribly predictable: nice middle-class girl – born and bred for nice middle-class marriage – suddenly kicks over the traces and goes in for modelling. There were hundreds like her on the circuit. All having their five minutes of rebellion before meeting Mr Right and settling down in the suburbs.

Except Liz wasn't so sure about this one. There was something wilful about her. Something wayward. It wasn't that she was spoiled, it was simply that this girl was used to getting her own way. It's the way she looks, Liz decided. She's a classy piece, people automatically pay attention when they first see her. It's only when they find out how soft she really is that they start to take advantage.

'What will you do?' she asked. 'Are there any friends who might help you?'

Vanessa shook her head. 'Not really,' she responded. 'One of the girls I worked with at Hartnell knows of a woman in Battersea who does abortions, but it sounds dangerous.'

'I can do better for you than that.' The words were out of her mouth before she had had time to think. Liz hadn't wanted to put herself out for this girl, there was really nothing they had in common, but she couldn't let her go to a back-street butcher.

'There's a man in Harley Street,' she went on. 'He's expensive and it's difficult to get through to him, but he won't hurt you. A friend of mine went to him last year so I can vouch for that.'

It was as if she had thrown Vanessa a lifeline, for the girl was all over her. In her earnestness to thank her she reminded Liz of a puppy or a new kitten and she found herself melting.

'I suppose you'll be looking for somewhere to stay too,' she said. 'You won't want to go on living with your parents.'

Vanessa shook her head. 'Do you know of anywhere?'

'Actually we have a spare bedroom here. Carole and I were looking for another girl.'

They fixed it on the spot. Vanessa had some money in a savings account which just about covered the Harley Street doctor and her first month's rent. She handed over a cheque without asking any more questions.

After she had gone Liz wondered what had come over her. She had never collected lame ducks before. It wasn't in her nature. Then she remembered the spirit the girl had shown earlier. Maybe she is worth saving, she thought.

Three days later Vanessa moved into the box room. As soon as she arrived she filled the bathroom with what looked like the contents of Harrods' cosmetics hall. Then she stuffed both Carole's and Liz's cupboards with all her spare ballgowns and riding gear. She got away with both these things because she wasn't pushy about it. Any other girl would have spread herself out and asked questions later. Vanessa said please and thank you. She also doled out little presents. For no reason she presented Liz with a bottle of Floris bath oil.

When she returned from one of her country weekends she always brought whatever she could lay her hands on – a brace of pheasant, a whole cheese, fruit from her father's orchard.

Liz found herself warming to this unwanted new flatmate, mainly because she didn't behave like a flatmate. The girls she knew used the places they lived in like hotel rooms, rushing in and out to change before going on to a club or a date.

Vanessa didn't see things that way at all. She had been brought up to view her surroundings as her home. She cleaned the place three times a week, taking towels to the laundry and making sure they always had loo paper in stock. Sometimes, when she was feeling flush, she actually went out and bought fresh flowers for the living-room. For the first time in Liz's memory they actually had food in the fridge.

Both girls put this domesticity down to the fact that Vanessa was pregnant.

'It's the mumsy thing,' Liz told Carole. 'She wants to turn the place into a nest. She'll change after the operation, you'll see.'

They had taken to calling Vanessa's abortion 'the visit.' It made it less sinister when they talked about it like that, less frightening, though as the time for it came nearer reality intruded.

The doctor Liz had found insisted that Vanessa went to see a psychiatrist before he would do anything.

'It's a way of getting round the law,' he explained. 'I have to be able to prove you might commit suicide if I didn't give you an abortion.'

Vanessa refused to go and see anyone if she had to do it alone and in the end Liz walked her round to the shrink, a disapproving looking woman who had rooms in Marylebone High Street. It was this experience that hardened Vanessa's resolve.

They both went to see the psychiatrist thinking it would be a brief, boring formality – a rubber stamp. But they didn't get away with it. The woman doctor seemed to want to prove something that day.

'Why are you getting rid of this child?' she demanded.

When Vanessa trotted out the answers she had rehearsed with the others at the flat, they didn't wash at all. Every argument against having the child was knocked down.

'It's a life,' the woman said. 'The start of another human being. If you have this abortion it will be like committing a murder.'

Liz expected Vanessa to dissolve in the way she had

done on the day they met, but she didn't. She stayed very calm and there was ice in her voice when she answered.

'If you don't allow me to have this abortion I will take the law into my own hands,' she said. 'I'll get rid of this child myself.'

The psychiatrist didn't say much after that. She simply pressed her lips together and concentrated on taking copious notes. When she was through she showed them the door and told them she would be in touch with the surgeon in Harley Street.

A week later he called with a firm date. The abortion was to take place in a clinic in South London the day after next. He gave Vanessa an address and told her what time to present herself.

'What do I need to bring?' she asked.

'Just yourself,' said the doctor briskly. 'You won't be staying overnight.'

Vanessa put the phone down and the wrongness of what she was doing began to hit her. What if things don't go according to plan, she thought? What if I get sick and the doctor isn't there to take care of me? A thousand doubts went round and round in her head. With an effort she made herself face reality. My only alternative is to have the baby, she thought, and that's out of the question.

She hired a mini-cab to take her to Streatham early in the morning. Liz went with her, and all the way through the South London traffic the two girls held hands and said nothing. The time for joking was over. They knew what was going to happen that day could save Vanessa's life. Or take it. All they could do now was pray that the surgeon was competent.

From the outside, the clinic looked like a drinking club and only when they were let through the door did they realize they had come to the right place. A nurse in a green uniform led them to a waiting-room and told them to hang on. When the doctor was ready for Vanessa, she would be called.

Liz looked around her. They were the only occupants of the cold, dismal room. On three sides there were rows of straight-backed wooden chairs, and there were no magazines on the table in front of them.

Liz looked across at Vanessa and saw she had gone very white. Please God, she prayed, see her safely through this. I won't ask for anything else ever again if you just make sure my friend survives.

Twenty minutes later a nurse came through and asked Vanessa to follow her. She turned to Liz.

'She'll be a couple of hours,' she said shortly. 'When you take her out, she'll still be dizzy from the anaesthetic.'

Liz raised an eyebrow. 'What if there are complications?' she asked baldly.

The nurse looked at her blankly. 'There won't be,' she said.

When Vanessa came round the pain hit her with the force of an armoured truck. She had known she would be sore, but this was more than soreness. Much more. She tried sitting up and the pain was so awful, she thought she would pass out.

The doctor was right behind her.

'Easy does it,' he said. 'You're nearly out of the woods. As soon as you can move, you can get going.'

'But I can't move,' Vanessa whispered. 'It hurts too much.'

The doctor patted her on the shoulder. 'The nurse will give you something for that.'

And he was gone. There were a million things she wanted to ask him. Had everything gone according to plan? How long would she hurt? Would she see him again?

Vanessa started to call out, but the nurse appeared amost immediately and told her to be quiet.

'If you're not careful, you'll get us all into trouble,' she said. Then she produced a phial with a needle on the end and inserted it into Vanessa's left arm. After that she didn't feel anything very much.

She came to and found Liz pushing her upright.

'Hold tight,' she said. 'I'm going to put your coat round you and try to get you into the cab. The nurse told me you're having a bad time, but you've got to expect it.'

Vanessa put an arm round Liz's shoulders and gave her the briefest of hugs. She thought she saw tears in Liz's eyes, but it could have been the light. She felt so fuzzy and there was a dreadful lump right in the pit of her stomach.

Somehow they managed to get into the minicab and she dozed fitfully until they got to Chelsea. Carole was waiting for them at the flat and the presence of the other girl reassured her. They were all of them together in this, three of them against the world. She was sure to make it.

The nurse had provided some pills for Vanessa: one sort for the pain, and half-a-dozen knock-out drops to get her through the nights. Liz administered the painkillers. The sleeping pills she kept in reserve. If her friend was going to be ill, she wanted her to be fully aware of it.

At two o'clock in the morning her fears were confirmed.

Vanessa wasn't just ill, she appeared to be dying. Liz and Carole had taken it in turns to look in on her at hourly intervals, and it was Carole who woke Liz.

'I don't know what to do,' she whispered. 'Vanessa's burning hot and she's asking for more painkillers.'

Liz got out of bed. 'Leave her to me. I'll try and make her more comfortable.'

She tried everything. Two of the blue pills, a hot cup of tea, more pillows. Nothing she could do was any good. Vanessa was in trouble and she knew it. So she just lay there, clinging on to Liz's hand praying for the pain to go away.

At three o'clock her pulse began to fade, and Liz took a decision: she was going to fetch a doctor. If the surgeon who did the operation wasn't available, then she would find someone else. The fact that they had broken the law didn't matter any more. Let them sue us, Liz thought grimly. All that counts now is that Vanessa gets help.

She didn't expect to get any response from the Harley Street number, but the telephone was picked up on the third ring. The person on the end of the line was the surgeon's wife.

Briefly, Liz explained the problem, stressing the urgency of the situation. The woman must have run up against this one before, for she took down Liz's address and told her not to worry.

'Someone will be with you in fifteen minutes,' she said.

An ambulance arrived at half past three and Vanessa was taken off.

Liz followed her to the hospital and spent the rest of the night sitting on a hard wooden bench in the casualty department. Then, at half past seven, she was allowed into the ward. Vanessa was still unconscious, but breathing and Liz sat by the side of the bed until she came round. She opened her eyes at last, and before she could say anything, the nursing staff moved in. A screen went up around the bed and Liz was pushed out into the waiting-room again. Two hours later she managed to see the ward sister.

'Is she going to be all right?' she enquired anxiously.

The nurse nodded and looked tired.

'It was a close thing,' she said. 'If you'd left it another thirty minutes, she wouldn't have made it.'

She sighed and sat down heavily beside Liz. 'Why do you girls do it?' she asked. 'It wouldn't have been difficult to have had the baby. The mother's a young woman. In good health, from what I can see. It might have done her good to have taken responsibility for her pregnancy.'

Liz looked at the sister carefully. She was a plain woman in her mid-thirties with a look of experience about her. She'd obviously been nursing for some years, and whatever happened in her life, she would go on nursing. A woman like this could take a baby, or even a husband in her stride. All Vanessa had was her looks.

'I don't think you understand,' was all Liz said.

Vanessa was allowed out of hospital a week later and went straight back to the flat in Old Church Street. Part of her wanted to go home to her parents, but she knew she wasn't a little girl any more. There was nowhere she could hide.

Not being able to retreat into her family was the hardest part. All the other times when Vanessa had been hurt her mother had been there to make it better. She could hardly ask her mother to repair this wound – it went deeper than a cut knee. She had lost a child, or more accurately, she had murdered a child.

The realization of what she had done came home to her when she was well enough to think about the future. The photographic session she and Liz had done with Sandy Boyd was out now in *Harper's Bazaar*. As she suspected, there was very little of her in it. All the shots featured Liz who looked thin and mysterious and somehow magical. The dark girl was over the moon of course and so were the Lucie Clayton School who were inundated with bookings for her.

Vanessa found it difficult to join in with all the excitement. She knew she would never be another Twiggy or Shrimpton like Liz, yet it wasn't jealousy that held her back. It was simply that the whole game seemed pointless suddenly.

She saw herself working for Hardy Amies or Victor Steibel season after season. Going to the latest club, wining and dining with the latest crop of young men about town and getting nowhere.

The only thing she had done of any real importance was to conceive a child. If she had valued it at the time, that child could have been born and grown into a statesman or a hero. Now what did she have? A career that lasted as long as her looks. The depression lasted long after the rest of her had healed.

When she got really low Liz could be relied on to cheer her up.

'It's not over yet,' she would console her. 'One day a real man will turn up for you and your whole life will change.'

He never did of course. Vanessa's biggest asset turned out to be her biggest curse. Her beauty, instead of attracting suitors, terrified them. All the men in her circle found her daunting. A woman who looked like Vanessa deserved no less than a prince, and because none of them were that they gave her a wide berth.

Not that she was neglected. There was always a coterie of camp photographers and designers who wanted her on their arms. Older men sought her out and so did married men. To them she presented no danger and she consoled herself with these temporary companions. From time to time she would have the odd discreet affair and while the liaison lasted she even convinced herself she was in love. But Vanessa's loves never lasted for none of them had any future. What she wanted for herself more than anything else was a baby to replace the one she had lost. She yearned for a home and a husband and a child. Her need burned a great aching hole inside her but she took care to show to no-one her emptiness. As far as the world was concerned, Vanessa was bright and beautiful and the envy of everyone she knew. Only Liz knew her secret and she guarded it jealously. The way a sister would.

7

Sandy Boyd surveyed the wreckage of his wardrobe and felt sorry for himself. All the sleeves of his jackets had been cut off at the elbows, and his trousers – even his jeans – had been reduced to shorts. Whoever was responsible for this wanted to cause him a great deal of embarrassment and a certain amount of inconvenience.

Eve, he thought. It has to be Eve. It couldn't be anyone else. He and Eve Turner had been together for eighteen months now, and they complemented one another perfectly.

Black, sleek, excitable Eve was the hottest model on the Paris catwalk and Sandy was the hottest talent to wield a camera. Together they made a fortune. Like Shrimpton and Bailey, Twiggy and Justin, they were one of those teams that just couldn't fail. Except they did fail. One day, after the mother and father of all rows, Sandy had stormed out of his house in Holland Park and Eve had taken her revenge. With a pair of garden shears she had laid into his clothes and when she had rendered them all unwearable, she had packed her own things and walked out of his life.

The whole thing depressed Sandy utterly, though it wasn't the loss of the clothes that got him down. He could replace them without too much trouble. It was the loss of Eve that hurt. Particularly now.

It was coming up to collection time and he had assignments from top magazines on both sides of the Atlantic.

Sandy racked his brains thinking of possible replacements. There was a very good German girl doing the circuit at the moment, Junoesque and Nordic-looking. He made a note to call her agent. Then there was a healthy, statuesque Texan who had made her mark during the last Paris Season.

Sandy sighed. It would be easier if he could find a decent English girl. Someone on the spot who hadn't made too much of a name for herself. The trouble with all these girls was that once they found their feet they became impossible. His mind went back to Eve. She was too famous, he decided. She wouldn't do what she was told even in the very beginning. The next girl he took on wouldn't be like her at all. The next girl would be a pussycat.

When Liz was signed as Sandy Boyd's model for the International collections she knew she'd finally made it. Her agency realized it too, for they upped her rates the minute the booking came in.

'If you survive the next six months,' Janelle told her, 'you'll be in the Verushka class.'

The last remark confused Liz. 'Why shouldn't I survive?' she asked. 'I've worked for Sandy once before and he's a piece of cake.'

Janelle wondered whether to tell this rising star of hers the truth about Sandy Boyd. That he wanted a mistress as well as a model. Then she thought, no. The new contract was going to bring a lot of money and a good deal of prestige into the agency. What was the point in giving the girl cold feet?

She decided to tell half the story.

'I was worried about your stamina,' she replied. 'Sometimes the collections can be very demanding.'

In the middle of her first week in Paris, Janelle's words came back to Liz. The woman had known what she was talking about. Liz had been up every morning at dawn, and even before the sleep was out of her eyes an army of hairdressers and make-up men had descended on her room.

By seven, Sandy appeared with hot coffee and croissants which he consumed in front of her. On her first day she had made the mistake of reaching for her own breakfast, only to find her hand slapped by the make-up artiste.

'You'll smudge your lipstick,' he screamed. 'You can have something after the session.'

But there was never time. While everyone else broke for lunch, Liz had to go back to her hotel where the same people she met at breakfast were waiting for her.

Over the next hour, her entire look was changed. If she was an innocent in the morning, they re-did her to look like a vamp in the afternoon. The heated rollers that burned her scalp five hours previously were shoved back and her hair was bent in yet another direction. Layer of paint was applied over layer of paint and she ended up feeling submerged. I'm not a person at all, she would think as she stood in front of Sandy's cameras. All I am is a bendy doll. A creation of other people's fantasies.

Nevertheless, she loved what she was doing. There was an excitement about working with Sandy she didn't feel with anyone else, and she suspected it was something chemical. When she stood in front of him and he looked at her in a certain way, she responded. Their communication became so complete that he only had to raise an eyebrow and Liz knew exactly what he wanted.

In the evenings when it was all over Sandy took her out for dinner with the rest of the team. Half a dozen camera-men and fashion assistants in jeans and the leather jackets that they all wore off duty trooped down to one of the Brasseries on the Left Bank where they would consume crudités and thin-grilled steaks. On those nights everyone except Liz, who needed to look dewy-eyed the next morning, drank quantities of rough red wine and talked shop till past midnight.

Liz was always sent home to get her beauty sleep at around ten and she went without complaint. She knew she was employed for the way she looked, yet she couldn't help feeling as if she had been cheated. She had gone into this life for glamour and excitement, yet here she was living like a student nurse.

On her fourth night in Paris she took stock of the situation. She was staying at the Plaza Athénée just across the road from Christian Dior. The foyer was so grand it reminded her of a constant cocktail party. Every time Liz walked through it she saw a succession of women wearing the clothes she was being paid a fortune to model. They all wore diamonds and they were all accompanied by rich grey-haired men and Liz knew without having to ask that they were all having the time of their lives.

What's the point, she thought, of looking like a cover girl if it's all going to waste. I had more fun when I was posing for knitting patterns.

Her dissatisfaction must have been apparent for Sandy noticed it and came to her rescue. He gave her a morning off, then he asked her out to dinner on her own.

'I've been working you too hard,' he told her. 'You need a breather.'

Liz's spirits picked up. Like all the other girls in their group, she was half in love with Sandy. None of them really knew him of course; he was too aloof for that, too wrapped up in his work. But there was something sexy about him. It was more than a combination of faded blue jeans and long black hair. Sandy looked as if he had seen it all and done it all and the whole thing bored him to tears. Surprise me, his expression seemed to say. Do something, anything to spark my interest.

Liz decided to take up the challenge. On the night they were going out, she got out her most expensive dress. She had been saving it for an evening like this and the moment she put it on, she knew something exciting would happen. It was by one of the new Italian designers and consisted almost entirely of intricately worked black lace cobwebs held together by chiffon. It was low in the front and very short and Liz couldn't wait to see Sandy's face when she met him in front of the hotel.

It was her first disappointment that evening, for she made no impression on that photographer at all. He behaved towards her in the way he always did. She might have been wearing jeans for all the notice he took.

She climbed into the waiting taxi and began to make small talk. This was her first real evening out since she had arrived in Paris. She wanted to know where they were going, if it was smart, and who she could expect to see when they got there. Sandy answered her questions absent-mindedly, as if there was something else he wanted to say to her. As they drew up in front of the restaurant Liz discovered what it was. Sandy wanted to talk business. He had taken her to Fouquets at the top of the Champs Elysées. The place where film stars and millionaires drank champagne and all Sandy wanted to do was discuss camera angles.

Liz sighed. Damn you, Sandy Boyd, she thought. You might think Fouquets is old hat, but I'm going to enjoy myself.

It was a big, bright, L-shaped restaurant with the best tables in a conservatory section at the back. Liz was glad to discover that Sandy had at least got them a special table and by the time she sat down and the waiter had brought her a Kïr, her mood had improved. As well as his work, Sandy was fascinated by old Hollywood movies. He had a fund of anecdotes about the stars of the 1930s and Liz found herself listening to him and laughing. It wasn't her subject at all, yet the photographer injected all his improbable tales with such off-beat humour that she was entranced.

On all the other first dates Liz had had, her escorts had told her highly edited versions of their life stories. It was what she expected of the men in her life. Sandy didn't go in for the obvious and it liberated her, for she didn't have to play the woman any more. She could relax and enjoy the wine and not give a damn what she looked like.

Somewhere towards the end of the meal Liz realized she was slightly drunk. She noticed she was talking too much, asking too many questions, but she couldn't stop herself. She half expected Sandy would tell her she was going too far, but he didn't seem worried. I can say anything I like to this man, she thought. He's unshockable.

They were talking about liaisons they had had in the past and Sandy started to tell her about Eve. Liz had read about them in the gossip columns and she felt privileged that he was confiding in her.

'Why did it end?' she asked him. 'I always thought you were an unstoppable combination.'

For a moment Sandy's eyes looked very black.

'Eve was a deeply conventional girl,' he told her. 'She looks exotic, but it's all an affectation.' He paused, thinking what he was going to say next. Finally he went on.

'When I'm with a girl, I like to try different things. You've seen the way I am when I'm taking pictures, I don't have any truck with the standard poses, the obvious angles. It's the same when I'm in bed and Eve didn't like it.'

Liz didn't know why the conversation turned her on, but it did and she realized she was finally getting somewhere with this man.

'What do you do?' she asked. 'What do you get up to that's so shocking?'

Sandy refused to be drawn. Almost imperceptibly he retreated behind a veil of sophistication he always put up in front of him and Liz felt like a silly little girl.

It's finished, she thought. I had his attention and I blew it by being too pushy. I'll never get a chance to get close to him now.

Sandy was distant with her for the remainder of the week. Then they moved on to Milan and his mood changed. It was as if the Italian fashion capital breathed a different kind of life into him.

The designers themselves were less formal than their French counterparts. They drank more, and they shouted more, and they were less stuffy about the clothes.

If Sandy wanted to photograph dinner dresses at dawn in one of the medieval churches that dotted the town, nobody minded. In this town they could play at fashion any time of the day or night as long as they were communicating ideas. As long as they were selling, Milan was laid out at their feet.

One day Sandy dressed Liz in a bridal gown and took her into a smoky restaurant where he made her stand on the table with a glass of wine in her hand. Another time he hired a body artiste and made her pose half-dressed, half-painted while he took roll after roll of colour exposures.

Liz was exhilarated, intrigued and frightened all at the same time because she knew this new situation was leading somewhere. She knew that she was losing control of what was happening to her.

The whole thing came into focus on the last weekend. She and Sandy were shooting a final session for American *Vogue*. Most of the team had already left Milan and were on their way to New York for the American shows. Because the set-up was a simple one, Sandy allowed Liz to do her own make-up and hair and he dispensed with his usual assistants.

They were to shoot the clothes in a studio Sandy had hired for the afternoon, then they would have a quiet dinner in town before packing up and getting the plane across the Atlantic the next day. There was an end-of-term feeling about the job and Liz hadn't even bothered to enquire about the clothes she would be wearing. When she got into the dressing-room behind the studio, she wished she had, for she had never seen such outfits. The man who had dreamed them up was obviously into bondage or something kinky, for all the garments seemed to be made of leather with bones and wires in the most curious places.

When Liz walked in front of Sandy's cameras she felt like Jane Fonda in 'Barbarella'.

She had on a short black mini-skirt in soft nappa with high-heeled boots that came up to her thighs. Her midriff was bare and she was wearing a complicated bra which made her breasts look like two ice-cream cones. Round her neck was a dog collar with studs on.

Liz thought Sandy would burst out laughing when

he saw her, but he looked deadly serious. After only the briefest of instructions they went to work. Usually in the studio they were more relaxed than this – there was always a make-up girl or a hairdresser in attendance and they would break and drink coffee and discuss what they were going to do next. Now, without the distractions of other people, they completed the session in record time.

With a certain amount of relief Liz made to get up and change into her own things, but Sandy stopped her.

'I want to try something else,' he said.

Liz sighed. Bang go my plans for a long bath and a hot cup of tea she thought. She listened while he told her to stand up against the white paper backdrop with her legs slightly apart. Then he came over to her and started to adjust the clothes.

She was used to him doing this. In studio after studio Sandy had moved shoulder straps, arranged hems, pushed her hair out of the way and she hadn't paused to change position. Now it was different, for instead of touching the clothes, he touched her skin.

Liz knew in that instant exactly what he was going to do next. I should slap his face, she thought. This is not part of the job description. But she didn't move.

She had spent too many nights dreaming about Sandy making love to her to pull back now. She would have liked him to be more romantic, but she was in no position to dictate terms, so she took what she was given.

When Sandy leaned forward and started to kiss her she made no protest. Instead she parted her lips and let his tongue explore the inside of her mouth. His hands came into contact with the ridiculous conical bra and Liz reached behind her back and undid the catch so that it fell to the floor. She could feel Sandy's hands on her and started to respond to him, arching her hips and pushing against him. They fell to the floor, Sandy's hands underneath her leather skirt, pulling at her panties. Liz felt them slide off her and she knew the time for playing was over. She started to undo the skirt, but he stopped her.

'I want you exactly like this,' he told her sharply. 'In the boots and the stockings.'

And before she could protest, he pushed the leather skirt up around her waist and knelt on top of her.

Liz expected him to take her quickly. To return the urgency of the moment. Instead he prolonged it, stroking her body and staring at her as if she was some private dirty postcard. Then very slowly, he unzipped his jeans and took her with such passion that she climaxed almost immediately.

Sandy Boyd was a very skilful lover. So skilful that nothing he made Liz do shocked her at all.

Several times that afternoon, he made her go back into the dressing-room and get into different combinations of the Italian designers' clothes. He didn't seem to be interested in her nakedness at all. It was as if he was making love to the clothes, the images of fashion, as well as to her. If he hadn't turned her on so much she might have worried. In the back of her mind was the memory that Eve, his last girlfriend, had left him because of this strangeness. But Liz didn't think about it too much.

Eve had been a conventional woman Sandy informed her. Liz knew that, whatever else, she wasn't conventional. She was a working-class girl from a poor background. Her life had been too hard to acquire manners or pretensions or false ideas about herself. What she and Sandy were doing might not be entirely to her taste, but it didn't repel her either. Because of that, she went on with the affair. Sandy had things that she needed. He could take her to places she had never visited before, introduce her to people she would never meet in the ordinary way of things, work with her in a way that would make her name.

In return for all that, he wanted her to dress up in different disguises while he made love to her. It's a fair exchange, she thought. There is, after all, no such thing as a free lunch.

8

Janelle at Lucie Clayton had been right about Liz. The next few months did push her into a different class. Before, she had been in demand with advertising agencies and women's magazines because she was dark and dramatic looking and the latest fashions looked good on her. Now it was more than that. With Sandy behind the camera, the latest fashions looked different when she was wearing them. It was as if the two of them were interpreting what the designers were trying to say.

When long boots came into vogue, Sandy got hold of a pair of waders and photographed Liz wearing them with hotpants and tiny mini-skirts. Liz was one of the first girls to wear aviator's sunglasses, dresses made of plastic discs and kaftans. The other women she came in contact with admired her and began to imitate the way she looked.

Twice in six months, Liz made the front cover of *Vogue*. After that, Vanessa started to read about her in the gossip columns.

When the affair first started, Liz joined the ranks of Sandy's other romances. She was just the latest in a line of beautiful model girls. Yet this liaison was different from the others because it looked more serious. The two collected around them a coterie of followers; other photographers, stylists, hairdressers and film actors. They became known as trendsetters and soon there was speculation about their future. Would they get married like the Quants, or would they simply set up home the way Jean Shrimpton and David Bailey had?

The columnists weren't the only people asking questions. Vanessa also wanted to know which way the wind blew. Yet every time she opened up a conversation about Sandy she was met with a blank wall. Liz, who had never kept anything from her friend, suddenly became secretive.

Vanessa often wondered whether there was anything wrong between them. Then she thought there couldn't be. If Liz was unhappy she would have shown it, and she didn't.

The only thing that was bugging Liz was that she wasn't getting on fast enough. Now she was famous she wanted to be something else. She wanted to be smart. She started asking Vanessa the sort of questions that went out with Miss Manners. How should she address a Duke if she met one? Should she wear a hat for Ascot? Was it acceptable to light a cigarette before or after the cheese?

Vanessa thought she was joking.

Then one evening she discovered Liz tucking into a steak an hour before she was due to have dinner at the Savoy and she realized something was up.

'What on earth are you doing?' she asked. 'Has your evening been cancelled?'

Liz shook her head.

'No,' she replied. 'Sandy's coming for me in forty minutes. What's the problem?'

Come off it, Vanessa thought. It's me you're talking to. Aloud she said, 'The problem is you're eating half a pound of the finest rump when there's another full meal waiting for you any minute now. Are you on some kind of diet?'

Liz looked embarrassed.

'No, I'm not,' she said quietly.

'Then what is it?'

The two girls looked at each other and Vanessa wondered if she had gone too far. Then Liz smiled.

'It's to do with manners,' she admitted. 'I haven't got any. That's not quite true – I have got manners but not the kind that go down like a bomb at the Savoy. I'm never quite sure whether I'm holding my knife properly. Sandy told me the other day I brandished it about like a pencil. Then there's the place setting. That's completely beyond me.'

She paused, adjusting her smile.

'Anyway,' she said brightly, 'I've worked out a way round all that. I always make sure I have something before I go out, so I'm guaranteed not to make a fool of myself. If anyone notices I'm not eating they automatically assume I'm struggling to keep my figure.'

Vanessa was irritated. Liz's obsession with doing the right thing had been getting on her nerves for weeks. Now she was putting herself through this.

'What's happening to you?' she asked. 'You never used to be like this.'

Liz pushed her dinner away and when she looked up to face her friend a shutter seemed to have come down over her eyes.

'It's no use explaining,' she told her. 'You'd never understand.'

But Vanessa had had enough.

'Try me,' she said.

There was something in her voice that made Liz sit up. An autocratic note, as if she expected a straight answer. It was at that moment she saw the difference between them. Vanessa had been raised from birth to give orders. She had grown up to take them. Liz sighed.

'It's very simple. I come from nothing and I get

worried when it shows. Before I got successful it really didn't matter. There was nobody much around who knew the difference anyway. Now there is. Sometimes when I have dinner with Sandy's smart friends, I do something wrong and everybody looks at me. The really awful thing is I never know exactly what it is I do to offend them.'

'Hence all those questions about how to talk to a Duke if you happened to run into one.'

Liz nodded. 'You're getting the picture.'

Vanessa wondered what she was going to say next. Liz was dead common, there was no point in denying that, but she didn't want to insult her either. Finally she said:

'Why do you worry about yourself so much? You're miles prettier than all these dreary people you want to impress. Half of them would give their manners and their accents to have your kind of style.'

Liz cut in on her.

'It's not enough,' she said. 'I can't walk about for the rest of my life knowing that people look down on me. You may think it's dreary and commonplace to behave like a lady, but that's because you were born one. I wasn't, and every time I drop an "H" or eat peas off my knife I get reminded of it.'

She looked at Vanessa, sleek and well-bred, and fought down a feeling of resentment.

'Have you any idea what it's like to be the odd one out?'

The other girl walked over to the window and stared into the street. The light was fading and the last of the shoppers and office workers were disappearing into the pubs. Once Liz had been like them. Happy and ordinary and wanting nothing more than all the other girls she knew.

Something has changed her recently, Vanessa

thought. She wondered if it was Sandy, this new lover she refused to talk about. Then realized it wasn't him. What's changed Liz is all this success she's having. Now she's got more, she expects more. More of life. More of herself.

Vanessa knew she shouldn't encourage this new ambitious Liz. Then she thought, what the hell, if I don't tell her the facts of life, somebody else will.

'You don't have to stay the way you are,' she said slowly. 'If you want to, you can make yourself over.'

'I suppose you're talking about flower-arranging classes at the polytechnic. Well you can stuff that. It won't make any difference at all.'

Vanessa looked her in the eye.

'I wasn't talking about that at all,' she said. 'If you must know I was talking about your bloody awful accent. If you can scrape up the money a long course of elocution lessons wouldn't come amiss at all.'

9

It began as a challenge. An experiment to see if she could actually change herself into someone else. Altering her appearance had been one thing, but changing the way she sounded, the way she was – that was a bigger hurdle.

Liz enrolled for a course of lessons with a voice coach, an elderly actress whose name she found in *The Stage*. Right from the start she hated it. It wasn't the lessons that got her down, it was the woman herself.

Her name was Daphne Tremain, a dyed blonde somewhere in her fifties who used too much paint and insisted on calling Liz 'darling'. When she drank a cup of tea, which she did half way through each session, she stuck her little finger in the air. For reasons she didn't quite understand, these little mannerisms irritated Liz. If I ever become a lady, Liz vowed to herself, I don't want to be like Daphne. But Liz showed no signs of turning into anyone but herself. 'How now brown cow,' she would chant furiously, Eliza Doolittle style, but the sound that emanated from her was the sound of cockles and whelks and brown ale.

She was given a tape and a set of voice exercises to practise night and morning, but no matter how hard she tried, nothing seemed to make any difference. After three weeks, Vanessa offered to lend a hand.

'If you imitate the sound of my voice,' she said, 'maybe that will help.'

It made it worse.

When Liz followed Vanessa's vowel sounds, she sounded like a caricature of a pantomime dame. In the end she decided to call it a day. She made up her mind to stop the lessons at the end of the fourth week.

'It's no good,' she informed Daphne. 'I'm not making any progress. Maybe I wasn't meant to sound any different.'

The tutor shook her head sadly.

'You're too impatient,' she said. 'It took you over twenty years to speak the way you do. You need time to undo it now.'

Liz settled her bill and turned to go.

'I don't have the time,' was all she told her.

That weekend she was going down to visit her family. Her brother was a real boy now, and because he was grown-up enough to be off his hands, her father had re-appeared on the scene. He didn't actually live at home – Brenda Enfield had too much pride to take him back – but he visited frequently, and when he had learned his daughter was going to be at home, Ernie had invited himself to Sunday lunch.

Liz wasn't looking forward to it. She had managed to keep clear of her father for years now, and that suited her. He had disappointed her a long time ago, but she had managed to put the disappointment aside and go on with her life. She thought she had, at any rate. Seeing Ernie again might prove her wrong. Stirring up all that long forgotten bitterness was the last thing she needed.

As Sunday approached she became increasingly nervous. What if I go home early, she thought. Mum can cope on her own, she doesn't need me there – I can always go down some other time. But something made her hesitate. She remembered how her father used to buy her presents and take her to the carnival. And with this memory came the memory of love.

Ernie Enfield arrived the way he always arrived for Sunday lunch: forty minutes late, after the pubs had tipped out. Liz was surprised at how he had aged. She remembered her father as being very tall, with jet-black hair and a military moustache. He was still tall, but his hair – what there was left of it – was greying. He had shaved off his moustache, and now he looked like a shabby old man. This wasn't Liz's father. The man who had broken her heart. The man who had left her for dead. It couldn't be.

Liz helped her mother bring the food to the table. It kept her busy for a while and it gave her time to think. What was she going to say to this pathetic stranger – what was there left to say? In the event, it was her father who made the running. He wanted to know all about her life. Most of all, he wanted to know which famous people she had met.

He's like some starfucker, Liz thought. Some bloody groupie who reads the *News of the World* to get the inside track.

Liz struggled through lunch as well as she could, trotting out names and places and boring anecdotes she thought she had long forgotten. Suddenly, she realized she had an audience. Her mother was gazing at her in rapt attention, and her little brother, Tom, was hanging on every word.

'You should write a book about your life,' he said. 'I bet it would be a bestseller.'

Her parents chimed in agreeing with him, and Liz felt surrounded by admiration and something else – hero worship.

I should feel flattered, she thought. I should be tickled pink. Only she wasn't. She felt sick instead.

For she thought she belonged to this family unit and now she wasn't sure.

She noticed for the first time how expensive her clothes were. She was only wearing jeans, but the jeans had a designer's label on them, and her hair had been cut in Bond Street.

It's not fair, she thought. They're the shabby ones, yet they make me feel like an outsider.

Liz considered playing down her success. Even lying about it to make them accept her in the way they used to. Then her mother made one comment, one ill-considered remark, and Liz changed her mind about everything.

'You can tell that Liz knows a lot of posh people,' Brenda said turning to her husband. 'Just listen to the way she talks.'

Liz was frozen to attention.

'Are you out of your mind?' she said. 'I sound just the same as I always did.'

Her parents shook their heads, and in their eyes there was a look of unmistakable pride.

'You sound like a lady now,' said Ernie. 'No-one could mistake it.'

Liz had come to the point of no return. Before she started having her voice trained she might have just been able to go home. Now there was no way. She sounded wrong in Southend. She may still sound off-key in London, but she could change that. With time and practice she could polish her voice the way she was polishing her appearance. In the end, when she was finished, she would be a new person.

She looked at her father, the man she had loved and then hated with such a passion, and she felt nothing. Even her mother was growing away from her. Growing towards the down-at-heel past, the down-at-heel man who had come to claim her. Soon there would be nothing left of any of them: brother, parents, uncles, aunts. All of them would be lost. Eclipsed by her success.

She shivered slightly and made ready to go back to London.

10

In six weeks Liz's voice started to improve. It was nothing startling, but she did sound different. She felt that people began to pay more attention to her. Before, she could sit at a dinner party and be ignored all the way from the soup through to the cheese trolley. Now, the other guests were interested in her conversation. What tickled Liz was that she didn't say anything particularly different. She chattered on in the same way that she always did, but she chattered in the right accent and that made her fit in.

She decided to educate herself. She went to lectures on modern art at one of the Cork Street galleries. The sessions were tucked in between photographic jobs, so nobody was put out by them, and when she found she enjoyed learning about pictures she applied her mind to other things. She visited antique shops, she did a course of French cooking. Her temper improved, too, because she no longer felt inferior. In the past, girls like Vanessa had made Liz feel less of a person. Now she knew she was equal to everyone she met.

There was only one person left to convince: Sandy.

Since Liz had been sharing his bed, the two of them had become close. She was spending more and more of her time at his house in Holland Park. Half her clothes were already hanging in his wardrobe and she knew the time was approaching when she would move in with him.

'It's a logical step,' he kept telling her. 'Why spend

your hard-earned money paying rent on Old Church Street, when you spend all your time with me?'

Liz knew she would give in in the end, but she held back because their relationship worried her. The whole world acknowledged the change in her, yet Sandy behaved as if nothing had happened at all. He still expected her to bow to his superior authority. If she had an idea of her own on one of their photographic sessions, he brushed it aside and told her she didn't know what she was talking about. He always decided exactly what clothes to use and Liz didn't have any say about the way she presented herself. As far as Sandy was concerned she was simply a doll. A living doll to be taken out and dressed up and put in front of the cameras.

Even when we go to bed, Liz thought bitterly, it doesn't change. All I do is put on another costume. I'm a leather lady, or a French maid or a tart in a brothel. Why is it that when Sandy makes love to me I have to pretend to be somebody else?

11

New York, 1968

Ever since he could remember, Dan Levin had pursued two kinds of girls. The girls he could get – Jewish girls who lived in his suburb and played at his tennis club, and the girls who were far beyond him. The second kind were the ones who really turned him on.

Dan was to lament his sexual preferences most of his youth, for tall, fair debutantes didn't waste their time with the likes of him. He was too big, too clumsy, too rough round the edges. Until he was in his early twenties, Dan had his heart broken regularly by a succession of snotty little blondes. Then he wised up. He wasn't such a bad catch, he decided. His parents had a thriving clothing business, a business he would join when he left design school. He was good looking, great at sports – it was time he found somebody who appreciated these qualities.

Six months later he found Ruth Gold. She was taking the same course as he was at the New York School of Design. When she graduated she planned on a career in fashion, or so she said. After they had been dating for three weeks, Dan knew she was lying. The only thing on Ruth's mind was getting married. The lucky guy had to be rich, or have rich parents. He had to be Jewish and he needed to be good in bed.

Dan won this final qualification one weekend when Ruth's parents were away in Miami. It decided his future, for Ruth was simply the sexiest girl he had ever known.

No woman, even a blonde from Smith College,

could move him the way Ruth moved him. He couldn't leave her alone. He couldn't get enough of her, and in the end, because he couldn't see any other way of sleeping in her bed every night, he asked her to marry him.

Both sets of parents were overjoyed by the news. The Golds set them up in a big swish apartment on the West Side. Sid Levin took his son into the family business and made him head of design. It was then, just weeks after his honeymoon, that Dan realized he could have all the classy blondes he wanted.

Levins was one of the biggest garment manufacturers in the USA. They made high-class dresses, suits and evening wear for the big department stores. They had three labels: Bonniwear was the cheap range for salesgirls and secretaries; Maxi-modes, the more expensive label, was aimed at the affluent wives of rising executives; Madame Xavier was a heavily beaded and bowed evening collection that catered for the richest women of all. Every spring and autumn the showrooms were filled for six weeks with tall, slender models showing the ranges to the buyers. They were the kind of girls Dan spent his youth breaking his heart over. Now they broke their hearts over him. He was the head of design, the boss's son. Of course he resisted them. He was married to Ruth now – the sexiest girl in the world. She was quite enough for him. Then she learned how to be the wife of a successful Seventh Avenue tycoon. She got pregnant and learned to cook. One day, ten years after he got married, Dan turned round and discovered he had married his mother.

After that he stopped resisting the models. It was one of the best times in his life. He had a wife he liked, two beautiful children, an apartment in Manhattan and a house in Long Island. He also had a succession of the kind of mistresses he had only ever dreamed of.

Dan rented an apartment in an exclusive building on West 57th Street. It was a very old, historic building with a vaulted ceiling in the lobby, but the best thing about it was that it was half way between his office and his home. That made it very convenient for seeing his girls.

Ruth knew about the girls, of course. She wasn't a fool, but she didn't begrudge her husband his pleasures, since she knew they were passing pleasures. Sometimes Dan discussed them with her. He didn't admit straight out that he had girlfriends, but Ruth knew that Angela who had looked so wonderful in the autumn line, or Stephanie who was popular with the buyer from Saks, did more than just model the clothes. She didn't let on that she knew of course. She simply shrugged her shoulders and looked the other way. The Angelas and the Stephanies were just icing on the cake. All men, all successful men needed girls like that, but they also needed wives like Ruth. Wives and houses and children and possessions. Ruth never forgot that. So when Dan was home late for dinner, or was away more days than he said he was going to be, the knowledge of how necessary she was gave her courage.

Dan's girls provided the inspiration for his first fortune. At the beginning of every season, Dan would go to the offices of the Eileen Ford agency and choose which models he wanted for his lines. Due to his personal preferences most of the girls he booked were thin and upper-crust looking. One year when the showroom seemed to be crowded out with debutantes, Dan's father called him into his office.

'It's got to stop,' he said. 'I know what you get up to, and I'm prepared to turn a blind eye, but what I won't have is every girl here looking like a candidate for your bed.'

He paused and regarded his only son with despair. 'We don't make clothes for the social register,' he told him. 'Levins manufactures for the woman in the street – working women, New York women. I want you to send these models back and get some all-American girls.'

Dan gave the matter some careful thought. He was a typical New Yorker, yet he aspired to having a grand lady on his arm and in his bed. So what about all the other typical New Yorkers? They probably wanted exactly the same thing. He began to canvass his friends and discovered he was right. Then he started on his wife and her friends. If the men fantasized about conquering debutantes, what did the women dream about? He had a hunch he already knew what they would say. And he was right. All the women, without exception, wanted to look classier than they really were. Even rounded women with black frizzy hair wanted to look like elegant ladies.

Dan took his design pad and retreated into his office where he stayed for five days. When he came out he had the basis of a whole new collection. Everything in it was designed for an aristocrat as seen through the eyes of a New Yorker. The suits were simple: slips of skirts under jackets cut like a man's. The dresses were unwaisted tubes, and all the trousers were cut like jeans. What made the line different to anything else on the market was, though, the fabric he used. It gave a touch of class. Tee shirts were made out of satin; the simple, thigh-skimming cocktail dresses were cut out of rich brocade, and he used suede and thin supple leather in everything from shirts to jeans.

Sid Levin was appalled.

'We'll never sell it,' he protested, 'it's too impractical.'

Dan laughed at his father.

'Whoever heard of a woman going to a fashion store to buy something practical? When she buys clothes, she buys dreams, and the dream I'm selling is the beautiful high-born lady.'

This last remark sent Dan's father wild with rage.

'No gal in this town wants to look like that,' he shouted. 'That's your fantasy. It's got nothing to do with real life.'

He motioned to the sketches on Dan's pad. 'None of this has a hope in hell. I wouldn't waste my money making it up.'

Dan picked up his pad. 'I don't need your money,' he replied shortly. 'I've got plenty of my own.' Those were his last words on the subject. Sid ranted on for days, but his son refused to be moved. He was going to finance the new range and that was the end of it.

He even gave the range its own name. It was to be called Royal Enclosure and he was going to launch it that spring.

By February everything was on the rails. An ad agency had been hired to do a press campaign and a poster campaign, and all that remained was to find a girl who looked good in the clothes. Eileen Ford could provide any number of American girls who could model the clothes, but what was needed was a new face, a face that summed up the Royal Enclosure look. Dan took on this job himself.

Dan needed a model who could show clothes, but who also looked good in photographs. It wasn't as easy a hunt as he thought it would be. Most of the good catwalk girls simply weren't photogenic, and the few who were had already been snapped up by other designers.

Dan went through the books of every model agent in the city. At the end of a week he was nowhere. The girl he was looking for, a girl with high cheekbones and long pale hair and fine white skin simply did not exist in New York City. He looked further afield, getting the agents he knew to cast around their European associates. Peter Stanford in London finally came up with the answer he was looking for. Her name was Vanessa Grenville and most of her experience was on the catwalk. That didn't matter. The pictures the agent had sent told Dan she had no problem in the studio. From every angle the face was perfect. It breathed exactly the kind of class, the kind of breeding he was looking for. When he closed his eyes, Dan could imagine this girl in the suede jodhpurs and white silk shirts he had designed. He gave a little moan of pleasure. Vanessa was sporty, but not hearty. She would look just as wonderful in his dresses as in his shapeless unstructured suits.

Dan called Stanford in London and booked the girl. He wanted her for three months for the ad campaign, to model his clothes for the press and to show the collection to the buyers. He needed her to be put under exclusive contract and money was no object.

Half an hour later Dan's secretary came back with the blueprint for the deal. The money wasn't outrageous, and most of Stanford's terms and conditions could be met. There was only one outstanding request. Vanessa wanted to stay somewhere decent in New York.

'She's heard it's a rough town,' Dan's secretary informed him, 'so, she's a little nervous about where she's going to be for three months. Apparently she doesn't like the idea of staying in a hotel for that length of time, and she doesn't have any friends who can put her up.'

Dan smiled. 'Ring Stanford back and tell him Vanessa can have the use of my apartment on West 57th. Tell him it will be a pleasure to lend it to her.'

12

Vanessa had no idea New York was so tall. As she came off the airport freeway the buildings reared up around her, black, glittering and predatory. They frightened her a little. They also excited her. For she was here to conquer the city.

When Peter, her agent, had told her about Dan Levin's call she didn't believe him at first. It seemed almost too good to be true. Three months in New York, all expenses paid, was the offer. All she had to do for that was to show a new range to the buyers and have her pictures taken for the magazines.

Then Peter had told her how much Levin was offering to pay for her services and she knew it had to be a joke.

'Ten thousand dollars,' she had exclaimed. 'Come off it. That's ten times more than I get paid for a season. There has to be a catch.'

But the American designer was on the level. Top models pulled in that kind of money to promote a new line.

'You won't just be walking up and down a catwalk,' explained the agent. 'You'll be used in all the advertising. The sales team will want you at conventions. Who knows, you might even have to do the odd TV chat show.'

Vanessa was staggered. Nothing like this had ever happened to her before, and she hadn't been expecting it. Liz was a star because of the way she looked and because of Sandy. Her success had been a kind of fluke. A miraculous fluke, but a fluke nonetheless. Vanessa saw her own career as more mundane. She was always in work because she was the right height and she knew how to show clothes, but she had few illusions about herself. She knew she was pretty in an English kind of way, but that was all. Then this offer came from America and suddenly she was going to be famous.

Liz was thrilled for her and gave her a list of things to do and sights to see while she was in New York. On her days off Vanessa was to make sure to see Central Park and the Empire State building. Then there were Macys, Gimbels and Bloomingdales to be toured and appraised and raided. Finally she had to go up to Greenwich Village and poke around the book shops and the art galleries and the street market.

'With this schedule,' Vanessa protested, 'I'm not going to have any time at all to work.'

Liz and Sandy laughed at her.

'Don't worry about the work,' they told her. 'Dan Levin will make sure he gets his pound of flesh.'

She leaned against the seat of the limousine and thought of her new boss. Vanessa had half expected Dan to meet her at the airport and when she had been greeted by a liveried chauffeur holding a notice with her name on she had felt slightly let down. She was the new star model, wasn't she? She should have some kind of reception committee. Then she remembered what she had read about Dan Levin in the gossip columns and she laughed at her own arrogance.

Levin was a big tycoon, not some small time dress manufacturer from Hampstead Garden Suburb. He had a yacht and a private plane and a big house on Long Island. A man like that had better things to do than hang around airports.

Vanessa peered out of the window. They were

approaching Times Square and she had never seen so much bustle. Everyone out there seemed to be going somewhere and the sheer energy of the town lit her up from inside. There was a break in the traffic now and the car gathered speed, taking them down Broadway and up into the West Eighties. The sidewalks were broader now and the dark tenements gave way to sleeker buildings with elegant entrances. Vanessa saw restaurants, tourist shops, the towering Rockefeller Center. At last they slowed down, coming to a halt outside a grand apartment block. She had arrived.

The chauffeur helped her out of the limousine and as he was doing so, two porters appeared from the doorway of the building and hurried towards them. The man who appeared to be in charge asked how many bags there were and before Vanessa had even finished telling him the second-in-command had whisked them out of the boot of the car and disappeared back inside the apartment block.

Seeing her worried expression the head porter gave Vanessa a sympathetic smile.

'They'll be waiting for you inside the apartment as soon as I let you through the door.'

Vanessa knew she was staying in an apartment owned by the man who was employing her, but nothing – the reports in the gossip columns, Sandy's tales of Levin's wealth – had prepared her for it.

The first thing Vanessa noticed when she walked through the front door of the apartment was the scent of roses. On every surface were great silver bowls of the freshly cut blooms. The place reminded her of a florist's shop or a funeral parlour. Surely, she thought, he hasn't gone to all this trouble on my account. Vanessa wandered through into the main room. It was a big room with a huge window at one end overlooking Central Park. But it wasn't the view that held her attention. It was the furniture. She had lived with antique furniture all her life. It didn't impress her. Levin's collection was something else. At first, Vanessa was struck by the vulgarity of it, for all the wood was carved and polished and inlaid with mother-of-pearl and gilt. Then, when she looked at it properly she realized that what she saw went beyond vulgarity. The pieces were all French Empire and rightfully belonged in a museum. Instinctively her eyes went to the walls and she recognized a Degas ballet dancer and two Renoir country scenes.

It was then she realized that Dan Levin hadn't gone out to the florist just because she was coming to stay. Someone did the flowers every day. Someone Levin employed specially.

Vanessa wandered down the hall to the main bedroom, which boasted a four-poster under a canopied ceiling. She threw her case down and went in search of a place to hang her clothes. She found a walk-in closet, and it was in this oak-lined cupboard the size of a box-room that she found her first clue to the identity of the man who lived here. Half the space was taken up by his clothes: navy blazers with the imprint of the New York Yacht Club on the top pocket nestled side by side with white tie and tails. Vanessa found immaculate suits which could have only come from Savile Row, and everything in front of her was sponged and pressed and looked as if it belonged in a gentleman's outfitters.

She heard the door open behind her and turned round to find herself face to face with the owner of the clothes.

She didn't know what she expected Dan Levin to be, but one thing was for sure. He was nothing at all like his press pictures. The man in the gossip columns had been smooth and urbane, a regular jet-set playboy. The man facing her was well . . . tacky. She imagined if Liz Taylor had been born a man he would have looked rather like this, for his hair was black and wavy and combed back into a pompadour. The eyes, fringed with the longest lashes she had seen, were a startling violet. The rest of him was hung about with gold chains and medallions.

He came towards her holding out his hands in welcome.

'So you finally got here,' he said. 'Sorry I couldn't be there to meet you when you got off the plane, but there was a crisis over at the warehouse, and I was called away.'

For a moment Dan looked worried. 'Staff,' he said. 'You employ the best you can find, pay top dollar for the privilege and the moment there's a little problem, they all come running to you to sort it out.'

The voice was low and cultured and the manner was confident. Close up, he seemed less of a barrow boy and Vanessa took hold of one of his outstretched hands intending to shake it.

'Dan Levin,' she said, a formal little smile on her face. 'I've heard so much about you.'

The handshake never happened. Instead he pulled her towards him and kissed her roughly on both cheeks.

'I hope you heard only good things,' he grinned. 'A lot of people seem to think I'm a playboy.'

Vanessa pulled away from him, maintaining her smile with a certain amount of effort.

A playboy? Vanessa wondered. Not a chance in the world. If you came to London you probably couldn't even get into The Pickwick Club.

Dan took her silence for a form of acceptance, for

the next thing he said was obvious to the point of crassness.

'Can I offer you a glass of champagne?'

Vanessa looked at her watch.

'It's four o'clock in the afternoon,' she said. 'Nobody drinks champagne at tea-time.'

She had intended it as a put-down, but it had the opposite effect. A smile lit up the too-handsome face.

'I should have known it,' he said. 'I search the world for the classiest dame I can find, then I insult her with my American habits. Can I offer you a cup of Earl Grey tea. I take it that's what you drink at this time of day.'

In the ordinary way of things Vanessa would have been irritated. Dan Levin was almost too eager to please. Tea was served by a butler in uniform. There were cucumber sandwiches cut thin, there were muffins, strawberry jam, Cornish cream.

Dan, she noticed, drank straight bourbon. She also noticed he didn't apologize for doing it.

Vanessa began to ask him about himself. For her, the questions were routine small talk. What does your father do? How did you get into the fashion business? She almost switched off when he responded, but then he started talking about his childhood in the Bronx and she was glad she had paid attention after all. It was riveting stuff, all the more so because she had had no knowledge of this kind of existence. The people Vanessa grew up with had parents who were stockbrokers or land agents.

Nobody she had ever met had a father who sold cheap clothes in a market and was proud of it.

'My father was the best salesman in the district,' Dan announced, 'because he wasn't just interested in turning a buck. He saw the bigger picture. He saw hundreds and hundreds of needy people, all of them with money in their pockets. All of them looking to buy style. What people forget about the poor,' he went on, 'is how many there are of them. Individually they spend peanuts, but get enough of those peanuts and you could end up rich. He sat down one day and figured it all out,' Dan went on. 'He wasn't an educated man. Not what you'd call educated, but he had instincts. His gut had told him what made poor people buy things, and he reckoned if he knew that, then it wasn't hard to know what made rich people buy things. After all it was the same transaction. All he needed to do was find the right merchandise. The sort of merchandise that would make rich women part with their money.'

As Vanessa listened to the story, she found herself changing towards this man. She wasn't exactly fascinated by him, but she respected what he had to say. Dan Levin knew his business backwards. Better than that, he loved it.

He started to tell her how his father haunted Fifth Avenue observing fashionable women as they shopped. It was like a fly fisher talking about landing a trout, or a painter discussing the merits of working in oils. Levin was simply fascinated by the mechanics of selling and the minds of women themselves. As he matured he saw his father grow rich from understanding his customers, for Sid Levin could dress any woman on the street. She could be the wife of a dustman or a rising executive, she could even be married to the chairman of the board and Sid knew how she wanted to look that season. He put his money where his instincts were and produced that look. Then Dan joined the business.

'Tell me about Royal Enclosure,' Vanessa said. 'I mean, what made you do it yourself?'

Dan looked at his watch.

'It's a long story,' he told her, 'and I'm due at the Met in twenty minutes to see "Don Giovanni".'

Vanessa was disappointed. She didn't particularly go for this great gangster of a man, but she enjoyed his company. He told her things she didn't know, rather than treating her like an airhead the way a lot of men did.

'Maybe I'll see you tomorrow,' she ventured, 'and you can tell me then.'

Dan smiled. 'Maybe,' he said. 'One thing is for certain. I need to see what you look like in the collection.'

13

Vanessa saw Dan Levin every day. He was there through all the shows, and when he wasn't taking buyers to lunch he would shepherd a group of them to the local deli, where they filled up on bagels and pastrami on rye. He spoiled them all outrageously, like an over-indulgent father on a school outing.

As the weeks went on, Vanessa talked to the other girls and she stopped seeing Dan as someone to be trusted. He had had affairs with several of them, though when she first heard about it, Vanessa found it hard to believe. The guy was so obvious, so rough round the edges. What on earth, she wondered, did he have to offer? It wasn't as if he was even eligible. He had a wife and family out on Long Island.

She remembered the married men she had been in love with. All of them, without exception, had been figments of fantasy. They had taken her to exclusive restaurants and flown her to Paris for the weekend. There had been presents too: a diamond from Cartier, a ranch mink coat that reached to the floor. Elegant little touches that somehow dignified the liaisons.

If the other girls were anything to go by, this man didn't go in for elegant little touches. He could afford them, but he wasn't prepared to spend his money that way. Dan Levin's girls got taken out to dinner at Irish Steak houses, yet none of them had any complaints. They felt comfortable with him, and he wasn't mean either. Dan might not shower a girl with jewellery, but he made up for it in other ways. When one of his regular mistresses had a sick mother, Dan paid all the hospital bills. For some reason that particularly amused Vanessa.

'He's the sort of lover a girl needs when she's down on her luck,' she observed. At the time she didn't realize she was seeing into her own future.

After a while Vanessa's life fell into a routine. She was collected by a chauffeur driven car every morning and taken to the showroom on Seventh Avenue. Most days there were two or even three shows. Then there were photo sessions with Norman Bracken, the ad agency that handled the Levin account. Vanessa didn't enjoy these much. Norman himself was usually there, which filled everyone with terror. He and Dan went back to the days when the company was in its infancy, though for the life of her, Vanessa could never understand why the two men were such friends. Norman was so tall and elegant and chilly. How could anyone want to spend half an hour with him, she thought, let alone the whole of dinnertime? Then she pulled herself up. I'm being naive, she told herself. Norman's a single guy, it's obvious he provides girls for Dan. There's no way the two of them spend dinner alone together.

At the end of each day Vanessa would soak in a long, luxurious bubble bath, then she would raid the icebox and watch television. The kitchen was surprisingly well equipped. There was a food processor, a stainless steel cocktail shaker, an eye-level oven and two vast fridges. Every night when she opened them it was a bit like Aladdin's Cave, for their contents never failed to impress her. Sometimes she would discover a whole cooked chicken and a ready prepared salad in a crystal bowl. Other times there would be lobster, shrimp and a variety of smoked fish that could never have come from American waters.

Once she found a whole tin of caviar with a note on it from Dan.

'Eat and enjoy,' it said. 'After what the buyers are saying about you, you deserve it.'

Vanessa felt cosseted and cared for. The man was a lecher and definitely not her type, but she enjoyed being with him and staying in his apartment.

Days later she was mugged, and after that she didn't take anything for granted again. She was on her way home from a photographic session at the ad agency. Normally she would have been in one of Dan's company cars, but she had no idea how long she'd be so she told him she'd grab a taxi. She was nearly at the apartment when she realized she needed some shampoo and she asked the driver to drop her at the drugstore. When she'd bought what she needed, she noticed a couple of shabby looking individuals eyeing her. They were a couple, a man and a girl, not that she gave them much thought. She was still in the make-up she wore for the cameras and she was used to strangers staring at her. They probably thought she was appearing in some theatre show. She was nearly back at the apartment block when she realized they were following her. She turned up the collar of her coat and walked faster. They can't be after me, she thought. I'm in my working clothes. I don't even look rich.

She knew she was in trouble when one of them came up behind her and asked for a light.

'I don't smoke,' she said.

The guy took hold of one of her arms and twisted it behind her back. His accomplice grabbed hold of her bag. Vanessa didn't struggle. The girls at the showroom warned her something like this could happen.

'Let them have your bag,' they told her, 'but always

carry something in reserve tucked away in one of your shoes.'

Someone must have told her assailants about these instructions. For after they ripped open her purse, the girl asked her where the rest of the money was.

'What money?' she asked. 'I don't have any more money.'

They both called her a liar. Then the girl knocked her to the ground, kicked her and ran.

Vanessa struggled to her feet and made it half a block home. The doorman, who realized what had happened, made her sit down while he rang around and found Dan Levin. He was in luck. Dan was still in his office.

He was with Vanessa in twenty minutes and the minute he arrived he didn't waste any time. He wanted to know exactly what was in her bag, the names and numbers of the credit cards, what keys she had on her. He seemed to have an intimate knowledge of the criminal mind and how to deal with it. When he had finished interrogating her, he cancelled all her cards and arranged to have the locks on the apartment changed.

Only when he had made sure that Vanessa was in no more danger from her attackers did he start to look at her properly. He had made her a sizeable bourbon as soon as he got there, and when he saw she had finished it, he made her another.

'Poor Vanessa,' he said softly, 'you have been in the wars.'

Vanessa realized she must look like hell. The suit she was wearing was filthy and torn and she bet her mascara had run. She realized Dan had only ever seen her at her best and she was momentarily embarrassed.

'I think I should go and clean myself up,' she

apologized. She saw the look of surprise in Dan's eyes.

'Don't go and get all self-conscious on me,' he said. 'You got mugged for Christ's sake. You're not meant to look your best.'

Dan insisted Vanessa finished her drink, then he went through to the kitchen and started to organize supper.

'Go take a long bath,' he instructed, 'and don't bother getting done up afterwards. It's an informal meal, jeans are perfectly correct for the occasion.'

There was something nice about being fussed over by Dan. It made Vanessa feel cared for and valuable. She had few illusions about why he was putting himself out like this: Dan had a reputation for helping damsels in distress and reaping the rewards afterwards. Only she didn't care now. She had been through too much today to protest loudly about her honour. I'll go with it, she decided. If he does anything I don't like, I can always change my mind.

They had supper in the kitchen. There was a scrubbed pine table at one end of the room underneath a window where Vanessa had all her meals when she wasn't watching television and she was glad he chose to eat here. The dining-room with its shiny antiques overwhelmed her at the best of times. Now it would have rendered her speechless.

Dan was a surprisingly accomplished cook. She had expected something like spaghetti. A peasant dish to suit a rough man. Instead he had prepared quenelles with freshly minced pike that owed nothing to a packet. They drank Beaujolais with the meal and when Vanessa had finished, Dan offered her a rare Armagnac with her coffee. In a way she felt Dan had restored her, and she revised her earlier opinion of him. Dan hadn't cooked for her as part of a seduction plan. He'd looked after her because he was genuinely concerned that she had been hurt. In a cold, uncaring city, Dan was one the few inhabitants who liked his fellow men. He wasn't prey to any of the usual emotions Vanessa found in his type: there was no envy, no carping, no compulsion to succeed at the expense of his friends. Dan had come up the easy way, courtesy of his rich father. He had no axes to grind.

They drank their coffee in the main room with its panoramic view of New York. It was clear that night and beneath them the city twinkled like a magic carpet. Dan poured the brandy then he turned to Vanessa.

'When you're tired just say the word and I'll be on my way.'

Suddenly she didn't want him to go. She had been frightened today, and the idea of being on her own chilled her.

'Do you have to go back tonight?' she said. 'Would your wife miss you if you stayed in New York?'

Dan looked at Vanessa for a long moment, the violet eyes glittering in the half light, then he reached out for her.

Vanessa had expected something cut and dried. Comfort sex to lull her through the night. Dan Levin destroyed all her illusions – she knew that the moment he kissed her, for there was a fire about him, an electric, liquid excitement that made her heart thud and her breath short. When this man kissed her and touched her skin it was as if he had pressed a trigger inside her. All her inhibitions melted away and for the first time in her life she was truly herself. Just for a second Vanessa considered the indignity of it all. She should have been in bed with the covers pulled up instead of on her back with her jeans around her knees, but as she lay on the sofa and Dan leaned over her and started to stroke her naked breasts, she watched his face. He was half smiling and in his eyes there was a look of such concentration, such pleasure that Vanessa could have been the first woman to have given herself to him. She parted her legs and drew him down to her but Dan refused to be hurried. With a delicacy she didn't know he was capable of, he took each of her pointed pink nipples in his mouth, circling them with his tongue. Then when he was finished, he traced the line of her body down to her navel and beyond.

His tongue was at her entrance now, probing and exploring and Vanessa knew she couldn't hold out much longer. She started pleading with him to take her, arching her back and moaning like a bitch on heat. And he finally came to her.

Vanessa was no stranger to love. Richer, older, tougher men than Dan had feasted on her, yet when he pushed himself between her legs, the experience felt new to her. Passion was no longer a solo performance – the man enjoying, the woman pretending. They were both in this together, and when the climax came she gave herself completely, and Dan took care of her.

They spent every night together after that. Neither of them discussed what was happening with anyone else. As far as the other models and the buyers were concerned, theirs was a strictly business relationship. The only people who knew different were Vanessa, Dan and Dan's wife, for when the affair started he stopped going home until the weekends.

In her saner moments Vanessa wondered where it would all lead. This wasn't just any affair, there was more emotion to it than that. Not that Vanessa wasted too much time torturing herself about the future. As far as she was concerned, the future was already mapped out. She was going home in six weeks. Home to Liz and the Christmas that was waiting for her.

She was mad about Dan of course, but she had to be sensible: it was, after all, only a holiday romance.

14

Liz was worried. She was expecting Vanessa back for Christmas. Now it was half way through December and there had been no word from her.

'She might have called,' she grumbled to Sandy. 'How does she know we hadn't planned to go away for the holidays?'

They were having a late breakfast on Sunday morning, surrounded by the papers. A picture special of Sandy's was being featured in one of the colour supplements and the whole spread was torn out and strewn around the bedroom.

Sandy got up and threw on a pair of jeans.

'How long is it,' he asked, 'since you and Vanessa actually talked?'

Liz thought.

'It must be going on for over two months,' she told him. 'Why?'

'Because she's got no idea of what's happening in your life. She probably thinks she's coming home to find Christmas as usual in the flat.'

Liz looked at her lover padding around the bedroom and decided she had made the right decision after all. With the sleep still in his eyes he looked soft and somehow unfocused. I was silly to worry about living together, she thought – things are good between us.

What had finally decided Liz was the lease of the flat in Old Church Street coming to an end. The landlord wanted double the rent to renew it and

Carole was the first one to express doubts. She had wanted a place of her own for some time now and the only thing preventing her from moving on was money. Now she had a good job and decided to look elsewhere. Vanessa had felt much the same and then the American job came up. Liz found herself the odd one out. She felt no yearning for a bachelor flat, because she was already spending all her time round at Sandy's. When he heard about her lease ending, he forced her hand.

'You more or less live with me anyway,' he said. 'Why not make it formal?'

Liz looked at Sandy with a fondness. He was a difficult bastard, she thought, but he suited her. They suited each other.

'Maybe we should have one last Christmas in Old Church Street,' she ventured. 'The place has a lot of memories for all of us.'

Sandy surveyed the chaos around him. Liz's wardrobe overflowed from the cupboards on to every available surface and hanging space. An old-fashioned hair-dryer was wedged in one corner of the tiny room and her suitcases, piled on top of each other, occupied the remaining floor space.

'Holland Park's a better idea,' he said shortly. 'We'll invite Vanessa if she's got nothing else to do.'

Two days before Christmas Eve there was still no communication from Vanessa. Liz decided to call her agent, Peter Stanford, and when she spoke to him, she was thoroughly confused. Vanessa had come to the end of her contract two weeks ago. Dan Levin hadn't asked for any extension and Peter assumed the model was taking an extended holiday.

'You mean she hasn't been in touch?' Liz asked.

'Not a word. I was just about to call you and ask what was going on.'

'Don't worry,' Liz told the agent, 'I'll call her at her apartment tonight. I'll be in touch when I've got some news.'

Liz finally got hold of Vanessa at seven o'clock New York time. She was on her way out and seemed in a rush.

'I can't talk now,' she said, 'but I'll ring you tomorrow. Will you be in during the morning?'

Liz informed her drily that she was putting up Christmas decorations and would be around all day. Nevertheless, Vanessa didn't call, and Liz thought the silence ominous.

If she had told Sandy of her worries, he would have asked her to pull herself together. Vanessa was just busy – it was Christmas, after all. She would call when she had a moment free.

But Liz knew there was more to it than that. She and Vanessa had been closer than sisters. Each knew what the other was doing, wherever they were. In the normal course of events Liz would have told Vanessa about Sandy and moving out, but she was saving it up as a surprise for when she came home. Now it didn't look as if that was going to happen.

She's in some kind of trouble, Liz thought. I know it. I can feel it in my guts. Then she made her mind up. She would jump on a plane to New York, leaving a note for Sandy. Liz picked up the phone and called the airport. There was a plane leaving in two hours. If she hurried, she could just make it.

15

There were snow flurries at Kennedy, and as Liz was driven into the city, the weather built up into a blizzard. She looked at her watch. It was half past eight in the morning. She hoped Vanessa hadn't decided to go out and do any last minute shopping.

All night long on the journey over the Atlantic, Liz had been wondering about the girl she thought she knew so well. Of the two of them, Vanessa was the reliable one. When she was in charge of the flat, they always had milk, eggs, cotton wool. All life's essentials.

If she was called out unexpectedly, she always left a note saying where she was, and if she wasn't coming home, she always rang ahead and said so.

What on earth could have happened, wondered Liz. Had she met someone? Had she fallen in love and addled her brain? Had Dan Levin given her more work and not told her agent?

Then it hit her. Dan Levin. He was the problem – the reason Vanessa had suddenly gone quiet on her. Why hadn't she guessed before. As they checked their way through the toll gate, Liz cursed her stupidity. I might have known, she thought. Vanessa is exactly the type that kind of man goes for. The classy English lady. I wonder what brand of bullshit he's been feeding her.

She stared bleakly at the icy road in front of her. Whatever lies Levin's been telling her, she decided, it's high time she wised up. I can see I've arrived just in time.

Vanessa was in when Liz reached the apartment. In and alone, and Liz was glad of that. The thought of sharing breakfast with Dan Levin daunted her. At least this way she had her friend to herself.

Vanessa wasn't surprised to see her. It was almost as if she had been waiting for Liz. She kissed her briefly and ushered her in.

'I'll tell the maid to organize hot coffee and croissants. You must be frozen through.'

For a second Liz was startled. The maid, she thought. Since when did Vanessa start ordering maids around?

She followed her into the main room with its panoramic view of Central Park.

'Nice place,' she remarked. 'Whoever's keeping you here must make a packet.'

Vanessa looked irritated.

'This is Dan's place,' she said. 'Peter arranged it so I could stay here. It was part of the deal.'

'And was it part of the deal that you slept with the owner?'

For a moment neither woman said anything. They stood there in the centre of the room looking at each other. She looks different, Liz thought. She's been here for four months and already I hardly recognize her.

The change wasn't something that Liz could easily identify. Vanessa hadn't had her hair dyed, nor was she wearing any exotic new fashion. It was more subtle than that, it was something about the way she held herself. In London she had always been open and free and ordinary. Now she was none of these things. Vanessa had things to hide. Things she didn't want to share with anybody, not even her dearest friend. Liz suddenly felt tired.

'I'm sorry I said that,' she said, breaking the silence. 'It wasn't fair.'

Vanessa was wearing a long, soft robe that looked like cashmere and she huddled into it now, retreating from the situation.

'Why don't you come into the kitchen,' she said. 'It's easier to talk there.'

The maid had set the coffee up on the pine table in the window and Liz guessed her friend was in the habit of having it there. She wondered what other habits she had got into while she had been in New York.

Almost as soon as they sat down, Vanessa told her the whole story: how she had been mugged on her way home; the way Dan had come to her rescue; the way she had fallen into his bed.

Liz felt irritated.

'You don't mean you've decided to spend the rest of your life in New York just because Dan Levin is a good lover. He was an expert in that department well before you came along and he'll go on demonstrating his talent to every other model who says yes long after you've gone.'

There was a long silence while Vanessa poured more coffee and Liz noticed she wasn't eating anything. The table was piled high with waffles, croissants and fresh fruit and Vanessa ignored it all.

'It's not the way you think it is,' she said tightly.

'So tell me what's different?'

Again Vanessa didn't reply, and Liz reached out for her hand.

'I'm sorry,' she said softly. 'I didn't mean to sound tough. It's just I've been so worried about you.'

Vanessa smiled thinly.

'You shouldn't worry any more. You've got your own life to live.'

Now Liz was really alarmed. There was something final about her pronouncement. She was almost saying goodbye. 'What is it?' she demanded. 'What's up?'

Now there was warmth in Vanessa's smile and she looked almost serene.

'I'm pregnant again, and this time I'm going through with it.'

There was a sense of *déjà vu* about the situation. The first time they met, Vanessa had been pregnant. Pregnant and wallowing in a pool of misery. The girl sitting across the pine table didn't look troubled at all. Liz wondered if she was quite sane.

'Do you know what you're doing?' she asked. 'Dan Levin isn't Mr Wonderful, you know. He's a bastard – a well-known bastard. He's not going to leave his wife and break up the happy home for you.'

Vanessa simply smiled her maddening Mona Lisa smile.

'We've been through all that,' she said. 'And now I know the facts, I wouldn't expect him to leave Ruth.'

Liz was stumped.

'What facts?' she demanded.

'Ruth hasn't been well,' Vanessa told her. 'It's more than that. Ruth has a heart condition that keeps her a semi-invalid.'

She paused while some of the colour came back into her cheeks.

'Look, one of the reasons Dan has such a bad reputation is that he and Ruth should have parted years ago. He told me himself, the marriage was virtually over well before I met him. The only thing that held them together was the children and the fact that he feels sorry for her.'

She is mad, Liz thought to herself. That's the oldest line in the book – my wife's ill, I can't leave her. How can she swallow it?

'How do you know he's not having you on?' she asked.

'I don't,' Vanessa said shortly. 'But I'm willing to take the chance.' She sighed.

'Look, what alternative do I have but to trust Dan? I don't want to go through another abortion. I'd rather die than get rid of another child. I like it here – I've got plans for being here. If this collection I'm showing is a success, Dan is planning to launch a perfume to go with the clothes. He's already told me he wants me to be the Royal Enclosure girl, and I think that's great. It's exciting. Can't you see that?'

'Sure I can see it,' Liz said wearily. 'But let me ask you one thing. How do you intend to live? Will you have your illegitimate child and bring it back to Mummy and Daddy in Kensington? Or will you stay here and be kept by your married lover?'

Vanessa pulled a face. 'Why do you have to make it all sound so tacky? It isn't, you know. Dan genuinely cares for me. He wants me to have his baby. Our baby. And he wants me to live here.'

A feeling of intense hopelessness threatened to engulf Liz. She helped herself to some more coffee.

'Does he want to leave his wife?' she asked.

'Eventually, though I'm not going to push him.'

Liz thought about Sandy and settling down.

'Maybe you should push him,' she said. 'There's nothing wrong with commitment. Even I'm going in for it. Sandy asked me to live with him again and I finally said I would in the New Year.'

This latest bit of news had a remarkable effect on Vanessa. Instead of looking dreamy and slightly sorry for herself, she brightened up as if there was something to hope for after all.

'But that's marvellous,' she said enthusiastically. 'Why didn't you call me?'

Liz laughed at that one.

'I was saving it up as a surprise for when you came

home. The three of us were going to have a big party on Christmas Day in Holland Park. Now it will only be the two of us.'

She thought about Sandy's house and the way they had both covered it in glitter and paper chains. There was a Christmas tree that reached the ceiling and rows and rows of cards from all their friends. It was cosy and welcoming and completely different from this formal palace where Vanessa lived.

Liz looked around her, but try as she might she could detect no sign of Christmas at all. It could have been January or midsummer for all the difference it made. This isn't a home, Liz thought. It's a cage where a rich man keeps his mistress.

'What will you do, over the holiday?' she asked. 'Will Dan be there?'

Vanessa shook her head.

'One of the other models who works with me said she'd come over and help me eat my turkey, though I haven't got much of an appetite right now.'

Vanessa saw the pity in Liz's face, and winced slightly.

'Don't feel sorry for me,' she said. 'I know what I'm doing and I want things this way.'

She seemed terribly isolated sitting in her high-tech kitchen, wrapped from head to toe in cashmere. She could have been the Lady of the Lake, she was so remote. So that's what it means to be a kept woman, Liz thought. I'm glad it's not me.

She turned to her friend. 'Is there anything I can do for you? Do you want me to send anything from the flat or will you leave me to sort things out?'

'Will you really do that . . . you are kind.'

Liz was reminded of that first time again, when she agreed to take Vanessa in and organize the abortion. Vanessa had thanked her profusely then, just as she was doing now. She felt tears pressing against the back of her eyes.

'I'm not being kind,' she said gruffly. 'I'm just being normal and doing what all friends do.'

Now the tears gathered momentum and started to spill down her cheeks.

'I'll always be there for you, Vanessa. No matter what happens to either of us. You only have to ask me.'

16

London, 1969

Liz began the year by moving out of Old Church Street. She had few regrets. Her whole life had been spent moving from one situation to another. What pleased her was that each time she pulled up her roots she went on to something better.

The house in Holland Park was a definite step up. There was more space there: you could actually sit down and have dinner in the kitchen. There was an office for Sandy, a dressing-room for her, and a spare bedroom where she could keep the rest of her stuff. Liz had no idea how she managed to collect so many things. She had three winter coats, two fun furs, four pairs of boots and so many shoes she couldn't count them. Liz knew she should throw some of it out, but she couldn't bring herself to do it. Her possessions were all she had. Her voice belonged to her elocution teacher, her appearance belonged to her make-up box, her diet doctor and Vidal Sassoon. Even her opinions were the product of one of the numerous classes she attended.

She took comfort in the fact that Sandy knew her as she really was. But did he? He knew very little about her background, and even when her accent changed he didn't seem to notice.

Sometimes I feel I'm just a body to him, Liz thought. Someone he can look at through his camera lens. I'm not real to him. I'm not real to anybody but Vanessa, and now she's gone away. She threw herself into her work for she was aware of time passing. At twenty-two there were only a few more years she could stay at the top as a model. After that she supposed she would settle for marriage – probably with Sandy. She could do worse. She could do better too, but she wasn't looking – not at the moment.

Now she was in demand, she worked with a number of other photographers as well as Sandy. It left them both free to explore different styles. When they did work together, they made sure it was something special. The session at the *Morning Chronicle* fell into that category.

They were shooting cocktail dresses for *Harper's Bazaar* and because Sandy didn't play things by the book, they decided on an off-beat setting for all the glitter. They picked a newspaper office because it was such a contrast.

Chiffon on the city desk, thought Sandy. How bizarre. How perfectly delicious.

After lengthy negotiations with the paper's Managing Editor, permission was granted for a night-time shoot. From midnight onwards nothing much happened in Fleet Street. Most of the editions had gone, and the offices were manned by a skeleton staff who kept an eye out for last-minute stories.

Liz, Sandy and two assistants showed up just after twelve. By that time the Managing Editor had gone home to his wife and a messenger boy was left to show everyone to an empty office.

It was on the main floor of the *Chronicle*, right next to the news room, and appeared to be occupied during the day by the fashion editor. On the desk overflowing with torn carbons, Sandy spotted a pile of magazines, and a light box.

'We've come to the right place,' he announced. 'Liz, start getting into some of these things.'

He turned to his assistants. 'Set some lights up

on the main floor,' he instructed. 'I want to get going.'

Liz began to worry. She had expected one or more of the paper's executives to clear the way for them. In other locations there was always someone telling them what they could do and what they had to avoid. Here there was no-one, except for a messenger in his shirtsleeves, and even he had disappeared.

With a certain curiosity, she looked around her. The office they were in was on one side of a huge open-plan floor. Round its perimeters were a number of offices, all closed off from it. Liz supposed they housed editors and pen-pushers.

The main players, she knew, would be in the news room. That's where she would be tonight on the deserted desks with their ramshackle typewriters and old-fashioned telephones. Like the fashion editor's desk, everything was covered in carbons and pages torn out of newspapers. Buried in the debris were ashtrays full of decaying cigarette butts. Liz shuddered. She was wearing thousands of pounds' worth of French couture. After this session everything would have to go to the dry cleaners.

She looked to the end of the floor from where the murmur of voices was coming, and she saw a long desk with a line of chairs behind it. In the centre sat a man who seemed to be in charge of things, for every so often he barked a command to one of the men sitting on either side of him.

Liz felt excited. None of this was anything to do with her, yet she felt drawn into the tableau. These men were moulding the paper she would buy on the streets in a few hours' time. The shouting into telephones and issuing of orders would result in a banner headline. For reasons she didn't understand, she wanted to be part of it.

She sensed Sandy standing behind her.

'This place really gets to you, doesn't it?'

She turned to him.

'Yes,' she said tightly. 'You'd have to be dead for it not to.'

He led the way on to the floor. 'We should get some interesting pictures tonight,' was all he said.

Liz was wearing a shift made out of silver cobwebs. It was almost completely backless and the skirt skimmed her thighs. With it she wore high strappy sandals and her lipstick was scarlet.

She looks like some exotic bird, Sandy thought. They were at the far end of the room, some way from the tough-looking executives on the back bench. Sandy had an idea. The men in their shirtsleeves and their day-old stubble were the last people on earth a girl like Liz would be seen with. He needed to get them all in the same shot. It was the same technique he had used in New York. Liz had been fraternizing with hobos then. Now it was news room hacks. Sandy shrugged – the effect would be the same.

He took Liz by the arm and guided her to one of the deserted desks a few yards from the centre of the action. Nobody looked up. The last edition was more absorbing than the antics of a group of freaks from the fashion world. Sandy breathed out and signalled his lighting men to bring things into position. They worked fast, and within ten minutes he had the picture set up.

When Lord Dearing's son and heir walked into the news room of the *Chronicle*, Liz was lying face-down on the main desk. She appeared to be wearing very little, apart from her silver sandals, and she was pouting with crimson lips, right into the camera.

'Just what the hell's going on over there?'

His voice cut through the room, shocking everyone into silence. All the men on the back bench sat up and looked frightened. The two lighting men started backing away, and even Sandy stopped what he was doing.

Liz looked up to see where the voice was coming from and it was then that she saw David Dearing.

At first she thought he was some kind of lunatic, for he had very black hair which seemed to be standing on end. He was in his shirtsleeves with his tie hanging loose. His eyes, which were as dark as his hair, seemed to be on fire.

Cautiously, she pulled herself up into a sitting position. As she did, the madman advanced towards her.

'What the fuck do you think you're doing?' he demanded to know. 'This is a newspaper office, not a strip club.'

The impact of his words winded her. Liz wasn't used to men shouting at her, and she certainly wasn't used to men she didn't know shouting at her.

'I'm not a stripper,' she said softly.

'Well, you bloody well look like one,' Dearing snapped. 'Why don't you go and get some clothes on before you give one of these men a heart attack.'

Slowly, with enormous care, Liz rearranged her legs, crossing them demurely, at the knee, slanting them away from her.

When she next spoke her voice was clearer and colder than it had been before.

'I don't know your name,' she said, 'but I do know you have no authority to speak to me like that.'

Dearing ran outstretched hands through his long black curls and sighed heavily.

'And how did you work that one out?'

Liz pursed her lips into a smile.

'Because,' she said sweetly, 'you have the manners of a pig, and nobody who behaves like a pig could possibly hold down a position of any importance.'

She noticed Sandy signalling to her out of the corner of her eye. He looked nervous. Worse, he looked terrified.

The man who seemed to be running things on the back bench left his post and hurried over to where they stood.

'There's been a misunderstanding,' he said to the black-haired man. 'I didn't sign in any of these people. This looks like one of Harry Black's cock-ups.'

Liz could see that the man she had just insulted was staring at her. He didn't look angry. He didn't even look like a lunatic any more. Instead he looked amused. His eyes crinkled up at the sides and she saw the indentations of laughter on either side of his mouth.

'What's your name?' he enquired.

'Liz, Liz Enfield. I'm a model.'

Now he relaxed.

'That explains it,' he said. 'All you girls go around looking like tarts nowadays.'

Liz slid down off the bench.

'Suppose you tell me who you are,' she said bluntly.

They were inches away from one another and the buzz Liz had felt earlier when she saw the edition being made seemed to be emanating from this man. It was almost as if he was giving birth to the paper.

Liz knew instinctively that he was in some way vital to this whole operation.

'My name is David Dearing,' he said. 'My father, Lord Dearing, owns this paper. I think that gives me every authority to order you off the premises, don't you?'

Liz glanced over her shoulder to see that Sandy, his

two assistants and all the equipment were waiting by the door, waiting for something or somebody. With a start, Liz realized she was holding them up.

She turned round and looked Dearing full in the eye. Then she held out her hand.

'It was not a pleasure to meet you,' she said coldly, 'and you don't have to order me from this dreary hole you call a newspaper. I'm on my way.'

Dearing took her hand and held it for a moment too long.

'You're a very sexy girl,' he said. 'Next time we meet, I'll try to mind my language.'

17

David Dearing wondered about Liz for days afterwards. It wasn't her looks that made him pause. He knew lots of pretty girls – too many pretty girls. It was her rudeness that caught him. 'You have the manners of a pig,' she had said. 'It was not a pleasure to meet you.'

He could still remember the cold, clipped little voice passing judgement on him. That and the look of disdain on her face. He knew he had to see her again, if only to prove her wrong.

David Dearing was not used to women putting him in his place. His mother, a warm, rather docile Admiral's daughter, had spoiled him rotten.

All the years that his father had worked himself silly building up the Dearing empire, she had been the one rock he and his elder brother Charles had clung to. At Eton, when he was bullied by the other boys in his class, it wasn't his father who told him to fight back. His father wasn't there, most of the time.

It was his mother who told him he was strong and he could win. All through his childhood he had run to her when life had hurt him, or was simply unfair. She had explained the world to him.

As he grew into a man, there were other women who unravelled the mysteries of the world, the girls who wanted to marry him and the girls who went to bed with him. Because of his mother, he expected love from the females he knew, and he wasn't disappointed. For David had a way with them. A dangerous charm. Every woman he had ever encountered had been prepared to sacrifice her interests to his. They took him seriously, they paid close attention to what he said and they never disagreed with him.

Then two nights ago, some snippy little model had had the temerity to call him a pig.

The story of Liz and her rudeness had spread like wildfire through the newspaper's office. The night editor and the other two executives who had been there had all gone down to the pub and told their colleagues. By the end of the week, the story had turned up as a paragraph in *Private Eye*. David did not come out of it well. Now he faced a summons from his father and thought the *Eye* story must be behind it. It can't be for any other reason, David thought.

David and his father had been at loggerheads ever since his schooldays. David resented his father for only being interested in matters of work. When he was out negotiating with the banks for bigger loans to buy bigger offices in Fleet Street, David longed for him to be home teaching him how to play cricket. He could never understand why his father had to eat so many dinners without him, or spend evenings at the opera or theatre without his family.

But Lord Dearing didn't neglect his sons entirely. They were the reason he was building his vast empire. He needed his network of provincial papers, his American interests, his Fleet Street flagship – the *Chronicle* – to pass on to them, and he groomed them accordingly.

Reginald Dearing wanted his boys to go on from Eton to Oxford. He got his wish, because when either boy showed the slightest sign of falling behind, they were given extra tutorials. When Lord Dearing wanted something, people obeyed. If they didn't, their jobs were on the line.

David and his brother, Charles, both did well at Oxford. After that, they were ready to start their training in earnest. Charles was sent to Harvard Business School, David was put to work in the provinces on his father's newspapers. My eldest son will run the business, Lord Dearing had decided. David will keep it alive.

He had seen David's flair before he even knew he possessed it. Unknown to the boy he had read all the essays he wrote at school, and to make sure his hunch was right, he arranged to be sent a copy of the thesis that won David his first-class degree. After he had read it, his mind was made up. David was that rare animal, a creative man. As a manager he would never be more than competent, but as an original thinker he outstripped even his father.

'Long after I'm dead,' Dearing had told David in a rare moment when they were alone, 'you will keep the name of our family alive. With your contribution my papers will stay at the top.'

Pompous fart, David thought. Why can't the old man ever talk in plain English. I'm glad I've got a talent for newspapers – I look forward to making pots of money at it – but does he really have to present it as if it was some fucking gift from God.

'I'm going to be a newspaper man, Pa,' he had said. 'Not the Pope.'

They were drinking whisky in the library of the family's house in Eaton Square. It was after dinner and everyone else was either out or in bed. Lord Dearing regarded his youngest son with a mixture of love and exasperation.

'Don't be facetious, David. I just wanted you to see how serious I was about having you in the business.'

David knew how serious his father was. He had been working in the North of England for nearly five years then. Five years of training from scratch to be a news reporter, a sub editor and a production man. There was not one department in any of his father's papers where he hadn't been kicked from one end of the room to another. When Lord Dearing had told his staff to treat his youngest son as one of them, they had taken him at his word.

The training had paid off. David had gained a comprehensive knowledge of how a paper worked – he could bring out an edition single handed, if necessary. Now he wanted more. He was nearly thirty then, and he had been kicking his heels for long enough. He wanted to come to London.

'Exactly how serious are you,' he asked his father, 'about having me in the business?'

'Why?' Lord Dearing asked. 'Have you had an offer from somebody else?'

There was a silence while David went over to the sideboard and splashed some more whisky in his glass. When he turned to his father again his face was impassive.

'Yes, actually,' he said. 'The *Mail* want me to join them in their London office. There's a vacancy for a foreign editor and Vere thought I could do the job.'

Lord Dearing displayed as little emotion as his son. There was no point in wasting energy at this point. The time to get excited was if David failed him.

'What did you tell Lord Harmsworth?' he enquired politely.

David grinned. 'I said, I'd think about it – that my father had his eye on me for something similar at the *Chronicle*.'

The two men stared at each other across the book-lined room. I should keep him in the North for at least five more years, thought Lord Dearing. If nothing else it will teach him discipline and a knowledge of who runs the show. But he knew he was fighting a losing battle. David had exactly the kind of impatience he had had himself at that age. If I don't let him come to London now, he thought, he just might go on to the *Mail's* payroll, and then where would I be?

He broke the silence.

'I can't give you the foreign desk,' he said. 'The job's filled, and even if it wasn't I wouldn't want you down among the ranks. That was fine for the provinces, but if you're going to run the paper one day, you have to keep some distance between you and the rest of the men. No, the job I have in mind for you is overseeing the editorial floor, starting with the news room. I keep an eye on the paper's policies and I will until I die, but the key departments need some fine tuning.

'I want you to spend six months looking at the news operation, then I want your suggestions for how we can improve it. After that we'll play it by ear.'

Now, David looked around his huge office overlooking Ludgate Circus. His father had been as good as his word. He had handed news over entirely to him, and for nearly a year now the department had been pulling slowly and imperceptibly ahead of the nearest competition. In another six months the *Chronicle* would be picking up awards, with or without mocking stories in *Private Eye*.

He sighed and straightened his tie. It was time to go upstairs and face the music.

18

Liz knew nothing about the story in *Private Eye* until Sandy called her from Scotland and told her about it. He was up there photographing a hunt ball for *Tatler* and before the festivities began in earnest, he thought he'd put in a call to Liz.

She was furious she hadn't seen the item and made Sandy read the whole thing out to her. Then she relaxed.

'It makes David Dearing look like the twit he is,' she said. 'Serves him right.'

Sandy was exasperated. 'You shouldn't hate him so much,' he told Liz. 'All the man did was to tell us to stop disturbing his newspaper. He was within his rights, you know. I was surprised when we got away with it in the first place.'

Liz made a face at the phone. Ever since that night at the *Chronicle* Sandy had been on at her for her rudeness. Well, the man deserved it. She was glad she stood up for herself. The likes of David Dearing were altogether too arrogant for their own good.

'Anyway, what are you up to tonight,' Sandy asked.

His voice was very casual when he said it, but Liz knew him better than that. Ever since they had been living together Sandy had been acting possessive. He didn't like her to go out on her own any more – even if she was only seeing a girlfriend.

Liz didn't take him too seriously. After all, it wasn't as if they were married or anything. She changed the subject.

'What will you do when you've finished photographing the debs?' she asked.

'I expect I'll go back to the hotel and have dinner with the lads. We'll probably spend all night talking about camera angles.'

It was the opening she needed. 'I've been invited to a sort of business dinner as well,' she told him. 'Charlotte de Courcy has asked me to make up numbers tonight.'

It was stretching a point. Charlotte gave the best dinners in town. To get invited you had to be either famous and influential or very beautiful. Liz knew it was going to be fun and so did Sandy.

'I don't like the idea of you going there without me,' he said. 'You'll probably meet some American tycoon and I'll never see you again.'

Liz toyed with the idea of cancelling the evening – she could do with a quiet evening in front of the box. Then she thought, no, I won't let him railroad over me.

'Don't be silly, darling,' she said to Sandy. 'Charlotte doesn't know any Americans.'

After she rang off Liz thought about the evening ahead. She had been going to wear a tailored black suit. Now she changed her mind. She went to her wardrobe and drew out the dress made of silver cobwebs she had worn for the shoot at the *Chronicle*. She had managed to mark it and although the cleaner had eradicated the flaw, the designer didn't want it back and sold it to Liz at a knock-down price.

After she had put it on Liz rummaged in her dressing table and brought out a pair of long silver tassels. These she attached to her ears. She gave her mouth a last lick of scarlet lipstick and stepped into her high strappy sandals.

I might be spoken for, she thought, but that doesn't mean I have to look like it.

Charlotte de Courcy lived in a small, rather beautiful house in Belgravia. From her main room on the first floor you could see Hyde Park Corner. Nobody who knew her quite understood how she came to be living there for she was not an heiress, nor was she married to anyone rich. She was a single woman – of good stock – somewhere in her late twenties who decorated houses for a living. The fact that the houses she designed were owned by multi-millionaires meant that she was paid well – but not well enough to afford a half million pound pile of property in the middle of the most fashionable few acres of London.

She has to have a lover, thought Liz as she pressed the bell of the glass and wrought-iron front door. Somebody rich keeps her – an Arab or an industrialist.

The door was opened by a manservant in a white apron, who appeared to double as the cook. He took Liz's coat and ushered her up the wide, curving staircase to the drawing-room where people were having drinks. As she made her way towards the sound of voices, Liz felt herself being looked down on by the canvases that followed the curve of the stairs. At a casual glance she could see that the paintings were of Charlotte's family. Ancestors, she thought. Everywhere I go people have ancestors and pasts they can be proud of. She remembered the last time she had seen her father. They had been having Sunday lunch in Southend with the rest of the family. 'Tell me about your famous friends,' he had asked her, admiringly.

Liz looked up again at the stern portraits on the stairs. None of these men wanted to know the secrets of the stars. They would be above that sort of thing. For an instant she wondered what on earth she was doing in this house. Then she saw Charlotte at the top of the stairs holding out a glass of champagne to her and she put aside her doubts. She belonged here, courtesy of her face and the manners she had learned at night school. She would have preferred a father with a title and a public school education, but God hadn't decreed things that way. He had given her beauty and drive instead. With that equipment she would have to get all the other things she wanted.

Liz saw him as soon as she walked into the room. He was standing in the bow-fronted window that overlooked Hyde Park. Tall, black-haired, intense-looking. Even in repose, drinking champagne and making small-talk there was an energy about him, and Liz remembered how rude she had been to him.

Charlotte followed her glance and looked surprised.

'I'd no idea you knew David Dearing,' she said. 'I've been rather keeping him under wraps until now.'

Liz was intrigued. 'Why all the secrecy?

The impassive face with its patrician nose and high, arched brows suddenly came to life.

'We're not exactly engaged,' Charlotte said. 'It hasn't come to that yet, but you can definitely say we're an item. He took me to see his parents in the country last weekend. The verdict is, I passed muster. So I can relax now and let things take their course.'

Liz felt let down, as if somebody had cancelled a *Vogue* cover or a trip to the States. However, she took care not to let Charlotte see it.

'That's wonderful, Charlotte,' she said with as much conviction as she could. 'I'm afraid when I did meet David, I rather put my foot in it.'

Charlotte started to laugh.

'Of course,' she said. 'The *Private Eye* story. How silly of me to forget. His Lordship was quite huffy about it over lunch. He said . . .' Her voice trailed off.

'He said girls as pretty as Liz shouldn't be allowed to take their clothes off in the offices of national newspapers.'

Neither woman had seen David approach, and now he was standing beside her, Liz was angry and tense all over again. It was as if the squabble they had had a week ago had somehow been left in the middle. Now she was face to face with him, she felt no choice but to go on with it.

'Why is it,' she asked, 'that whenever I see you you seem to patronize me?'

David Dearing stared at her, his eyes very black.

'What are you objecting to?' he questioned. 'The fact that I despise modelling, or the fact that I think you're pretty?'

Before Liz could reply, Charlotte had put her arms round both their shoulders and was moving them down towards the dining-room.

'Ricardo announced dinner five minutes ago,' she said. 'If we don't move quickly everything will be cold.'

There were ten of them at dinner, all grouped around an oval walnut table that nearly filled the cosy red-painted room. Charlotte was good at this sort of party. The gossip columns christened her home, 'the salon where the middle-aged meet the middle-class.' As Liz looked around the rest of the guests, she realized it was an accurate assessment. The men there were all in their thirties and forties. Clever, powerful and much divorced. All the girls, apart from her, were glamorous-looking Sloanes. She knew without having to ask that they were all single. I wonder, Liz thought, whether interior decoration is all Charlotte does. Then she banished the notion from her mind. Whatever her hostess did to get her grand house, she wouldn't have to do it for much longer. David Dearing was loaded. She had read about his house in the country with its own pheasant shoot, the private jet, the yacht in the Mediterranean.

'Charlotte's a lucky girl,' Liz said, turning to David who was sitting on her right. 'I bet you have a lot of fun together.'

He leaned back while the waiter spooned soup into his bowl.

'If that isn't patronizing,' he grinned, 'I don't know what is. There's nothing lucky about having an affair with someone. Now if Charlotte was going to marry me, it would be another story. But she isn't.'

Liz was astonished by his candour. When she had first met David she had thought him arrogant. Now she realized he always expressed himself this way. David Dearing told the truth. He didn't dress it up with charm or social lies. He said things the way they were and if the person who was listening didn't like it, then that was their lookout.

Liz looked at him curiously.

'Does Charlotte know any of this?'

'Not yet. I'll tell her soon though,' David said. 'I wouldn't like her to think I was wasting her time.'

He spooned up some of his soup and Liz noticed how elegantly he did it. He didn't have to learn not to slurp or splash, and he was doubtless born knowing exactly where to put the spoon when he'd finished. She felt a moment of pure envy. Then he turned to her.

'Let's stop talking about me,' he said. 'I'm interested to know more about you. Do you always walk around in indecent silver dresses, for instance. Or do you have another life that's nothing to do with fashion?'

Liz considered lying to him. There was no real reason why she had to go into her background. She was just another girl at a dinner party and she probably wouldn't see David Dearing again. Yet David Dearing had treated her as an equal. He hadn't been particularly polite to her, but that didn't matter. He respected her sufficiently not to dish out a line of bullshit. Now she returned the compliment.

She told him that she started out as a beauty queen who won a modelling course.

To her astonishment David was fascinated and bombarded her with questions. He wanted to know how she felt about leaving her family to come to London. Did she ever go home? Did she ever feel guilty about earning so much money?

Every time Liz answered him, there were a thousand and one more things he wanted to know. In the end she called a halt.

'I'm not some kind of social study,' Liz told him. 'If you want to know more about the working classes, there are plenty of books written on the subject.'

David looked at her for a long time after that.

Finally he said, 'You're very angry, aren't you. You know what you remind me of? You make me think of a cat. Not some back-yard moggy, but something proud like a Siamese. On the surface you're all sleek and beautiful, but disturb that hide of yours and you spit and scratch. I could imagine you clawing someone to death if you took against them.'

'Are you saying you behave any differently?'

David leaned back in his chair and laughed. 'I asked for that.' Suddenly he turned to her.

'Liz, any moment now, our hostess is going to usher us all upstairs to drink coffee and brandy, and after that I won't get another chance to talk to you. So I'm going to ask you now. Will you have lunch with me tomorrow?'

Liz hesitated. Whatever he might say, this man was more or less spoken for, and the woman in his life was one of her friends. Then there was Sandy. He would never understand. Not in a million years. She began to say no, but she reckoned without David's forcefulness.

'I'll reserve a table at Wiltons,' he said standing up. 'I'll see you there in the bar, at one o'clock.'

Then he was on his feet and moving towards Charlotte, who was in the doorway. I could go up to him, she thought, and refuse. Tomorrow is very short notice, for all he knows I could be shooting a cover or flying to Paris for a show. Even as the reasons for not going formed in her mind, Liz knew this man would not listen to her. He thought modelling was a pointless activity. He had even told her as much. No, if Liz wanted to turn down David's invitation, she would have to tell him she didn't want to see him. Straight out and to his face. She looked across the room to where he was standing, flirting with Charlotte. He had his hand underneath her chin and he was gazing deep into her eyes. There was no mistaking what he wanted to do next.

For some unknown reason Liz felt furious. He shouldn't be doing that, she thought. Not in front of all these people.

She realized she was being childish. What am I getting all steamed up about, she wondered. It's not as if they didn't know each other. Then she realized what the problem was. She didn't want David to flirt with Charlotte because it made her jealous. This is all I need. As if I didn't have enough to contend with, she thought. All the same she didn't turn down having lunch with him.

19

Wiltons was the stamping ground of old men, because senior politicians and chairmen of the board were the only men with expense accounts big enough to afford it.

David Dearing fell into the last category and Liz couldn't help noticing how young he looked compared to everyone else, and how handsome. She had arrived at the fish restaurant off Jermyn Street at ten past one and was immediately blinded by the tablecloths. Acres and acres of starched white linen came between her and David who was waiting for her at the back of the restaurant. When she sat down, she wasn't sure what impressed her more: the movers and shakers who eyed her as she negotiated her way through the tables, or the tables themselves.

David was pleased to see her and she noticed that there was an open bottle of champagne standing in an ice bucket in front of him.

'I know you drink this stuff, so I ordered a bottle,' he smiled.

A waiter came over and filled their glasses and while he did Liz observed her host. He looked exactly the way he had done the night before. Urbane and unruffled. Then she remembered him the first night they had met. There was nothing very smooth about him then and she wondered about the effect newspapers had on him.

She started asking him about his profession, the way he had asked about hers, and he seemed to come to life. The careful, almost courtly manner disappeared as he talked editions and deadlines and Liz began to find herself liking him. If she closed her eyes she could imagine she wasn't in this chic, inhibiting place at all, but in some pub in the city. I bet he drinks with the boys, Liz thought, as David told her about his life in the provinces. When his father isn't looking, I bet he's the life and soul of the saloon bar.

A waiter came to their table and without consulting the menu, Liz asked for a Dover sole and a melon to start. David looked amused.

'I didn't know you'd been here before,' he said.

'I haven't,' Liz replied, 'but I've yet to go to a fish restaurant that doesn't serve those two items.'

David gave the waiter his order, then he turned to her.

'You're very confident, aren't you,' he observed.

'Not as confident as you. How did you know I'd be here today? Or did you just take it for granted?'

David thought for a moment. Finally he said, 'If you must know, I wasn't sure whether or not you would turn up. But I'm glad you did.'

Briefly, Liz remembered Sandy hurrying back from Scotland. She wondered if he was making plans for a more permanent future – a future with her. She started to feel guilty.

'Are you glad?' she asked doubtfully. 'I don't know if I am.'

'And why is that?'

'Lots of reasons. Charlotte. My own complications. It might have been fun once, but now it's too difficult.'

David touched her then. It was nothing clumsy. He didn't grab hold of her hand or attempt to kiss her. He just reached out and with his finger traced the line of her cheekbone down to her mouth.

'I don't think it's difficult at all,' he said. 'We don't have to tell anyone about it.'

The waiter arrived with their food then, but it was too late. She had gone off the idea of eating altogether. She regarded the sophisticated man sitting opposite her. How cheap he must think I am, she thought. I bet he had it all worked out. He takes me to an expensive restaurant, impresses me with his great importance. Then, when I'm all softened up and lunch is nearly over he leans forward and comes in for the kill. She sank back in her seat and as she did a feeling of nausea washed over her. That routine of his, caressing my cheekbones. He probably thought I'd fall apart at the seams with lust. He probably thought I'd roll on my back right after lunch.

David looked at her sharply.

'Is anything the matter?'

Liz gathered up the remnants of her dignity. 'Nothing's the matter,' she replied. 'Only next time you try to take a girl to bed you might come up with something a bit more original. Not everyone goes for a straight proposition, you know.'

David rang Liz for three weeks after that. Discreetly. He always seemed to pick the times Sandy was out, and he never left messages. Nevertheless it worried Liz. What if he got hold of Sandy by mistake? What if he started leaving his name with the secretary?

In the end Liz told David to stop.

'There's no point in this,' she said. 'You're wasting your time.'

'I'd like to hear you tell me that to my face.'

She arranged to meet him at the Savoy for a drink. She was seeing Sandy later that evening at a restaurant in Knightsbridge, so she was safe. David could say what he liked but he could only say it for half an hour, forty minutes at the most. After that she had to be on her way.

David was waiting for her in the American Bar and despite her misgivings she was glad to see him. There was something about David that put her at her ease. She didn't feel comfortable with him, the way she did with Sandy, but seeing him, talking to him, laughing with him put her in a good mood.

This man desires me, she thought as she sat down. He can have any girl he likes, but it's me he wants. The knowledge made her feel valuable. If a lesser man had wanted her, she wouldn't have cared, and she despised herself for revelling in this new flirtation, but she couldn't resist it either.

Liz left David on the dot of seven, but only after she had agreed to see him again the following week.

After that, they started to see each other on a regular basis. Sometimes they would have lunch, sometimes just a drink before they rushed headlong back into their lives. And each time they met, they left something of themselves behind when they parted. Finally, the tension between them became impossible to contain.

'I know about Sandy,' David told her. 'I always have, just as you know about Charlotte. But this is something different. You have to let me take you away.'

They were drinking martinis in the lobby of the Ritz where there was a fountain and a marble statue and a lot of little round tables snuggled together at the back end of the huge entrance hall.

Liz looked at David across the rim of her glass.

'Are you suggesting a dirty weekend?' she asked.

'Of course I am. You don't really think I want

to take you on a tour of Europe's ancient monuments?'

'So it's Europe you're talking about.'

'Unless you have a special preference for Bognor Regis?'

Liz grinned.

'I'm not that old fashioned.'

David signalled the waiter for another drink.

'That settles it then. I'll take you to Paris. How soon can you get away?'

He's done it again, Liz thought. Decided on a course of action before I even had time to consider it. He's gone ahead and made plans.

'Look,' she said firmly, 'I know you're used to ordering people around on this newspaper of yours, but I don't work for you so don't expect me to fall in line every time you raise your little finger.'

David sighed.

'Stop behaving like a grand lady, will you? You're a nice girl who I happen to have an itch for. There's nothing wrong with that. Grown-up men and women do this sort of thing all the time. Look Liz, I like you. I like being with you, I like talking to you, I like listening to you. As well as all that I want to take you to bed. I wish I could fall on one knee and swear eternal love, but I don't go in for that kind of bullshit. So either you come away with me and we find out if there is anything more to this relationship, or we call it quits right now.'

Liz weighed the options and decided to follow her instincts. For she knew she had reached the point of no return.

'I'll come away with you,' she said slowly, 'but can we make it somewhere other than Paris?'

'Why's that?'

'Because Paris is such a cliché,' she said crossly. 'It's

a place you take your mistress to, or some tart. I'm neither of those things.'

David looked at the girl sitting opposite him. His eyes took in the silky black hair that hung like a curtain round her face, the delicate fragile bones, the white skin. If that was all there was to her, he would have walked out at that moment. But this girl had something else. She had her anger.

It was the most vibrant thing about her and it seemed to light her up from inside. I want to feel all that energy, David thought to himself. I want to sink deep inside her and feel her coming alive around me. I have to possess her, if only for a weekend.

He leaned across and took her hands.

'We could go to Amsterdam. All the tarts are on sale in windows of the red light district, so nobody ever takes girls there. Would that suit you better?'

Liz considered for a moment.

'I've never seen a tart in a shop window before,' she said. 'It might be fun.'

20

Liz told Sandy she was off to see Vanessa for a long weekend. Her baby was due in weeks now and it seemed to Liz to be a good time to visit.

'Can't you wait until the child is born?' asked Sandy. 'If you're going to go all that way, you might make the trip worth your while.'

Liz thought about David and the fact she was going to Amsterdam, not New York.

'You don't understand anything,' she told Sandy. 'Vanessa needs me now, not afterwards. Anyway, when she has her baby, she won't want to see anyone for a bit.'

She thought about ringing Vanessa and telling her what she was up to. Then she decided not to. The less anyone knew about this weekend, the better. She told Sandy she would call him on Sunday, then she packed a suitcase and headed out to the airport.

David was waiting for her at the departures gate and the moment she saw him Liz wondered what she was getting herself into. Most of the men she knew would be wearing jeans for this kind of weekend. But not David. He was in grey flannels and a cashmere sweater. Flung over his shoulders casually, but not too casually, was a vicuna overcoat.

It was the coat that irritated Liz most. It was so obviously expensive, so jet-set playboy. She glanced down at her own denims and cowboy boots. How the rich separate themselves from the rest of us, she thought bitterly. No matter where they are, they always have to wear their money. But she couldn't be distant with David for long for he seemed hell-bent on spoiling her this weekend. He had brought with him all the latest glossies for her to read on the journey. Even though they were travelling first class, he made the stewardess bring them a whole bottle of the best champagne.

By the time they landed at Schipol airport, Liz was relaxed and starting to enjoy herself. All her life she had done things for a reason. She had flirted with the local councillor when she was a little girl because she needed to win a modelling course, she had flirted with Sandy later on, because he was a photographer who could help her with her new career. David could give her nothing except for fun and flattery and sex.

Sex, Liz thought. The reason I'm here. The reason we're both here. She looked at David pushing his way through passport control.

I wonder if he's that pushy in bed, Liz thought, and as she wondered, the vision of David alone and naked with her invaded her senses. She had not allowed herself to think this way before, for if she had, she couldn't have resisted him all these weeks. Now the resisting was over. She could do what the hell she liked this weekend. Whenever she liked. However she liked. She glanced at her watch. It was nearly eight. Quickly she caught up with David as he strode through the customs hall.

'What plans do you have for tonight?' she asked.

'I've booked dinner at the Amstel. After that I thought I'd take you to see the red light district. You told me you hadn't seen it before.'

Liz took hold of his arm.

'I've got a better idea,' she said. 'Why don't we stay in our hotel room instead. We can always order room service later if we get hungry.'

David sighed, and when he looked at her next he was the same chilly rich man Liz had met at Heathrow.

'You don't understand anything at all, do you?' he asked. 'We've waited a long time for this moment. We've built an appetite for it, a sense of anticipation. Now you want to ruin everything by rushing at it like a little girl.'

They rode into the city in silence. David had booked a suite at the Pulitzer, an old-fashioned five star hotel on one of the canals. Normally Liz couldn't have waited to check in and unpack. Now she didn't want to do any of it. What had seemed like a great adventure just a moment ago, had overtones of the squalid.

She trailed behind David as he made his way across the lobby. The Pulitzer was one of the most romantic hotels she had ever seen. It was in fact two old Dutch houses knocked together with all the original beams on display. The discreet lighting made it seem cosy, and everywhere she looked she saw antique furniture. The fact that she had dreamed of being taken to a place like this depressed Liz even more. David will order more champagne when we get to the room, she thought moodily. Then we'll have dinner somewhere expensive. Then, just to whet my appetite and get his juices flowing, we'll end up at some live sex show afterwards.

The whole scenario sickened her. It was so self-conscious, so obviously planned. He does this all the time, she thought. He has Charlotte as his public, respectable girlfriend. Then he does things like this in between. It's just a game to him, an illicit thrill. His words at the airport came back to her.

'We've built up an appetite for this,' he had said. 'Don't ruin it by rushing at it.'

He makes me feel like an oyster, Liz thought. He should be squeezing lemon and pepper sauce on me in order to appreciate the whole thing better. All of a sudden she didn't want to know any more. She walked up to the desk where David was getting the keys.

'Does the hotel have another room?' she asked loudly. 'I'd like to have some space for myself.'

The concierge looked surprised, but David took the whole thing in his stride.

'I'll find out,' he said pleasantly.

Within three minutes Liz was holding the keys to her own suite. She was staying down the hall from David on the first floor. As they got out of the elevator, he turned to her.

'I'll meet you downstairs in half an hour,' he said matter-of-factly. 'We'll have a drink in the bar, then a car will take us to the Amstel. Unless you'd rather walk.'

Liz had expected David to protest and ask questions about her sudden change of direction, but her companion didn't seem in the least perturbed. It was everything as usual. Champagne, dinner, the red light district. And bed. Liz swallowed hard. She needed to sort things out and do it fast.

'Before we even unpack,' she said, 'I need to talk to you.'

'Where?' David asked patiently. 'Your suite, or will you risk mine?'

'As long as it's not in the bedroom, I don't really care,' Liz snapped.

David led the way down the carpeted corridor to where he was staying. Then he opened the door, put his bags down and walked straight to the telephone.

'Send up a pot of tea for two,' he instructed room service. 'Make it fast.'

Liz was surprised.

'I thought champagne would have been more your style.'

'Champagne is for seductions,' David said wearily. 'Now that is no longer on the agenda, I might as well have what I really want.'

Suddenly Liz liked him better. It had been a long day and a tiring journey. A cup of tea at the end of it seemed more normal. Almost human.

'Do you want to know what made me change my mind?'

David shook his head. 'Not really. We'll only end up quarrelling about it, and there's no point. We're here now. I don't know about you, but the excuses I made mean I'm stuck in Amsterdam till at least Sunday, so we have two alternatives. We can split up and make the best of the situation on our own or we can spend the time together as friends. Or we can do a bit of both.'

Liz relaxed a little. 'Why don't we play it by ear?'

David grinned. 'Why not? We could still have dinner at the Amstel. The table's booked.'

Liz shook her head.

'If the Amstel's as grand as your usual places, I'll take a raincheck. All I really want to do tonight is to walk along the canal and find a glass of beer and a sandwich. Do you mind?'

David laughed.

'What you have in mind sounds fine to me.'

He was silent for a moment, considering. 'Would it bother you terribly if I joined you?'

Liz raised an eyebrow. 'Not if you put on a pair of jeans.'

It was bitingly cold that weekend. Exhilaratingly cold, and Liz was reminded of her days by the seaside as she walked along the canals. The air had the same quality, for it was raw and clean and made her cheeks tingle.

Now she no longer cared about making an impression, Liz left her make-up off and tied her hair back and turned all her attention to exploring the city. She wanted to see everything: the Rembrandts at the Rijksmuseum; all the modern paintings in the little galleries dotting the canals; the flower market; the curio shops; the places where they sold fresh herrings.

To her surprise David did everything with her. In the beginning Liz thought he was slumming – the rich man on a tour of the sights. Half way through Saturday, she realized he wasn't putting on an act at all. He seemed genuinely at ease in the little bars by the canals where they perched on hard wooden seats and got jostled by backpackers and students. He could have been a student himself, or a professor, for now he had let go, she began to see David as he really was. She discovered he needed to wear glasses to read the menus and the booklets in the museums. And like his penchant for tea, they humanized him. He had bought a duffel jacket during the day to wear with his jeans, and that made him more approachable too. They found a little restaurant on one of their walks. It was tucked away in a back street and seemed shabby on the outside, but when they peered through the door their noses were assailed by the most fragrant, most delicious smells.

'Do you want to have dinner here,' David asked her, 'or do you plan to go somewhere on your own tonight?'

Liz shook her head.

'As long as we're friends, I'd love to have dinner. But you must let me pay my half. It wouldn't feel right otherwise.'

David laughed and took her arm.

'I'll do a deal with you,' he said. 'You can buy lunch in the bar that serves fresh herrings, if you leave dinner to me. That way I'll have some of my masculinity left after this weekend.'

For a moment Liz felt regret. It could have been so different, she thought. We could have been cosy and tucked up in bed instead of behaving like tourists. She stifled the thought. It's better this way, she decided. I'm not a tramp and I won't be treated like one.

They both found they could talk to each other with ease. Liz had started telling David about her life at Charlotte's party, but it had been a carefully edited version, sanitized for the consumption of a powerful man. Now she let rip. She told him about her father and how he had left her and her mother in poverty. She recounted the days of her girlhood when she carried condoms around in her handbag so she didn't get pregnant. She even told him about Sandy.

'I'm surprised you live with him,' David said. 'I always thought your relationship was based on business.'

Liz pulled a face. 'It was to start with. Business and sex. But then it changed. It's impossible to go to bed with someone and feel nothing. Impossible for me anyway.'

'Do you love Sandy?'

Liz thought about it for a moment, then she shook her head.

'It's not love,' she replied, 'but there's an affection and a warmth and a kind of belonging. I would never hurt Sandy. Not intentionally.'

For a moment David was silent. Then he reached for her hand.

'I'd no idea,' he said. 'I had you down for a tough little good-time girl out to make a quick conquest.'

'Why?'

'The way you behaved. Offering yourself, then withdrawing at the last moment. The last few weeks have been like some kind of mating dance. First you wanted me, then you ran away. Courtesans play that game and in the end I brought you here because I wanted to know what the deal was.'

Liz felt insulted, but she was also curious. She swallowed her pride and made him go on.

'What kind of deal did you have in mind?' she asked.

David shrugged and even in his jeans and chequered shirt there was no mistaking his worldliness.

'I thought you wanted me to buy you something,' he said. 'A diamond necklace or a Cartier wristwatch. A lot of girls do. But the price could have come higher.'

'How much higher?'

Again he gave a shrug and Liz noticed how tense she felt.

'You may have wanted me to keep you in some fancy flat in the West End.'

'And would you have done?'

He was smiling now. 'Yes, I would have actually. You have no idea how much I wanted you. It got to the point when I couldn't think of anything else. It was driving me insane. I came out here with my mind made up to give you whatever you asked for.'

Desire hit Liz out of the blue. One moment she was sane and in control of herself, the next she was weak and finished. What she wanted now was to be close to this man. Somewhere quiet, somewhere without people.

'What a fool you were,' she said softly. 'All I ever wanted from you was your body. Only I had no idea it had to be such a production.'

He must have known what she was feeling for there was a subtle change in him. Without moving or even saying anything her bookish, professor-like companion turned back into David again. He beckoned the waiter to bring him the bill. Then after he had paid, he took Liz's arm and pushed her gently into the street.

'We're going back to the hotel,' he whispered. 'We're going to my room, to my bed, and the minute we get there all this negotiation has to stop.'

This time when they got back, she didn't bother to ask for her key. The concierge looked slightly bewildered, but Liz was beyond explaining anything. He can think what he likes, she thought. I'll be on my way back to London tomorrow.

They held hands in the elevator going up to David's room. And when they got there he didn't offer her a drink.

They had got to a place beyond champagne and small talk. Instead he took her in his arms and held her close. They stood like that for a long time, warming themselves on each other. Then delicately, almost shyly, he started to kiss her.

She had spent weeks wondering about this moment.

21

In her mind, Liz had devised scenarios where she and David tore one another's clothes off, devoured each other like hungry animals. What was happening to her now bore no resemblance to those fantasies, and she was glad. She didn't want this man to seduce and ravage her. Not now. Now she wanted David to love her.

The kissing went on for a long time, until Liz started to tremble. Then David drew her into the bedroom and started to undress her gently, then he quickly undressed himself.

Liz couldn't take her eyes off his body. Even though it was the middle of winter, he was very tanned. And his chest, right down to his stomach, was covered in black curls. It was like being in a bed with some primaeval god. With a hunger she could no longer contain, Liz reached out for him, and it was like coming home.

With the others, even with Sandy, she had always been on stage. She never made love without all her make-up on, and she always knew exactly what effect her hands, her tongue, her lips were having. With David, none of this mattered, for he wasn't another lover, separate from her. He was her. Where she finished, he started, and in the middle of it all when he finally came astride her and into her, she felt they had melted into one.

Liz slept in David's arms, waking now and then to make sure he was still there. Each time she opened her eyes, she saw him watching over her with such concern, that all the things that had once frightened her no longer mattered.

In the morning David ordered a huge breakfast, Dutch style. There were eggs and muffins and plates piled high with slices of cheese and sausage. Liz laughed out loud when she saw it.

'If we eat all this,' she protested, 'there won't be any room for lunch.'

David looked at her rosy and naked beside him. 'What makes you think you were going out for lunch?' he asked, smiling.

The day seemed to slip through their fingers. They made love tenderly, then they had breakfast. They took a shower and made love again. They couldn't stop making love. They experimented with all the positions they had learned with other people, and when they were exhausted they invented some of their own.

The night before, they had loved like sweethearts. Now their coupling had more urgency, for they both knew they were running out of time. Tonight they would be on the plane to London and Liz would be going home to Sandy. David would be going back too, and it would never be like this for them again.

They packed as it was getting dark, teasing each other and talking lovers' nonsense. As she fastened her case, Liz wondered what would happen next. Do we go on this way, meeting in secret? Or is there more to it? She thought about asking but she held back. If she declared herself now, she invited rejection, and she didn't want that. She didn't want to hear David say, 'It's been nice. I'll call you.' So she went on making little pleasantries and avoiding his eyes.

It was a fine evening, and they decided to order a car and wait for it outside. It was then that

David spotted the flower seller. The old man had positioned himself on the opposite side of the road and he was surrounded by spring flowers: hyacinths, and daffodils, all pale and papery and tinged with yellow.

'I want to buy you the whole barrow,' David told Liz.

Before she could say anything, he was off, striding across the road. Idiot, she thought fondly, I'll never get them through customs. When she looked at him again, she saw he had been as good as his word, for his arms were piled high with flowers. He'll never see his way across the road, her eye told her. Then the porter came up to her carrying their baggage and her attention was momentarily deflected as she fumbled in her bag for a tip. She looked up as she heard the squeal of tyres and the sound of car horns.

'What on earth . . .' She never finished the sentence.

Daffodils and hyacinths were scattered all over the road, and at the centre of them was David, spreadeagled in front of a black Peugeot. The car had hit him almost as soon as he had stepped off the kerb and already a crowd was gathering around him.

Liz screamed his name just once, pushing her way through the cars and the people until she knelt by his side. David was unconscious and very white. Liz noticed his arm was sticking out at an odd angle, then she saw the blood. It was coming from a wound just under his ribcage and already his suit was stained with it.

Her head came up.

'Has anyone called an ambulance?' she demanded. Everyone started to talk at once, but nobody had an answer for her.

Damn it, she thought. If I don't do something he's

going to die. She struggled to her feet and headed towards the hotel.

David was still alive when they arrived at the hospital. After that Liz had no idea what happened. One minute he was being taken away on a stretcher, the next she must have fainted, as she found herself lying on a hard bed in a cubicle. She sat up as the door opened to admit a tousled-looking young man in green overalls. He held his hand out.

'Dr Weiss,' he said. His English was perfect, with just the slightest trace of an accent. 'You want to know how your friend is?'

Liz nodded, feeling sick. 'He's going to make it, isn't he?'

The doctor smiled. It was an automatic expression containing little humour. 'I can't make any promises,' he told her, 'but we should know more in the next few hours.'

'Can I see him?'

Now even the automatic smile was switched off. 'I'm sorry, I can't allow that, Miss . . .' He floundered for her name and as he did she saw her chance.

'Mrs Dearing,' she said. 'I'm his wife. I have to be with him.'

The first time David woke he felt only pain. White hot, searing agony that made him cry out. For a moment he felt the touch of a hand on his. It was a firm touch, his only link with life and he clung on to it. Then he heard the sound of bells and hurrying footsteps, as someone approached the place where he was lying. He felt a needle go into his arm. After that there was only blackness.

The next time he opened his eyes the pain was still there, but he could cope with it. He couldn't move his body, but he had the energy to look around him, and it was then that he saw her. She was sitting by the side of his bed and when she saw he was awake, she took hold of his hand again.

'It's going to be all right,' she said reassuringly. 'You're going to live.'

David tried to speak, but only unintelligible sounds came from his lips. He felt the pressure on his hand increase.

'Hold on tight,' she said. 'I'll get you through this.'

David woke several times after that, and Liz was always there waiting by him. He started to equate her with living itself. I have a chance, he thought, as long as she stays.

One day he found he could speak. 'How long have I been here?' he asked her.

'Nearly a week,' Liz told him. It was then he remembered who he was and what had happened, and he was assailed by a terrible fear.

'You shouldn't be here,' he whispered. 'You should be in London going on with your life.'

'I know,' Liz said, 'but you needed me more than my life did.'

'And now,' he said, panic rising in his voice. 'Now I'm making sense, will you go away?'

Liz reached over and smoothed the hair out of his eyes.

'I'll only go away when you want me to.' After he heard that, David was able to sleep again.

In the morning the nurses came and took all the tubes out of his arms. Sitting him up and plumping out the pillows behind him. His right arm was in plaster and one of his legs was strapped up and suspended by wires from the ceiling. Every time he drew breath a shooting pain went right through him, but before he registered any of those things, he checked to see where Liz was.

She was sitting at the end of the bed, her face screwed up in concentration as she attempted to do a piece of tapestry. Even at the distance he was sitting at David could tell she wasn't very good at it.

'Why don't you put that down and come and say good morning?'

Liz looked up and smiled. 'Saved by the bell,' she said.

As she came near to him, David realized she hadn't been sleeping for there were great dark smudges underneath her eyes. She looked like she'd lost around ten pounds in weight and aged ten years. If I told anyone here that this girl was a top model, they'd laugh at me, he thought. It was at that precise moment that he fell in love with her.

'You haven't been here all the time?' he asked, wonder in his voice.

Liz shook her head. 'Not all the time. I moved myself into a little pension down the road from here. I eat and sleep there when they throw me out at night.'

'Who knows about the accident?' David asked sharply. 'Do my office know? Have you told your boyfriend?'

Liz brushed a dirty tangle of hair out of her eyes and looked weary.

'If you're worried about your reputation,' she said, 'don't be. I called your office as soon as I knew you were going to be okay and told the secretary you were delayed on business. So your accident won't make the front pages, unless you want me to ring the *Chronicle* again with a different story.'

David reached out for her hand.

'You did the right thing, I'm proud of you. But what about your side? Surely Sandy doesn't believe you're on an extended business trip.'

Liz pulled a face.

'Before I left I told him I was going to New York to visit a girlfriend. I also told him I'd call him from the airport when I was on my way home.'

She stopped talking for a moment, while she considered how she was going to finish the story. Finally she said, 'As things turned out, I didn't make the call in time and Sandy got hold of my girlfriend. I don't have to tell you the rest.'

David looked at her. 'I think you do,' he said slowly. 'Does Sandy know you're here with me?'

Liz sighed. 'He knows I'm here with a lover, but he doesn't know it's you.'

David was about to say something when one of the nurses interrupted him with his breakfast.

'Mr Dearing,' she said, 'I understand you have not been eating your breakfast. This is not good. You have to eat to build up your strength.'

She turned to Liz. 'You tell him to eat. Maybe he'll listen to you.' She bustled away, leaving David in a state of mild confusion.

'Why should I do that?' he asked. 'You didn't tell her you were my mother, did you?'

For the first time since the accident, Liz felt shy. I came away with this man for a dirty weekend, she thought, and I've ended up taking over his life. Christ, I even told everyone here I was married to him. She found she couldn't meet David's eyes.

'I didn't tell anyone I was your mother,' she said. 'I did worse than that. I told them I was your wife.'

Her shoulders were bowed as she stared at the floor and David was overcome with a wave of pity. She put herself on the line for me, he thought. Her boyfriend will throw her out of course – he has to after what she told him. And all because I was scared of dying and wanted someone to hold my hand.

He wondered what he should do. What present would be good enough for her. Liz wasn't like the other girls he knew. She didn't take things from men, she was too damn proud. He marvelled at this new lover of his. She was like no-one he had ever been close to. Even his parents would have put themselves first when the push came to the shove.

'Why did you say you were my wife?' he asked gently.

She looked at him now, and he saw she was blushing.

'I had to,' she confessed. 'They wouldn't have let me in here if I said I was just your girlfriend.'

David considered her reply for a moment.

'I don't ever want to hear you lying again,' he said. 'So the moment I get out of here, you and I are going to get married. It's the only way I can make an honest woman of you.'

22

New York, 1977

Freddie grew up knowing she would never see her father at weekends and it made her feel like an outcast. Not because she particularly needed to see him on Saturdays and Sundays, but because it set her apart from all the other kids at Dalton where she went to school.

Her classmates were always talking about their fathers taking them to the ball game, the movies, or the toy department at Macy's. Always at weekends. When she was old enough to care, Freddie asked her mother where her father got to.

In the beginning, Vanessa didn't like to talk about it. She compensated for it instead. At weekends she took Freddie to the park and the movies and toy department all at once. Then during the week her father came and collected her early from school and took her out to tea at the Plaza. It didn't stop Freddie asking questions.

'Why do we always have to go to the Plaza during the week?' she asked Dan. 'Why can't we go on Sundays?'

Her father always went very quiet when she said things like that. He didn't get angry exactly, but he had a way of making Freddie feel bad when she did anything he didn't like, so she didn't press him.

Her mother was different. She could say anything she wanted to her mother and she always loved her. No matter what. So when she found the right moment

Freddie returned to the weekend question. In the end Vanessa couldn't hold out any longer.

'Daddy isn't around on the weekend,' she told her daughter, 'because he has another family who live in the country and he has to go and see them.'

This kept Freddie quiet for a bit. But when she passed her eighth birthday, she started wondering about her father again. She asked some of her friends at school about their parents. She wanted to know if their fathers had other families they had to go away and see, and she found they did. The more she talked about it to her friends, the better the arrangement sounded, because the fathers with other families sometimes brought them home. Her friends had brothers and sisters to play with. This idea particularly appealed to Freddie. The next time she had tea with her father, she asked him about his other family in the country. Her questions seemed to bother him.

'Why do you want to know so much about them?' Dan asked.

Freddie grinned and asked for another ice-cream soda.

'Well, a lot of the kids at school have other families too. When they get old enough, their fathers bring them home and they all play together.'

Freddie thought her father couldn't be very well, because he asked the waiter for the check, and as soon as it came he threw a pile of dollars on the plate and hurried her out of the hotel. He was quiet all the way home in the taxi. Later on, when she was in bed she heard her father and mother shouting at each other. It didn't bother her too much because she was used to her parents shouting.

They were always arguing over somebody called Ruth. She was the lady her father went to see at weekends. Freddie wasn't stupid, and she realized that Ruth was part of her father's other family. She wondered whether she would ever get to meet this Ruth, and if she did, whether she would like her.

There were days when Vanessa wondered how all this had happened to her. Those were the days she blamed Dan. At other times, when she collected her daughter from school or she tucked her up in bed at night, she blamed herself.

For Freddie was the real reason she lived the way she did. If Vanessa hadn't been pregnant, she would have left this married lover of hers and gone back to London. She might have missed him for a while, they might have even gone on seeing each other occasionally, when it was convenient, but she wouldn't have loved him, because she wouldn't have known him well enough to love him.

Why does nobody ever tell you, she asked herself bitterly, that you become part of a man when you have his child? She had changed towards Dan almost as soon as Freddie was born. In the beginning when they were new lovers she had been the independent one, the one who had to be pleased and placated and courted. When she was off her food, Dan would take Vanessa out to ludicrously expensive restaurants where he would tempt her with everything on the menu. If she was bored he would buy her things – a record from her favourite show, a new pair of earrings. Dan never bought presents for women, so she knew he had to be crazy about her.

Then Vanessa had Freddie and the courtship stopped. Vanessa knew it had to happen of course. They couldn't be star-crossed lovers for ever, but what scared her was how much she needed Dan now.

Before, when he went home to Long Island at weekends she hadn't really missed him. There was always plenty to do in New York and Monday came round soon enough. Now, every moment he was away from her, her life stopped.

For the first year or so, Vanessa didn't tell him how she felt – she didn't dare. Then as Freddie grew into a little girl, she started to make herself clear. Vanessa loved Dan too much to share him any more. It was time he left his wife.

She had imagined it would be easy now he knew the score. But Dan went on at length about Ruth's illness, her total dependency on him, the fact that a shock like this might put her back even further.

Vanessa had believed Dan when he talked like that, especially when there seemed to be hope. Sometimes Dan would come home and say, 'Ruth is thinking of moving out to the coast. The climate would suit her better.' Or, 'Ruth says she can't go on living with half a marriage. She seems to be coming to a decision.'

Vanessa would then fantasize and talk of moving to a bigger place so that the three of them could be a real family. She even considered changing her name to Levin, so Freddie wouldn't have any problems at school. But every time she made a positive plan, Ruth had a relapse. At times Vanessa wondered if Dan's wife had put a bug in the apartment, for she timed her bouts of ill health to coincide almost exactly with the moments Dan talked of insisting on a divorce.

Then Freddie starting growing up and asking questions and Ruth got really sick.

'She has to be putting it on,' Vanessa would say. 'Every time she hears something she doesn't like her heart flutters.'

Dan was furious. He turned on Vanessa.

'Are you trying to say Ruth is manipulating me with her illness?' he shouted. 'Because if you are, you disappoint me.'

Vanessa would back down then. She hated it when Dan was cross with her, and she went out of her way to make things up to him. Most of their quarrels would end up with them in bed. As time went on, she became adept at turning her lover's anger into passion.

Then one day Vanessa ran into Ruth quite by chance, and after that she knew that making love to Dan was no way to solve her problems.

She bumped into Ruth, standing in the reception area of the Levin showroom on Seventh Avenue. Vanessa didn't model the range any more, but she was involved with the Royal Enclosure perfume promotion. The morning Vanessa saw Ruth, she had stopped by to collect some clothes for a photographic session at the Norman Bracken agency.

She probably wouldn't have noticed her at all if Ruth hadn't asked for Dan by name.

'Who shall I say wants to see him?' the receptionist enquired.

The dark woman standing by the desk looked bored. 'Tell him it's his wife,' she said.

Vanessa did a double take. It can't be Ruth, she thought wildly. Ruth's too sick to come into the city. She had a vision of Ruth that had never altered. In her imagination she saw her as a faded matron of uncertain age. The facts in front of her didn't quite match with the fantasy, for this woman was anything but matronly. She was around medium height and very curvy, with a bosom she wore like a fashion accessory. There was something aggressive about the bosom and she didn't hide it. The black suit she was wearing clung to every inch of it – she even had a cleavage. For a moment Vanessa couldn't believe what she was seeing.

She took a hold of herself and went up to the reception desk.

'You must be Ruth,' she said boldly.

The dark woman turned to her and Vanessa saw how good looking she was. Nobody could call her a beauty, for there was nothing classic about her features, but she had a vitality that more than made up for it.

'How come you know my name?' she asked. 'Do you work here?'

Vanessa was stuck. If she told Dan's wife who she was she might provoke a scene so she lied.

'I'm from the Norman Bracken agency,' she said. 'In one of our meetings, Mr Levin mentioned he was married to somebody called Ruth.'

The other woman smiled. 'I don't believe a word of it,' she said. 'You're far too pretty to be an account executive. Still, I'm flattered that my husband talks about me. He usually forgets to mention he has a wife when he's with someone who looks like you.'

There was something about Ruth, a confidence and a good humour, that worried Vanessa. The woman Dan had talked about all these years was nothing like this. If he was to be believed his wife didn't have the energy to come into the city, let alone doll herself up and show her cleavage with such enthusiasm. Vanessa decided to push her luck.

'What are you up here for?' she enquired.

The other woman smiled and patted her hair into place. 'Dan's taking me out for lunch. We always do this on Wednesday – it's been one of our little routines ever since we moved out to the country. I don't generally come into the showroom, though.'

Vanessa went cold all over. So Dan was on good

terms with his wife. Worse, he took her out to lunch during the week. Why hadn't he told her anything about it?

The phone on the reception desk shrilled and the girl picked it up. After a couple of seconds she nodded and replaced the receiver.

'That was Mr Levin,' she said to Ruth. 'He says he'll be out in five minutes.'

Vanessa realized that if Dan came out now and saw her talking to his wife, the game would be up. Just for a second, she was tempted to let it happen. It was time things came out into the open. There would be an almighty row but she might find an answer to some of the things that were bothering her – Ruth's apparent health and fitness for instance.

Then her courage deserted her. I can't face it, Vanessa thought. Not yet. I have to get hold of some facts first.

Norman Bracken, the agency chief and Dan's old friend finally wised her up. She had been suspicious of him at first, for his coldness frightened her. But time had changed all that. Time and familiarity. Now they were firm friends. She arranged to have Sunday lunch with him at the Oyster Bar on Grand Central Station.

As soon as she got there Vanessa spotted him. He was so formal in his blazer and flannels. So businesslike.

He stood up when she arrived.

'Where's Freddie?' he asked. 'I thought this was her favourite restaurant.'

Vanessa grabbed a bar stool. 'It is,' she said shortly, 'but there's something I want to discuss with you today that I'd rather she didn't hear.'

'In that case,' Norman said, 'do you mind if we

move next door. The Tavern is slightly more grown-up than the Oyster Bar.'

Vanessa got to her feet. The thing she most liked about Norman was his sensitivity to others. She had been nervous about today. Ever since she had run into Dan's wife, her whole life seemed to have been out of kilter, and Norman had understood her mood without having to ask questions.

She let him escort her into the handsome tavern with its soft lighting and wood panelled walls. For the first time that weekend she started to relax. Whatever the truth was about Ruth, she was no longer worried about it. As long as she was with Norman, they would face it together. Drink in hand, Vanessa began to tell Norman about her encounter with Ruth. She didn't miss out any of the details. At the end of her monologue, Norman looked weary.

'Where do you want me to begin?' he asked. 'Do you want me to tell you about Dan's marriage before he met you? Or would you like to know about it now?'

Vanessa took a gulp of her drink.

'Tell me all of it,' she said. 'I need to know the truth.'

Norman gave her a quizzical look.

'The truth,' he said, 'will make you very unhappy. Are you sure you want to hear it?'

Vanessa frowned, considering her options. She had been living a half life for eight years now, but it was the life she had chosen because she loved Dan and she believed him when he told her it would change. Now she wasn't so sure. She regarded the flint-faced man in front of her with a certain trepidation. What he tells me could change everything, she thought. Do I want that?

He saw her hesitation and smiled.

'I think you like the fool's paradise Dan makes you live in,' he said softly. 'So I'll shut up and we'll talk about something else.'

But things had gone too far, and Vanessa knew too much to go back now.

'I want to know why you think I live in a fool's paradise.'

Norman sighed. 'In words of one syllable?'

Vanessa nodded and signalled at the waiter for another drink.

'Dan,' Norman said in his clipped East Coast voice, 'is a married man with a beautiful mistress. The arrangement suits him down to the ground and he has no intention of changing it.'

Vanessa had suspected it all along of course. It was the logical explanation for the way things were going and had always gone. Nevertheless, Norman's words hurt like hell. Vanessa floundered around trying to take the sting out of them.

'Does Ruth know about Dan's arrangement, as you call it? Does she know Dan has an eight year old daughter living in New York city?'

Norman looked embarrased. 'Ruth knows everything there is to know about Dan,' he told her. 'She knows the bottom line of his business better than he does. She came to terms with his other women years ago, and when you came on the scene she allowed him to stray, just as long as he didn't stray too far.'

Vanessa wasn't quite sure she had heard him right. Ruth knew about her and she wasn't screaming blue murder. It was impossible to believe. Then she thought back to the woman she had met, and how confident she seemed.

'Does Dan really talk about me in front of someone as pretty as you?' she had said. 'Normally he doesn't mention his wife.'

Suddenly it all made sense. Vanessa was an extra – an affordable accessory to a millionaire's marriage. Her eyes filled with tears, threatening to spoil the perfection of her pan-cake.

'So Ruth isn't ill at all. It's just a story Dan made up to keep me quiet.'

Norman reached into his pocket and fished out a clean linen handkerchief.

Handing it over to Vanessa, he said, 'Ruth's illness wasn't a complete fabrication. There was some trouble a long time ago; and at the time the doctors thought it was her heart. As it turned out it was a false alarm. Ruth had some kind of virus, which cured itself. She's been one hundred per cent ever since.'

Vanessa put her hand over her face. What am I to do? she thought. I staked my whole life on a lie and now I'm in so deep there's no going back. How naive can you get? I can't walk out on Dan because there's nowhere to go. My parents won't take me in with a daughter in tow. They don't even know she exists. Nobody does except Liz, and she's got problems of her own.

She looked up to see Norman watching her. There was sympathy in his eyes.

'I've got a suggestion to make,' he said. 'You don't have to tell Dan we had this conversation. You don't have to do anything, until you're good and ready.'

'When will that be?' Vanessa asked bitterly. 'When Prince Charming comes riding by on his white horse and rescues me?'

Norman smiled.

'What's so silly about that?'

'Everything, starting with the fact there's no Prince living in Manhattan.'

There was a silence and Vanessa realized that

Norman was looking at her intently. The penny dropped.

'You don't look very far, do you,' he said.

Vanessa felt a rush of gratitude, but even as she did she realized it would be impossible. She lived with Dan because she had come to love him. It was the reason she had never left New York, the reason she had believed his lies. Lots of girls, she thought, would adore a man like Norman. He's rich, he's not all that bad looking. He would make the perfect Prince Charming. But not for me. I can't settle for anything less than love.

She reached out and took Norman's hand.

'It can't work,' Vanessa said. 'I wish it could, because I think you could make me very happy. But not now, and not with Dan in my life.'

'So you're going on with it?' Norman asked.

Vanessa nodded. 'I have to. No other way feels right.'

Norman took his hand away from hers, then he leaned across the table and planted a kiss in the centre of her forehead. It was a chaste kiss. A brotherly kiss.

'Dan may seem right for you now,' he said. 'But nothing lasts for ever. Things will change. You'll see.'

23

Out of all her friends, Freddie had by far the prettiest mother. She had more hair than any of the other mothers, and when she took it down it flowed down to the centre of her shoulders like a shower of gold. Freddie helped her brush it every night. One hundred strokes it took with her mother sitting in front of the bedroom mirror all the while. They both did the hair brushing routine after tea, before Vanessa got ready to meet her father in the evening.

Now that Vanessa was working again she and Dan were hardly ever home nowadays. But the whole thing cheered her mother up so much, that Freddie didn't dare complain about not seeing her. Another thing she noticed was that they didn't shout at one another any more. Freddie knew she should have been relieved about that, but she wasn't. She couldn't quite work out why she wasn't, but she knew it was something to do with the way Mom behaved towards Dad when he was home. Before, even when they shouted, it was okay because they were both so easy with each other. They were always kissing and touching and now all that seemed to have stopped.

It was true that Mom didn't shout any more, but she didn't do anything else either. When Dad was at home she was kind of quiet with him, almost as if she was frightened of him. Freddie knew that couldn't be true at all, because they'd known each other for ever and ever. She decided to ask her mother if anything was the matter.

'You'd tell me if Daddy was ill,' she said, falteringly, to her mother. 'Promise me you would.'

Vanessa was nonplussed.

'There's nothing wrong with Daddy,' she told her daughter. 'Whatever gave you the idea there might be?'

'Because of the way you're treating him.' The words seemed to burst out of Freddie's mouth, and the moment she said them she started to feel very sad, as if the world was coming to an end.

Vanessa gathered her daughter up in her arms and held her close.

'Don't cry, darling,' she soothed. 'There's nothing to worry about.'

Her words fell on deaf ears, and the tears were flowing thick and fast. Freddie sobbed her heart out for over an hour and in the end the cook had to promise to make her favourite strawberry cake before she would stop. Vanessa resented her daughter for making the scene. I want to cry too, she thought bitterly. But I can't afford the luxury. As long as I stay with Dan I can never afford to be anything but perfect.

Vanessa knew she was losing her touch the day she passed her thirtieth birthday. It was nothing obvious. Nobody at the ad agency told her she was last year's model, because nobody dared. She had been the Royal Enclosure girl for years now, and the perfume had caught on in a big way. She was also Dan Levin's girlfriend and that counted for something.

So why did Norman keep talking about Cindy Chase every time the three of them met for dinner?

To be fair to Norman, he didn't start the Cindy Chase conversation. Dan did. The blonde model had just done a big campaign for Ralph Lauren and everyone in New York was raving about her.

'She's only a kid,' said Dan. 'She can't be more than twenty-one at the most, but she's got such class.'

He turned to Vanessa and chucked her under the chin.

'You know who she reminds me of?' he said knowingly. 'Cindy looks just like you did when I first met you.'

He swung round in his seat until he was facing Norman. 'Check her out for me, will you? There has to be something we can use her on.'

Vanessa started to worry about herself after that. In the past, she had taken the way she looked for granted. Her huge pale eyes were her father's eyes. Generations of Grenvilles looked like she did and if their faces changed as they got older, that was just part of the natural way of things. Like all the women of her class, she cut off her long hair the day she passed thirty. The moment she had done it, she lived to regret it, for the very same week Cindy Chase did her first modelling assignment for Levins.

Dan didn't use her on Royal Enclosure. He had some consideration for Vanessa's feelings. Instead, he gave her Maxi-modes to show. The design house was starting to spend money on the line and before Dan put his advertising agency behind it, he wanted to see how the trade received it.

Dan knew he was on to a winner the moment he saw Cindy in the clothes. There was nothing special about Maxi-modes, except for the quality. The line was aimed at executives' wives, so all he needed to sell was an expensive look, a value for money look. What Cindy provided was an extra dimension, an oomph, which sent all the buyers hurrying for their order forms.

It's sex, pure and simple, Dan thought as he watched the slender blonde go through her paces on the catwalk. Cindy makes these respectable dresses look less starchy. You feel you want to undo the buttons or push the skirt up when she's in them. As he put himself into the minds of his buying public, Dan felt an uncontrollable frisson of lust. I wonder, he mused, what it would be like with Cindy. She was so young, so wild looking, so different from Vanessa yet so much the same.

If Cindy hadn't been the star that she was, he would have approached her there and then. After all, she was just another model girl – a body for hire, a buyable commodity. But this girl was more than that. She had a talent for making women want to buy clothes and Dan needed her in his business. So rather than settling for a quick seduction, Dan began to court Cindy Chase.

She wasn't exactly a pushover. For a start she knew all about Ruth and Vanessa, so she wasn't all that flattered that Dan was chasing her.

'How come you have time to take me to dinner,' she enquired when he invited her to the Four Seasons. 'I thought you had your hands full already.'

'I thought so too, until I saw you,' Dan said, laughingly. Cindy dimpled and smacked his hand. 'Naughty,' she trilled.

Three days later, Dan asked her to have a drink with him, but Cindy couldn't do that either. As far as Dan was concerned Cindy's schedule was chock-a-block. Each time he asked her to do something she was either rushing off to another job, needed to go to the hairdresser or was having her nails done. He tried another tack. The next time he ran into her, he handed her a package, gift wrapped. Inside it was a tiny sapphire brooch in the shape of a Praying Mantis. Cindy was delighted with it.

'It reminds me of you,' she giggled.

The fact that she accepted his gift gave Dan hope. This girl meant business. All he had to do now was determine her price. In the weeks and months to come, he discovered that Cindy came expensive – too expensive for him. What the model girl wanted was to step into Vanessa's shoes. She wanted to be the Royal Enclosure girl.

'It's out of the question,' Dan protested. 'Vanessa and Royal Enclosure are one and the same thing. When you see a pack shot of the perfume, you immediately expect to see Vanessa's face next to it. The public would never buy anyone else's image.'

Cindy was unconvinced.

'They said the same thing about Marilyn Monroe,' she told him, 'then Jayne Mansfield came along and proved them all wrong. The public gets bored with old faces and old images. If Monroe hadn't died when she did, people would have got tired of her.'

'This is not the film business,' said Dan crossly. 'And I'm not Cecil B. DeMille. Vanessa has been selling Royal Enclosure across America for years now, the clothes and the fragrance. I can't just pension her off.'

But Dan was tempted. Vanessa had been very tiresome of late. Always asking questions, always wanting to know where he was every second of the day. In the past he had kept her in touch with his movements because he liked being near her, but recently he felt she was fencing him in. It was one thing volunteering his whereabouts, but it was quite another being ordered to give out the details of his diary.

Vanessa was turning into another wife, and the notion depressed him. Dan had set her up in the first place because he needed some excitement in his life. He had always been surrounded by responsibility: a wife, a business that needed running, possessions that needed maintaining, children that needed educating. Vanessa had been his escape from all these things, for when he was with her he could imagine he was young and free and sexy. Now she had gone and changed all that.

Over the years Vanessa had saddled him with a child, and any number of demands he couldn't satisfy. These days he felt about her the way he felt about Ruth – guilty and beholden.

Dan thought about Cindy, wanton and baby-faced, and spoiled beyond measure. She hadn't even let him touch her hand and already she was demanding the starring role in his advertising campaign. He was furious with her arrogance, yet at the same time he was intrigued. When he made Vanessa his Royal Enclosure girl, she had been so willing to please. This girl wasn't like that at all.

Cindy knew her own worth. She knew she was hot, and she felt that what she asked for was only her due.

From out of the blue a thought assailed him. What if Cindy is right? What if Royal Enclosure is in danger of looking dated? He put it out of his mind. The girl was holding him to ransom. She would use any argument to get what she wanted. Anyway she was a model girl, an airhead. What did she know?

Dan started to dream about her, and in his fantasies he was touching her and kissing her and she was allowing him to do anything he wanted. Sometimes when he was making love to Vanessa he closed his eyes and pretended it was Cindy. Then she would whisper, 'I love you, darling,' and the spell would be broken. Cindy would never sound so grateful.

Vanessa continued to irritate Dan. He loved her dearly, but did she really have to rely on him so much?

She didn't seem to be able to make even the simplest decision without consulting him first. On the days he left the apartment without instructing the cook Vanessa was on the line an hour or so later asking what he wanted for dinner. When he took her to a gala evening at the Met, she wouldn't get dressed without his approval on what she wore. There were times, he decided, when it was less stressful to be with Ruth than with Vanessa. At least his wife knew her own mind.

Then there was the problem of Freddie.

When she was younger it had been easy to hide her away, but as the years went on she became more and more of a handful. Other people's daughters did as they were told, even Freddie's mother did as she was told. But Freddie was a law unto herself. Dan smiled fondly remembering her latest obsession.

She had developed a passion for board games. First it was snakes and ladders. Now it was draughts. She was a tough little player, never giving an inch and screaming blue murder if anyone tried to take advantage of her lack of experience. Dan wondered what kind of woman she would grow into. Would she be like Vanessa, beautiful and passive? Or would she be more like Cindy, a ballbreaker? He had an awful premonition it would probably be the latter.

Young women nowadays were becoming far too independent for their own good, Dan decided. They didn't seem to need men at all unless it suited them. Cindy and my daughter, he thought. What did I do to deserve them?

Once a month Dan had lunch with Norman Bracken to go over the latest advertising. The agency was currently handling two campaigns for Levins. There was the perfume promotion which was mainly posters and television, and the new Maxi-modes campaign which ran in women's magazines. Of the two, Maxi-modes was gaining ground because of the public's fascination with Cindy. She was fast becoming the face of the seventies. Every time she went out in public, she would have her picture taken, and the next day one of the gossip columns would record the fact that Cindy Chase had been at a gallery opening in Greenwich Village or an Andy Warhol party.

'She's a difficult bitch,' said Dan, 'but we're stuck with her. Nobody moves the goods like she does.'

Norman agreed with him.

'Vanessa could do with taking a leaf out of her book,' he said. 'Royal Enclosure sales are down on last year.'

Alarm bells sounded in Dan's mind. Wasn't this exactly what Cindy had been warning him about, when she told him the public got bored with old faces?

'How long have we been using Vanessa in our advertising?' he asked.

Norman thought for a moment. 'She's been doing in-store promotions for the clothes for going on eight years. The perfume has been around for nearly as long. Why are you interested?'

Dan signalled to the waiter to bring another pitcher of martinis. This was going to be a more difficult lunch than he thought.

'I have a feeling her image is getting out of date. She's still as lovely as ever, there's no denying that, but are good looks and breeding enough these days? Aren't young women looking for something else as well?'

'Like what?' Norman asked.

Dan frowned and a ran a hand through dark, wavy hair.

'I don't know – aggression, assertiveness, a kind of fuck-you attitude. I see it all around me. On the streets, on television. I think women are beginning to identify with that kind of feeling.'

The advertising supremo leaned back in his chair. Dan was right of course. He had been having this conversation with his executives for a couple of years now, but if he agreed with his client, he would be selling Vanessa down the river. Could he do that to her, he wondered. Did he have the heart to destroy her?

Then a thought occurred to him. If Dan dropped Vanessa from the advertising and substituted Cindy Chase she wouldn't be able to tolerate living with him too much longer. She would have to consider an alternative and Norman was the only one she had.

'I can only agree with you,' he said slowly. 'In my opinion Vanessa belongs to yesterday.'

24

The day Freddie left home, all her dolls and her toys and the backgammon board her father bought her for Christmas were packed into a tea chest and put on the back of a removal van. She cried a little when she saw all her things being taken out of the apartment, but her mother calmed her down.

'We're moving to a nice neighbourhood,' she told her. 'You'll love Gramercy Park, I promise you.'

Freddie set her chin.

'But I won't love Uncle Norman,' she replied. 'I won't love anybody any more – especially not Uncle Norman.'

Vanessa had told her she and Dad were splitting up a few days before they moved, but Freddie had known there was something wrong ages before that.

It started when her parents stopped touching and holding hands. She hadn't minded when they shouted because of the touching, but when they started going quiet on her, she knew something terrible was going to happen. And she had been right.

The worst part about the whole thing was the way they treated her. Daddy behaved as if nothing had happened at all. After Vanessa had told her they were moving, he took her out to the park and tried to explain things.

'Mommy needs a change,' he had said, 'so you're going to stay with Uncle Norman for a bit.'

Freddie was nearly nine and her father was treating

her like a half-wit. Nobody could believe a story like that. Not even a baby.

'If Mommy needs a change,' she asked her father, 'why doesn't she go away on holiday? Why do we have to go and live with Uncle Norman?'

Dan went very quiet.

'Darling,' he said slowly, 'I don't expect you to understand any of this, I don't know if I understand it myself. Your mother is very angry with me at the moment. She's so angry that she doesn't want to live with me any more.'

'So why do we have to go to Uncle Norman? I hate Uncle Norman.'

Dan took her hand when she said that and pulled her close. When she looked up at him she noticed there were tears in his eyes.

'Uncle Norman isn't as bad as you think he is,' he told her. 'He's very kind to you – you have to give him a chance.'

Freddie pouted.

'I tried as hard as I could,' she wailed, 'but he frightens me, Daddy. He's not like you. When you smile at me and tell me you love me, I know you mean it. But when Uncle Norman smiles only his mouth smiles. It's scary.'

Dan gave his daughter a friendly pat on her cheek.

'That's quite enough,' he admonished. 'Norman's very fond of you. He told me so himself. So make an effort and try to be nice, for my sake.'

Freddie went on pouting and Dan sighed.

If Freddie persisted with this line none of them would get anywhere. He cast his mind back to the week before when he and Vanessa had their final fight. She was kicking up about Cindy being used in the new Royal Enclosure campaign. She accused him of betraying her and in his heart he knew she was right. But what could he do? Put his perfume business in jeopardy to satisfy her vanity? He tried explaining it to her calmly and rationally. He even quoted the research figures at her, but she didn't take any notice. All she could talk about was Cindy.

Somebody had told her the blonde model had replaced her before he could do it himself, and if he had known who it was he would have cheerfully strangled them, for Vanessa had taken the news very badly indeed. She looked as if she had been crying for hours on end, for her eyes were all swollen and puffy and she had a dishevelled look Dan hadn't seen for years.

Part of him was devastated – the part that had loved her. But there was another part of him that refused to be involved. That part observed this woman he had just destroyed and judged her without mercy. She was too old, too clinging, too boring to put up with any longer.

'Stop whining,' he had told her harshly. 'I gave you a good run, didn't I?'

'And what will you do with me now?' Vanessa had demanded. 'Turn me out to make way for a newer model. It's what you want, isn't it?'

Looking back, Dan wished he hadn't said what he did next, but she pushed him into it.

'Sure it's what I want,' he replied, 'but I don't have to house and clothe her for the pleasure.'

'You mean Cindy opens her legs free of charge.'

There was no point in going on with the discussion after that. Dan walked out before Vanessa could say anything worse. Then it was all a matter of negotiation.

Norman came to his office that evening and told him he was taking Vanessa away. He didn't argue until they came to the question of his daughter and then Dan saw red. Norman wanted to adopt Freddie and bring her up as his own.

'Forget it,' Dan said tersely. 'Freddie belongs to me. If you try to take her away I'll fight you in every court in the land.'

The advertising supremo was not amused.

'What will your wife and sons have to say about that?' he had asked.

The question had stopped him. Ruth didn't know Dan had a daughter, and he saw no reason to tell her until Freddie was older. Now there was no reason at all.

'I can't just abandon her,' he said desperately. 'She'd never forgive me.'

'She'll get over it,' Norman told him. 'Little girls have short memories, and it will be for the best. The thing with you and Vanessa is finished. You don't want to leave any loose ends.'

He accepted what Norman had said. He had had to, but he drove a hard bargain. A trust fund was to be opened in Freddie's name to take care of her education and welfare until she was eighteen.

He and Norman would be co-contributors; and in exchange for Norman's input, he agreed to forgo all visiting rights. Dan promised not to try and see Freddie until she had come of age. Now, as he walked her in the Park for the last time, he regretted his promise. She was tiresome, this daughter of his, there was no denying that. But she had guts and she was fun. He was going to miss her. He made one last attempt to talk her into making the best of her new situation.

'If you can't be nice to Norman for my sake,' he said patiently, 'then do it for your mother. Your uncle has told me he's going to look after her. If things work out he could be doing that for ever and it won't be easy on her if you play up the whole time. Try and be grown up, Freddie, you're stuck with him – whatever you do.'

Freddie let go of her father's hand and walked on ahead of him.

'I can always run away,' she called over her shoulder.

25

The advertising for Royal Enclosure was launched just before Christmas. It was the most ambitious campaign Dan had ever mounted, and overnight Cindy seemed to be all over town. Her face stared down from the city's main poster sites and every women's magazine carried a double-page colour spread of her. There were prime time commercial breaks featuring Cindy drinking champagne at the races and driving all the men wild with desire for her body and the perfume she was wearing.

The whole thing made Vanessa feel physically sick. Everywhere she turned she came face to face with her own failure. The gorgeous, arrogant Cindy Chase. The model had moved in with Dan almost as soon as Vanessa had moved out, and if it hadn't been for Norman she couldn't have coped at all. He understood what she was going through and did his best to make life bearable for her. It wasn't easy. From the moment she moved into his apartment she had to make certain adjustments. It wasn't as big as where she had been living. Where Dan's place had five bedrooms and living quarters for a maid, Norman's had two. One for them, and a tiny guest room for Freddie. There was no provision for staff whatever, but then there wasn't much in the way of help anyway.

A Spanish woman came in once a day for two hours. She dusted and tidied and once a week she had a blitz on the bathroom and kitchen, but that was it. When

Vanessa suggested that now there were three of them, Carmen should come in for longer, Norman didn't seem to hear her.

'You know how to clean a bathroom,' he said. 'Every woman knows that.'

Vanessa didn't argue. Norman had been so good to her, so good to both of them that she didn't want to seem ungrateful.

Sometimes it was an effort, though, for she had never had to look after anybody in her life. When she had been with Dan, he had seen to it that all the everyday things had been taken care of. When Freddie came along, there was a nurse, a nanny and finally a governess. Vanessa had had nothing to worry about. If she wanted a new dress, she went along to any one of half a dozen stores on Fifth Avenue, picked something out and charged it to Dan's account. Dan opened an account for her at Ardens, where she had her hair done; Maud Frizon, where she bought her shoes, and Weiss, which supplied her stockings and her underwear. Vanessa had never had any idea what all this cost, but Dan didn't like talking about money so the matter never came up.

With Norman the subject never stopped coming up. He wasn't exactly a pauper, but he seemed to have the mind of one. Everything Vanessa did, she had to account for. Norman gave her five hundred dollars every week to spend on food and liquor and cleaning bills. If she went over her limit, she had to come to him and tell him how much more she needed and what she needed it for. It nearly drove her insane.

In the first week she realized that a pair of shoes cost almost as much as Norman had given her to live on. It didn't seem possible, but she needed the shoes to go with a new outfit she had got the month before so she went ahead and got them. The shoes were the subject of the first row she and Norman ever had.

Vanessa had never seen Norman angry. In the past months he had been cool and controlled. When he found out about the shoes, it was a different story.

'I don't believe it,' he shouted. 'How could you think a pair of shoes was more important than the groceries – don't you and your daughter ever worry about what you're going to eat?'

Vanessa felt out of her depth. 'I thought we'd all go out to a restaurant. That's what we've always done before.'

The colour drained out of Norman's face and Vanessa noticed for the first time how thin his lips were. In this mood he was hard and more than a little frightening. She wondered if she knew him as well as she thought she did.

'You're a spoiled little hussy,' he said quietly. 'Did you ever lift a finger in your life, or did some man always pay for your first class ticket?'

Vanessa felt cheap and ashamed. This man had no right to say things like that.

'I'm not a kept woman,' she told him hotly. 'I never was. Before I met Dan, I earned my own living and I only stopped working when Freddie came along. You know very well that that happened because I thought that Dan and I were going to be married one day.'

Norman looked at her and there was a sneer on his face.

'You can go back to work any day you want,' he said. 'Find yourself a job and I won't stand in your way.'

Vanessa was in trouble. The only work she had ever done was modelling. She was a good model, a marvellous model, but she was a model past her time and Norman and she both knew it. If she was lucky she might get a catwalk job, but she would have to crawl for it and the money would be minimal.

She sighed. She simply wasn't qualified to do anything else, because she never thought she would have to. She began to cry and Norman realized he had gone too far. He crossed the room and gathered her in his arms.

'I'm sorry, baby,' he murmured, 'I didn't mean to hurt you. I never want to do that. Not as long as I live.'

He started to kiss her and Vanessa let him. Her quarrels with Dan had always ended up in bed and she realized that she was stuck with this scenario. For some reason it bothered her, yet for the life of her she couldn't understand why.

'Dan and I did this all the time,' she reasoned. 'There didn't seem anything wrong with it then.'

But Vanessa knew what was wrong. She knew it, but she hid from it. Norman didn't turn her on. She had tried not to let it show. On their first night together when he moved her into his apartment, she had made herself lovely for him.

She remembered sneaking into the bathroom while Norman got ready for bed. While he thought she was creaming off her make-up, she slipped into a lacy bra that made her breasts look huge. Then she added a pair of pants she bought in Paris that were almost transparent. And over the top she donned a satin nightdress slit all the way up to the thigh. Then she fluffed out her hair and dabbed perfume into her cleavage and behind her knees. She was ready.

Norman was waiting for her by the night table, in his dressing-gown, nursing a bourbon. Vanessa wondered if he was as nervous as she was.

'Darling,' she said, 'there's nothing to worry about. It's going to be beautiful.'

Norman started to fondle one of her breasts, and as the nipple came erect, he pushed down the top of her nightie. Then he saw the bra. Vanessa knew it would arouse him. The girl in the shop told her it was guaranteed to drive a man crazy, and she was right, for he couldn't wait to tear it off her. He couldn't wait to tear everything off her.

Then his hands and his tongue were all over her and Vanessa was reminded of a greedy little boy. Norman didn't try to please her – he hadn't even kissed her properly – all he could do was think of himself.

She tried to step away from him but he was having none of it. Instead he took her by the waist and pushed her down on to the bed. Then he opened his dressing-gown and she saw he was fully erect. In an involuntary movement she brought her legs together. All it did was inflame him further.

'What a beautiful bitch you are,' he said softly. 'I'm going to have a lot of fun owning you.'

Then before she could react, he was on top of her. Vanessa felt she was being plundered. Norman wasn't tender or even considerate. He simply forced her legs apart and pushed himself into her. Then he fucked her. There was no other word to describe what he did, and when he was finished, he turned his back to her and fell asleep instantly.

It was the same thing every night. Vanessa would spend hours getting ready for bed, hoping against hope that Norman would relax and show her a little affection, but all he ever did was get into her as fast as he could and spend himself.

Now they had quarrelled for the first time, and her new lover was kissing her and telling her he didn't want to hurt her.

What a liar you are, she thought bitterly. The moment you get me into the bedroom, you'll start treating me like dirt again. For the first time since she moved away from Dan, Vanessa began to wonder where her life was heading.

26

London, 1977

On her thirtieth birthday David gave Liz a party at Annabel's. The event made the social pages both sides of the Atlantic for David took over the exclusive premises on Berkeley Square and invited a mixture of café society and old money. Bianca Jagger nibbled caviar alongside the Earl of Lichfield and the Duke of Westminster. Princess Margaret came with Roddy Llewellyn, the American Ambassador put in an appearance as did David Bailey, Jean Shrimpton and Cilla Black. It was a wow of a party where money was no object and style was everything. David had flown in a five-piece dance band from Paris and the chef from Maxim's. When one hundred people sat down at the circular tables suspended under pools of light, they dined off oysters from Colchester, followed by wild Scottish salmon, and pheasant shot on the Dearing estate. Afterwards there were fresh strawberries and chocolate gateau because Liz insisted she didn't want a birthday cake.

'I want everyone to remember this party,' she told David, 'but I don't want them to recall why you gave it.'

He had laughed at her for that. 'Don't be a goose,' he said fondly. 'Thirty is no age at all.'

But Liz knew otherwise.

She had always been meticulous with her diets and her beauty routines and just because she was married she saw no reason to give up on herself. Then she got pregnant and there was even more reason to keep herself up to the mark.

She had heard of marriages that went wrong because the women became complacent and she was determined not to let that happen to her. While the waiters cleared away the dinner she threaded her way through the dimly lit nightclub to the powder-room. It was always something of a sanctuary at Annabel's, and reminded Liz of an old-fashioned boudoir. She loved the frilly dressing-tables and the pink lighting. It was empty for once, and Liz sat down and took a close look at herself.

I haven't worn badly, she thought. She was wearing a long strapless tube specially created for her and automatically she checked the tops of her arms, pinching the skin inside her elbow. It was still tight and elastic. The Swedish massage was a good idea, she thought. She made a mental note to step it up to three times a week.

Next, she peered closely in the mirror at the skin on her face. It still glowed the way it always did, but tiny lines were beginning to form above her eyebrows and at the sides of her mouth. She turned first her left profile, then her right profile to the light. Then she took a decision. It was too early for a lift, but there was something she could do. One of her girlfriends had been telling her about a doctor in Harley Street who eradicated lines. He did it by injecting a substance called collagen. According to her friend who had had it done, it was a very painful experience, but it did the trick. After one or two sessions there were no creases to be seen.

Gently, Liz prodded the skin underneath her eyes. It's a pity collagen can't take care of that as well, she thought. Then she straightened up quickly and fumbled in her bag for a lipstick. Charlotte de Courcy had just come through the door. The two women had barely spoken to one another since Liz's marriage to David. At the time Liz didn't blame the interior designer for being furious. She had walked off with her boyfriend, hadn't she? Stolen him from under her nose. But as the years went on the situation seemed increasingly silly. Liz and David had a daughter now, and Charlotte had changed lovers several times since, yet still she insisted on treating her as if she didn't exist.

In the end, Liz had written to her, inviting her to lunch.

Charlotte didn't bother to write a proper reply. Instead she had sent back the letter with a note scrawled across the top. 'I only lunch with friends,' she had written, 'and you will never be one of those.'

It was the rudest thing she could have done and Liz threw the whole thing into the wastepaper basket. If Charlotte wanted a vendetta it was fine with her.

Because the powder-room at Annabel's was so small, the two women were forced to stand side by side as they repaired their faces. Liz got out as fast as she could. What the hell is that woman doing at my birthday party, she wondered. I must ask David who she came with.

Back at her table she got the answer. Charlotte was there with Vic Chirgotis, the Greek shipping tycoon. According to the gossip columns she was refurbishing his ten-bedroomed house on Eaton Square. But there was more to it than that: Charlotte had moved herself in to supervise operations and it was becoming apparent that she was also supervising Vic. Liz was fascinated with what her husband had to tell her. Vic was in the Onassis class, but with a better pedigree. If Charlotte landed him, she was made.

'Is Vic enjoying the situation?' she enquired.

David grinned. 'Why not ask him,' he said. 'He's standing right behind you.'

If Liz hadn't been in love with her husband, she might have felt jealous of Charlotte, for her Greek had glamour. He was one of those macho men, all burning black eyes and muscular physique. For a moment she was tempted to flirt, but she stopped herself. Instead she said,

'I just ran into your girlfriend in the loo. She's looking very happy tonight. Very radiant.'

The Greek made a face and took a slug from the brandy balloon in his hand.

'Good,' he said. 'I'm glad Charlotte's looking radiant.'

From the way he said it, Liz realized she'd made some kind of faux pas, and she had no idea what to say next. Vic saved her the trouble of making any more conversation.

'Come and dance,' he said. 'They're playing my favourite tune.'

Liz let him lead her to the tiny floor and hold her close as they moved among the other couples. Vic's favourite tune was 'Tender is the Night' and for the next five minutes Liz gave herself up to the syrupy music. She wasn't sure how it happened: one moment she was smooching in the dark, her cheek against Vic's, her body pressed into his; the next, she was uncomfortably aware that the man had an erection.

Quickly, she pulled apart from him.

'I don't think we should go on with this,' she said.

The Greek took hold of her hand and pulled her in the direction of the circular bar in the corner of the room.

'Let's have a drink,' he said. 'I need to talk to you.'

In the normal way of things, Liz would have made

an excuse and gone back to her husband's table, but Vic intrigued her. He was rich, he was sexy and he was virtually living with her worst enemy. So, for a fraction of a second, she hesitated.

'If you want to talk about what just happened on the dance floor,' she told him, 'I'm not interested.'

They were standing by the counter now and a barman was hovering, waiting to take their order. The Greek looked her over, his eyes telling her it didn't matter to him whether she was interested or not. If he wanted her he would have her. Liz started to move away, but he grabbed her wrist.

'The bed thing can wait,' he said. 'I need to talk about Charlotte.'

Liz thought about putting up a struggle, but her curiosity won out.

'Tell me about her,' she said. Vic smiled and dropped her hand. Then he signalled to the barman for two cognacs.

'You don't like her, do you?'

'Not terribly. I think she's rude. But what's my attitude got to do with anything?'

He added the new brandy to what remained in his glass.

'Your attitude is very important. You see, I want you to help me get rid of her.'

For a moment, Liz didn't say anything. She didn't go in for dramatic revenges. Of course, Charlotte had snubbed her, but she was too busy with her husband and her daughter to care. Now Vic was handing her retribution on a plate and despite herself she warmed towards the idea.

'Why do you want to involve me?' Liz asked. 'Surely you're old enough to send your own girlfriends packing.'

'Normally yes,' he replied. 'But Charlotte is a

special case. You see she is living with me. I didn't intend her to, but with all the renovations it seemed convenient. Now it's almost impossible to disentangle myself. My whole family seem to think I'm going to marry her, and they certainly didn't get that idea from me. Last week one of the Sunday tabloids actually rang me to find out when I was going to name the day.'

He ran a hand across his eyes and looked weary. 'The whole affair has run out of my control. If I'm not careful, I'll find myself standing at the altar saying my vows, and not knowing how the hell I got there.'

Liz felt an insane desire to laugh. The man standing in front of her ran one of the biggest merchant fleets in the world. She knew politicians who trembled and grew short of breath when he came on the line, yet Charlotte had managed to tie him in knots.

'I'd love to help you,' she told him, 'but I don't see how I can.'

'I have a plan,' Vic said, and moved closer.

Liz shaded her eyes and looked across the room. If David was watching her now, he was bound to get the wrong idea. Then she saw him and she realized she didn't have anything to worry about. He was sitting where she had left him deep in conversation with another newspaper proprietor. He appeared to be brandishing a pencil and making sketches on the tablecloth and she smiled. He was talking about newspapers and that meant he'd be oblivious to anything for the next two hours at least. She gave the handsome Greek her full attention.

'Explain it to me,' she said.

Vic's plan was very simple. He wanted to give an interview to a respected newspaper categorically denying he was going to marry Charlotte. Because of the nature of the story a gossip columnist had to feature it, and the best columnist was working for the *Chronicle*.

'If Harry Davis runs it,' said the shipowner, 'all Charlotte's friends will sit up and take notice. After that, the woman's pride won't allow her to go on with the affair. With any luck she'll walk out on me then and there.'

Liz nodded. It would work of course.

'I suppose you want me to tell him,' she said.

The Greek looked relieved.

'Will you?' he asked.

It was unprofessional, but Liz couldn't resist it.

The item ran in Monday's diary and Harry Davis had gone to town. In the centre of the page was a picture of Charlotte looking glum at a point-to-point. Next to it was a shot of Vic with a fluffy young actress. The headline proclaimed, 'Chirgotis calls it off.'

Charlotte moved out of the house on Eaton Square the same day and that evening Liz received a parcel from Cartier. Liz retired to her bedroom to open the gift wrapped package and was glad she did, for the Greek hadn't sent a gold pen or a monogrammed address book: his gift belonged in the mistress, rather than the dear friend category. It was simply the most perfect pair of sapphire clips Liz had ever seen. They must have cost at least fifty thousand pounds, maybe more, and Liz wondered if she should send them back.

She had no business allowing strange men to send her expensive jewellery. Then she thought again. Vic hadn't sent her the clips because he wanted to seduce her. He had sent them as a thank you for a very special favour. A favour only she could grant. For the first time since she had been married, Liz realized she had power. Because of David, she could persuade columnists to do her bidding. She could break people like Charlotte who snubbed her if it suited her mood. The possibilities of what she could do made her head spin.

A few nights ago, she had been worrying about losing her youth. That particular worry wouldn't go away, but she had another weapon in her armoury now. She could make people listen to her.

Liz decided to make herself known to Harry Davis. She arranged to meet him for a drink at the Connaught. The old-fashioned bar in the hotel was the haunt of advertising men and visiting Americans. None of the Dearings' friends went there in the evening, so Liz could be discreet. She didn't want it getting round that she consorted with professional gossips, even if that was her plan.

Harry Davis had arrived before her and had taken a table in the window overlooking Mount Street. He was nursing a large whisky as Liz came through the door which gave her a chance to study him. He was very handsome, she noticed, in a flashy, barrow boy sort of way. His jaw was just a hint too square and his hair just a little too well-barbered to pass for a real gentleman. She was glad, for it put her at an advantage. Eight years with the Dearings had taught her how to behave like the grand lady. She would be in control of this meeting. In command of the entire situation. She hurried towards the table.

Davis put down his drink when he saw her and stood up.

'Mrs Dearing,' he said enthusiastically. 'What can I get you?'

She asked for a glass of champagne and settled herself on one of the large, soft sofas that were a feature of the Connaught Bar. When the drink arrived she came straight to the point.

'I think we can be of use to each other,' she told the columnist. 'I know most of the people you write about and from time to time it would amuse me to give you snippets.'

Harry considered this, without too much surprise. In his experience 'snippets' were the province of proprietors' wives, but why did Liz Dearing bother to have a drink with him? Why didn't she just ring him up when she had something to tell him? Surely she knew he could be relied on to jump to attention.

'I'm delighted you're taking such an interest in the column,' he said as smoothly as he dared. 'Is there anything special you want from me?'

It was easier than Liz thought. The man was like a trained poodle. All she had to do was raise a finger and he would scurry all over the place to do her bidding.

'There is something special now you ask,' she said. 'You see I like to think newspapers can change things. I'm not thinking about any real upheavals but say, for instance, someone is putting on a play and you'd like to see it succeed – would you be able to start a rumour about a movie deal?'

The columnist looked uneasy.

'I've never gone in for that kind of manoeuvre,' he admitted. 'There are always so many real dramas going on, I haven't needed to manufacture them.'

Liz drummed her fingers against the glossy surface of the table. She always did this when she was nervous and Harry caught her mood.

'That doesn't mean that making things up isn't a good idea,' he said quickly.

'It all depends which things. You'd have to be careful.'

27

Now she knew she could influence events, a change came over Liz. When she first married David she had been nervous. She knew who she was and where she came from and she was forever frightened of being found out. What if her accent was spotted as being phoney? What if somebody met her family? What if a former lover rose up from her past and denounced her as a tramp?

None of it happened, and with the birth of her daughter Barbara, she started to settle down. David had bought a seven-bedroomed house on Cheyne Walk and her entire time was taken up with running it and entertaining David's friends. Apart from that she was alone. She kept in touch with Vanessa in New York, but no-one else got close. She didn't see her family any more and there were no confidantes, because she didn't really believe in herself.

Then Harry Davis came into her orbit and Liz felt her life coming into focus. Amongst a very small circle it became known that Liz, through the *Chronicle*, could influence the social scene, and because of it she was lionized. Slowly, she developed an entourage to go with her new persona. David didn't entirely approve. He felt Liz was jeopardizing his professional integrity.

'Did you know your latest girlfriend used to hang out with an arms dealer?' he said to Liz. 'My father told me about her only the other day. You should be careful who you get close to.'

Liz brushed his objections aside. 'Natasha's fun,' she replied. 'She takes my mind off my problems.'

David looked at the girl he married with a certain surprise. She dressed at the most fashionable couturiers in Paris. Her jewellery was insured for half a million. She dined with princes and politicians. What problems could she possibly have?

'What is it,' he asked. 'What's getting you down?'

Liz frowned and wondered what to say next. At last she made up her mind.

'Barbara is getting me down,' she said.

Her daughter had been a disappointment. The extent of her shortcomings hadn't shown themselves when she was a baby, for during her first few years she was a chubby little angel. When she was five Barbara stopped being an angel and was just plain chubby. She was nearly eight now and with every passing year she became fatter and more clumsy. If she had inherited Liz's personality she would have risen above it. She would have charmed her way into her parents' and her grandparents' affections. Yet she seemed to owe nothing to her mother. She was slow where Liz was quick, serious where Liz was frivolous, and in the presence of people other than her immediate family she was self-conscious and shy.

Liz found it intensely frustrating. 'What am I going to do with her,' she complained. 'I've done my damnedest to turn her into something, but all I seem to have on my hands is an elephant.'

David looked sad.

'You're too hard on her,' he said. 'She's only a little girl – no more than a baby really. Why don't you leave her to her own devices for a bit. She'll grow out of this awkward stage, you'll see.'

Liz was unconvinced, but she took her husband's point. She knew Barbara well enough to realize that all her pushing wasn't going to make the slightest difference. Barbara would do exactly what Barbara wanted to do. So Liz backed off and hired a governess for her daughter. Miss Spencer was a tight-lipped, strait-laced woman from the Scottish highlands. If she did nothing else she would teach Barbara deportment. Liz sighed in resignation. Maybe David was right, maybe the girl would grow out of this phase.

In the meantime it was probably better to ignore her, and get on with her exciting new life.

She totted up the sum total of her achievements. She had virtually launched two new restaurants and put an art gallery on the map, but her greatest coup had been to interfere with an expensive production of 'Die Meistersinger' at Covent Garden. This had been achieved by making Harry Davis run an item about the diva's private life. The singer had been so upset that she completely lost her voice.

This last piece of chicanery proved Liz's undoing, for the opera house put in a complaint that ended up on Lord Dearing's desk. In essence the opera house demanded that the gossip columnist be removed, and because Lord Dearing valued his staff he mounted an investigation into the affair.

It took him several days before he got to the bottom of it. On the way he discovered that Harry Davis didn't write all his own stories. He had contributors – press agents, night-club bouncers, paparazzi all rang in with the latest dirt from the social world. In the last few months another name had been added to the list. The name was Liz Dearing, his daughter-in-law.

He had prised this piece of information out of his editor during a particularly spectacular row. The man was so scared he supplied the entire list of Liz's contributions and when Lord Dearing realized the extent of her interference, he decided to put an end to it. Liz had to be stopped before she turned into a monster.

When Lord Dearing's son announced he was to marry a doe-eyed model he had been disappointed. In his heart he had hoped David would end up with the daughter of one of his friends. A proper girl with a pedigree. He had, in his wilder dreams, wished he would marry into a title. The boy had the charm for it, and the looks. But David had let them all down when he said he was going to marry the model he had been to Amsterdam with.

Lord Dearing had her investigated of course. The first thing he did when he found out exactly who Liz Enfield was, was put one of his investigation teams on the case. They turned up some extremely interesting facts. The girl looked like a lady, but in fact she came from the gutter. Her father was a used car dealer in Southend. The sort of man he wouldn't have trusted to walk his dogs.

Liz's track record hadn't been all that savoury either.

When David met her, she was living with a photographer who seemed to have no intention of marrying her. Lord Dearing was furious. If the girl's lover didn't want to make a respectable woman out of her, what was his son doing? He summoned David as soon as he learned everything he needed to know about Liz.

'Are you out of your mind?' he shouted at his son. 'The woman who you want to make your wife is used goods. You keep that sort of baggage, you don't marry them.'

To his intense fury, David laughed at him.

'Father,' he chided, 'you're just about a hundred years out of date. Women these days don't have to present their credentials if they want to get hitched.'

'I know that,' Lord Dearing said crossly. 'I'm not a complete old duffer but I still think you might have chosen a respectable woman to marry.'

David paid no attention.

'Liz is respectable,' he insisted. 'Her family might not be much, but that's got nothing to do with her. As far as I'm concerned she's kind and she's tough when she has to be, and she'll make a very good mother for my children.'

'What about that photographer she was living with?' Lord Dearing protested.

'What about him?' retorted David. 'She's not with him any more. She's with me and that's where she's going to stay.'

Lord Dearing was not fobbed off that easily.

He threatened to disinherit his son, if he didn't drop Liz. David responded by running off to Paris and marrying her by special licence. After that, Lord Dearing retired beaten. David was his favourite son, because he was the one who showed a genuine flair for newspapers. Charles, his eldest, was a solid enough businessman. He ran the family's overseas investments creditably, but he had no feeling for print. No, David would inherit his mantle. David would take the family name to even greater glories. So if he insisted on tying himself up with an unsuitable girl, then they would all have to learn how to live with it.

As soon as David and Liz returned from their honeymoon, Lord Dearing invited them down for the weekend. He and his wife wanted to look over this new addition to the family, and they got their first taste of Liz when she responded to their invitation. She didn't ring up, the way he expected she would. She wrote a letter instead. In it, she declined their kind offer to stay the weekend.

Her marriage had been very sudden, she informed them. She also communicated the fact that she knew that neither of David's parents really approved of her. So, she pointed out, it would be very uncomfortable knowing all this if she was to spend two whole days with them. She suggested that they all meet for dinner on neutral territory. Lord Dearing was so cross when he opened the letter he nearly had a stroke. When he recovered himself, he had to admit a certain grudging admiration for the girl. In her position he would have played the situation in exactly the same way.

Only a complete idiot would walk into the lion's den with no preparation at all. He rang his son and told him he had received Liz's letter. Then he arranged to have dinner with them both the following evening at the Connaught.

His second surprise came when he actually met the girl. He had seen pictures of Liz, so he knew what she looked like, but nothing had prepared him for the sheer impact of her beauty. It was something more than the combination of flawless bones and luminous skin. It even went beyond the cat's eyes and the handspan waist. In the end he decided it was not the ingredients themselves that made this woman remarkable. It was the way they all worked together.

The fashion photographers had captured her elegance, but no-one could duplicate her animation, her energy. When she talked, her eyes sparkled, her features formed and collapsed and re-formed. For the first half hour Lord Dearing was so fascinated that he didn't say very much. Then he asserted himself. This woman had put herself up for his inspection, it was up to him to put her to the test.

He began by asking about her background. He didn't let on he knew all about it – that would have given her an unfair advantage. Instead, he bombarded her with tough questions. Questions that demanded an answer. Then he sat back and waited to see what lies she was going to tell. He had a long wait, for Liz didn't lie. She didn't give herself away either. She simply told him her family lived in the country and she had lost touch with them. Beyond that she refused to go.

Years later, when they all knew each other better, he had asked her why she had been so secretive about her background.

Liz didn't pull her punches.

'I have always been rather ashamed of my parents,' she said in that crisp, clear little voice of hers. 'So it was better not to say anything about them on our first meeting. If I had told the whole story you would have had a reason to despise me. And if I had lied, you would have found me out sooner or later.'

The answer summed Liz up completely. She was tough, she was calculating and she played him the way she played every other man in her life. To perfection. Right from the start he had fallen for her completely, and by the time dinner at the Connaught was finally over, Lord Dearing was eating out of her hand. He went home to Eaton Square a happy man. David had married a beautiful eccentric. A woman who couldn't be judged by the ordinary rules, because she didn't play by them. She reminded him of himself as a young man carving out his empire. He just hoped his son was equal to her.

Now, when he least expected it, she had let him down. He had no idea what he was going to do about it, but she would have to be stopped, there was no question of that. He couldn't have her using the *Chronicle* to settle her personal scores. He spent days worrying about it, until finally he decided to face things. He did this by putting himself in Liz's shoes.

What would his daughter-in-law do if she caught him out in some kind of chicanery? The answer came almost immediately. She would give him hell.

Lord Dearing smiled in a grim satisfaction. Liz wasn't going to enjoy it one little bit, but it was the only course of action. She had to understand once and for all that she had gone too far.

Lord Dearing invited Liz and David for lunch in the country. He ran a large estate in Leicestershire which he went to at weekends when he wanted to hunt. There was stabling there for his horses, there were indoor and outdoor tennis courts and a huge floodlit swimming pool for his wife, who didn't ride.

When he wasn't beating up the countryside, Lord Dearing liked to socialize. To this end there was a ballroom bigger than the one at Claridges where the local hunt ball was held. There was also a dining-room of such grandeur that the Prince of Wales was heard to complain that it was far too formal for the country. This was the setting that Lord Dearing decided on for the difficult lunch ahead of him.

When he wandered into the room half an hour beforehand, he rather regretted his choice. There were only five of them and the butler had put them up at one end of the vast walnut table. To his eyes, the whole arrangement looked damn silly. This was a table that sat two dozen. He was used to seeing all the crystal and silver on display.

What greeted him now were five miserable little places, perched like refugees on the edge of a sea of polished wood.

He summoned his butler.

'Dress the rest of the table,' he told him. 'Make it look like the entire county is coming to a grand party.'

His servant looked confused. The kitchen had only catered for the family. It was too late now to do anything else inside an hour.

'Have you changed your plans, sir?' he asked nervously. Lord Dearing shook his head.

'I wouldn't do that to you. I just want it to look as if there is a party for twenty-four. That way, the table does justice to the room.'

At one o'clock sharp Liz found herself lunching with her husband, her daughter and her parents-in-law at a table ready to host a banquet. It worried her. If Lord Dearing had wanted a big lunch party, why hadn't he organized one instead of this awkward family conference? None of them was in the habit of cosy little get-togethers. What on earth was it all about?

She soon found out. When the last of the roast pheasant had been cleared away and replaced with a vast sherry trifle Reggie went into the attack.

He started on David.

'I didn't know your wife had ambitions to become a journalist,' he said.

His youngest son looked startled.

'Neither did I,' he replied. He turned to Liz. 'Do you mind telling me what this is all about?' Liz felt the first flutterings of panic. He must be talking about the Harry Davis business, she thought. How the hell did he find out? She decided to play the whole thing down.

'I'm not interested in being a journalist,' she said crossly. 'But I do like talking to them. There's no law against that, is there?'

Lord Dearing inclined his massive head towards

her. 'This scribe you talk to,' he said, 'it wouldn't be Harry Davis by any chance?'

Liz paused, considering. 'The name rings a bell,' she said bluntly.

'So it bloody well should,' Dearing thundered. 'My informants tell me that you and Harry have regular little tête à têtes in the Connaught Bar.'

Liz felt the first rush of cold fury and she thanked her stars for it. Fury was the only way to handle Lord Dearing.

'You've been having me followed,' she said, bitterly. 'How dare you?'

'I'll tell you how I dare,' Lord Dearing replied, with menace in his voice. 'I dare because I need to protect the good name of the *Chronicle*; and the good name of this family.'

He rounded on David. 'I think it's time you realized what your wife gets up to when your back is turned.'

Then without preamble he launched into details of the Covent Garden fiasco.

'At the time I didn't believe it,' he said. 'My paper has never had any use for blackmail. It's not the way we operate. I had the whole business investigated, and guess what I turned up? Little Liz feeding the gossip column with choice titbits of her own making.'

David was torn between two emotions. His love of his wife, and his fear of his father. Fear scored a temporary victory.

'What do you have to say about all this?' he asked Liz. Liz put her spoon down and pushed the cut-glass bowl of strawberries over to one side. Then she set her chin and decided to brazen it out.

'You all talk as if I'm doing something I'm not entitled to do, and that's nonsense. Proprietors' wives have been planting news in the gossip columns since the beginning of time. I'm very surprised you're taking me to task like this.'

Lord Dearing fought down the impulse to cheer. Anyone else would have burst into tears, or run out of the room, but not Liz.

He might have pushed her into the corner of the ring, but she'd come out fighting. He was about to say something, when David intervened.

'You don't convince me,' he said coldly. 'No-one else would ever have mounted a plan to humiliate the Royal Opera House. Other people deal in tittle tattle, not death blows. What in God's name were you playing at?'

This time Liz was lost for words, and it was left to Lord Dearing to come to her rescue.

'I don't think it's productive to start looking for motives,' he said. 'Liz got carried away. Let's leave it at that, shall we? What I want to establish now is that she doesn't repeat her mistake.'

He turned to her and wagged a finger.

'As long as I'm in charge of the *Chronicle*, I don't want you interfering any more, is that understood? When I die, and David takes over from me, it's a different story. If you want to influence the columns at that stage, you work something out with him. But for now you keep your nose out of it, or I'll have your guts for garters.'

Liz was silent during the remainder of lunch. She was silent when the family trooped through to the drawing-room to take coffee, and shortly afterwards she had a quiet word with her husband and asked if they could go back to London early.

Lord Dearing sighed as he saw them into the Silver Cloud. He'd had it out with Liz, well and truly, but he knew it wouldn't end there. His daughter-in-law had enjoyed her first taste of power and he strongly suspected it had gone to her head.

Now he'd reduced her to being a housewife again and he knew she wouldn't be satisfied. She was too headstrong not to want to have people sit up and listen to her.

He wondered what she'd get up to next.

28

New York

Freddie realized she would never see her father again three months after they went to live with Norman. She had expected she would continue to have tea at the Plaza, the way she always had. When Dan didn't show up in their first week in Gramercy Park she began to worry. Maybe Dad's giving me time to settle down after the move, she reasoned. In a week or so, things will go back to normal. But they weren't. Every Wednesday Freddie waited for her father to drive up in his chauffeur-driven car and whisk her away to the Plaza, and every Wednesday she was disappointed.

'What's happening?' she asked her mother. 'Where is Daddy? Why don't we see him any more?'

Vanessa had no answer for her. One day Norman took Freddie for a walk in Central Park. It was on that walk he told her he was going to be her new adopted father.

Freddie didn't want a new adopted father and made that plain. She was perfectly happy with the old one. Why did grown-ups always want to change things? But there was nothing she could do, since all the papers had been prepared and signed. She was now officially Freddie Bracken. It was the worst thing that had ever happened to her, because it was so final. Before when they moved away from her father she had been able to hope. Life might be terrible now, but things could change. Her parents could make up their quarrel, they could all go home and live as a family again.

Now she was Freddie Bracken she would be stuck with Uncle Norman for all time and never see her father again. She stayed awake at nights wondering what she had done wrong.

Vanessa thought it was very sweet of Norman to became Freddie's legal guardian. In the early days she had worried that he might take against the child. Freddie was very hostile when he was there, always picking fights and comparing him to Dan. Vanessa wouldn't have blamed him if he had wanted to send her away, but he seemed to understand that her daughter had problems adjusting to the new situation.

'She'll settle down,' he told Vanessa. 'Children are very flexible.'

Vanessa forced herself to believe him, but then she had to force herself to do a lot of things nowadays, including cooking. When she lived in London, she always seemed to eat out, and with Dan there had been servants to prepare meals. Now Vanessa was the cook and it wore her nerves to a frazzle.

It started with breakfast. Norman left for the office early in the morning, but not so early that he didn't have time to eat first. He required poached eggs, crispy bacon and waffles covered in maple syrup. Vanessa had to have everything on the table at seven thirty sharp. Norman could get very bad tempered if she was even five minutes late, and she took care not to be.

It was the same thing in the evening. Dinner had to be ready half an hour after Norman returned from the office. It had to be piping hot, and it had to be done just so. If it wasn't then Vanessa would go back into the kitchen and cook the whole thing over again.

Freddie couldn't believe what her mother was doing. One night when Norman didn't like the asparagus Vanessa had prepared for him, Freddie got down from the table and followed her into the kitchen. She was just in time to see her mother throw the whole first course into the rubbish bin.

'Why don't you make him take us out to a restaurant?' she whispered.

Vanessa didn't answer. Her daughter was too young to understand the complexities of male-female relationships. Norman was fussy about his food: it was a failing, but it was a failing she was forced to accept and understand. The alternative was to risk a fight, and she didn't like fighting with Norman. Or to be more honest, she didn't like making things up with Norman.

'No, it's fine. Run into the other room and talk to Norman,' she told her daughter. 'I'll have things ready in a few minutes.'

My life isn't that bad, Vanessa consoled herself. At least he takes me out two or three times a week.

Norman socialized with the people he did business with. Once a week they would go out to a fancy restaurant where he would entertain a client. The other times they would dine with his employees at the agency. During the time she had been living with Dan, Vanessa always thought of Norman as a mild man. Now she knew better, for in the company of the people he deemed to be his inferiors, he was an intolerable bully. Vanessa discovered she wasn't the only one who suffered if the food wasn't to Norman's liking.

His executives panicked for days if he was scheduled to dine at one of their houses, and several of the wives confided their feelings to Vanessa. She did what she could for them.

If Norman was going through a phase of not liking pasta, or spinach, or beef, she would ring ahead and warn her hostess. It saved everyone's nerves. Then came the day they were invited to Ted Bloom, the creative director's apartment and there was one dislike not even Vanessa could foresee.

Ted had never given them dinner before. His wife had left him several years previously and he found it difficult to entertain on his own. Now he had a new girlfriend and made up for lost time by inviting Norman and Vanessa for Sunday brunch. It was an intimate occasion. Ted had asked a couple of other people from the agency with their children, and Freddie was asked along as well.

It was a bright, warm Sunday in late spring – warm enough for Ted to open the doors to the terrace. When Vanessa arrived the whole apartment had a festive air. Ted had filled the place with spring flowers: jonquils, daffodils and great branches of mimosa. To complement the mood Ted had made up pitchers of champagne and orange juice. Every surface boasted a cluster of crystal glasses frothing with the drink, and Vanessa's heart sank. Norman liked orange juice. He enjoyed champagne. But the combination of the two gave him dyspepsia.

Vanessa hurried into the kitchen where she found Patsy, Ted's new girlfriend. As gracefully as she could, she explained the problem. The girl didn't understand it at all.

'I haven't got anything else to offer him,' she told Vanessa. 'We've mixed everything together now. Can't Norman just sip a little to be polite?'

Vanessa was stuck. If she told this new girlfriend that Norman was never polite to his staff, she would make him sound like an ogre. Yet if she didn't find an alternative to the cocktail, Norman would be furious. She made a decision.

'There's a liquor store on the corner,' she said. 'I'll

shoot down and get some Californian Chardonnay. Keep an eye on Freddie for me, will you?'

If Norman hadn't caught sight of Vanessa sneaking out of the front door, things might have been different. As it was, he reached out his arm and stopped her.

'Where do you think you're going,' he asked.

'Just to the liquor store. I've forgotten something.'

Norman looked puzzled. 'This isn't our party,' he said. 'What do you need to get?'

Vanessa decided to come clean. Keeping her hand on the doorknob, she told him about the champagne and orange juice. Norman's mouth arranged itself into a tight disapproving line.

'You're not going anywhere,' he told her. 'Our hostess here is the one who does the running around.'

Patsy appeared in the kitchen doorway.

'What's the problem?' she asked.

Vanessa looked at Norman nervously. The colour had drained out of his face and a muscle under one of his eyes started to twitch. Christ, she thought, there's going to be a row.

Norman took hold of one of Vanessa's arms and shoved her into the room. Then he turned to Patsy.

'It might interest you to know that these drinks you're serving give me wind.'

Patsy simply stared. 'So they give you wind,' she said. 'I can make you a cup of coffee instead.'

'I don't want coffee,' Norman roared. 'I want a drink. It's midday for Chrissakes.'

'I know,' said Patsy. 'Vanessa was going out to get you something.'

The room suddenly went quiet. Freddie, who had been playing on the terrace, came back inside. Everyone focused on Vanessa.

'It won't take a moment,' she said. 'Honestly, I'll be back before you know it.' She edged her way back to the door, but Norman was too fast for her.

'You're not going anywhere,' he said grabbing hold of her.

Now Vanessa was embarrassed. She was used to Norman's tantrums, but in front of all these people, in front of the children, it was too much.

'Stop it,' she hissed. 'Stop ruining the party.'

She didn't see it coming. One moment she was standing with Norman hanging on to her arm. The next, he had let go of her and was raining blows about her head. She tried to get away, but he went on hitting her until she sank to the floor.

At that moment the room, which had frozen into a tableau, came alive. Both Patsy and Ted rushed over and pulled Vanessa out of the way. Then Freddie burst into tears and ran over to her mother. Norman did nothing to make amends. He turned furiously, and stalked out.

Vanessa stumbled to the bathroom. No man, no human being, had ever hit her before. One of her eyes was red and angry and starting to swell up. There was a gash just above her temple and two of her teeth were loosened. He might have killed me, she thought. If the others hadn't dragged me away when they did, I could have been in the hospital. She turned both taps on and filled the basin with water, splashing her face to wash the blood away. When she looked at herself again, her eye had almost closed up. How am I going to handle this? she thought wildly.

Patsy came in looking shaken.

'I've sent everyone home,' she said. 'The best thing you can do right now, is to see a doctor, or have a stiff drink. Why not have the drink? You need it.'

Vanessa followed her into the living-room.

'Swallow that,' Patsy instructed, handing her a glass of bourbon. 'It will settle your nerves.'

Vanessa made a wry face and sat down on a sofa. 'If you had offered this to Norman in the first place, maybe the mess wouldn't have happened.'

Ted came into the room with Freddie in tow, who hurried over to her mother and buried her face in Vanessa's skirt.

'Yes it would,' he insisted. 'That son-of-a-bitch was looking for a fight. If he hadn't picked on the booze, he would have picked on something else.'

Vanessa took a mouthful of her drink. 'But why me?' she asked. 'Why did he have to lay into me? I never did him any harm.'

Ted looked sad.

'He did it to you,' he told her, 'because he knew you couldn't hit back. That's the way Norman operates. All the years I've known him, he never picks on someone his own size. It's always a junior employee, someone who can't return the shot.'

Freddie began to cry. 'Can we go home now,' she wailed. 'Take me home to my Daddy – please.'

Vanessa's eye began to throb. Ted was right, horribly right. Norman had picked on her because she couldn't defend herself and she had nowhere else to go. She had no money, and no job.

She sighed and picked Freddie up in her arms.

'We're not going home to Daddy,' she said gently. 'Daddy lives with someone else now. In an hour or so, when things have calmed down, I'll call Norman and he'll come and pick us up.'

The child started to sob. 'But Norman hit you, Mommy. You can't go with him now.'

'Shush, darling,' Vanessa crooned. 'I know it looked terrible, but it wasn't that bad. How many times do you get into fights with your friends at school?'

Her words had no conviction. And it was Patsy who came to the rescue. She took the little girl out of Vanessa's arms and put her to bed in the spare room. Then she pushed Vanessa and Ted back into the comfortable lounge and sat them down.

'Whatever you say, you can't go back to Norman,' she said firmly. 'Until we think of something you can stay here in the spare room. Now, it's nearly three and high time we all had something to eat.'

Two hours later the buzzer sounded on the front door. Ted went to answer it and was confronted with Norman.

'I've come for Vanessa,' he said sharply.

Ted was tempted to tell him to get the hell out of it but then he thought about his job. The Bracken agency paid him a hundred thousand a year. He wouldn't find anything like it without a long search.

'I'm not sure she wants to see you,' he said cautiously.

The tall, greying man started to push past him.

Then he saw Vanessa across the room and stayed where he was. The whole of one side of her face was the size of a pumpkin, both her eyes were black and there was a jagged gash over one temple.

'Darling,' he whispered. 'What have I done to you?'

Vanessa started to cry then, the emotion of the afternoon breaking down the last of her defences. She had been strong for Freddie's sake, but now, as she stood face to face with her attacker, she could hold out no longer.

Norman went over to her, taking her in his arms and stroking her hair.

'I'm so sorry,' he said. 'So terribly sorry.'

Ted took hold of Patsy's hand and pulled her out into the hall.

'It's better that we leave them alone now,' he told her. 'I've been through this with Norman's other girlfriends. He always begs their forgiveness after he beats them up.'

Patsy looked at her lover aghast. 'And do the girls take him back?' she asked.

Ted shrugged. 'What do you think?' he said.

29

When she and her mother had returned to Norman's flat, Freddie did some hard thinking. She wanted to run away. It had always been her plan to leave school early one afternoon and turn up at her father's apartment. The porter knew her well enough, and so did all the servants. In her imaginings they would have made her a cup of hot chocolate and let her wait until Dan came home, then she would have thrown herself on his mercy.

'Uncle Norman is mean and cruel and horrible,' she was going to say. 'Please don't make me go back to live there.'

Because this was her own private daydream, her father didn't argue with her but understood perfectly that this new adopted father wasn't good enough. He scooped Freddie up in his arms and told her that he would make everything right. Then they both went to Gramercy Park in his chauffeur-driven limo, collected her mother and returned home together.

Only it couldn't happen. Daddy had someone else to live with now – another lady, perhaps with a little girl of her own. When Vanessa had told Freddie after the big fight with Norman she could hardly believe it. The next day, she asked her mother about it again, just to make sure. It was true, they really didn't have any other place to go except Norman's.

All Freddie could depend on now was Norman. She didn't count her mother in her reckoning, because Vanessa wasn't that good at looking out for herself, let alone her. Now if she had been Nanny Worth or the cook, she would have felt differently. They were strong women, both of them. She would have been safe with them. But they weren't there for her any more. She had to make the best of Norman all on her own.

Freddie decided she had been rubbing him up the wrong way. She had always been honest in her dealings with the world, because the world had played straight with her. Norman hadn't told her the truth when he said he was going to look after her and Vanessa. He proved it that terrible weekend when he lost his temper with Vanessa.

This realization liberated Freddie. If Norman could pretend to be somebody he wasn't, so could she.

She decided to be Miss Goody-Two-Shoes. Norman liked people sucking up to him. So she became the queen of the toadies. She started telling him how handsome he looked in his city suit. Every time he did something for her – gave her an ice-cream or took her to the movies – she went overboard with delight.

'Norman, you're so good to me,' she would squeal. 'Such a wonderful adopted father.'

Freddie thought he would see right through her. They were such big lies and she wasn't all that good at telling them, but he didn't seem to notice at all. Instead he started to smile when she came in the room. Overnight she changed from 'that terror' to 'my good girl'.

Freddie wondered if she could keep it up. It wasn't easy being Miss Goody-Two-Shoes when Norman yelled at her mother for not doing the dinner right, but she persevered, because somebody had to handle Norman.

The best way to get round him, she discovered,

was asking him to show her things. One weekend he showed her how to ride a bike, even though she'd learned ages ago in school. When she stayed upright after half an hour's tuition, he was really pleased with himself. He went all pink and sort of puffed up and Freddie had to hide her face in case he could see she was laughing at him.

Then she got him to show her the baseball game in the park, getting him to explain the rules she already knew. She even asked him to show her how to look after her kitten. After that she got bored.

There must be something Norman could show her she didn't understand? She finally hit the jackpot with backgammon. Her father had bought her the game the Christmas before they left but had never got round to showing her how to play. It made Freddie sad and she would sit in front of it for hours and try to understand how it worked. Norman found her one Sunday afternoon, setting out the counters and frowning over the instructions.

Out of interest, he showed her one or two opening moves, and the child latched on surprisingly fast.

'Have you played this before?' he asked.

Freddie shook her head. 'I wish I could,' she told him. 'It looks like a good game.'

Norman wondered whether she was having him on. He didn't mind Freddie pretending she couldn't do half the things she was good at. All children played silly games. Then he laughed at himself. How could she know backgammon, he asked himself. She's a baby. Most of the grown men I know don't do that well at it.

He began by showing her how to move the counters round the board. This time when she looked interested, he knew it was genuine. The child had an instinct for boardgames, a flair that was something to do with intelligence and naked aggression.

She's not as sweet as she would have me believe, he thought, but she's cute. Maybe I'll give her another chance. Norman knew it had been a wrench moving Freddie away from Dan. There were times when he felt guilty about it. Now at last he had found a way of making her happy. At least one of my women likes me, he consoled himself.

He thought about Vanessa and the growing silence between them. It was stupid hitting her in public, he thought. I should have saved my temper until we were alone. That way I could have got away with it.

There were times when Vanessa didn't think she could keep going. When that happened she thought about her daughter and the roof over their heads. As the months went on and Norman's beatings became more frequent, she concentrated her mind on Freddie. The child had surprised her by settling down. She actually seemed to get on with Norman.

Vanessa wondered after that first fight if she had stood up to Norman whether things would have been any different. Ted often told her she was a fool for going back to him, but what could she have done? Stayed with him and Patsy in the apartment? They would have soon got tired of that.

Vanessa thought about Ted again. He had been surprisingly kind after that disastrous brunch. Something must have told him she was in need of a shoulder to cry on, for he called her a couple of days afterwards and asked her if she was free to have lunch with him.

She let him take her to Charlie 'O's with its black and white bar and louche atmosphere. Art directors and advertising writers went there, and

Vanessa appreciated the change from the formal places Norman took her to. She remembered she wore a pair of tight black leather trousers that day, and a loose plaid shirt. She could easily have been mistaken for somebody who worked in the business. The problem was that she was recognized. She had been the face on Royal Enclosure perfume for too long to go unnoticed. People kept coming up to them and asking her how Norman was. The less well informed enquired after Dan. After a bit Ted looked worried.

'You're a lovely girl,' he said regretfully, 'but I don't know if we should go on meeting. I mean Norman could get the wrong idea.'

Vanessa's heart missed a beat. Ted Bloom wasn't just a lifeline. The man had something for her. She regarded him over the remains of her steak tartare. He was casual looking in the expensive sort of way that was fashionable in the latter half of the seventies. Like her, he was wearing leather jeans and he wore his hair long, way past his collar. It was his eyes that riveted her, though. They were black like sloes. Black and secretive and sexy.

If only I was free, she thought. If only I didn't have a boyfriend who might get the wrong idea. Ted interrupted her reverie.

'I've got an idea,' he said. 'You and I don't have to lunch in such a high profile joint. If we went to a deli, say, or a Chinese, nobody would know the difference.'

Vanessa felt better immediately. For the first time since Dan, she had met a man who made her feel female. Nothing would come of it, of course. Ted was tied up elsewhere, but just seeing him gave her something to hope for.

'I don't mind lunching in a deli,' she said, 'if it's easier.'

They took to meeting once or twice a week in little out-of-the-way places. Sometimes Ted took her to Chinatown or the Bronx or Brooklyn Heights. Wherever they went didn't seem to make any difference to Vanessa's appetite. She simply couldn't eat anything when she was with Ted. She put it down to nerves. If Norman discovered she was seeing his creative chief on the quiet, he would kill her.

But she couldn't stop. There was between her and Ted a growing bond of warmth. They talked about anything and everything. He told her about his ex-wife and Patsy. She told him about Dan and Freddie. And finally Norman.

At first, she had refused to discuss him at all. In her heart she was ashamed of the way the advertising supremo treated her, but as things became worse between them, she needed to confide in someone, and Ted wanted her to unburden herself. When she admitted that the beating he had witnessed hadn't been an isolated incident, he was shocked.

'But I never see any of your injuries,' he told her. 'The first time you looked like the victim of a hit-and-run.'

Vanessa made a face.

'Norman really regretted that,' she said. 'He hated everyone knowing what he did to me. He's been more careful since. When he hits me these days, he takes care not to let it show. If you saw my body, you'd know what I was saying.'

Ted leaned closer to her in the crowded deli.

'I'd love to see your body,' he told her softly, 'but not because of Norman's handiwork.'

Vanessa felt the blood rush to her face. She hadn't been wrong after all. Ted desired her the way she desired him. She put her hand out towards him and he took it in both of his.

'What happens now?' she asked.

For a moment neither of them said anything. They just stared at each other and Vanessa felt a moment of panic. I'm getting in deep, she thought. It can only end in tears. Ted broke the silence.

'We could go back to my apartment,' he said. 'Nobody's there in the afternoon.'

By nobody, he meant Patsy, and Vanessa felt cheap. Patsy was the one who had stood up for her against Norman. Now she was betraying her friendship by seducing her boyfriend.

Ted increased the pressure on her hand.

'This was meant to happen,' he whispered. 'Stop fighting it.'

Vanessa looked at him again, losing herself in the dark eyes.

'What about Patsy?' she asked.

Ted looked tough then.

'This is nothing to do with Patsy or Norman or anyone else. What I feel for you is between the two of us. It stays that way until one of us decides otherwise.'

It had been too long now since Vanessa had known any true happiness and Ted was giving her the chance to start living again. Whatever the consequences, she had to grab it.

They left the deli before one thirty, and hailed a yellow cab on the street. By the time they were back in the apartment it was nearly two. Neither of them wasted any time. As soon as the front door was fastened, Vanessa was in his arms. She had expected Ted to be in a hurry – after all he had a job to get back to – but this afternoon it didn't seem to be on his mind. He sat her down on the long leather sofa and started covering her face and neck with kisses.

'I love you,' he murmured. 'I've been crazy for you from the time I first saw you with Norman.'

The mention of his name made her stiffen.

'This has to be a secret,' Vanessa said. 'Promise me you won't tell anyone.'

Ted laughed at her then. 'What kind of bastard do you take me for?' he asked.

He made love to her, gently peeling off her jeans and unbuttoning her blouse. If he noticed the weals on her body, he didn't make any comment. Instead he caressed her, his hands lingering on the soft, full breasts, his fingers trailing down her stomach until they reached the damp triangle below. Still he was in no hurry to conquer her. Slowly, achingly slowly, he found the opening between her legs. First with his fingers. Then with his tongue. It seemed as if he couldn't kiss her enough and Vanessa felt her body come alive. Her hands connected with his head and slowly she lifted his face until his eyes were level with hers.

'Do it to me now,' she demanded with an urgency she had long forgotten. 'I want you inside me.'

Ted took her then, sliding inside her until he filled her completely. Then, tentatively, like teenagers, they found each other's rhythm, building to a climax that left Vanessa breathless. Afterwards Ted took her in his arms and carried her into the bedroom.

'Shouldn't you be on your way back to the office?' Vanessa asked, worried.

Ted grinned. 'Probably,' he said, 'but as I'm planning to change my job, I don't see too much point in going there. Anyway I've got better things to do.'

It was at that moment that Vanessa fell in love with him.

30

London, 1981

Liz looked at her watch with a certain impatience. She had been waiting in San Lorenzo's for twenty minutes and Melanie still hadn't put in an appearance. She looked around the crowded basement. You can tell it's Friday, she thought. All the beautiful people are out in force.

The Italian restaurant in Beauchamp Place was the unofficial headquarters for the jet-set. If a pop star wanted to talk business with his manager, he went to the Savoy Grill or Morton's or the Rib Room at the Carlton Tower. If he wanted to impress his latest blonde, he took her to San Lorenzo. Visiting movie stars from Hollywood went there, as did minor members of the British royal family.

Nobody patronized it for the food, which was adequate and expensive, or the location, bang in the centre of the Knightsbridge shopping area. They went there for one thing only. To see and be seen. If you were a woman lunching there, you wore your Chanel suit or the latest designer leathers. For men it was blue jeans, because even though it took a lot of pre-planning to get the right table, it wasn't done to look as if you had tried. Part of the fantasy was to appear as if you had just been in an all night recording session or stepped off a plane from Los Angeles.

This lunchtime, Liz had put on a country look, which consisted of a tweed hacking jacket and riding breeches. She achieved the same slightly phoney effect as everyone else in San Lorenzo, for Liz hadn't been near the country in months.

David's sprawling estate in Leicestershire had been largely unoccupied, due to pressure of work. All week and most weekends nowadays, he stayed in his office in the *Chronicle*. The paper was going through a bad time and it was David's task to make sure it didn't get any worse.

The only time I ever get David to myself, thought Liz as she waited at her table, is when we go to bed, and then he's usually so tired, he turns over and goes to sleep instantly. She sighed. David was still the sexiest man in the world when he got round to it. Maybe we should take a holiday, she mused. Perhaps I can persuade that father of his to lend us the house outside Antibes.

Her reverie was interrupted by the arrival of Melanie Fox. She was not alone. With her was a very young, rather scruffy boy who Liz identified as her latest lover. The other member of the party was Vic Chirgotis. She hadn't seen the Greek since her birthday party in Annabel's, but she hadn't forgotten him. No-one apart from her husband had ever given her jewellery, and no-one she had ever known looked at her the way this man did. Even now, as he approached the table he was undressing her with his eyes. It bothered her. She was a married woman with a child and a place in the world. A very important, powerful place. So what was Vic doing looking her over as if she was some chorus girl? She made her mind up to be cool with him.

When he finally got to where she was sitting at the bottom of the stairs, she didn't offer her cheek to be kissed, but extended her hand instead. Vic turned it over and kissed the palm and Liz snatched it away in fury.

'You weren't meant to do that,' she said.

The Greek smiled. 'I know.'

She turned to the woman she was lunching with. 'I didn't know you were bringing a party,' she said crossly. 'You might have told me.'

Melanie Fox pulled a face, and half the men in the restaurant turned round to watch her doing it. To say she was beautiful would have been an understatement. Melanie was one of those women who held her place in society simply because no-one else had the remotest chance of looking like her.

There was something awesome about Melanie and Liz put it down to the combination of long legs, flame red hair and eyes the shape and hue of fine-cut emeralds.

She was wearing the regulation Chanel suit that Friday, except it didn't look regulation. This wasn't something you could buy in Bond Street. The cut was too clever, the braiding too unusual, and Liz recognized the mark of the couturier. That little number set someone back the best part of ten grand, she thought. I wonder who's buying her clothes nowadays?

Melanie wasn't a kept woman – not in the strict sense of the word. No Arab millionaire kept her closeted away in a luxury penthouse, but a string of other millionaires of all nationalities vied with each other for her favours. She was picky with all of them. It was as if she was born with the knowledge that men, particularly rich men, appreciate best the things they can't get, and Melanie deliberately made herself unavailable. A Turkish Sultan could shower her with diamonds and she wouldn't give him the time of day. If he complained at her treatment of him, she would send the jewels back where they came from. Her gesture implied she had no need of diamonds, and because she was so cavalier with her suitors she couldn't move for expensive presents. She lived variously in an apartment in Manhattan, a mews house in Belgravia and a town house in the second arrondissement in Paris. Men had provided all three residences, and Liz wondered how long Melanie could go on getting away with it. She was lovely now, there was no arguing with that, but in ten years from now would she still be lovely, or would there be cracks in the porcelain surface? She shuddered fearing her own mortality.

'Sit down,' she told the redhead, 'and tell me which one of these two men you're with today.'

Melanie raised carefully pencilled eyebrows.

'I'm with both of them of course,' she said. 'Now if you mean which one am I sleeping with, that's different.'

Everyone at the table started laughing and Vic asked the waiter to bring them a bottle of champagne. Then he turned to Liz.

'I didn't know you cared,' he said.

'I don't,' replied Liz, embarrassed.

'Then why ask?'

She thought about walking out. She hadn't planned to spend Friday this way. All she had on her agenda was a friendly lunch, an exchange of confidences and maybe if there was time a shopping trip afterwards.

She regarded the Greek with caution.

'I'm not in the market for a lover,' she told him. 'And even if I was, I wouldn't pick on you.'

'Might I ask why not?'

Liz heard the faint sound of alarm bells in her ears.

'Because you're too rich, you're too well-known and you're too damn pushy. Just sitting at this table with you is enough to get me in the gossip columns.'

'I was coming on to that,' he said.

That stopped her. Her run-in over the Harry Davis page had been years ago now – but Liz still didn't feel entirely rational about it. Lord Dearing had been very public about the way he had removed her from working behind the scenes at the *Chronicle*, and she had been humiliated.

With her chums, the people she lunched with at Morton's and San Lorenzo, she had held sway.

Now she was just another pretty woman with too much money and too much time on her hands.

'I don't want to talk about gossip columns,' she told Vic. 'If I hear one word on the subject, I walk out right now.'

He put his hand over hers.

'You wouldn't do that,' he said. 'Not while we're getting to know each other.'

Liz set her jaw.

'Watch me,' she said.

Melanie interrupted them.

'Stop fighting,' she pleaded. 'Juan hates fighting while he eats. It gives him heartburn.'

It was the first time she had acknowledged the young man sitting beside her and Liz was intrigued. She smiled at the scowling, scruffy boy.

'My name's Liz,' she said warmly. 'Liz Dearing. I don't think we've met.'

The boy turned to Melanie and said something in Spanish. She smoothed his hair back and replied in the same language, then turned to the others.

'I found him in Regine's last night,' she explained. 'He was waiting on the tables and I asked if I could take him home with me. Madame handed him over, as a sort of present.'

Vic lifted the bottle of champagne and filled up all their glasses.

'Regine should have thrown in a language course,'

he observed. 'Unless you decide to live in Madrid, Juan could get very boring.'

'Don't be silly,' Liz said. 'Juan won't be around long enough to get boring.'

For some unknown reason Melanie was offended. She might have treated her other lovers with disdain, but this one was clearly an exception. She smacked her drink down on the table.

'Come off it,' she said sharply.

Vic did his best to placate her.

'You told me just now the man was a present. Why all the fuss?'

But Melanie was having none of it. 'How we found each other is nothing to do with it,' she said. 'Juan is a man. A proud man. I won't have him insulted.'

Liz groaned inwardly. It's going to be one of those lunches, she thought. Experience told her that Melanie would go on getting more and more irrational, Juan would look insolent until it was time to go and Vic – she had no idea what Vic would do.

She soon found out. With a dapper little smile, the Greek turned to Melanie's companion and said something in rapid Spanish. The boy got up from where he was sitting and fled up the stairs to the street.

The redhead grabbed her quilted leather bag, called Vic a pig in three languages and ran after him.

Despite herself Liz was amused. 'What on earth did you say to him?' she asked.

The Greek pushed away his food and lit a small cigar.

'I told him that Melanie was married to a rich, jealous old man who took his revenge on her lovers by cutting off their balls.'

Liz grinned. 'Was that fair?'

'Not really,' Vic acknowledged, 'but I don't have a reputation for playing fair. Take you for example.

Some people would say it was against the rules to get you to cheat on David. I say that's nonsense. You need to take time off from your husband. Every married woman needs it. How else can you keep looking young?'

Liz supposed she should have been angry, but it was difficult with this dark, extravagant man. He didn't take women seriously. That was apparent from everything he said and did. If she did have a fling, she knew it wouldn't mean anything to him, and the strangest feeling came over her. A kind of nervy excitement, as if she was walking a tightrope.

The last time she had it was when she was manipulating people's lives through the Harry Davis column, and she realized her excitement had something to do with power and everything to do with danger.

'If we did get together,' she said slowly, 'and I'm not saying we will, would you tell anyone about it?'

Vic gave her a rueful smile.

'Don't be silly,' he told her. 'Half the charm of this kind of thing is in the secrecy. The fear of being found out is one of the greatest aphrodisiacs known to man. Or to sophisticated man at least.'

Liz stared at the dark man sitting beside her. Even though he was obviously expensively barbered, his chin was slightly blue from where the beard was growing through. He probably has to shave twice a day, she thought. Underneath that fine lawn shirt of his, he probably looks like a gorilla.

It was as if he could read her mind.

'Why don't you stop playing the English lady,' he said. 'It doesn't suit you.'

Liz looked at him, bleakly now. 'The role may not fit completely,' she replied, 'but it's the best one I've got.'

* * *

The next day Liz spoke to David about Antibes. His father had a château in the hills behind the town. They had been down there three summers ago and the visit had stayed in Liz's memory. The house was magnificent of course, all grey stone and secret courtyards covered in bougainvillea, but it wasn't the setting that imprinted itself on Liz's mind – it was the South of France itself.

The whole area from Cannes to St Tropez had a dangerous glamour for her. She and David had spent hours exploring the old village of Ez which overlooked Monte Carlo on one side and Cap Ferrat on the other. They had played boules with the locals after a boozy lunch in St Paul; they had sat in the sunshine on the Croisette in Cannes and imagined they were Scott and Zelda Fitzgerald.

'If we can just go back there for a week,' she said, 'we'll have some time to ourselves. You're at the paper so much these days, I feel I hardly know you any more.'

David sighed and felt weary. The latest newspaper circulation figures had just been published and the *Chronicle* was showing a ten per cent drop on last year. They had fallen way below a million now and for a popular newspaper they were in dangerous waters.

'I have to be in Fleet Street,' he said heavily. 'Someone has to save the family fortunes, though the way things are going, I often wonder whether there's anything to save.'

Liz looked disbelieving. 'Come on,' she said, 'it can't be that bad. Your father isn't exactly a pauper. Nor are we come to that.'

David looked at the beautiful spirited girl he had married and prayed for patience.

'You'll always be able to pay the dressmaker,'

he said, 'but that's not what I'm talking about. There's no point in living well if there's no purpose to your life. My purpose is producing newspapers. It's not some divine right as my father would have everybody believe, but I love it all the same. It would break my heart if we had to fold the *Chronicle* because we can't keep up with the competition any more.'

'Has it come to that?'

David considered for a moment. If the *Mail* went on taking circulation from them, they would have to close within the year. From a financial standpoint, they just weren't viable any more, but should he tell Liz that? It would panic her. Worse, it would send her flying off to all her friends begging for sympathy, and once the world knew they were in trouble, they would close even sooner.

David put on the best face he could.

'We don't have to close down yet,' he said. 'If father would just agree to let me run things my way, we might not have to close down at all, but he won't hear of it.'

Gloom settled over Liz. She had been hearing this argument for years now. Almost since she got married. Recently, she had been hearing it more often.

'Now things have got this bad,' she said, 'surely he'll listen to reason.'

David grinned. 'Have you ever known my father listen to reason? I don't think reason is a word he understands. No, I'm just going to go on with the battle and hope the economy picks up. That could save us, you know.'

Liz went over to the fire where her husband was sitting nursing a whisky. They were due at the theatre in half an hour and she knew that once they were in the car she wouldn't get another chance to talk to him in private.

'What are we going to do until the economy picks up? I can't go on living like this, you know.'

'And I can't take time off to go to the South of France, if that's what you're pushing for.'

David realized he had said the wrong thing. Liz had been banking on this holiday, and now he had hurt her. He decided to sweeten the pill.

'I've got an idea,' he said. 'It's not the South of France, but at least it's a way we can be by ourselves for a bit. Why don't you go down to Leicestershire and open up the house. Take Barbara with you, if you like, she could do with the fresh air. Then I'll come down and join you both for a day here and a day there. With luck I can manage to stretch my breaks to more than just a day. How does that sound to you?'

She looked mollified. It wasn't the ideal solution, but at least he was meeting her half way.

'If I go down next week, when can I expect to see you?' she asked.

David frowned.

'I'm not sure, but I'll be down there, you can depend on it.'

Liz took the empty glass out of his hand and returned it to the silver tray on the library table. As she did so, she caught sight of herself in the mirror above it. Leonard had styled her hair that morning in a new short cut that made her look like an Italian boy. Now she regretted it. She was really too thin to wear her hair that length. And too old. She wondered whether it was time to have her eyes done now. She made a mental note to speak to the plastic surgeon. Her husband hadn't lost interest in her, after all, she decided. She must make sure he never did.

* * *

Liz went down to their house outside Market Harborough the following Monday. They were fifteen miles as the crow flies from Lord Dearing's estate, but the way they lived in the country couldn't have been more different.

Where Reggie had styled himself as the grand lord living extravagantly in the shires, David had done the opposite. He genuinely loved Leicestershire with its gentle hills and rolling acres. He had been brought up in this county and as a boy had been able to ride almost as soon as he could walk. Now when he went back there he wanted to do the simple things he had always done. London was for parties and get togethers and business. Leicestershire was for taking time off.

The house he and Liz had chosen after their marriage was up in the Laughton Hills. It was a Georgian pile, probably owned by a wealthy manufacturer, and the stables in the back were big enough for a riding school. Not that the equestrian quarters held any interest for Liz. David might be mad about hunting, but Liz was mad about comfort. If she was going to spend time out of London, she wanted to do so with as little inconvenience as possible. In her heart, she would have loved a house like her father-in-law's, but when she realized she couldn't have it, she compromised. David could have his stables and his trout stream and his vegetable garden, but she wanted a drawing-room with a fire you could sit in. She wanted a conservatory with orange trees imported from California and central heating so hot you could wander round in your nightie and never feel cold. Above all, Liz wanted luxury of the kind only understood by people who were born and bred in London. And she had her way.

The inside of Liz and David's country retreat looked a little like a high-class health farm, with one difference: the paintings and the furniture were genuine. Liz knew the local gentry sneered at the way she lived, but she didn't give a damn. Let them freeze to death in their shabby, draughty halls if they wanted. As long as she was snug and insulated from the horrors of country living, that's all she cared about.

She and Barbara got down to the country just in time for tea, which Liz had served in the conservatory.

Liz and her daughter hadn't spent that much time together in the past year or so, and now Barbara was nearly a teenager Liz felt it was high time to get acquainted again. While they talked about the subjects the girl wanted to study for her 'O' levels, Liz scrutinized her. She was starting to grow tall now like her father, and it made her look less podgy. Barbara would never be slender and graceful the way Liz was herself. She could see just from looking at her bones she would be powerfully built, and Liz felt worried. How was Barbara going to find a husband with that shape? She switched her attention to the girl's hair. At least in this respect, God had been kind. Her daughter had a thick, chestnut mane which she wore in a braid. With the right styling, her hair could be her best asset. It needs to be, thought Liz grimly. She had a very strong face, Liz conceded. In a man it would have been considered handsome, but girls weren't meant to look commanding, they were meant to be meek and pretty. Nobody could call Barbara meek. She had grown out of her shy, self-conscious phase, and the girl that faced Liz today was bossy and rather jokey in a jolly-hockey-sticks kind of way. Liz didn't understand her at all. How could I have given birth to this Amazon, she wondered. What on earth am I going to do with her?

Barbara was going through exactly the same kind of mental torture, but in reverse, for she couldn't stand her mother. When Liz decided out of the blue to bear her off to the country for a week, she thought of a million ways of getting out of it.

'I can't just take a week off school during term time,' she had protested. 'The headmistress wouldn't hear of it.'

Her mother had killed that argument stone dead.

'The woman will do exactly as I tell her to do,' she had replied. 'She wants me to go on paying her exorbitant fees, doesn't she?'

There was no answer to that, so the next thing Barbara did was to invent a cold. She sniffed and snivelled all over the weekend, dabbing her nose with water from the tap in order to be more convincing. All her mother said was that she was clearly in need of a rest and the country would do her the world of good. In the end she resigned herself to her fate. There was only one thing that remained to do. She called the woman who ran the riding stables and said she was coming down. She and Martha Hill had been best friends ever since Martha taught Barbara to ride when she was four. Who knows, Barbara thought, maybe if I'm staying a week, I'll be invited to go out with the hunt.

Now as she made stilted conversation with her mother, her thoughts returned to the hunt. She looked surreptitiously at her watch. It was nearly five. Martha should be at home by now. Barbara gave Liz her best smile.

'Would you mind if I made a phone call?' she asked.

Liz nodded.

'Go ahead,' she said, 'but tell Martha I'm not letting you off the leash until tomorrow. It's high time you and I spent some time together, and there's no time like now.'

Barbara groaned inwardly. When her mother talked about spending time together, what she really meant was she wanted to deliver a lecture. Barbara had lived through years of her mother's lectures and they were all a load of rot. Who wanted to know how to behave like the perfect lady for heaven's sake? That sort of thing had gone out with stiletto heels and hair dyes and all the other things Liz's generation went in for. She made a face.

'We spend lots of time with each other in London, Ma. I thought you said I should get out and about in the fresh air.'

Liz ignored her protests.

'You can get out into the air tomorrow,' she said firmly. 'Tonight I want you to be washed and dressed for dinner at eight sharp. We'll eat in the dining-room.'

The dining-room. That was the final nail in the coffin. Barbara stomped off into the hall, fighting off a gathering depression. Not only would they be talking about the way her mother liked her to behave, she would actually be going through the motions. Damn it, she thought as she climbed the polished wood stairs to her room, I'll have to wear a dress.

At ten to eight Barbara slid into the elegant drawing-room. There was a fire burning in the huge grate and despite everything she felt herself beginning to relax.

There was no doubt about it, her mother knew how to make a room comfortable. She had furnished it simply enough with long pale sofas and leather armchairs you disappeared into. But what gave the whole place a glow and made you never want to move from it, were the floors. Liz had kept the original wood, but instead of leaving the boards as they were, she had polished them to a skating rink gloss. Over them she had thrown a selection of rugs. There were kelims and flokatis and right in front of the fire was a vast throw made of real animal fur. That particular rug made Barbara feel guilty. Some perfectly nice bear had died so that her mother could satisfy her need for luxury. Poor bear, she thought stroking the lifelike head with glass eyes and a leather nose, what did you do to deserve this?

Her thoughts were interrupted by Liz, who had come into the room.

'How many times have I told you not to sit on the floor,' she said crossly. 'You'll ruin that skirt.'

Barbara got up unwillingly and went across to the sofa. Sod the dress, she thought. It makes me look like a streetwalker anyway. She was dressed in a Saint Laurent creation that was made for someone with an entirely different build. It had a short tight bodice and a flirty fluffy little skirt that ended in handkerchief points. She had an entire wardrobe full of things like this chosen by her mother, and she felt a fool in all of them.

A butler came into the room and offered her a drink. Barbara asked for a tomato juice even though she knew she was allowed one glass of sherry before dinner. She didn't like alcohol particularly and could never understand her parents' need to get slightly sozzled on château-bottled claret. Then she arranged her features into the blandest expression she could muster and prepared herself for the boredom to come. Liz had chosen that night to talk about diets, so she opened the discussion with a few observations about her daughter's shape. None of them were complimentary.

By the time they had gone into the dining-room and

the butler had served the first course, Barbara's appetite had gone completely. She pushed the chilled melon around her plate and wondered why her mother was so obsessed with the way people looked. Surely what mattered was whether they were interesting, or intelligent, or funny. The way they looked was a bonus, like the icing on the cake. It was nothing to do with the real person underneath. Barbara was about to put this point of view to Liz when she realized that they would only end up fighting. She tuned her mother out, while she focused her thoughts on what she could do tomorrow.

Usually she got away with smiling and letting Liz talk through the meal, but tonight it wasn't enough.

'Try to offer an opinion when I ask you a question,' Liz said crossly. 'It's like talking to a brick wall.'

Barbara pulled herself together. 'Sorry,' she said. 'I didn't quite catch the last thing you said.'

'I was talking about the time I lost over a stone when I wanted to work as a model.'

Barbara looked blank. Why would she want to do that, she wondered. She's scraggy enough as it is. Aloud she said, 'You don't need to lose anything Ma, you're perfect as it is.'

Now Liz looked irritated.

'I know all that,' she said. 'I wasn't talking about me. I was discussing your figure.'

Barbara glanced up from her half-eaten melon.

'What's wrong with it?'

Now Liz was really cross.

'Haven't you been listening to a word I've been saying all evening? I told you when we sat down it's time you thought about fining down. The way you look now is okay on the hockey field, but when you get older and start going to dances you're going to look out of place.'

'That's okay then,' Barbara said. 'I won't go to dances. It will spare both of us a lot of embarrassment.'

Liz's palm itched to smack her daughter right across those pink, too chubby cheeks, but she stopped herself.

'You will go to dances,' she said as firmly as she could. 'And you will go looking the right shape. We've got plenty of time in hand to slim you down.'

Now it was Barbara's turn to lose her cool.

'Mother,' she said furiously, 'I don't want you to slim me down. I'm perfectly happy with myself the way I am. Can't you understand I don't want to look like you?'

There was a short silence while both women looked at each other across a sea of silver cutlery and polished mahogany.

Liz was the first one to speak.

'And what's wrong with the way I look?' She said it coldly, cutting off her words at the ends the way her elocution teacher had taught her. Barbara shivered in the overheated room. She might resent her mother and challenge her authority, but when it came to it Liz still had the ability to terrify her.

'There's nothing wrong with you,' she said quickly. 'You're a beauty – everybody says so. It's just that your kind of thing doesn't suit me at all. Look at the dresses you make me wear,' she said warming to her theme. 'Most of the time I look a clown in them, and it's not because I'm too heavy. You could slim me down to a wafer and I still wouldn't look right.'

Liz pushed her plate away and picked up a little bell. She rang it twice and two servants appeared and served the main course. It was beef, very rare. On the side in a serving dish was a pile of green beans, with no butter on them. And there were no potatoes to be seen. Typical, thought Barbara. She diets even when she doesn't mean to.

Her mother waited until the maids had left before she went on. Then she said, 'I don't want to be difficult with you Barbara, but I don't think you know what you're talking about. You like to act the tomboy now but quite soon you'll grow out of that, and then you'll come to appreciate just how useful I can be to you.'

Barbara speared a mouthful of rare steak angrily. She would never make her mother understand what she wanted, or even who she was. All she could do was sit here and play the dutiful daughter.

Roll on ten o'clock, she thought. At least then we can watch the news on the telly. On a night like this it was any port in a storm.

Barbara awoke at the crack of dawn the next day, threw on her riding clothes and ran across the yard to the stables. She found Martha in the tack room getting ready to saddle the horses.

'You're just in time to get Samson ready,' she observed. 'Have you had any breakfast this morning?'

Barbara shook her head. 'No time,' she said.

The older woman smiled.

'I guessed so. If you go inside the cottage, you'll find some toast and cereal. Help yourself, but don't take too long. The hunt won't wait.'

Barbara did as she was told, and fifteen minutes later she was sitting astride the huge chestnut roan she was hunting that season. As she and Martha made to leave, there was a great kerfuffle in the yard and all the dogs started yapping at once. Barbara looked round to see what was causing all the fuss, and saw a very old, very beaten-up sheepdog running around in circles. It was clear from the look of him that he had been trying to make friends, but the resident stable dogs didn't want to know. On the contrary, they were taking it in turns to chase him around the yard.

'Who on earth does that belong to?' asked Barbara.

Martha sighed.

'Nobody, as far as I know,' she said. 'He showed up three days ago begging for food and I didn't have the heart to send him away, but he's not exactly popular with the others. He's too pushy and boistrous.'

The yapping and chasing increased in intensity and Martha pulled her horse to a halt.

'Go on ahead of me,' she said. 'I'll sort this out and catch you up.'

But Barbara wouldn't hear of it. Instead she got out of her saddle and ran to the rescue of the sheepdog. The moment she reached him everything came to a stop. The stable dogs backed off and the old dog stood stock still for a moment and started to whimper. In that instant Barbara's heart went out to him.

'Poor baby,' she crooned, stroking his ears. 'What's the trouble? Doesn't anybody love you?'

In answer the animal hurled itself at her, licking her face and her hair as if his life depended on it. After that she was completely lost, for Barbara had come face to face with another creature who was just as misunderstood as she was.

Martha, who recognized a love affair when she saw it, was worried.

'If we don't get a move on,' she told Barbara, 'we'll miss the meet.'

This didn't seem to bother Barbara at all.

'Go without me,' she said. 'Tommy needs me to be here for him.'

Martha remounted her hunter.

'Tommy? So that's what you've decided to call him,' she said turning to wave goodbye. 'It's a good enough name, though I don't know what your mother will think.'

Liz thought Tommy was the most disgusting animal she had ever seen in her life. Not that she liked animals much anyway. She always thought they were vaguely unhygienic. Now her daughter was visiting a smelly old stray on her, and she was having none of it.

'I don't care if you do love him,' she said crisply. 'I'm not having Tommy, or whatever you call him, in the house.'

'But Mummy,' Barbara wailed, 'he's got nowhere else to go. If we don't take him in, he'll die of neglect.'

Liz was unmoved.

'Then let him. We can't take responsibility for every stray in the county. You'll be setting up a dogs' home next.'

Barbara knew better than to argue any more. If she wasn't going to be able to save Tommy with her mother's blessing, then she would do so without it. Over the next few days she set about making her new pet a home in the outhouse. She went into Market Harborough and bought a kennel and a big supply of tinned dogfood. Then she felt uncomfortable about the tins.

'I'll cook for you in London,' she told Tommy, who liked to accompany her on all her outings.

Using a mixture of lies and old-fashioned deceit, Barbara managed to keep Tommy's continuing existence a secret for nearly a week. Whenever she could, she was out of the house seeing her friends and rambling around the fields with her new pet.

Only in the evening did she and her mother see each other. At those times Barbara did her best to placate Liz by agreeing to a dietary regime. She cut out all carbohydrates and sugar in her coffee, she counted her calories ostentatiously, and at the end of five days she had actually lost three pounds. This seemed to please Liz, who felt she had little to be happy about.

For Liz the break had been a complete waste of time. David hadn't shown up – not even once. They had spoken at length on the telephone every evening before dinner, but there always seemed to be some crisis or other that kept her husband at the newspaper. In the end Liz admitted defeat and made plans to return to London at the weekend. At least if she was living under the same roof as her husband, she had a chance of keeping tabs on him. This way they could be at opposite ends of the earth.

On Friday morning, an hour or two before they were due to go, Liz spread all her clothes out on the bed for the maid to pack into her suitcase. With a certain sadness she surveyed the things she had brought. There were two Bruce Oldfield dinner dresses, a beautiful silk suit from Chanel, a Calvin Klein catsuit and all her best Janet Reger lingerie.

Some second honeymoon this turned out to be, she thought petulantly. At least Barbara hadn't been a total pain in the neck, she consoled herself. There had even been times when the girl seemed to be listening to reason.

Liz took one last look at her unworn finery and went downstairs. There was just time to have some coffee and make a couple of phone calls before they left.

Half an hour later, when she returned to her room she had difficulty believing the sight that confronted her. For right in the middle of the bed, tangled up in her dresses and petticoats and lacy basques, was Tommy. He must have been swimming for the animal was covered in mud which he had splashed all over the carpet as well as the bed.

If Tommy hadn't been so enormous, Liz would have picked him up by the scruff of his woolly neck and hurled him through the window. As it was, she stood stock still and called out for her daughter.

Barbara came running into the room and the instant she saw Tommy she burst into tears of relief.

'Where have you been?' she panted. 'I've been looking everywhere for you.'

Liz was aghast. 'I thought you'd got rid of this thing a week ago,' she screamed.

The girl ran over to the bed and picked Tommy up in her arms.

'He's not a thing,' she said with as much dignity as she could muster. 'He's a dog. My dog. And I'll never get rid of him.'

Liz squared up to her daughter. 'We'll see about that,' she said shortly.

In the event, Tommy went back with them to London. He rode in the back of the Daimler, sitting next to Barbara in a special basket she had bought for him. Liz, who had ceased all communication with her daughter, sat in the front of the car with the chauffeur. It was a difficult journey, punctuated by the chauffeur pulling over to the hard shoulder to allow Tommy to be sick.

'He'll be better when we get him home,' said Barbara reassuringly. 'Cars don't suit him.'

Liz was speechless. When her daughter had insisted on bringing the fleabitten old dog back with them, she had refused. There were tears after that and for the first time in her life, Barbara had fought back.

'If I can't take Tommy with me, then I'm not going home,' she had said.

Liz weighed her options. She could stand firm and risk a shouting match; she could ring David and asked him to mediate; or she could accept the situation for the moment, then squash Barbara when they got home. She decided on the last solution. She knew she could win this fight, but she wanted David on her side when she went into battle. On her side in person.

They rode back to London in silence. When the car eventually pulled up in front of the house in Cheyne Walk, Liz asserted herself.

'You're not bringing that animal in with you,' she told her daughter. 'The driver can take it into the gardens at the back.'

'But it's cold outside,' Barbara wailed. 'Tommy will be miserable.'

Now Liz really had had enough. 'Tommy is a dog,' she said, her voice cold with rage. 'He's wearing a big woolly coat and he's used to living outdoors. Now stop fussing and come inside. Your father will be home in an hour or so and when he comes in we'll all decide what to do with the animal.'

Some hope, thought Barbara. In this house Mummy decides what to do and Daddy agrees with her. Tommy doesn't stand a chance.

David returned early that evening. He felt wretched about letting Liz down and not going to the country but the dramas at the *Chronicle* continued unabated. Their big series was in danger of being spoiled by a rival paper who had managed to lay hands on the copy and were threatening to pirate extracts. Legally they couldn't do it, of course, but they were bluffing and the readers were convinced that they would be getting 'Secrets of a Russian Spymaster' in both morning papers. David had managed to pour cold water on that plan, but it had taken time.

By the end of the week, the *Chronicle* was in shape, but David was still in London. I'll make it up to my family he thought. I can't have my wife and daughter playing second fiddle to a printing press.

He breathed out deeply as he came through the front door. His home with its elegant Georgian furniture had a calming effect on him. It was like stepping out of a world of grubby turmoil and into a more peaceful age. Here, there were always fresh flowers in the hall, the carpets were thick and old and precious, and the butler always knew exactly what he wanted to drink and what strength to make it.

David walked through into the drawing-room where a fire was burning brightly and his whisky was waiting for him on a silver tray. Next to it was a glass of dry white Chablis. So Liz is home, he thought. I'm glad of that.

David had missed his wife. He hadn't been able to spend all that much time with her recently, but he liked to know she was there. The fact that she was in the house reassured him. He had married her because she was the only girl who had truly cared for him, and he still valued that quality in her. He didn't like her friends all that much and sometimes her ambition terrified him. But underneath, her loyalty was beyond question. When the chips were down, that's what really counted.

As David sipped his whisky he thought about Liz. What is it that makes me love her, he wondered – her belief in me, or her determination to win at all costs. He smiled inwardly as he pondered over his wife's fierceness. It hadn't been easy living with a tigress over the years. There were times when he'd wondered if her claws weren't a little too sharp, but he had dismissed the thought. Okay, Liz could be a bitch, but she was never dull. He looked up as she came into the room and he allowed himself a moment to admire her. She had cut her hair very short that season and it looked good, giving her a stylish, devil-may-care kind of dash. The suit she was wearing underlined the effect. David recognized it as a Saint Laurent. Liz had chosen to wear black leather that evening: the short, tight skirt emphasized the leanness of her hips; the bodice, cinched by a wide belt, showed her curves.

David had been starved of her for a week, and at that moment he was overcome with desire for his wife. It was then he remembered that they were to dine with Michael Mander, the Foreign Secretary, in the House of Commons that night. Damn, he thought. Damn and blast. Isn't there one evening when we can be left alone? But David knew the answer already. As long as the *Chronicle* was losing circulation, he had to keep up a presence. Only by seeming confident and coming on like a winner could he stay ahead of the situation.

As Liz came towards him, David noticed her looking troubled and wondered if he was to blame.

'I'm sorry about the country,' he said straightaway. 'You know I tried.'

She came close then, circling his neck with her arms and kissing him softly the way she always did at the end of the day.

'You're forgiven,' she told him. 'Though next time you won't get out of taking me to Antibes so easily.'

They smiled at each other. 'I'm glad you're back,' David said.

The pleasure faded from Liz's face. 'You won't be quite so glad when I tell you what I've brought back with me.'

David took hold of his drink again, feeling he was going to need it.

'What?' he asked.

Liz didn't change her expression.

'A dog,' she said dully. 'A great, woolly, sloppy sheepdog that should have been put down at least three years ago.'

Later on he wondered whether the situation would have been any different if he had resisted smiling. He thought not. He liked dogs. He couldn't help himself any more than he could help being amused at the prospect of having one in his house.

'Does this dog have a name?' he asked curiously.

'Tommy.' Liz spat the name out like a curse. 'Barbara named the mutt herself.'

'So the woolly monster belongs to our daughter. How did that come about?'

Liz walked across to a table and picked up a cigarette. She made a great performance about lighting it, snapping open a gold Cartier flint and inhaling deeply.

'Our daughter,' she said sarcastically, 'found this new pet in the stable yard. It was a stray. If you ask me, its owners turned it out when they couldn't stand the smell any more. Barbara fell for this thing and when I tried to make her get rid of it, she hid it in the outhouse. I only realized what she was doing when I found it in the bedroom. It must have been rambling in some mud, because the carpet was completely ruined.'

With a certain effort, David managed to contain his mirth.

'What was the dog doing in our bedroom?'

Liz took another puff on her cigarette. 'It was sitting right in the middle of the bed. It had made a nest of my clothes – you wouldn't believe the mess.' She shuddered, as if she had come upon a massacre rather than a stray dog. It was this theatrical gesture that finally finished David off.

The laughter which he had been trying to contain

burst out of him in a great bellow. 'The dog was buried in your clothes,' he spluttered. 'Your precious designer kit.'

The more he thought about it, the harder he laughed. At last, he calmed down to see his wife facing him with an icy stare.

'I'm glad you think it's so funny,' she said tightly, 'because Tommy's coming to live with us if you don't do something about it.'

'What do you mean?'

'What I say,' she went on grimly. 'Barbara has taken it into her head that she wants a pet. She's at that age, and Tommy is the first candidate she's laid eyes on. If I'd known what was going through her mind, I would have taken her to Harrods and got a peke or something.'

'A peke?' Now it was David's turn to look horrified. 'That's the last thing we want – nasty, yappy little things. At least Ba has fallen in love with a proper dog.'

Liz set her mouth into a tight line. 'I suggest you meet Tommy first,' she said, 'before you apply that description.'

David and Tommy were formally introduced after dinner. It was then Liz knew she had lost her battle, for the dog took one look at her husband and jumped into his arms. Three stones of curly grey wool nearly knocked David off his feet, then one very pink tongue licked his face until it shone.

'Down boy,' he said, disentangling himself. 'Sit.'

Tommy sat, his ears cocked, his eyes gazing into David's with adoration.

'He's chosen you, Daddy,' said Barbara with joy. 'He did the same thing to me.'

Liz asserted herself one last time. 'Well, you're not keeping him,' she said sharply.

Father, daughter and dog lined up against her.

'Why don't we try it for a few days?' David suggested. 'If you really can't live with it, then I'll send him away, I promise.'

Liar, Liz thought savagely, but she knew she was beaten.

'I'm sure Tommy and I will come to an understanding,' was all she said.

She saw to it that Tommy was confined to the kitchen and the library. The bedrooms, the drawing-room, all the bathrooms and the dining-room were strictly out-of-bounds. It was a partial victory, yet Liz still felt betrayed. There had been a time, right at the beginning, when she and David had been one person. In those days they had clung to each other, but over the years the world had come between them.

David's interfering family had made the first cracks. They weren't really cracks, when Liz thought about it – just tiny divisions, like the way her father-in-law took her to task for interfering in the *Chronicle*. Then there was her daughter. No matter how hard she tried, she and Barbara could never seem to see eye to eye. At times, Liz felt a complete outsider. There were these well bred, civilized people with their passion for the great outdoors and hairy, smelly animals. Then there was her, the ex-model from Southend-on-Sea. She suspected when she wasn't there, they all talked behind her back. She wondered if David ever came to her defence. Then she remembered the way he had laughed when she told him about the dog ruining all her things, her precious, expensive dresses.

I'm being irrational, Liz told herself. There's nothing wrong with the way things are between us. I just sometimes wish there was more passion. I want to be made love to, she thought bitterly. I want to be seduced and ravished by someone who's hungry for me, not someone who goes through the motions after a hard day at the office.

Liz thought about Vic Chirgotis and the way he had looked at her in San Lorenzo's. He would never make love to her as a duty, she knew that. He had virtually told her that what he had in mind was dirty and decadent and deeply erotic. Liz thought about his darkness, the strength in his hands, the way the hair sprang out of his head as if it had a separate life all of its own.

Lust hit her like a tidal wave, flooding over her and leaving her weak and light-headed. I want you, Vic, she decided. And what's more, I'm going to have you.

31

New York

Norman considered himself to be a patient man. He knew he had his peccadillos: he was fussy with his food; he didn't suffer fools gladly. Underneath all that though, he had reserves of kindness, tolerance and sheer generosity that would have done credit to a saint.

Who else would have taken in a woman and child belonging to a married man. All his friends had told him Vanessa was a tramp, a shop soiled tramp, but Norman had defended her.

'She's had a lot of bad luck,' he had said. 'Her family in England are a class act. You'd see Vanessa differently if you met them.'

At his insistence, Norman had met Vanessa's parents when they visited London. She hadn't wanted to see them at first – apparently they hadn't spoken for some years – and Norman didn't blame them one bit. What parents in the world would condone a daughter who shacked up with a married man then had his child?

He had virtually said that one night when they were having drinks with her folks. Then he cursed himself for being such a heavy-footed American. It seemed Vanessa hadn't actually got round to telling her mother about Freddie and there was a big silence while everyone figured out what to do next.

In the end Vanessa said that she and her mother had a lot of catching up to do, and suggested that Norman should take her father out. Which is how

Norman Bracken from New York City got to eat in a real gentleman's club. For that alone, it was worth the trip to London. For the rest of his life, Norman would never forget the Guards and Cavalry on Piccadilly. He imagined it was a lot like Buckingham Palace, only in miniature. All old stonework and high ceilings and the sort of grand staircases you only ever saw in Hollywood films.

Over dinner, old man Grenville had asked Norman about his plans for marriage. It was then that Norman played his trump card.

'I haven't made up my mind about marriage yet,' he said. 'But I have done the right thing and taken on the girl. From the time your daughter moved into my home, I became Freddie's legal guardian.'

That seemed to satisfy Vanessa's father and Norman made a note not to get into the habit of having any more chummy little dinners like this. If he wasn't careful he could end up tied to Vanessa for life, and that was the last thing he needed.

Norman realized how wise he had been not to commit himself a few months after he and Vanessa returned to the States, for it was about that time that he found out about Ted.

He should have smelt a rat when his creative director quit on him. If Ted had been going to a better job, Norman could have understood his decision, but he wasn't. If anything, he was taking a step down when he handed in his notice. But there was no talking him out of it.

'I've been around you too long,' was the reason Ted gave for leaving. 'I need some space.'

What Ted really meant was that he was worried that his affair with Vanessa might come to light if he stayed around the agency. He was right, for he was always taking long lunches and it was only a matter of time before Norman found out just who he was spending the time with.

Then, out of the blue Vanessa announced she was moving on. She had had enough of living with Norman, the feeling between them had died. She and Freddie were leaving.

At first, Norman didn't understand what Vanessa was saying. The whole thing was so unbelievable. He had envisaged that one day he might get rid of Vanessa, but the other way round? What was she thinking of?

He tried reasoning with her.

'I haven't been so bad to you, have I?' he asked. 'I gave you a roof over your head when you had nowhere to go. I didn't mess around with other women. I even took on your daughter. Why do you want to go now?'

Then Vanessa told him there was someone else and Norman saw red. The lazy, good-for-nothing tart had been eating his food, taking up space in his apartment and all the while she had been putting out for another guy.

'How long has this been going on?' he demanded.

Vanessa refused to speak and Norman grabbed hold of her arm, telling her he would beat the shit out of her if she didn't give him dates, times and the name of the guy involved.

Vanessa gave him a funny sort of smile when he said that. Then she threatened to go to the cops.

'You raise a hand to me again,' she said, 'and I'll have you in court. I let you get away with beating up on me in the past, because I had to. I had nowhere to go. It's different now.'

Norman hit her anyway, just to show who was boss. This time though, she didn't yell. Vanessa just got up and left the room, locking the door behind her. The next thing Norman heard was the front door slamming.

That was a week ago. Now Vanessa was shacked up with Ted and was endeavouring to sue Norman for assault. But Norman had gone one better. The stupid woman seemed to have forgotten the most important thing of all: Norman was still her daughter's legal guardian. She could fuck who she liked. She could even go on the streets if she wanted. The one thing she couldn't do was take Freddie away from him for no good reason. When her firm of lawyers contacted him with the assault charge, he delivered his bombshell: he would sue Vanessa for custody of Freddie, and with her record, he knew he'd have no problem getting it.

Freddie made her mind up to run away the day before they were due in court. She had been thinking about it ever since her mother dragged her out of Norman's apartment; and now she had made her decision. She had had quite enough of being carried around New York as if she were a sack of potatoes, and she had no intention of being squabbled over by two men she didn't particularly like. She didn't belong to Norman and nor did she belong to Vanessa's new boyfriend. She had a perfectly good father of her own. The time had come to go and find him.

It had been years now since Freddie had seen Dan and she wondered whether he would recognize her. She had been a little girl then, a skinny little girl with long pigtails and a squeaky voice. She had filled out since and she didn't squeak any more. She had also had her hair cut. Uncle Norman had paid for her to go to Lily Dache and the stylist there had cut off the pigtails and given her a mass of golden curls. It surprised Freddie how quickly it had all happened, one moment her hair was straight and heavy and hung almost to her waist, the next it bounced above her shoulders in waves and ringlets. She had turned round and looked at the man who had worked the miracle.

'I didn't know I had curly hair,' she said.

The stylist laughed. 'If you had it the length you were wearing it I'm not surprised. You weren't giving your curls a chance.'

Her mother had loved her new look.

'In a couple of years you'll be able to model,' she told her. 'These days girls start younger and younger.'

But Freddie had no intention of following in her mother's footsteps. Modelling was something brainless people did. Any girl who was smart didn't let herself be used as a living clothes peg, and Freddie was smart. She knew it because her teachers told her so. She was top of all her classes, and she already had her name down for a scholarship to Radcliffe.

So far, Freddie hadn't made her mind up what subjects to specialize in, because she didn't know what she was going to do with her life. However, she did know one thing: when she came out of college she would do so with qualifications. She would be equipped to go into a profession so that no man, no matter how important he was, would be able to push her around.

Freddie wondered, as she often did these days, exactly what it was that made her father stop loving Vanessa. She had no doubt whatever that it was Dan who had ended things. Men behaved that way around her mother, and it made her feel sad. She was so good, she had so much to give, yet people got bored with her.

Freddie had seen it happen with Norman, and she remembered her father being irritated by her mother.

Now she was older, she understood why. It was partly because men were so bound up with their lives that they didn't have time for women's talk. Norman always wanted to talk about Wall Street or who the next Mayor of New York was going to be. Because her mother wasn't all that fascinated with those things, Freddie made sure that she could keep the conversation going. She read the papers and she watched television. After a bit she found that talking to men wasn't so difficult after all.

Now she was glad of this new skill she had acquired. If she was going to run away and find her father, she had to make absolutely sure that when she found him, he wouldn't turn her out again. I'll dazzle him so completely, he won't want to get rid of me, she decided.

Freddie knew that Dan had a showroom on Seventh Avenue. Now she looked him up in the New York directory to make sure he hadn't moved. He was still there. The address was 550 Seventh Avenue and Levins was on the twelfth floor. Freddie didn't pack a suitcase. Once she knew where she would be living, her mother could send her things on. For the time being she put a toothbrush and a clean change of underwear in the leather satchel she always carried. Then she took the subway to Penn Station.

It always came as a surprise to her that this grimy part of town was responsible for the manufacture of three quarters of all the clothes in the United States. When her mother first told her this fact, Freddie had imagined the district to be inhabited by elegant women dripping with diamonds and chauffeur-driven cars. It wasn't like that at all of course, and when she told her father his precious garment district reminded her of Times Square nearby, he had laughed at her.

'What do you expect?' he teased. 'We're not trying

to woo customers here. That's the job of all the fancy Fifth Avenue stores. Down here it's strictly business.'

Freddie could see what he meant. Clothes were a commodity, like cars or washing machines, and the people who made them thought nothing of loading them up on racks and shunting them around the streets.

She walked up the Avenue until she got to her father's building. She hadn't rehearsed what she was going to say, and now as she swung into the reception area of Levins she still had no idea how to present herself. It occurred to her that if she announced her name, it might frighten her father off. After all he hadn't contacted her for years. There had to be a reason for his silence. In the end she decided to give her best friend's name. Laura Mason.

'I'm here to see Mr Levin,' she told the receptionist. 'Mr Dan Levin. I'm Laura Mason from Bloomingdales.'

She knew her father supplied the store – he must see hundreds of people from there every day. The girl behind the desk rang through to Dan's office and after a brief conversation on the internal phone she looked up at Freddie.

'The secretary here says Mr Levin isn't expecting any Laura Mason.'

Freddie started to worry. If the girl thought she was an imposter she really would be in trouble. She smiled at the receptionist as calmly as she could.

'I must have come to the wrong place,' she said quickly. 'Sorry to bother you.'

She left the room as fast as she could.

In the hall she went over to the elevator and started to press the button, then she thought again. Nobody could tell her to move on if she stayed right where she was, and sooner or later her father had to get out of the building. All she had to do was wait.

Her patience was rewarded. At six o'clock, three hours later, Dan and and another older man came out of the doors. Her father was greyer than she remembered, but apart from that he was still the same. She didn't waste any time.

'Daddy,' she said hurrying over to him. 'It's Freddie. You haven't forgotten, have you?'

Dan looked terrified and for a split second Freddie thought he would walk straight past her. Then he stopped, the look of surprise giving way to a broad smile.

'How could I forget?' he said softly. 'How are you, my darling? And what are you doing here?'

The words came tumbling out of Freddie's mouth. All the time she spent waiting for Dan, she had gone through some form of greeting, but now it came to it, everything she had thought of sounded silly. So in the end she said what was on her mind.

'I ran away,' she babbled. 'Mommy walked out on Norman to live with Ted, and I couldn't take another father, so I left.'

The man with Dan registered alarm. 'What the hell is this all about?' he asked. 'Who is this girl?'

Dan put an arm round Freddie. 'This girl,' he said proudly, 'is my daughter. Pretty, isn't she?'

The older man drew himself up to his full height. 'The mother was the shiksa you kept in that love-nest of yours. I heard there was a child, but I thought you put that business behind you.'

Freddie began to feel worried all over again. She knew her father and mother had never been properly married, that had been explained to her, but this old man made it sound as if her mother had committed a crime. She glanced up at her father and saw the look of fury on his face.

'I think it would be better if you went on ahead of me,' he told his companion. 'I'll catch up with you later.'

Then he turned on his heel and led Freddie back into the offices he had just left. 'That was my father,' he said shortly. 'He never did have any style. Now, I want to know everything that's been happening to you and I want to know why Mommy and Norman have split.'

They were sitting in a vast office which had a plate glass window that ran the length of the entire wall. At one end of it was an imposing polished wood desk, at the other was a white sofa and a couple of leather chairs. Dan went over to a bar in the corner and brought out a bottle of bourbon, a Perrier and two glasses. He handed Freddie the mineral water.

'Go ahead, Freddie,' he said. 'I'm waiting.'

It took Freddie nearly an hour to tell him the story of the past few years, and she held nothing back, including the way she had waited for him, and her devastation when he didn't come.

Dan looked at her warily. 'It's been a tough time for you, Freddie,' he said, 'but it's been tougher for your mother. Tell me about the beatings again, will you? I want to get it all clear in my head.'

Freddie did as she was told, then she asked her own questions.

'Why did you let Mommy go?' she said. 'I thought you loved her.'

Her father looked at her seriously.

'You know I was never married to your mother, don't you.'

Freddie nodded.

'Did Vanessa tell you the reason for that?'

'Not properly,' said Freddie slowly, 'though she did tell me there was a lady called Ruth who you lived with on Long Island. She was your real wife, wasn't she?'

Dan sighed. 'Ruth was my real wife. She still is.'

'What did that make Mommy?'

Dan thought for a moment. Freddie was in her teens now. She was old enough for the truth.

'Your mother and I were lovers,' he said slowly. 'That means we loved each other. It wasn't just an arrangement with Vanessa. I truly cared for her.'

'But not enough to marry her,' Freddie interjected.

Dan opted for candour.

'No, not enough for that. But I stuck by her – I took full responsibility for the relationship. After all, you were my daughter, too.'

Freddie looked at him and now there were tears in her eyes. 'If you cared so much, why did you desert me?'

'I had no choice. Norman threatened to create a scandal if I didn't stay away, and that would have hurt my real family. In the end I put some money into a trust fund for your schooling and made Norman do the same. I had no idea things would turn out the way they have.'

Freddie wiped her eyes with the back of her hand.

'How embarrassing for you,' she said. 'I bet you wish none of this had ever happened. I bet you'd be really relieved if I just disappeared back into the elevator shaft and you never saw me again.'

Dan reached out for her then and took her into the circle of his arms the way he used to when she was very small.

'Don't be a goose,' he said gruffly. 'I don't wish anything of the sort.'

Freddie wanted to believe him. She wanted it more

than she had wanted anything in her life before, but she knew he was lying. She and her mother were surplus to requirements. Freddie had known it the moment the old man she had met earlier was so rude about them. The fact that he turned out to be her grandfather made it even worse. No, her father didn't want her, and that was the end of it. She drew away from him.

'I'm not a goose,' she said. 'And you don't have to be frightened of hurting me either. You stopped doing that years ago when you went out of my life.'

Dan looked at her, wondering whether or not to believe her. She dispelled his doubts by jumping up and going over to the drinks cabinet.

'I know the Perrier water's very trendy,' she said, 'but have you got a Coke or maybe a glass of wine. I refuse to hammer out my future over a bottle of fizzy water.'

Dan looked at the young woman standing in front of him and felt like a heel. All those years ago when he had last seen Freddie she had been a child.

In those days he could promise her anything that came into his head and she would have taken it on trust. Now it was different. She had grown suspicious and so hard he could scarcely believe it. What did I do, he asked himself, to turn her into this? But Dan knew very well what he had done, just as he knew there was no going back.

'You'll find some Coke on the bottom shelf,' he said drily. 'I'd rather you stayed away from wine at your age, though I know I can't stop you drinking if that's what you want.'

Freddie smiled then, and she looked so confident and pleased with herself that he realized in some subtle way he had given her the advantage.

She found a Coke and brought it over to the table

where Dan sat. Then she waited to see what he would say next.

Dan decided to face all his problems head on.

'What do you want from me?' he asked.

Freddie had him now and she knew it. I could ask for almost anything she thought, and he'd have a tough time turning me down. Then she brought herself back to reality. There's no point in going right over the top, she decided. He can't take me home with him, he's already told me about his real family. He can't really love me either, except as a cute baby, and I grew out of that years ago. So what can this father of mine do for me?

She considered asking him to buy her an apartment of her own, but rejected it. That wouldn't stop Norman trying to claim her, nor would it help her mother either. From nowhere, a great feeling of love and longing came over her.

My mother, she thought. In that moment she knew what she had to do.

She looked at her father carefully.

'I'll tell you what I want from you,' she said. 'I want you to stop Norman taking us to court. I want him out of the way so that Mommy doesn't have to worry any more.'

Dan frowned. 'Is that all you want? Or is there more?'

Freddie leaned back into the deep padded sofa.

'Stop looking so worried, Daddy,' she told him. 'You're off the hook. I don't want any more of your money, and I won't embarrass you with your family. Just fix dear Uncle Norman for me and I'll be on my way.'

'You're very cynical aren't you?' Dan said quietly. 'Too cynical if you ask me.'

But I'm not asking you, Freddie thought. The only

person I'm ever going to ask, the only person that counts for me now is my mother, because she's the one that cares.

Freddie looked back on the way she had taken Vanessa for granted. Everything she owned she had shared with her daughter. When times were good they ate in grand restaurants, when times were hard they dined on hamburgers. More than all the material things though she knew her mother had given her something this man with all his riches was simply not capable of. She had given her love.

She regarded her father with sadness.

'I suppose I am cynical,' she told him. 'But all girls my age are cynical. It's the fashion at school.'

Then she pouted and twinkled her eyes, the way she did with Uncle Norman when she wanted to get round him.

'It's been lovely seeing you, Daddy,' she said. 'If you just do this one thing I ask, I won't be cynical with you any more. I won't be tough, and I won't be demanding. I promise . . .'

Later on that evening, when Freddie had finished supper, the phone rang in Ted's apartment. It was their attorney. He had called to tell Vanessa that the court case was cancelled. Norman had dropped all claims on her daughter, with one provision: he never wanted to see her or hear from her again.

'What this means,' said the lawyer, 'is that we have to drop the assault case. Otherwise Mr Bracken will reconsider his position.'

Vanessa gave a great whoop of joy. 'Tell Mr Bracken,' she said, 'that I agree to his terms. As far as he's concerned we cease to exist from this moment on.'

She put down the phone and came back into the lounge. 'Norman has decided to get off our backs,' she told Freddie. 'We won't be hearing from him again.'

Ted got up from the table and gave both of them a hug, then he went into the kitchen and opened a bottle of wine he had in the fridge.

'I'm sorry it's not champagne,' he said, 'but it's the best I can do.'

Freddie looked at her mother drinking cheap Californian plonk with the new man in her life. She noticed Vanessa had lines at the sides of her mouth she had never seen before, and as she saw these first signs of age, she saw something else as well. She saw the decor of the place where they now lived.

Ted had fitted out his apartment in the manner of all trendy advertising men with shag pile carpets and splashy abstract paintings. For a moment Freddie thought of how her father had lived. Then she remembered Norman's home. The last home they had left.

This new place was nothing like either of the other apartments she had known. Ted's apartment was cheap and tacky and somehow impermanent. She shook her head in wonderment. How funny, she thought, how very peculiar. I must have been here hundreds of times, yet I never really noticed that before.

32

The high point of Liz's year was the spring couture collections in Paris. Serious dressing for Liz meant tweed, leather and fur for the day, followed by brocade and beads for the evening. Every winter she spent between fifty and one hundred thousand pounds on clothes and her favourite designers were Chanel and Yves Saint Laurent because there was nothing understated about them. When you wore a suit by Saint Laurent everyone knew exactly where it came from, and certain hostesses even knew how much it cost which pleased Liz. What was the point in spending thousands of pounds of your husband's money on a new outfit if nobody noticed? If you wanted to melt into the background you shopped at department stores. If you wanted your photograph on the social pages of the glossies, you made the twice yearly pilgrimage to Paris.

Spring of 1982 was the year of the shoulder pad. The shoulder pad, the short tight skirt and the stiletto heel. For Liz it was the year of the affair, and when she went to Paris at the beginning of March, she reserved two suites at the Crillon. The second suite was for Vic Chirgotis.

There was something very frightening about her relationship with Vic. Liz knew that any moment she could be found out and it kept her on edge. She often wondered what it would be like loving Vic without the fear, but she dismissed the notion.

Without the fear they would be like any other

well-to-do couple. Dressing up and going to parties, watching their horses cover the course at Ascot and Trouville, looking after their grand properties.

The man Liz was married to had houses in London and the country, plus an apartment in New York. Vic also had an apartment in Manhattan, but his houses were in Greece. Take away Vic's Greekness and he and David were virtually interchangeable, which was why Liz needed to hang on to the fear. Fear, she discovered, bred passion. And passion was the reason she was risking everything she had to see this man.

Liz would never forget the Greek's reaction when she finally contacted him. She had been feeling neglected. Her husband preferred his office to her company. Her daughter was spending all her time with a stray sheepdog. Liz wondered if anyone still noticed if she was even alive. She decided to put it to the test. She sent a telegram to Vic's offices in Athens. It said simply: *Call me. Liz.*

Vic did better than call her. He turned up. One morning, when Liz was getting ready to go out to lunch, a long black Lincoln Continental drew up in front of her house. Liz was duly informed that her car had arrived for her, which surprised her. She wasn't expecting to be collected for another half hour at least.

'Tell the driver he's early,' she said to the maid. 'I'm not due at Langan's till one fifteen.'

Five minutes later the girl came back.

'The man who came for you says you must go down now,' she told Liz. 'He wouldn't give me a reason, but he seemed in a flap.'

Liz felt annoyed. There was probably a crisis at the paper and David wanted the car in a hurry. She thought about telling it to go away and ringing for a taxi. Then she changed her mind. If she took the car as far as Bond Street, she could go to a gallery before going to Langan's. The idea pleased her. The Fine Art Society had a Monet exhibition she hadn't been able to get to. This would be the perfect moment.

Liz threw on the dark mink she always wore in London and hurried downstairs. It was only when she saw the car that she knew something was wrong. David didn't own a Lincoln. A more cautious woman would have sent one of the servants to find out who the car belonged to, but that wasn't Liz's style. If there was a problem she liked to sort it out herself. She drew her coat around her and approached the Lincoln. When she was yards away from it, the back door opened and Vic got out.

'I came to take you away from your husband,' he said. 'I had a feeling you needed me to.'

Liz was aware that she could be seen from the house.

Any one of the people who worked for her might let on she had disappeared into the back of a long black car. A car she wasn't expecting. She turned to Vic.

'I'm waiting for David's driver to take me to Langan's,' she told him. 'Can I meet you later?'

He shook his head. 'No,' he said. 'Either you come with me this minute, or we forget the whole thing.'

Her head started to spin. 'Where are you taking me?'

'Round the corner to my flat of course. Where did you think I was taking you?'

The whole thing was crazy. Vic expected Liz to cancel everything, to compromise herself in front of the servants and miss her lunch appointment. All to go back to his apartment and let him make love to her.

She looked at him, and as she did, she felt her heart beating in her ears.

'I can't go back with you,' she said.

Vic didn't move.

'Yes you can,' he told her. 'You want to.'

And Liz did. More than anything else in the world she wanted to be alone with this foreigner she hardly knew. The urgency of her need terrified her.

'But I made plans,' she said. 'People will ask questions.'

He shrugged.

'That's half the fun – or didn't you know?'

Liz let Vic hussle her into the back of the Lincoln, and while the car drove round to Eaton Square she didn't say a word. She was too busy thinking. I can tell the maid a friend of mine was taken ill and I had to dash round and see them, she decided. I'll give the same story to my lunch date. That way I won't be found out.

Vic cut into her reverie.

'If you spend all day thinking up excuses, there won't be time for anything else.'

The car had come to a stop outside a modern apartment block. Liz hurried inside, worrying if anyone had seen her on the street. Then she pulled herself up. I must have walked into hundreds of houses without my husband and never given it a second thought. It's guilt that's making me feel this way. Guilt about something that hasn't even happened. She forced a smile on to her face. It was her hostess smile. Vapid and polite.

Vic looked at her and took a decision. He was going to wipe that expression off this woman's face if it was the last thing he did. He led Liz into the elevator and closed the gates.

'I live on the top floor,' he told her. 'The penthouse.'

Then before Liz could comment he leaned over and kissed her. It was a lover's kiss, experienced and passionate. Without thinking, Liz felt herself respond.

Vic had his hands underneath her coat and he was pushing her skirt up. At first Liz tried to stop him, but there was nothing she could do. Her dress was up round her waist now and Vic was pulling down first her tights, then her panties.

She pulled away from him.

'Are you mad,' she whispered. 'Anyone could see us here.'

Vic grinned then and Liz imagined he must have been very naughty at school.

'I am,' he informed her. 'Completely mad. And you are entirely in my hands.'

The lift jolted to a stop at the top floor and he pressed the 'down' button. Then he reached under her coat and slid his fingers between her legs. It was a light deft movement and Liz felt herself beginning to open.

'For Christ's sake stop,' she begged him. 'Any minute now we'll be back on the street.' But Vic wasn't listening. Instead he got on to his knees and started to kiss the place where his fingers had been. In that instant, Liz saw the lift doors open in the lobby of the building. She reached over and jammed her finger on the 'up' button. As they started to climb again, Vic buried his tongue inside her. It was then that she felt her knees start to buckle, but Vic wasn't having it. He got to his feet and pulled Liz to him. Then he stopped the lift by pushing all the buttons at once.

'Now,' he said. 'I want you to concentrate.'

The lovemaking in the lift set the pattern for the affair, for Vic had a flair for the dangerous, the unexpected. He would hire private rooms all over town, just to give Liz lunch. Then between the hors d'oeuvres and the main course, when the waiter had finished serving the wine, he would make his move. Vic, Liz discovered, could make love to her at any time and whatever the occasion. The more bizarre the encounter the better it was. There were telephone boxes in hotels, the private compartment of a train going to Edinburgh, the hostess's bedroom half way through a grand dinner party. Liz could never understand why she wasn't found out. She cancelled dates for the theatre and the opera with only the flimsiest of excuses. She was often late for the things she did turn up for, but her husband didn't seem to notice anything was wrong. Liz put the whole thing down to luck. David was so intent on saving the *Chronicle*, she had ceased to exist for him.

Then, one day, Liz's luck ran out. Her cover was blown in Paris. She was there to see the Spring collections, and was spotted with Vic in a discreet little restaurant on the Left Bank late one evening.

Normally when Vic was in Paris, he would dine in the second arrondissement, but because Liz didn't want to bump into anyone her husband might know, she made him take her to out-of-the-way places.

What Liz didn't count on was meeting the fashion staff of the *Chronicle*. They too went to out-of-the-way bistros. Not because they were avoiding anyone, but simply because it was all they could afford. The night Betty Smith ran into Liz, she and Vic were half way through coffee and making plans to head back to the hotel. The restaurant had seated them in the back, as they had requested. They were holding hands and whispering when Betty approached their table.

'Hello, Mrs Dearing,' she said. 'I'm sorry to interrupt.'

Liz had no idea who she was. 'What is it?' she said

crossly, imagining the tall woman standing in front of them was something to do with the bistro.

Betty looked nervous.

'I'm sorry,' she said. 'I just came over to say hello and find out what you thought of the Chanel collection. I could use a quote from you in tomorrow morning's piece.'

Liz went cold all over.

'Who are you exactly?'

'Betty Smith,' the woman blurted out. 'I write the fashion page for the *Chronicle*.'

The moment she identified herself, Liz realized it was too late. She had told David she was doing the Paris collections with a woman friend, she had even come up with a bogus name. She would have got away with the fabrication if it hadn't been for Betty Smith.

Now she knew she was sunk. Betty Smith would scurry home to report the incident. She could almost hear the woman's cultivated accent bleating out to David.

'I saw your wife in Paris. She was having dinner with the Greek shipowner who's always in the gossip columns. They were quite alone and they looked surprised to see me. I hope I haven't done anything wrong telling you.'

For days afterwards Liz carried a picture of Betty Smith in her mind. Betty was everything she most hated in a woman. She was tall, blonde and willowy with a soft face. Certain men, she knew, would find Betty attractive. It bothered her, for she also knew that Betty worked closely with David, and she liked him. More than liked him. Liz suspected the stupid creature had a king-sized crush on him.

She'll tell him, Liz thought. I can guarantee it. Betty wouldn't miss a heaven-sent opportunity like this one.

33

David started to let go when the seatbelt sign went off. Any minute now the girl would be coming round with the champagne. David looked forward to that. He had never felt more like drinking a toast.

I'm free, he thought. For the first time in my entire life I don't have to answer to anyone. He thought about his father sitting in his gloomy oak-lined office overlooking Ludgate Circus. He'd be back from lunch by now and wading through the pile of paper left by the news desk. I wonder when he'll get round to opening my letter, David mused. Will he tackle it before he calls his afternoon conference, or will he wait till he's dispatched Donald Evans for the second time that day? David had a vision of the crumpled, brow-beaten editor trying to make sense of his father's demands and for a moment he felt genuine compassion for the man. Then he dismissed the emotion. From now on he would be feeling no more regret for Donald Evans or the *Chronicle*.

When his father finally got round to opening his letter, he would discover he had one less person to push around. He would discover that David had finally resigned.

He let out a sigh and settled back in the first class seat while the stewardess arranged champagne and little biscuits covered with caviar in front of him. She was blonde and pretty in a plastic sort of way, and for the first time in years David allowed himself to notice the fact. The girl saw him noticing and started to flirt. David suppressed a smile. Liz wouldn't approve at all.

It was the first time that day that he had allowed himself to think about his wife. Really think about her. As he did so, the pain came back. David took a swig of the drink in front of him and wondered what he was toasting – leaving his job, or leaving Liz.

What in God's name made her do it, he wondered. I wasn't such a bad husband. I didn't beat her. I didn't carry on with other women. I gave her all the things she wanted. Or did I? He felt a tide of bitterness rise up inside him. If I had truly satisfied Liz, he thought, there would have been no need for the Greek. No need at all.

Betty had been in to see him late that morning. Blonde, willowy, lissom Betty who only wanted the best for him.

'I saw your wife in Paris,' she had told him. 'With Vic Chirgotis. I didn't know she was a friend of his.'

David's first instinct was to ask Betty for all the details. Where had she seen them? What were they doing together? There was no point in asking those questions, though. Not when he knew what the answers would be.

For David had known about Vic for a long time. He hadn't known his name of course, but he knew his wife was seeing someone. You couldn't be that close to another human being and not notice when things started to change.

It began with the way they slept. Liz had always stayed close to him in the big double bed. Now she kept her distance and he would wake in the middle of the night thinking she had left him, only to find her curled into a ball yards away from him. The evenings were different too. When he knew he was going to be home late David called in the afternoon and told her. When he did, Liz would always shout at him, complaining bitterly that the *Chronicle* saw more of him than she did. Now she no longer complained. She simply made other arrangements. Some nights she visited girlfriends, some nights the theatre. It was then that David knew there was someone else, for Liz never went anywhere on her own. She was too insecure for that. She always needed to have a man around. He thought about Vic Chirgotis – smarmy, macho, pleased with himself. Then he drained his glass of champagne and signalled to the blonde for another. He was going to drink a lot of toasts before he got this one out of his system.

David cast his mind back to the holiday they never had together when Liz had wanted to go to Antibes and he couldn't leave the paper. Did Liz fall out of love with him then, he asked himself. Or was it later? Did it happen after the row they had over Barbara's dog, or the row they had over the *Chronicle*? They never seemed to stop quarrelling these days.

Poor bitch, David thought. No wonder she took a lover, I couldn't have been much fun for her. Yet in the middle of all his sympathy and understanding came another less civilized emotion. Rage.

So Liz was bored, David thought – neglected even. So what? It happens to most women during the course of a long marriage and most women sweat it out. They soldier on through the barren patch and at the end of it they take up where they left off. What they don't do is throw in the towel. They don't betray the man they promised to love and honour to the end.

As David pondered on Liz's betrayal, he started to dislike her, then to hate her. Finally, the pain began to recede. If I keep this up, he decided, getting through the next few days won't be any problem.

* * *

David landed in New York where he spent forty-eight hours, putting up at the St Regis where he wasn't known. After a while he began to feel uncomfortable. He had an apartment in town, he had friends and business acquaintances. Christ, even Liz's best buddy Vanessa was here somewhere. With his kind of luck he could even run into her. No, if he was going to forget his wife, he had to move on.

He decided to go to Aspen. There was something clean about the mountains, clean and anonymous. He would go up as far as he could go, then he would hire a helicopter to take him to one of the peaks where there was virgin snow. Then, and only then, would he ski.

Three months after his retreat to Aspen, David decided to call home. It wasn't something he deliberated on. One morning he simply woke up and knew it was time. He called his secretary in London and told her he was in America. She almost jumped out of her skin.

'What on earth have you been up to?' she demanded. 'Lord Dearing is going frantic trying to find you. When you didn't make contact he worried you might have had an accident or you were dead.'

David laughed. 'I'm not dead,' he reassured her. 'I'm very much alive and in rude health.'

'Whereabouts in America are you?' she interrupted. 'And when are you coming back?'

There was a silence. Then David said, 'I don't know if I am coming back, and I'm not even sure if I should tell you my address. I don't want my father sending out search parties.'

'But what about Liz?'

The question burst out of the woman and David was surprised. He had the most formal of relationships with his secretary, only ever calling her Miss

Parker rather than Sarah. Now she was talking about his wife as if she were a cousin.

Liz must have been getting at her, David thought. If I know my wife she's probably been calling the office twice a day.

Aloud he said, 'How is Mrs Dearing? I take it she's none too pleased with my absence of leave.'

Sarah Parker took a breath. Something had happened between her employer and his wife, something that had made him go away without telling her, and now she was in the middle and she had no idea how to proceed. In the end, the feminist in her asserted itself.

'Surely you didn't believe your wife would be overjoyed with the situation?'

She said it as coolly as she dared and David took her point.

'What time is it in London?' he asked.

'Nearly six, I was just going.'

'Good, I'll call home straight away. With any luck Mrs Dearing should be there.'

Before he rang off, Sarah had one last question for him.

'Do you have any message for Lord Dearing?' she asked. 'He badly wants to talk to you.'

David hesitated. He owed his father some kind of explanation for walking out the way he did. Then he thought, if the old goat doesn't know by now how totally impossible it is to work for him, then he never will.

'Tell his Lordship I'll be in touch after I've seen my wife.'

Then he broke the connection.

When David called the house on Cheyne Walk, Liz answered the phone herself. David wondered if Sarah had rung ahead to warn her, for she sounded very calm, almost as if she knew she would be speaking to him. Then he remembered their almost telepathic knowledge of each other. The way in times of great trouble, they could almost link minds. He remembered how she had pulled him back from the brink of death when he was knocked down by the car in Amsterdam.

Liz didn't need my secretary to tell her I would be calling, David thought. She felt my presence half way across the world, the way I still feel hers. He wondered if the divorce he was about to ask her for would really separate them.

'Liz,' he said when he heard her voice, 'it's David. We have to talk.'

'Yes.' David could hear the strain in her voice now. 'I suppose your little fashion girl told you all about Vic?'

'She didn't go into details if that's what you think, but she didn't have to. I'd known that something was up for a long time.'

Liz didn't reply at first and for a moment David wondered if the line had died. Then he heard her again and there was no mistaking her worry this time.

'What are you going to do?' she asked him timidly.

If I was a harder man, David thought, I'd tell my wife about the divorce here and now. It's faster and it's cleaner. Then he thought about the years they had been married and he relented.

'I'm coming straight home,' he said. 'I think we need to talk about this situation face to face before we take decisions.'

Again there was a silence. Then Liz said, 'I don't want you to come here. I'd rather we met somewhere else – on neutral territory.'

David was surprised.

'Why on earth do you want that?'

'Because I've got something to tell you,' Liz said. 'And it's not something I care to talk about at home.'

David felt annoyed. He had rung his wife in the spirit of compassion, concerned that he might hurt her feelings by leaving her, and she had turned the tables. Liz obviously had plans of her own. Plans that no doubt revolved around her greasy Greek. Five minutes ago he was resigned to turning his back on her. Now he wasn't so sure. Losing out to Vic Chirgotis wasn't something David felt comfortable about.

'Where did you have in mind for this meeting?' he asked tightly.

'Zurich,' she said. 'Le Bar du Lac. I'll book a table for lunch there, the day after tomorrow.'

David was furious. She'll be talking about raiding my bank account next, he thought. Why don't I just put my lawyer in touch with hers and let them hammer something out. But he resisted. There was Barbara to consider, after all. And Vic. David wasn't prepared to hand over his wife without some kind of fight.

'My plane doesn't land in time for lunch,' he told her. 'Re-book the table for dinner and you've got yourself a date.'

He put down the phone wondering if he was doing the right thing.

34

The Bar du Lac where Liz had arranged to meet David was one of Zurich's grandest establishments. The restaurant was in fact the focal point of a hotel which overlooked the lake and David decided to simplify his life by taking a suite. If Liz wanted to talk he could hold meetings with lawyers in his room the following day.

David arrived at the hotel in the early evening and automatically went through a mild form of culture shock. America did not lack for amenities. Technologically it was streets ahead of Europe, but in terms of style Zurich made everything he had left behind look clumsy and amateurish.

As soon as he walked into the carpeted lobby he was surrounded by the kind of silence only money can buy. A porter in white gloves materialized by David's side and took his bags to his suite, the man on the desk seemed to know exactly who he was without going through the usual system of computer checks, and everywhere he looked there were fresh-cut flowers. David knew they were renewed every morning, just as he knew the antique furniture in the Bar du Lac was the best that could be found outside a private collection.

Something inside him started to relax. He understood this kind of luxury, he had been brought up with it. If he was going to have a tough fight with Liz, at least he would be doing it on familiar territory.

By the time he had showered and changed it was a

quarter past eight. Liz had said she would meet him at eight thirty in the bar and that gave David fifteen minutes to kill. He considered taking a short walk along the lake. The air would clear his head. Then he decided not to. If Liz arrived before him it would put her at an advantage and tonight he wasn't going to give her an inch.

When he arrived at the bar it was full. Old ladies with elaborate coiffures and inherited diamonds fought for space with sleek suited money-men. Zurich society was out in force that night and David wondered idly what kind of show Liz would put on. Would she go for heavy make-up and big shoulder pads or would she play the put-upon wife in understated Jean Muir? For a moment David stopped thinking about Liz, for along with everyone else, his attention was caught by a spectacular blonde. She had come in by the back door, but it didn't stop her from making an entrance. In that dress, nothing could stop her. She was all done up in a cocktail number. From where David was sitting, it looked as if it was made entirely of sequins held together with fine black gauze, and this girl certainly had the figure for it. High round bosoms, a stomach like a board and the kind of backside that spoke of hours every day in the gym. He felt a moment of casual lust. If he wasn't meeting his wife tonight he would have been tempted to ask the woman over.

He sighed and signalled to the bartender for a drink, then he turned round to take a last look at the blonde. She was nearer now, and David realized with a start that he recognized her.

It can't be, he muttered under his breath. It simply isn't possible.

But it was. Coming towards the bar where he stood frozen in disbelief was Liz. It was the hair that had fooled him. He was used to being married to an aggressive girl with jet-black hair. The woman standing beside him was fair and delicate looking, giving the impression she was made out of spun sugar. David wondered for a second whether it was the dress that gave that impression, or whether she had done more than just change her colouring. Then he knew what it was. Liz had done something to her face. Whatever it was, it was very subtle. There was nothing stretched or lifted about her, but she looked as if someone had waved a wand and made her twenty-eight again. He shook his head.

'I hope your new boyfriend is impressed,' he said slowly, 'but you don't fool me for a second.'

Liz laughed and ordered herself a glass of champagne.

'You don't change do you? What on earth makes you imagine I made myself over for the benefit of some man. I did this for me. If it pleases you, that's a bonus.'

For some obscure reason David was irritated.

'I didn't say it pleased me.'

'You didn't have to. I can see for myself how you feel about it.'

David took hold of his whisky and threw it down, then he took his wife very firmly by the elbow and steered her into the restaurant.

If he was going to deal with her, he wanted to do so without the benefit of a bunch of Zurich bankers looking down her dress. The waiter found them a table in the corner by the window and handed David the menu.

In this place David didn't need to read the Carte. He always had the soufflé followed by trout from the lake. Tonight though, he retreated behind the giant leather-bound booklet. He needed to put some space between himself and this new blonde Liz.

Who knew what other surprises she had for him tonight?

After five minutes he called the waiter over to place their orders. Then he dealt with the wine list, taking his time deciding between a Château Latour and a Lynch Bages. In the end he went for the younger vintage. Finally, because he could no longer avoid it, he turned his attention to Liz.

'I take it you want to talk to me about Vic,' he said tersely. 'Will you marry him quickly, or will you wait till the dust has settled?'

Liz frowned and David noticed it made little impression on her perfect face. Once more, he wondered what she'd had done to herself. Then he let it go, there were more important things to occupy his mind tonight.

'I'm not going to marry Vic,' she told him quietly.

He was surprised.

'Why's that?'

'Because I left him a few weeks ago. I never loved him you know, and I didn't see any point in running to him for protection just because you'd walked out on me.'

David felt a certain grudging admiration for his wife. She was well into her thirties now, too far to chance her luck on her own, but that was what she had decided to do.

'Do you want a divorce?' he asked her. 'It might be tidier for both of us – financially, I mean.'

Once more Liz attempted a frown.

'No, I don't want to stop being married to you,' she replied simply. 'And I don't care about being tidy either.'

There was a pause. 'Unless there's somebody else,' she said. 'Is there?'

David had come to Zurich to be perfectly honest

with Liz. In Aspen there had been girls but now things looked different. Liz wasn't the calculating bitch he had taken her for. She was just a woman who had taken a chance and miscalculated the odds. He decided to lie a little. For her sake.

'No, nobody,' he told her. 'We can postpone coming to terms till you're ready.'

The food began to arrive, and as it did, a thought struck him.

'You said you were meeting me here because you had something special to tell me. Can I ask what it is?'

Liz's head came up.

'I wondered when you were going to get round to that,' she said. 'Yes, there was something.'

She let the waiter put the fluffy cheese soufflé in front of David and the caviar on ice in her place before she went on.

'After you left,' she said, 'I sat down and had a long talk with your father. He wanted to know what prompted you to take off like that. He didn't believe your dissatisfaction with the *Chronicle* was the whole story.'

David looked at her.

'And did you tell him the whole story?'

Liz nodded.

'Actually I did. I didn't see any point in hiding things.'

Once more his wife surprised him. His father had never really approved of her but he admired her – that was common knowledge. He also thought she was headstrong and spoilt. Liz had taken one hell of a risk confessing all like that.

'How did my father take the news that you were carrying on with a Greek playboy?' he asked.

Liz looked at him over the rim of her glass and he noticed how becoming her new hair colour was.

He wondered why she never thought of going blonde before.

'He was very understanding,' Liz said bluntly. 'To be honest, he blamed the whole thing on you.' She paused. 'And himself,' she went on. 'You see, he reckoned if you both hadn't been at loggerheads the whole time the *Chronicle* wouldn't be in the mess it is today, and you would have had some time to devote to me instead of spending every hour propping up a dying newspaper.'

David felt sour.

'What a pity you had to take a lover before my father saw sense. If he'd listened to me once or twice in the past year or so, all that dirty business with Vic could have been avoided.'

Liz stretched a hand out and gently touched his cheek.

'Don't be sarcastic,' she told him. 'It doesn't suit you. Anyway what I'm going to tell you calls for a celebration, not a lot of griping.'

By now nothing she could say or do was going to surprise David any more.

'Why don't you just tell me what you came here for,' he said crossly. 'I'll decide whether or not I want to hang out the flags.'

She took a breath and let it out slowly. Then she said, 'Your father has offered to stand down and let you take over the running of the paper.'

David didn't say anything and Liz looked at him sharply.

'It's what you want isn't it?'

'Of course it's what I want,' he replied shortly. 'I'm just trying to work out what the catch is.'

Liz closed her fingers around her wine glass and for the first time that evening David noticed how tense she was.

'There isn't any catch,' she told him. 'All you have to do is go back to London and tell your father you accept. I'm not asking you take me back or anything. Credit me with some pride.'

He still wasn't satisfied. 'Why did you insist on presenting me with this news in Zurich? Why didn't you just tell me on the phone and let me come into London and settle things?'

'Because you need time to think about it,' Liz said frankly. 'I've known you a long time and I know how you react to things. You would have come flying into town and signed anything your father put in front of you. I don't think that's the right way to go about things.'

She leaned forward, intent upon what she was saying.

'Look, it took you three months away from me to decide you wanted to end our marriage. If I had been pressuring you for a decision, you might not have been so clear about it. It's the same thing with the *Chronicle*. You know the problems with the organization and you know what you have to do to put them right, if there's still time for that. You can't take on the whole caboodle in five seconds, and I wasn't going to give your father the chance to push you into it overnight.'

It was as if David was seeing her again for the first time. It wasn't just the way she looked, it was the way she was. Right in the beginning he had fallen for Liz because she had put his interests above everything else in her life. Now she was doing it again, despite the fact that he had walked away from her without allowing her to explain herself. He felt ashamed.

'I don't deserve you,' he said.

'You don't have me,' Liz replied.

Out of nowhere, David felt a sense of loss.

'It probably sounds crazy,' he said, 'but this news you brought all the way to Zurich doesn't exactly thrill me.'

Liz ran a hand through the glossy blonde curls.

'It will,' she said. 'You need to sleep on it and get over the shock. By the morning you'll be on top of the world.'

'I'd rather be on top of you.'

The words came out without warning. Crude and silly. The words of a schoolboy. He expected her to slap his face, instead she took his hand in hers.

'Are you asking me to spend the night with you?' Liz said quietly.

The lust David felt for her in the bar came back in earnest now. He wanted to take hold of that ridiculous provocative dress she was wearing and tear it off her body. He wanted to possess her the way he had possessed her in the past. This time he wanted to do it properly, so she would never look at another man again.

He got up from the table, pulling her to her feet with him.

'I'm not asking you to spend the night,' he said hoarsely, 'I'm ordering you to.'

Liz stepped out of the shower with her hair wrapped in a towel. From where David was lying he had an uninterrupted view of her and he marvelled. I've been married to this woman for all these years, he thought, and she still surprises me.

The night they had spent together had been a revelation. He had been hungry for her and she had shown him the dimensions of his hunger. Then when Liz had built his appetite, she set about feeding it. Looking at her as she paraded naked and unselfconscious around his suite David remembered some of the things she had done to him. He sighed. He supposed he should have been shocked. Grand English ladies didn't go in for that sort of thing – but then the woman he had married had never been a lady.

He called out her name and she stopped fussing with her hair and came over to the bed.

'How do you feel about breakfast?' he asked.

Liz smiled.

'Terrific, only you'll have to make it fast. I've got to be out of here in an hour.'

It was as if the sun had gone in. One moment David was happy and relaxed and wondering what to do with the rest of the day. The next, she had snatched it all away from him.

'Why all the rush?' he asked crossly.

Liz's face hardened.

'I have to be in London.'

David looked at her with something approaching despair.

'And I thought you had come back to me.'

'I have, only I can't change my plans.'

He felt the fury start to build inside him. I should have known, he raged. Once Vic had gone, Liz wouldn't have been content to sit around on her own. She'd have somebody else by now. Some other playboy who liked to put her through her paces in the bedroom. He picked up the phone by his elbow and ordered coffee and croissants. Then he turned to his wife.

'Who is it waiting for you in London?' he demanded. 'Has he got a name?'

Liz sighed.

'It isn't a man. It's a teenage girl called Barbara. She's due to sit her mock "O" levels at the beginning of the week. Had you forgotten?'

David felt like a fool. Three months had passed

since he last saw his wife and he hadn't even asked about Barbara. He hadn't even wondered about her much.

'I've been very selfish,' he said softly. 'What on earth did you say to her when I took off like that? What excuses did you make for me?'

Liz pulled a face.

'I said you had to go away on business. I was going to tell her we had parted, but I thought I'd wait until we'd both worked something out.'

There was a knock at the door to the suite and Liz pulled on a terry robe and went to receive their breakfast tray. The waiter didn't express any surprise that David had company. He was too well trained for that. Nevertheless, he made a great show of setting up a table in the bedroom, laying out napkins and arranging plates and knives and forks with such bluster that in the end Liz couldn't stand it any more.

'That will be all,' she told him crisply. 'You can go now.'

To underline her meaning, she pressed a ten franc note into his hand. Then she went and poured them both a cup of coffee before the man had had a chance to leave the room.

'If things are meant to be over between us,' David told her, 'do you think you could try to be a bit less bossy. You behaved remarkably like a wife just then.'

She regarded him thoughtfully.

'I still am your wife you know, and I didn't hear any complaints about it last night.'

David took hold of her hand and pulled her down beside him.

'I want you to go on being my wife,' he said. 'Look, we've both made mistakes. I'm still furious about Vic, but if I'd been in my right mind you would never have got involved with him. I left you alone too much, Liz. I got swamped by the *Chronicle* and by my father. Well, that won't happen again. No matter how many demands the paper makes, you'll always come first. You and Barbara. I don't want to lose sight of either of you again.'

He expected her to melt into his arms the way she had done the night before. Instead, Liz pulled her robe around her and went over to the window.

'What about the girls in Aspen?' she asked. 'There must have been girls.'

He was startled.

'How did you know about that? Have you been having me followed?'

Liz laughed.

'I didn't have to. I just know you would never have stayed away for as long as you did without there being someone around.'

For a moment David was silent.

Aspen had been fun. A fantasy land where love added up to a few hot nights. Liz was more than that. She always had been.

'Forget about the girls,' he said shortly. 'I already have.'

35

New York, 1985

Vanessa looked around her in despair. There were glasses everywhere. All the shelves, the glass coffee table, the pine trestle where they ate dinner, were covered with the debris of the weekend. Wearily her eyes took in the shabby apartment. It was Monday morning and Ted had gone to the office. The time had come for Vanessa to clean up after him.

Was it always like this, she wondered, or did things look different before? She picked one of the rugs off the floor and started shaking cigarette ash out of it. I must have liked this once, she thought. In the days when I had servants and women to do the house, I thought white fluffy rugs were really cute. She looked down at the scrubbed wooden floor that gave her splinters if she went barefoot. I bet I thought this was the last word in bohemian living as well.

She made her way through to the kitchen where she found a big plastic tray, then she carried it back to the other room and started to collect the dirty glasses, and the empty wine bottles.

Vanessa wondered if Ted knew anybody who didn't drink, then she laughed at herself. Don't be silly, she thought, that man of mine wouldn't hang out with anyone who wasn't good for at least two bottles. Because she had nothing else to think about, she considered Ted's drinking. It had been getting out of hand recently.

Vanessa accepted the fact that he spent everything he earned in the bars around town. She had learned to live with it very early on in their relationship. 'A little wine helps me cope,' Ted had explained to her. 'Men are under a different kind of pressure to women. They have responsibilities. I have to work in a shitty business called advertising because I need to keep us all in food and central heating. There are days when I feel like kicking it all in to go and sit on a beach. I know I can't do that, so I go down to Murphy's and sink a bottle or two and after that things don't seem so bad. I can go back to the agency and do my thing.'

Vanessa often wondered what Ted actually did in his office after two bottles or more. She had seen how he was when he had been drinking and she couldn't imagine that anyone in his state would be capable of writing his name, let alone an advertisement.

But she didn't say anything. Despite the fortune he got through in the wine shops of New York, Ted managed to pay for the apartment and the groceries.

Then a month or so ago, he lapsed. Vanessa first realized this when the landlord's representative paid a call. Ted was out and it was Vanessa who had to deal with him. It was then she found out that they owed three months' rent. If they didn't pay up, they would be out on the street.

Vanessa did her best to reassure the man that there had been an oversight. He had left, giving her seven days to rectify the situation.

Vanessa tried to have it out with Ted the minute he came home, which was past midnight, but she couldn't get much sense out of him. So she waited until morning when he had sobered up. She still couldn't get a straight answer. In the end, she worked things out for herself by calling the bank. She told the teller she was Ted's wife in order to get the information she needed and found that there was no money in his account. Worse, he was overdrawn to the tune of several thousand dollars. Vanessa did the only thing she could: she raided her own account and settled the rent bill with what she had left.

From now on, she decided, I'm going to keep a tight rein on Ted's money. Before he starts spending his salary on booze, I'm going to make sure he hands over something for the landlord. Only, things didn't work out exactly the way she had planned. Sometimes when Ted was in a good mood she got the money she needed, but often she didn't, and they would wind up having fights. Ted wasn't violent with her the way Norman had been. He didn't hit her or insult her in front of their friends. He preferred the subtle approach.

When they were alone, he accused her and Freddie of being a burden.

'When I paid my wife off after the divorce,' he would whine, 'I didn't plan on supporting any more bodies. Now I've got you two, you suck me dry. You eat too much, you take up too much space, you interfere with my drinking.'

After one of these sessions, Vanessa couldn't bear to be near to Ted, and she would leave the bed they shared and spend the rest of the night on the sitting-room couch. She would stay awake making elaborate plans to leave, then Ted would wake her in the morning with a cup of coffee and a big apology and her heart would melt.

She knew this new man of hers was a drifter and a bum. Of all the men she had known, he was the least likely to succeed, the least likely to protect her and her daughter against the world. Yet for all that she loved him. She had to. There was no other choice.

Then she met Lauren Evans and things changed.

Vanessa ran into Lauren in the course of business. Lauren was working at the time, though Vanessa didn't know that. She simply thought the girl was a friend of Ted's from another agency. A group of them were having dinner at the Four Seasons to talk over the latest plans for their main account, 'Minty Gel' toothpaste.

The 'Minty Gel' client was there in person that night. A bluff, tiresome Texan, who insisted on the most expensive items on the menu, then left them untouched. It was his way of demonstrating his importance to the agency. He could behave in the rudest possible way and everyone would pretend nothing was amiss.

When he had finished rubbishing the food he began on the dinner guests. Ted got it first, then Ted's boss. Finally he turned his attention to Lauren.

When it happened Vanessa was very worried, for the girl was elegant and lady-like and clearly not in the habit of dealing with ugly customers. Lauren, though, wasn't in the least bit ruffled. When the Texan started in on the men he had attacked them on their business acumen, which was fair game. When he went for Lauren he got personal. He wanted to know exactly what her relationship was with Kramer, the agency boss.

'You look young enough to be his daughter,' he told her. 'Surely you can't be going to bed with the old goat?'

Lauren looked him in the eye.

'It's none of your business what I do with Mr Kramer,' she replied.

The Texan wouldn't let it be.

'Everything Kramer does is my business,' he said. 'I'm his agency's biggest paying client.'

The girl started to smile.

'I work for an agency too,' she told him, 'and the day you become one of my clients, I'll tell you what you want to know. Until then you can shut it.'

Her reply was so firm and so matter of fact that the Texan backed right down, and Vanessa was impressed. Most of the women she knew were like her – put upon housewives. This girl was different and she was intrigued. She knew she could never have a career like Lauren. It took years to establish yourself in a field like advertising, but she still thought she could learn things from her, so she asked her if they could have lunch one day.

Lauren agreed to meet her and they arranged to get together in a sushi bar on Second Avenue two days later.

The restaurant was Vanessa's idea. Sushi was just becoming fashionable in New York, and if you stuck to the basic menu, it was a reasonably cheap meal. That was important to Vanessa. Now she could no longer rely on Ted she watched every penny. Lunch with Lauren would come out of the housekeeping money and she thought for the hundredth time about taking a job. It was a vain thought and she knew it for she simply wasn't qualified for anything except modelling, and she was too old for that. She was contemplating how much the sushi bar would set her back when Lauren arrived. The minute she set eyes on her, Vanessa realized that this girl was not in the habit of lunching in places like this. She was dressed for the 21 club or La Côte Basque in a fur coat and a simple black suit. Vanessa felt cheap and depressed.

Why did I come, she thought. Lauren and I have nothing in common. We might have had things to talk about once when I was living with Dan, but not now. Our lives are light years apart.

If the younger woman felt uncomfortable she didn't

show it. She simply took off the long sable she was wearing and flung it over the back of a chair. Vanessa was fascinated.

'That's wonderful,' she said. 'Where did you get it?'

The girl grinned. 'A grateful client,' she replied. 'Paying me in kind.'

'I didn't know you worked on fashion business?'

Now Lauren was really amused.

'I don't,' she shrugged. 'I'm a hooker, I thought you knew that.'

For a moment Vanessa didn't know what to say. Lauren was so elegant, so poised, so damn lady-like. She couldn't be what she said. She had to be having her on.

'Pull the other one,' she said. 'It's got bells on.'

Lauren put her hands under her chin and regarded the other woman with interest. As she did so, Vanessa noticed that there was something feline about her companion. Her eyes were green and slanty and she had very high, almost oriental, cheekbones. But it wasn't the arrangement of her face that reminded her of a cat. It was the fact that she was so obviously pampered.

'Why are you so resistant to the idea that I earn my living by selling my body?' she asked.

Vanessa was flummoxed. 'Because nice, well-educated women like you don't do that,' she said.

Lauren stared at her. 'And what do we do?'

Now Vanessa was indignant. 'What you should do,' she told Lauren with a certain irritation, 'is a high-powered job. Or if you don't have the temperament for that, then you marry a man with a high-powered job. It's what everyone does.'

The girl raised her eyebrows.

'Really,' she said. 'Is that what you did with your life?'

Vanessa felt the colour rise into her face.

'No it isn't,' she replied. 'But that's another story.'

'So tell me the story,' said the girl with a smile. 'We've got all lunchtime.'

Vanessa didn't mean to open up, but Lauren seemed genuinely interested and she found herself pouring out the details of her life in New York. She had never related this story to anyone before, and as she told it, she felt as if the events of the past few years had happened to somebody else. Somebody innocent and foolish. Somebody who had no idea about how to handle men at all.

While she talked, Lauren organized lunch. She seemed perfectly at home with all the waiters and they responded by showering her with more attention than she deserved. By the time Vanessa got to the end of her story, bowls of salad and plates of raw fish had magically appeared on the table. There was also a bottle of chilled Chablis and two glasses. Vanessa frowned slightly when she saw that Lauren had ordered an old vintage. Then she saw the wine was French and she really got worried. It was as if Lauren could read her mind.

'Stop worrying about how much everything costs,' she told her. 'I'm taking care of lunch. It's my treat.'

'But you mustn't do that. It isn't fair. I was the one who asked you.'

Lauren regarded her with her cat's stare.

'You can pay me back,' she said, 'when you have the money.'

Vanessa started to protest, but the other girl cut in on her.

'I know what you're going to say. You don't know when that will be because you can't be sure of Ted. Well that's baloney. Ted owes you a decent life-style because of what you do for him.'

‘Try telling that to him.’

Lauren took a sip of her Chablis and considered what she was going to say next. Finally she went on.

‘Has it ever occurred to you that you have an alternative to Ted?’

Vanessa laughed shortly.

‘I know what you’re going to suggest. Find another man. Look I’ve done that three times already and I’m getting a little weary of moving house.’

‘Actually I wasn’t going to say that.’ She paused. ‘When I told you just now I worked as a hooker, I was on the level. I am a hooker, but it’s not what you think it is. Listen, when I asked you about your life, what did you tell me? You lived with three men who you didn’t marry, but who kept you. Don’t kid yourself that they loved you, because they didn’t. They used you, and when you got tired of being used, you moved on. Well, being a hooker isn’t so different from that, except the money is better, and you get to do what you like in your spare time.’

It occurred to Vanessa to walk away while she could. What Lauren was saying made perfect sense. She *had* been used by the men she had loved, but what separated her from the likes of this girl was that she hadn’t accepted it. When she suspected Dan was exploiting her, she tried to change things. She attempted to get him to commit himself. If she had been a hooker she would have just taken the money and kept quiet. Then she thought about Norman. She’d even let him beat her without too much protest. In that moment Vanessa realized that she didn’t have to change her life at all. Her life had changed without her even noticing. All she was doing now was putting a name to it.

She focused her attention on Lauren.

'Tell me what you do?' she asked. 'I'd like to know the details.'

Now it was her companion's turn to talk about her life and she was as candid as Vanessa had been. Lauren had started out working as a space saleswoman for a glossy magazine.

'I got to work in a glamorous office with interesting people,' she said. 'The only snag was I got paid nothing. I worked my butt off from early morning till late at night, yet I could hardly afford to live. I got so desperate that one day I answered an ad for an escort service. They wanted dining and dancing partners for out-of-town businessmen, and I was so naive I believed them. I really thought some boring businessmen would pay for the pleasure of my company on a night out. The girl at the agency wised me up, and when I discovered I had to sell my body as well as my company, I nearly walked out.'

Vanessa looked at her.

'What stopped you?'

'The money actually. I'd answered the ad because I was flat broke and these people were offering me a way to make a hundred dollars for an hour's work. If I'd had an alternative, if somebody was going to pay me to write an article or appear on television I would have taken it. But they weren't. I wasn't even getting paid to do the job I was doing. So I went for it. Do you know something, after the first time it really wasn't so terrible. I didn't have to spend time with the guys I was sleeping with. I didn't have to listen to their boring problems for hours on end. All I had to do was perform a sexual service and get paid for it.'

It was the words 'sexual service' that made Vanessa think. There was something clinical about the way Lauren said it, as if she was talking about dishing up a meal or shining someone's shoes. Then without warning, Norman came back into Vanessa's mind. She remembered the first time he had taken her to his bed, she had put on her best French nightie and dabbed perfume at her pulse points. He didn't even bother to notice, all he did was ram himself into her as if she was a blow-up doll and not a woman at all.

With the vision of Norman, came the vision of Ted the last time he had made love to her. He was drunk of course, but then he mostly was these days. I could have been anyone, Vanessa thought. I could even have been a hooker and he wouldn't have known the difference. She wondered what would have happened if she had been a hooker. She would have made love to Ted the way she did every night but instead of turning out the lights and switching on the burglar alarm, she would have simply got out of bed, put on her clothes and gone home.

The idea of going back to her own home intrigued her. My own place, she thought. My own bed with my own clean linen and my own closet neat and tidy and well organized. There would be a separate room for Freddie and I wouldn't have bare boards, she decided. My apartment would have fitted carpets. 'Do you have your own apartment?' she asked Lauren curiously.

The other girl laughed.

'Where do you think I live? In a hostel? Of course I have an apartment, a duplex actually, on East 76th. I moved there after I'd been with the agency for six months.'

Vanessa thought for a moment.

'Will you do something for me?' she asked. 'Will you take me to this agency you work for.'

36

The offices of the Montrose Academy were in a rambling apartment building in Greenwich Village. Lauren accompanied Vanessa as far as the reception area, then she disappeared and left her.

'It's better that you meet Lila on your own the first time,' she said reassuringly. 'I've told her all about you and she knows you're coming so there's nothing to be worried about.'

Vanessa took a seat on the leather sofa running the length of the room and took stock of her surroundings. At first glance the place reminded her of an advertising agency or a chic photographic studio. The central area was dominated by a long marble reception desk behind which sat a golden-skinned Eurasian girl. Like Lauren, she was expensively dressed in the latest fashions and she wore a lot of gold jewellery. There was nothing tacky about her, though. She didn't look like a whore and Vanessa thought she was probably just what she appeared. A well paid receptionist.

She glanced down at the table in front of her. On it was an enormous leather bound volume. Out of curiosity, Vanessa picked it up and discovered it was a book of photographs. Each page held a different girl in several poses. For a moment, Vanessa was reminded of her modelling days. Then she looked at the pictures again and realized these girls weren't into fashion. The commodity they were selling was their bodies: in bathing suits, in lacy underwear and *au naturel.* Just to be sure the customers knew what they were getting, the girl's name, vital statistics, interests and occupation were listed at the top.

The receptionist called out Vanessa's name and she put down the book.

'While you're waiting for Lila,' she told her, 'you might like to look at this contract.'

The document she handed over asked for Vanessa's personal details. It also requested that she write down her interests, job aspirations and the names of three professional people who would vouch for her. Vanessa concealed a smile.

These people want a filing clerk, she thought, not a hooker. She put the contract on the table next to the book of photographs, folded her hands in her lap and tried to imagine what Lila looked like.

The name itself conjured up a million exotic pictures. Lila was a full bosomed European with black hair and wicked red lipstick. Vanessa had seen women like that in Hollywood movies. Then she laughed at herself for being naive. That kind of woman went out with the Ark. The Lila she'd be dealing with was probably more on the lines of a high-powered career woman. Someone who went with the glitzy office and the leather-bound photo album.

'You've got to be Vanessa,' said a voice at her elbow. 'You've no idea how glad I am to see you.'

The voice was Brooklyn Heights, low and husky and full of laughter. Vanessa looked up to see a homely fat woman of about fifty standing over her. If she hadn't been where she was, she would have taken her for the owner of a delicatessen.

The woman extended a hand. 'I'm Lila,' she said warmly. 'Why don't you come through with me to my office?'

With a certain disbelief, Vanessa followed the stout

woman through an archway and down a corridor until they came to the place where the work of the agency was done.

There was another, younger woman there operating what looked like a small switchboard. There were two desks next to each other, a filing cabinet and, to one end of the office, a small cubicle with a curtain across it. Lila indicated that Vanessa should go into the cubicle. The next thing she asked her took her breath away.

'Take all your clothes off,' she said.

Vanessa stood rooted to the spot.

'Why do you want me to do that?'

'Two reasons,' said the woman briskly. 'I want to know if you're on drugs. If you are, I'll soon see the track marks. The other reason is your marketability. If I'm selling your body, I want to know what I'm selling. A tattoo in the wrong place could affect your price.'

Her matter-of-factness was like a slap in the face. That and her ordinary appearance. With Lauren in the sushi bar the whole thing had seemed like a big adventure. A fun, slightly way-out way of earning extra pin-money. Lila was bringing the thing down to basics and it made Vanessa feel uncomfortable. With an effort she pulled herself together. If I feel queasy about taking my dress off in front of my agent, she reasoned, how am I going to be with a client?

She got out of her things as if she was getting undressed for the doctor. Then when she had done, Lila asked her to come across the office to the desk. There, the older woman turned the glare of a lamp full on to Vanessa. After a few minutes she seemed satisfied.

'You can go and get dressed,' she said. 'Then come back and sit down. We need to talk.'

Vanessa did as she was asked, yet she still felt uncomfortable. It should have been easier than this. She wasn't just any street girl looking to sell her wares. She was an English lady from a classy background. Only a few years ago, she had been a top model with her face on all the billboards. She shook her head. Why was Lila treating her like a piece of meat? She went back to the desk, her mind made up. She was going to get some straight answers out of this bordello keeper, or she was going to walk out. Before Lila could say anything Vanessa went on the attack.

'Exactly what is this all about,' she demanded. 'I didn't come here for the third degree. I came to work as a call girl.'

The older woman tried to look patient. 'I know all that,' she said, 'and with the right help you'll make a very good call girl.'

Vanessa wasn't going to be fobbed off. This woman was clearly trying to pull the wool over her eyes. What help could she possibly need for a job like this? She said as much to Lila and the fat woman started to laugh.

'Let me ask you something,' she said. 'What do you imagine you say to a client when you first meet him?'

Vanessa looked at her as if she was mad.

'I'd ask him if he wanted to get comfortable, or if he needed a drink?'

'Then you'd be a damn fool. The first thing you ask any man you're doing business with is to see his ID. In this game any one of your clients could be a cop. There are hundreds of them out there just looking to make an arrest. So you before you say anything or do anything, you get a good look at his papers. If you can, you check credit cards, driving licences, even a dog licence if he has one. And if the guy on the papers doesn't tally with the guy standing in front of you, then you call me fast.'

While she was talking Vanessa visibly deflated. One minute she was poised and in control of herself, the next she looked stricken.

'Is it always this risky?' she asked. For the first time since they met, Lila smiled, and to her surprise, Vanessa saw real warmth.

'If you're working for another agency, the answer is usually yes,' she told her. 'But I take more care.'

For the next half hour Lila told her how far she would go to protect her if she went on her books. Lila would cross-question all the clients. What city was the gentleman from? What hotel was he staying in? What room number?

As a rule Lila didn't send any of her girls outside Manhattan and she made sure most of her clients were regulars. Even then, she ran a check on their addresses and phone numbers. As an added precaution Lila promised she would never be out of contact with her when she was working.

'Before you get to see the client, I want you to check in with me. Then when you arrive call again. That way I'll know the ID's in order and exactly where you are. I'll be expecting a final call when you leave, and if I don't hear I'll know you're in trouble and start making my own enquiries.'

Vanessa was intrigued. 'What on earth can you do if something does go wrong?'

Lila made a steeple of her fingers, resting her chin on the top.

'Plenty,' she said. 'Most of the hotels and apartment buildings you go to will have porters and security men on duty. Believe me, they don't want trouble. If I come on and say there could be a problem with one of my girls, they go into action pretty fast.'

The older woman paused for a moment and rummaged around in her desk drawer. Finally she brought out a battered packet of cigarettes and offered one to Vanessa. Then she took one herself, and lit it before she continued.

'Look,' she said, 'there are a lot of bad things about this business, but there are a lot of good things too.

'You get to eat in some of the finest restaurants in the city and a lot of the men are generous. You saw Lauren's sable and that's not all she's got. I know this sounds crazy, but you get to be your own boss. I don't know whether you've been married, but I'd like to bet you've been dependent on some man or other for everything you have. You want to eat, you want a new dress, a roof over your head, then you have to ask nicely. And if you're really good then you're allowed to have these things. I'm not saying this is a wonderful job, but at least you never have to ask anyone for charity. The men you sleep with pay you for it. They give you a hundred dollars for an hour of your time, and they give me another hundred dollars for arranging it. You don't have to sleep with anyone you don't like the look of, and you don't have to do anything you don't choose to do.'

Vanessa drew on her cigarette and looked doubtful.

'I thought men went to call girls for something different. Kinky sex, you know what I mean.'

'Sure I know what you mean,' Lila looked at her appraisingly. 'If you want to make real money out of this job, you'll learn to do all the extras. Lauren can show you most of the angles. Maybe she'll even do doubles with you.'

'By doubles, you mean two of us making it with each other?'

'Two of you making it with the clients, each other

– anything you damn well like. I don't make the rules, you do.

'The whole point about out-of-the-ordinary sex,' she went on, 'is that it takes a certain amount of time. If you mix it in with drugs like cocaine, it can take a great deal of time. Let me remind you, you charge by the hour. The more hours you can rack up, the more money you make.'

Talking to this woman, Vanessa decided, was like taking a cold shower. A shower that washed away all illusions, all hopes, all dreams. To Lila, the fact that she had been a top model counted for nothing. Nor did she care about her achievements or her identity.

'I want you to use a different name,' she told Vanessa. 'It doesn't pay to be too public in your line of business.'

So Vanessa became Cheri, and with the shedding of her name came the final transformation. She became anonymous. She was told that when she started working, anonymous was the base line from where she began. If a client wanted a sexy Latin type, Vanessa would be expected to don a black wig and dark lipstick. If he wanted a pocket Venus, she would go to the job in flat shoes. From now on she would be all things to all men and nothing to any of them.

At the end of an hour Lila looked her over.

'You know most of the facts now,' she said. 'The rest of your education you'll pick up when you're working. When do you want to start?'

So this is it, Vanessa thought. The hard work. The final clincher. When do I want to start? It crossed her mind that she still had time to get out. She could say that she had cold feet, was frightened of being arrested, didn't want any weirdos beating up on her. But she didn't. Because the bottom line was that she'd had it with men. When she was younger she'd let them exploit her because she didn't know any better. Now the calluses had formed on her soul. I'm coming up for thirty-eight, she thought. Nobody wants to keep me except for Ted, and he can't afford me. This is the only option I have left.

For a moment Vanessa thought about her daughter. Freddie was in high school, dreaming of becoming a writer. Will she have to know how I keep a roof over our heads, Vanessa wondered. She's known all along I wasn't married to her father. She's aware I live off men, but can I tell her about this latest development?

She imagined herself going through the motions. 'Darling, I've got something to tell you. I've started a new job as a call girl.'

I can't do it, she thought. I've still got some pride, some self-respect. Then she hit on a solution. She didn't have to go into details about her job. All she had to say to her daughter was that she'd found a job in a fashion house. Freddie wasn't interested in anything except her studies these days. As long as Vanessa didn't bring clients home to the new apartment she would be renting, nobody need be any the wiser about what she did. Particularly if she wasn't even working under her real name.

She took hold of Lila's pack of cigarettes and helped herself. Then she turned to her new employer.

'I'd like to start work as soon as possible,' she told her. 'All I need is a few days to get my personal life sorted out.'

Lauren was waiting for her when she came out into the reception area. She was talking to the girl behind the desk, kidding around with her as if they had been pals for a long time and it made Vanessa feel uneasy.

She knew what Lauren did now. Really did.

Kidding about it didn't seem right. She headed for the door and Lauren was right there with her.

'How did it go?' she asked. 'Did you decide to go ahead?'

Vanessa nodded.

'I have to get one or two things straight though, like how I'm going to live and where I'm going to live. I don't expect Ted to go along with any of this. If he knew about it, he'd probably scream blue murder.'

The other girl looked her up and down. It was as if she was measuring her, assessing her for some task ahead.

'So you really are serious,' she said. 'Maybe I can help you.'

Vanessa remembered what Lila had told her. Lauren was looking for someone to do 'doubles'. So this was how it started. She returned the blonde's look with a stare of her own.

'Maybe we can help each other,' was all Vanessa said.

It was late afternoon when they got out on to the sidewalk. Ted wouldn't be home for another two or three hours. She decided to use the time to talk frankly with this new friend of hers. There was a bar on the corner of the block, a shabby affair which catered for the local artists and bohemians. The women stopped off there and had a beer.

To look at they could have been a couple of secretaries on the way home from the office. It was early spring and they were wearing jeans and open-necked shirts. Lauren had left her make-up off that day and it made her look fresh and slightly vulnerable. Who would have thought it, Vanessa mused, who would have imagined that this kid turned the kind of tricks she could go to prison for?

She took a swig of her drink, frowning slightly. Her companion looked concerned.

'Is something bothering you?'

Vanessa put her beer on the table in front of them.

'I'm having a tough time working out how to get started. You see I don't have any savings. Ted took the last of my money to pay the rent. If I move out on him, I've got nowhere to stay.'

Lauren smiled.

'I've been thinking about that. You could move in with me until you get on your feet.'

'It's not that simple,' Vanessa said. 'I have a daughter in high school. I don't want her to be mixed up with all this.'

'Then you have to start learning how to tell lies.'

The way Lauren said it was entirely matter-of-fact. Lying was part of the package. You lied about your name, you wore wigs and lied about your hair colour. Most of the time you lied about what you did. Vanessa turned to her companian.

'What kind of lies?' she asked.

Lauren considered.

'First you have to fix Ted,' she said. 'It will take you about a month to get together enough money for a down-payment on an apartment. So move in with me and tell lover boy you're going home to see your parents. He'll never know any different, as long as you stay out of his way.'

It's a good plan, Vanessa thought. Going home to London could easily take a month. Even longer. Then I can send for Freddie when I have a place of my own. She nodded her approval.

'I like it,' she said. 'I think Ted will buy it.'

'Good, then I can start making plans too. I work out of my apartment as well as using the agency. I see three or four private clients regularly and I could use some help.'

Vanessa smiled. Now she'll talk about doubles, she reasoned. She's been leading up to it for long enough.

Because she needed the money, she decided to make things easier for Lauren.

'I'll go along with anything you have in mind,' she told her. 'But you've got to remember I haven't done this before. You'll have to educate me.'

Lauren gave her the shrewd appraising look she had used earlier.

'I already figured on that,' she told her.

Lauren's apartment was in an exclusive block where the porter announced the visitors before they were allowed to go up in the elevator. It had two bedrooms, a big living area with a bar at one end of it, and a tiny cramped kitchenette.

'Don't worry about the cooking facilities,' Lauren told her. 'Food is the last thing you have to provide.'

Vanessa took the point. This was not the kind of place designed for a wife or a mother. Everything was in pastel shades: the thick fitted carpet; the velvet covered sofa; even Lauren's talked-about collection of original art was in tactful, muted shades. It was as if the place extended arms towards you as you walked through the door. Arms that wrapped themselves around you and didn't let go until it was time to leave.

'You have to think like a Geisha girl,' Lauren explained. 'Guys come here to be pampered. Sex is part of the pampering, but there have to be other things as well. My clients have to believe I'm putting on the ritz for them. They get chipped china and paper towels at home. When they come here, all they get is spoiled.'

It was an illusion of course, and like everything else in this new profession, it was tacky. There were crystal glasses to pour the cocktails into, but only two crystal glasses. If the client wanted tea and a dainty snack there was a bone china set of plates, cup and saucer, but just one set. There were two place settings of silver, two linen napkins, one set of bath towels.

Receiving a client was a bit like putting on a piece of theatre. Lauren would get out bottles of the most expensive colognes and put them in the shower. She'd make the bed up with satin sheets. Then she'd change into French lingerie. When the man walked in the door, it was a bit like the curtain going up on a Broadway show, and it was this fakery that made the whole thing possible for Vanessa.

If she convinced herself that what was happening wasn't real, that everything she did was just play-acting she could get through it. Lauren knew she was nervous, so she made things easy.

She told one of her regulars she had a cold and would he mind seeing her room-mate?

The guy didn't object and they both heaved a sigh of relief.

'Once you do this thing,' Lauren said, 'you'll feel differently about selling yourself. It's a bit like learning to swim. You have to know you won't drown if you take your foot off the bottom.'

Lauren's regular client, Budd, was a public relations executive for a broadcasting company. He was tall, thin and very bland-looking. Vanessa could imagine him taking the press out to dinner and sweet-talking them into giving him a puff for one of his programmes. His manners bore out her first impressions. When she led him across to the tiny bar and offered him a drink, he insisted on mixing Martinis for them both.

What on earth is this guy doing here, she asked herself. He could get any girl into bed without even trying. There must be hundreds of secretaries working in his building who'd jump at the chance.

She leaned up against the bar and did her best to concentrate on what Budd was saying. He was talking about a new documentary series he was promoting and in the normal way of things she would have been fascinated. Now she hardly heard a word. She was too busy thinking about herself and the way she looked.

Lauren had sent her out to get her hair styled and her sleek honey bob fell in rigid waves to her shoulders. The make-up echoed the mood of the hair: thick and bright and come-hither. It wasn't the make-up that bothered her, though. It was the way she was dressed, or rather, undressed.

She was wearing a black garter belt with black sheer stockings, five-inch heels and a lacy peignoir that hid nothing. If Budd ever stopped talking about his job, he would notice that her breasts were bare and she wasn't wearing any pants. She knew it was ridiculous, but she felt somehow ashamed to be standing here like this. She was in somebody's drawing room, making small talk with a thirty-five-year-old businessman. If she had been lying on a bed naked, it would have been different. But she wasn't. She was going through the motions of being a lady and she wished the ground would open up and swallow her alive.

Surreptitiously she glanced at her watch. They had been standing here for ten minutes now. That meant there were fifty minutes to go. Fifty minutes to fill. She wondered how long he would go on holding forth about programme making.

Budd held on to the subject for what seemed like

another half hour, but was in reality about five minutes. Then he put down his glass and asked her to open her negligée.

'Do you want to go into the bedroom?' Vanessa asked.

He shook his head. 'Stay where you are,' he instructed. 'I just want to get a look at you.'

She undid the fastener at her neck and the lace parted, displaying her breasts. The sight seemed to please Budd, for he reached across the bar and started playing with her nipples.

For some obscure reason it turned Vanessa on. She was selling herself to this Ivy League man, using her body as a business transaction, yet the sight of him caressing her aroused her. Her nipples started to harden, and as they did his hand travelled down her body until his fingers found the place between her legs. Vanessa felt herself respond to his touch and Budd caught her excitement and moved in closer.

Then the strangest thing happened. He started to kiss her. In all the stories she had heard about tarts, Vanessa knew they didn't go in for intimacies or shows of affection. For a moment she didn't know what to do. Then she thought, to hell with it, what difference does it make if I enjoy this? The man isn't going to take it out of my fee.

She returned his kisses and when he moved her over to the couch she didn't protest. Instead she let him remove the lacy dressing-gown, unhook the garter belt and peel down her stockings. Before she abandoned herself completely, she glanced at her watch. There were thirty-five minutes left. Things seemed to be going to some sort of plan.

She decided to help Budd off with his clothes. They were coming to the stage when the foreplay had to lead to something else, yet he seemed strangely shy.

He parted with his jacket, his trousers, his shirt, but he hung on like grim death to his boxer shorts. Vanessa gave a mental shrug. If that's what he wants, she thought, who am I to complain?

In a little while, when Budd had kissed her all over, he finally suggested going into the bedroom.

She showed him through to the spare room where Lauren had prepared the bed. In place of the everyday striped cotton, there were pale peach satin sheets. The air had been sprayed with a sweet, lingering perfume and the lights were turned down low.

At last, Vanessa thought, I get to earn my living. She lay on the bed and pulled Budd down on top of her. Once more, she felt his hands on her body and she arched her back in anticipation. Then she saw him. If he hadn't been who he was, if he had been a date or a boyfriend, she would have laughed. As it was she had trouble controlling her expression. For now she could see why Budd had to pay for his sex. He had the smallest penis she had ever seen. It wasn't underdeveloped looking, or even short. It was tiny, like a pencil stub.

She wondered if she was meant to notice his deficiency. Were there allowances she had to make? Services she was required to perform? Then she thought, that can't be so. Lauren would have told me if I had to do anything out of the ordinary.

Cautiously, Vanessa parted her legs, then she kissed and stroked Budd's body as if he really was her lover and there was nothing about him that was wrong. He reacted by climbing astride her and going through the motions of love. It was over very quickly and Vanessa hardly felt a thing. Afterwards Budd was very tender with her as if she was someone special.

When he was in the shower, she looked at her watch for the final time. There were ten minutes left on the clock and that made her feel sad for she knew Budd would never use the time.

What's happening to me, she wondered. I've just made love to a freak for a hundred dollars and here I am feeling sorry for him.

37

After Budd, Vanessa felt easier about going to Lila for work. She could do the job. She wasn't an expert, she knew she had a great deal to learn, but she had crossed the line that separated the professional from the inspired amateur. She could rent her body out for money and not feel guilty about it. At least that's what she told herself.

Lila sent Vanessa on half a dozen calls around town. She visited a Wall Street broker who didn't have time to cultivate a social life, a much married dentist who wanted sex without complications, a lawyer with a withered leg. All her assignations lasted around an hour. They were clinical, predictable and she had no complaints from anyone. At the end of her first week she had made six hundred dollars. The down payment on a decent apartment was going to cost her several thousand dollars. She wondered where she was going wrong.

'I need to earn more money,' she told Lila. 'Can you keep me busier?'

Her agent looked doubtful.

'If you were younger, say in your twenties, I could give you twice as much work but straight guys don't go for women your age. Not as a rule, anyway.'

'Are you telling me I have to do something kinky before I can fill my dance card?'

Lila thought for a moment before answering the question. Then she got out a cigarette and lit it.

'I wish I could say no, but I'd be lying. Most men

who go to hookers are looking for something they can't get at home. That means something younger and fresher than their wives, which you're not. Or someone who offers something special. I haven't sent you out on any of those jobs, because frankly I thought you weren't up to it. Lauren told me a bit about your background. Then I talked to you myself, and to be honest I nearly didn't take you on. There's no place in this business for ladies with feelings, and that's what you are, sweetheart. A nice, refined, well-behaved lady. When I asked you to take your clothes off, you nearly jumped out of your skin. Then when I mentioned you might use drugs – I thought you would walk out on me.' Vanessa bit her lip.

'You think I'm not tough enough. Is that what it is?'

The older woman nodded.

'I can't see you with a sadist or a cross-dresser or a guy who likes being beaten. Those feelings of yours would get in the way. How can I be sure you wouldn't lose your temper and scream rape if one of my clients wanted to do something unorthodox?'

Vanessa started to get irritated. She had done everything that had been asked of her.

She'd broken every convention she'd been taught, and now this fat, middle-aged madame was telling her it wasn't enough. She wasn't up to the job.

To hell with her she thought. Grabbing hold of her carry-all, she made ready to leave.

'I'm sorry things haven't worked out,' she said with regret. 'I guess I'll have to go and find myself another agent. One with more faith in my abilities.'

Lila's expression didn't change but she sat up straighter behind her desk.

'Don't go,' she said. 'Not without talking some more. Maybe I misjudged you.'

Vanessa did her best not to smile. You bet you misjudged me, she thought. Aloud she said, 'You were telling me you weren't sure if I could deal with cross-dressers and all the other crazies. Well there's one sure way of finding out. Let me do a double with Lauren.'

Lila seemed to like the idea for she softened. 'It could work,' she said. 'Lauren knows all the routines, so she can show you what to do, and she'll be there in case you lose your nerve.'

Vanessa looked at the woman sitting in front of her. The hard-bitten Brooklyn professional who doubted her resolve, her sheer desperation to escape from the financial trap she'd dug herself into.

'I won't lose my nerve,' she told her.

When Lauren heard about Vanessa's conversation with Lila, she came up with the perfect solution. His name was Burt Hamlyn, and he had a whole shopping bag of vices that needed to be catered to. He was a masochist, a fetishist, a cross-dresser and he loved his wife. He managed to reconcile these different needs by letting a professional take care of his fantasies. Lauren had been seeing him for two years. Sometimes in the company of another of Lila's girls, sometimes alone. The next time he called Lila explained to him she had a new girl she was trying out, could Lauren bring her along? Burt liked the idea and a deal was struck. They were to meet him in his suite at the Plaza Hotel. The fee for both of them was to be the usual hundred dollars an hour – with the proviso there was no limit on the time, they were at his disposal all evening. He would go on paying as long as they could keep him entertained.

The women arrived at the hotel at seven o'clock,

smartly but conservatively dressed. Lauren was wearing a black suit with a Hermès scarf knotted around her neck, Vanessa a mink thrown over a knitted dress. To the unpractised eye, they could have been a couple of women executives coming to the hotel for a drink or a meeting. The doorman knew otherwise, for there was one thing that gave both of them away: their hand luggage.

Both women carried heavy shoulder bags. The sort of thing a model girl humps from studio to studio, except the contents of Lauren's would have blown any photographer's mind. Her basic equipment consisted of a credit card printer, a few changes of sexy lingerie, several pairs of stockings, a vibrator, a spare washcloth and towel, two pairs of shoes, condoms, a wig, a diaphragm, a blindfold, a savage looking whip and a ping-pong paddle.

If either woman had been a model they would have been wearing jeans and they would have looked as if they were in a hurry. They would also have been considerably younger. The doorman of the Plaza knew this. He also knew Lauren and as they walked in he stopped her.

'Where are you going?' he asked her.

She didn't break step.

'The suite on the twelfth floor. We're expected.'

The man nodded. 'Just checking,' he said.

This was the first time Vanessa had been stopped going into a hotel and she felt a moment of panic.

She had lived in this town for years. She had friends here. She thought about Dan and the power of his family. She thought about her daughter, Freddie. I won't be able to walk into any hotel ever again without being recognized, she realized. Soon it will become known what work I do.

She considered the implications of this, then she

gave a mental shrug. None of her so-called friends were prepared to help her out financially. Dan wasn't paying bills. The only person that really mattered was Freddie, and her daughter was too young to visit grand hotels. By the time Freddie started getting around, she hoped she wouldn't be working as a hooker any longer.

As they got out of the elevator, Vanessa began to wonder about the man they were spending the evening with. Lauren had told her he was a cross-dresser and she dredged her memory for images of all the transvestites she had encountered. They were few and far between. The only men she had seen dressed up in women's clothes were pantomime dames or variety acts. She imagined Burt to be lean and camp-looking, so when he answered the door of the suite, she did a double take.

Burt had muscles. He was big and heavy with the shoulders of a baseball player and for a moment she wondered if they had come to the right place. Then Burt greeted Lauren like a long lost friend and she knew they were expected. The drawing-room of the suite reminded Vanessa of a miniature version of Dan's apartment, for no expense had been spared. The bookcase looked like a genuine antique. Some of the little gilt tables had to be Louis Quinze. And everywhere she looked there were fresh flowers. Glamorous out-of-season blooms, orchids and jasmine and lily of the valley.

Burt caught her expression and smiled.

'I keep this place on permanent loan,' he explained. 'My company uses it for entertaining.'

'It must be a huge corporation,' she ventured, nervously.

The big man nodded. 'How else do you think I could afford to spend my time with you?'

The response jarred Vanessa. Here, amongst the luxury and opulence of the Plaza, she wasn't prepared for rudeness. Then she checked her emotions. Quite soon a lot of other things she wasn't prepared for were going to take place. She needed to be ready.

Burt lumbered over to the drinks cabinet and brought out a bottle of champagne, then he popped the cork and filled three flutes. It was a signal for the party to begin and Lauren started to unpack her bag. Vanessa noticed she had come prepared for the session for she seemed to be carrying half a dozen pairs of shoes. They weren't the usual things she wore, they were too vulgar for that. They were very high heeled and most of them had ankle straps. But what really struck Vanessa as outlandish was what they were made of. There was a pair in red patent leather, another in black vinyl and even a pair of white suede. When Burt saw them, something seemed to happen to him. It was as if an invisible wire inside him had tightened and he looked tense and predatory. He shoved the glass of champagne he was drinking onto one of the little polished wood tables and moved across the room to where Lauren was sitting. When he got there he sank to his knees in front of her.

The next thing he did surprised Vanessa. He started kissing Lauren's toes. The big man kept putting the tarty shoes on her feet, kissing the fronts of them, then taking them off.

This went on for half an hour or so, then Burt got up and went over to the sofa where he had a Bloomingdales shopping bag. Out of it he took the biggest pair of shoes Vanessa had ever seen. They were the same sort of things he had been putting on Lauren, except they were three times the size. He gazed at them looking dreamy.

'My turn,' he said.

He disappeared into the adjoining bedroom and Vanessa went and sat down beside her friend.

'What happens now?' she asked.

Lauren got up. 'We all get undressed,' she said.

Both girls donned garter belts and stockings and Vanessa threw a sheer negligée on as well. The act of changing made her feel better. All the jobs she had done so far required her to put on tacky lingerie. It was almost like a uniform, and with her working apparel she put on her hooker's identity. Nothing could shock her now. No act, however obscene, could move her or touch her. She was protected by her new persona.

Vanessa expected Burt to walk back into the room when he was changed, but he didn't. Instead he called out to Lauren.

'Are you ready for me, Mistress?' he asked.

'Why does he call you Mistress?' Vanessa whispered.

Lauren tried to look patient.

'You'll see,' she said.

Vanessa had thought getting into costume had prepared her for Burt, but she had been wrong. When he finally made his entrance she gasped involuntarily. He's grotesque, she thought. Grotesque and scary at the same time. The worst thing about it was he was so hairy. He had thick vast legs covered in black down, like a gorilla. Over them he had stretched sheer stockings which he had fastened to a garter belt. Underneath all that were lace panties like the ones Vanessa was wearing, but through Burt's was the bulge of a penis.

Vanessa's first instinct was to run, to grab hold of her fur coat and make for the door. Yet she stayed exactly where she was. This situation required self-discipline of the kind she was only just beginning to learn. She inhaled the centrally-heated air of the Plaza and forced herself to be calm.

None of this is real, she told herself. It's a fantasy created just for this moment. When it's over, I can wipe it out of my memory and go on with my life.

Lauren caught her attention. She was going through an elaborate flattery routine. She told Burt the whole time how wonderful he looked. How sexy. How desirable. Vanessa wondered if she should join in. Then she decided not to.

Lauren seemed to be going through some kind of prepared ritual. Vanessa had a hunch the other girl recited the same lines each time she entertained this client. To break in on her now might put her off. As she was thinking this, Lauren changed her tack.

Now instead of flattering the dresser, she started to berate him.

'You've been a bad boy,' she intoned. 'A naughty, wicked boy. I'm going to have to punish you.'

Burt seemed to brighten visibly at the prospect, and Vanessa couldn't help thinking how silly he looked in his fancy dress. All the female impersonators she had seen made some attempt to look like women. This man looked like nothing she had ever encountered.

Lauren went on with her scolding and gradually the ritual began to make some kind of sense. It worked on buzz words. Punishment, wicked, pathetic little worm. With each insult, Burt would say, 'Yes, Mistress,' in a certain tone of voice, and Vanessa suspected they were both working up to some sort of finale. She was right. At a given signal from Lauren, the big man bent over the bed, so that his backside faced them.

Lauren grabbed hold of a hairbrush with one hand. With the other she pulled down the lace pants. Then she started laying into him. She hit both cheeks with the back of the brush, calling Burt names as she did so. After a bit she turned to Vanessa.

'Now you try,' she said.

At that moment Vanessa wished she'd had more to drink. I need my edges blurring for this, she thought. I need to be stoned out of my mind. Once more she breathed deeply on the scented, fetid air. Next time, she promised herself, I'll take something before I start this nonsense.

She took the brush out of Lauren's hand and imitated what she had been doing. She deliberately kept her touch light, but as the man in front of her groaned and started playing with himself something in her snapped.

'You scum,' she said, revolted now. 'You dirty, despicable piece of garbage.'

She brought the brush down harder, slamming it against the flesh. It was as if she was possessed by a demon who wanted to hurt, to kill, to revenge itself on every man who ever tried to use her.

He screamed out to her to stop, but she didn't hear him. Instead her rage continued unabated until she felt Lauren take hold of her and pull her away from the bed.

In that moment, her sanity returned. She saw, as if for the first time, the half-dressed man covered in the marks of her beating and she started to panic. I've killed him, she thought. Any minute now the hotel will call the police and they'll send me to the electric chair for murder. She looked up to see the other girl smiling.

'Who would have thought it?' she said. 'You're a natural. Lila will be pleased when I tell her.'

Now Vanessa was in total confusion. 'What are you saying?'

But before Lauren could answer their client was back on his feet and coming towards them. He had the biggest erection she had ever witnessed and the truth of the situation finally came home to her. She had been a success after all.

38

The code name for a cop was Gilda. If Vanessa had any doubts about a man she was visiting then she would call Lila.

As far as the cop was concerned she was just checking in with the modelling agency that sent her.

'Hello,' she would say, 'everything's fine here. By the way has Gilda been in today?'

The mention of the name would put Lila on full alert. One of her girls was in a hotel room with a member of the vice squad. It was her job to get her out without being arrested. Lila had a system she used on these occasions. They would carry on a normal sounding conversation. At least Vanessa's end sounded normal. Lila used the time to ask pertinent questions. If Vanessa answered her with a positive statement, it meant yes. Any negative, however outlandish, meant no. From this Lila could usually tell if her suspicions were founded. Then she would say, 'Okay, I've heard enough. Don't take any money and get out of the room.'

The system saved Vanessa's skin twice in her first few weeks. She prayed she wouldn't need it again for a long time.

Yet she didn't feel unsafe. The Montrose Academy looked after its girls. In a dangerous game, working for Lila was like working with an insurance policy. And it paid.

After five weeks Vanessa was able to move out of Lauren's duplex and take an apartment of her own.

She chose a converted loft in Soho because of the space it offered, and because she liked the district.

A designer had lived there before her and the place was done out in minimalist modern: white walls, black boards and plain white blinds in the windows. The occupant was leaving to take a job in San Francisco, so he threw in the furniture as part of the down-payment. Vanessa was glad of that. Now she was working full-time she had little energy left to browse around Bloomingdale's basement and the salerooms. The shiny black cubes that called themselves tables were hardly to her taste and she didn't understand any of the modern pictures, but for the moment she could live with them. More to the point, Freddie could live with them.

If there was one consolation in Vanessa's life it was her daughter. When the going was tough, all she had to do was think of Freddie and she was able to get to the end of the day. Freddie was seventeen now. Nearly full-grown and with such promise, such ambition that listening to her made Vanessa's head spin. She started out wanting to be a writer. Now she had abandoned that plan in favour of something more arty. Freddie wanted to make her name as a painter and she haunted the galleries and museums searching for inspiration.

As soon as she saw their new apartment she fell in love with it. It was the pictures that did the trick. The chaos of colours and textures that so confused Vanessa made perfect sense to Freddie. She demanded to know where her mother had found them and when she confessed they were part of a job lot, Freddie roared with laughter.

'You've got to promise me,' she said, 'you won't tell anyone at work about this. The guys at the fashion house will think you've got no taste at all.'

Vanessa told Freddie she had found a job consulting

for a Seventh Avenue dress house. To avoid complications she told her daughter she worked from home and Freddie swallowed the story. If she had told her she was working as a high-wire artiste Freddie would have believed that as well, for she couldn't wait to move into their own home.

Ever since they'd moved out from Dan, Freddie had felt like a refugee, an unwanted guest. She had dealt with the situation by piling on the charm. She'd even behaved that way with her father, only she hadn't meant it then. Walking away from Dan was the hardest thing she'd ever done.

There were days when she wanted to pick up the phone to his office and ask to see him, but she didn't. If he wanted to see me, she reasoned, he'd call me. That's what men do. What fathers do.

On the days when she missed him, the days when he didn't call, Freddie would weep. She didn't share her tears with her mother or her friends at high school, though. She crept away into a corner and did her crying alone. She was nearly a woman now. Nearly a college girl at any rate. Her grief was her own damn business.

The day Freddie sat her scholarship exams for the Pratt, a funny thing happened. Instead of her mother waiting for her when she got to the apartment, she found her mother's friend, Lauren, instead.

Freddie didn't like Lauren. She was one of those pushy Manhattan women who cared too much for appearances, and too little for people. She was always carrying on about which restaurant you were meant to be seen in, and what designer labels you should be wearing. She never seemed to notice that all the poseurs she was so in love with had very little between their ears.

'Did you ever have a sensible conversation with one of your social X-rays,' Freddie would ask.

And Lauren would wave her hands about and look vague. She and her mother always changed the subject when Freddie asked about the parties they seemed to be going to, and she didn't press the point. To be honest, she wasn't all that interested in what they did when they went out.

All she wanted was to be left alone to look at pictures and go to her art classes. She was going to a class the night she found Lauren in the apartment, but the moment she set foot in the place she knew the plan was doomed. The woman had something to tell her, something important from the look of her. So she put the books she was carrying down on the hall table and went to find out what was up.

Lauren didn't get to the point immediately. She kept thinking of things to keep Freddie busy. First she wanted a cup of coffee, then she discovered she'd lost her lighter so Freddie had to go searching for matches. Then the room was too cold, so she had to turn up the heating. Finally she ran out of things for Freddie to do. So she sat down on one of the leather sofas and motioned to Freddie to come and join her.

'Your mother's in trouble,' she said without any preamble.

Freddie felt a stab of alarm. 'She's not sick, is she?'

Lauren made an attempt to brush a stray curl out of the girl's eyes. It was meant to be a motherly gesture to reassure her.

'There's nothing wrong with Vanessa,' she said nervously, 'she's a hundred per cent healthy.'

'So what is it?'

The older woman seemed to have trouble finding the right words to describe Vanessa's problem. In the end she decided to change tack.

'Did your mother ever tell you what she did for a living?' she asked Freddie.

Freddie began to feel impatient. Her mother was obviously in trouble and Lauren wanted to make small talk.

'Of course she told me,' she replied. 'She works in fashion, as a consultant or something. What's that to do with anything?'

Lauren sighed heavily. This wasn't going to be easy.

'Vanessa wasn't telling you the whole story,' she said at last. 'She may have done some sort of fashion thing as a sideline, but her main living came from another source.'

It struck Freddie that she didn't want to go on with this conversation. She knew without Lauren saying another word that whatever happened next was going to change her life, and she doubted whether it would be for the better.

'Are you saying my mother is involved in something criminal?'

Lauren shook her head.

'Not criminal exactly. Actually she works for an escort agency.'

Freddie thought she had misheard.

'You mean an advertising agency, don't you? Escort agencies are for hookers.'

The older woman's expression hardened. 'You heard right the first time.'

Just for an instant the whole of Freddie's life seemed to go into slow motion. And as it did she took a good look at the woman sitting in front of her. If her mother was working as a hooker, then Lauren had to be a hooker too, yet there was nothing about her that gave the game away. She looked like any other middle-aged style victim.

'You're in the same profession, aren't you? How come I didn't know?'

Lauren looked impatient. 'Why should you know? We don't wear a sign on our foreheads.'

Suddenly Freddie didn't want to go on with this. Her mother was working as a hooker. It made her feel sick, but she had to accept it. What was important right now was that she was in some kind of trouble.

'What's happened to my mother?' she asked sharply. 'Where is she?'

'Down at police headquarters,' Lauren replied. 'She was picked up in a hotel room a few hours ago. They're throwing the book at her.'

Suddenly Freddie felt very afraid. 'What is she being accused of?'

Lauren got up from the sofa and made to leave.

'Prostitution,' she replied, 'and drug trafficking. When they found her, she was carrying several ounces of cocaine.'

Vanessa sat on the hard wooden bench and counted the hours until morning. It was past midnight. In five or six hours she would be moved to the Criminal Court in the Bronx. That's what the cop on duty had told her.

The court. Her mind fastened on the distant goal ahead. Once she was there with a proper attorney to defend her she'd be out of here. Maybe not permanently out, but out on bail at least. It was something to look forward to.

She looked around the cramped police cell where they had locked her for the night. There were three other occupants. All foul mouthed. All prostitutes. She was surprised how cheery and relaxed they all were. It was as if this stinking hole with its smell of stale urine was one of the hazards of the job, one of the things a working girl had to put up with like the creeps and weirdos they had to service.

That's what I am, Vanessa thought. A working girl. I may not walk the streets, I may look more expensive, but when push comes to shove, I do the same job as the women I share this cell with.

She shuddered and pulled her pale cashmere knit around her shoulders. The jacket had set her back seven hundred dollars at Bonwit Teller but it did nothing to warm her. There was a dankness about the place that got through everything. The soft suede pants, the thousand dollar boots, the fine silk shirt. As long as Vanessa lived she would never forget the filth, the cold, the sheer misery of this night.

The girl sitting opposite her started to vomit. She was very thin and wired-up looking, and she had been telling dirty stories earlier. It was all a big joke to her then, but now the fun had gone out of the situation and her body registered its protest.

She didn't throw up in any orthodox way. When Vanessa was sick as a little girl, her mother taught her to use the sink or the lavatory. She knew she had to be neat about it.

But the girl opposite didn't have her upbringing. She ignored the bowl in the corner of the cell and used her lap instead. The sound of the retching attracted the attention of the sergeant on duty. When she saw the skinny hooker with vomit all over her, she muttered disapproval.

'Filthy little cow,' she grunted. 'Looking for a washing down are we?'

Five minutes later she came back with a rubber hose and turned a jet of icy water on the girl. She screamed and yowled throughout the drenching, and after it was over she sat in the corner of the cell shaking. But she wasn't sick any more, not until the sergeant had disappeared down the corridor.

Vanessa wondered how the hell she had come to this. She had always been careful when she went to meet a client. Lila had checked him out on the phone and she ran her own routines when she got to the hotel room, but this one had slipped through the net. He seemed exactly the guy he said he was. A business consultant in New York for a sales conference. His ID seemed fine.

When Vanessa asked him what he was selling he told her video systems. He knew about video systems too, or at least he appeared to know. He also knew about cocaine, but that was what Vanessa was there for.

In the beginning it didn't seem any different from hundreds of other jobs. Vanessa was driving down Second Avenue when Lila called her on the car phone and told her to get over to the Regent Hotel in Gramercy Park.

'On the way stop off at the office, and pick up a package I have for you. The guy wants to get high and he's going for the full cocktail.'

None of this fazed Vanessa. Once or twice a month Lila had a request like this. Doing drugs wasn't out of the ordinary in this line of business, it was simply part of the service.

She did as Lila instructed, the dope was waiting for her with the receptionist, so she stuffed it in her carry-all and set out for the Regent.

The hotel had a parking garage in the back and Vanessa left her Cadillac in the underground car park. There was something eerie about these places at night. The amber lighting bleached everything out and every sound she made – the car door slamming, her footsteps on the concrete floor – was amplified.

Vanessa shivered as she called the elevator to take her to the hotel lobby. The sooner she was in there the better.

When she arrived she went over to the hotel security man and told him where she was going and how long she would be staying. The guard wasn't there to judge her, or to arrest her. He was there to keep the peace and make sure nobody got murdered. He was there for her protection. How was she to know he was working with the cops that night?

The truth of the frame-up came to her too late. Vanessa had taken off her clothes and was standing in her black lace teddy when the man started asking questions. What drugs was she carrying? How much extra would she charge for them? When would they have sex, before or after they got high?

Vanessa walked into every one of them. She even went into a striptease routine, undoing the front of the teddy and playing with her nipples, just to get the guy horny, and he let her do all of it before he walked over to her and put the cuffs on her wrists.

She screamed at him for that. Called him every dirty name she could think of and he laughed in her face.

'All this sweet-talk is going to do, is get you an even longer jail sentence,' he told her firmly.

Then the reality of the situation hit Vanessa. She would be locked away for selling her body and peddling drugs. But I'm not peddling drugs, she thought. I brought the cocaine because somebody asked me to. I was working, acting on instructions.

Vanessa knew she was fooling herself. The policeman would stand up in court and say she was a pusher. He was already hanging on to her bag containing the dope. What other evidence did he need? As she struggled back into her clothes, she wondered if there was a way out of this. Would Lila defend her? No, she thought, Lila will disappear if she has any sense. She has a business to protect.

Then she thought about Lauren, and she started to hope. Lauren was her friend, her mentor, her partner in crime. The woman might not go on the stand for her, but at least she could find her a decent lawyer.

The policeman took out his walkie talkie and signalled to his accomplice in the street. He was on his way down with a prisoner.

Vanessa was taken to a precinct on the West side, bustling and busy with night people – muggers, prostitutes, a couple of guys who had been caught breaking into an office building. She waited her turn behind them. Finally she came face to face with the sergeant on duty. He looked her up and down with a certain curiosity, then he turned to the policeman who brought her in.

'What's she here for?'

The man looked smug. 'Drug peddling and prostitution. I caught her at it in the Regent.'

Vanessa thought about protesting but changed her mind. Nobody was going to listen to her here.

'I want to make a call,' she said. The sergeant nodded wearily indicating her cuffs be removed.

'What number do you want?'

She reeled off Lauren's flat number. While the policeman dialled she glanced at the clock above his head. It was nearly eight. There was just a chance she wouldn't be busy yet.

She was in luck. The man spoke into the phone then handed it across to her.

'Don't stay on longer than three minutes,' he told Vanessa. 'That's the limit.'

Lauren sounded concerned. 'Where are you speaking from? The guy on the phone sounded like a cop.'

Vanessa didn't mince her words. There wasn't time.

'He is. I was booked half an hour ago at the Regent.'

She heard Lauren's intake of breath.

'Did he find anything on you?'

'Just the stuff in my bag. Some goods I picked up on the way over to the hotel.'

There was a brief silence, while Vanessa looked desperately at the station clock and saw she had fifty seconds left.

'What do you want me to do?' Lauren asked.

'Just get me a lawyer,' Vanessa said as fast as she could. 'And make it someone good. They're taking me down to the Criminal Court in the morning.'

She didn't get to say any more. The desk sergeant reached over and snatched the phone out of her hand.

'Time's up, honey,' he said. 'Move along.'

A policewoman took Vanessa roughly by the elbow and manhandled her into one of the cells.

Then she was left to her own devices. Among her own kind. She settled herself as best she could on the hard wooden bench.

In the morning she was herded into the back of a police wagon and driven downtown to the Bronx. The Criminal Court Building was a cheap-looking modern block on the edge of a giant parking lot. It was raining when they got to it and Vanessa began to worry about her clothes. It wasn't out of vanity. She wasn't looking to impress anyone here. The worry went deeper than that. It was as if what she wore somehow defined her. In suede trousers and designer cashmere she was still a lady.

She wasn't prepared for the sheer brightness of the court room. Everything was made of pale wood, cheap and modern and tacky-looking. For a moment

Vanessa wondered if she really was in a court at all. Then the bailiff called her name.

'The People against Vanessa Grenville,' he said shortly. The full import of the situation came home to her.

Vanessa looked over the wooden partition to the rows of people sitting in front of her. Lauren was somewhere among them. Lauren and the man she had brought to defend her. To get her out of this place.

She concentrated her attention on the sea of faces. None of them looked like Lauren. Not even remotely. Vanessa felt the first stirrings of panic. What if she hadn't come? What if she couldn't find anyone who would take her case?

Someone prodded her from behind and she felt herself being moved towards the bench. She noticed the judge was a woman. Middle-aged and immaculate with steel-grey hair and half glasses. She reminded Vanessa of a headmistress she had had at school and she was suddenly aware of how dishevelled she must be looking. The expensive suede pants were baggy now and streaked with mud, and the silk shirt which Ralph Lauren had insisted would suit every occasion had gone yellow in the rain.

The judge turned to look at her, her expression impassive.

'How do you plead?'

She thinks I'm a whore, Vanessa thought. I can see it in her eyes. She's already condemned me as a drug-peddling whore.

Frantically she looked around the courtroom. To one side of her was the District Attorney, a tall, stooped man who bore the expression of a person who had seen it all before. She looked across to the other side of the room, expecting to see the man who was representing her. But there was no-one.

The judge repeated the question.
'How do you plead?'
She broke down now, her body heaving with despair.
'I didn't do it,' she sobbed. 'I didn't do anything to deserve this.'
The District Attorney was on his feet now.
'She's lying,' he said. 'This woman was arrested in the Regent Hotel after she'd taken off most of her clothes for the policeman here. If she wasn't hustling I'd like to know what she was doing.'
Vanessa tried to break in, but the judge silenced her.
'I'll come to you in a moment,' was all she said.
The DA continued with his indictment.
'When she was asked if she had drugs, she replied she was carrying marijuana and cocaine. She said she would charge extra for the coke. When her bag was searched later on the stuff was found in a package inside.'
There was a brief silence after that. Where can Lauren have got to, thought Vanessa desperately. Why isn't she here?
The DA approached the bench.
'The state requests that Vanessa Grenville be held for prostitution and selling drugs. We do not believe it will serve the interests of justice to allow this defendant to go free on bail.'
Now she knew she was finished. Lauren, the last hope she had, had let her down. There was no lawyer to let her out on bail. No-one on her side at all. She doubted if Lauren had bothered to tell anyone, even Lila, about her predicament. All she was now was another hooker on a drugs charge. They'd probably lock her away without even hearing her side of the story.

The woman judge interrupted her reverie.
'Do you have an attorney?'
For the first time that day she saw kindness in someone's eyes. Maybe I was wrong about her, she thought. Aloud she said, 'I thought I had a lawyer, but the friend who was meant to be arranging one isn't here.'
The woman sighed.
'I take it you can afford to pay an attorney.'
'Of course.'
'Fine, the court will appoint someone for you. Until then I'm afraid you'll have a short stay in jail.'
She turned back to the pile of papers in front of her.
'Next case please.'

39

There are a lot of things that people know without openly acknowledging them. Freddie had always known her mother was weak, but she preferred to think of her as vague, or slightly dotty. She loved her mother and she didn't like to put her down.

Freddie had realized her mother couldn't support herself either, but she had a whole raft of excuses for that one as well. Vanessa needed to be looked after by a man, she needed to be cosseted and cared for. The female in her demanded it.

Deep down Freddie knew this was a lot of rubbish. That was before they moved into the expensive new apartment. When that happened Freddie had to come up with a whole lot of new reasons for the change in her mother, but she couldn't do it. There was no way she could justify or explain how a former cover girl could land a job that would pay for the way they lived now.

In the beginning she didn't ask her mother too much about her new job. She was terrified of finding out too much about it, in case it was what she suspected it was. For Freddie, who was born and raised in Manhattan, could see the truth at all times. It was an impediment she had, like a limp or a bad case of myopia. Sometimes she wished she could believe in fairy tales, but it was no good. Try as she might, she didn't believe her mother could earn a vast amount money without a catch.

It didn't stop her from being shocked when Lauren

told her the truth though, yet she didn't have time to wallow in the emotion.

Her mother was in jail for selling her body and selling drugs as well. She had to find a way of getting her out. It was her first priority. After that she could fall apart.

She went to Lauren for help. She was her mother's best friend, after all. She didn't get very far. Whenever Freddie rang her she got the answering machine. In desperation, she went round to Lauren's apartment only to find she didn't live there any more. The janitor told her the apartment was vacant and there was no forwarding address.

Freddie rang the work number her mother had given her, but the woman who answered the phone said there was no record of anyone called Vanessa Grenville. After that she knew she was on her own. None of her friends at school would understand her mother's predicament. They might not stay her friends if she told them about it.

There was nowhere to go. No-one to run to. Except for one person. Dan. She hadn't seen him for over two years. Not since the time when she asked him to get Norman off their backs. She promised she wouldn't bother him again after that, and she would have kept her promise if this hadn't happened. Now she had no choice. She had to go to her father again. If she didn't her mother would perish through her own stupidity.

This time Freddie didn't go to her father's office. Hanging around in lift chutes was for little girls. She was grown-up now. Nearly eighteen. The least she deserved was lunch.

After all this time she hoped he'd think of somewhere half decent to take her. Dan didn't fail her.

He arranged to meet her upstairs in the 21 Club and Freddie felt honoured. Anyone could go in the downstairs bar and grill, but to use the upstairs room was special. You had to be very rich or very well-connected to get a table there. As she pondered on the meeting with her father, she felt a sudden stab of panic. What on earth was she going to wear? She had her schoolgirl skirts and navy blazers, but they would never do. Her weekend track suit and trainers wouldn't be right either. Then she had an idea. Her mother had clothes and they were both nearly the same size. Freddie was broader in the shoulders and fuller in the bosom, but from the waist downwards they could have been twins. She felt bad about it though. Vanessa never let her go near any of her things. In the old days it was because she didn't have much to call her own and she liked to keep her good things in reserve. Now her mother had more, but she still didn't encourage Freddie to borrow anything. She sighed. Beggars can't be choosers, she thought.

Freddie had never looked inside her mother's closets and now she felt like an intruder. It was as if a whole different personality was housed along these rails.

For opening the cupboards was like walking into a fashionable boutique. There were pant suits, skirt suits and leather suits, all by well-known designers. Freddie saw two fur coats, one fox, one mink, hanging side by side. A clutch of day dresses took up a good part of the cupboard and there was another closet just for evening clothes. Why all these outfits, she wondered. Why all this expensive glitz? Then she laughed at her own naivety. Mother was a hooker. A high-class hooker from the looks of it. The clients evidently expected her to look the part.

She started pulling things out and laying them on the bed and she was now less dazzled than before. Some of the dresses were gaudy, too low-cut. And there were too many cute little trimmings on the jackets. Freddie suddenly felt repelled. Everything in front of her had the stamp of luxury, yet she hated it all. She had a memory of her mother done up to the nines in a velvet and black lace suit she saw on a hanger. Freddie hadn't known it at the time, but Vanessa had probably been on her way out to meet one of her clients. Now the memory made sense.

No wonder she looked so glamorous, Freddie thought. She looked at the pile of clothes on the bed and she felt sad, for she knew she would never try on any of it. Instead she would meet her father in plain navy serge. She wouldn't turn any heads in the outfit she had in mind, but at least she would feel clean.

Freddie took the subway to the city, and walked down West 52nd Street until she got to the 21 Club. From the outside, the plate-glass double doors daunted her. Then told herself she was meeting her father. She had nothing to be frightened of.

Freddie gave the hem of her blazer a tug, put her head up and marched in. To her left she saw a bar full of middle-aged men in suits. There was a hum about the place, an excitement that reached out to her and beckoned her to join. But she knew this wasn't where she was meant to be. Her rendezvous lay at the top of the red-carpeted staircase in front of her. As she made her way to the restaurant, a waiter intercepted her. 'Could you tell me the name of the reservation?' he asked.

She repeated her father's name and the man's reaction confirmed everything she'd thought. In the 21 Club, Dan Levin was a king.

Freddie walked a little taller as she entered the opulent room. She had been taken to places like this when she was a little girl and the sea of starched white linen tablecloths brought back memories of childhood. She was approached by a second waiter.

'Mr Levin isn't here yet,' he told her, 'but I'll show you to his table, or would you like a glass of champagne in the bar?'

Freddie toyed with the idea of champagne. Nowadays she didn't have many treats and the thought of it, fizzing gently, slightly chilled, tempted her. She turned to say yes, but something stopped her. It was the thought of her mother. I'm not here for fun, she berated herself. I'm here to get help. Then she sat down at the table and waited for her father to arrive.

The moment he laid eyes on her, Dan thought he had seen a ghost, for the girl sitting in his regular spot in the corner of the restaurant was the image of Vanessa when she had first arrived in New York. Freddie had the same long neck, the same fine aristocratic face, the same clear blue stare. The tumble of curls was different of course, but kids today liked that style.

Dan stood and looked at her before crossing the room. It wasn't shyness that made Dan hesitate, it was curiosity. Is there anything of me in this girl at all, he wondered? A waiter came to the table to fill Freddie's glass and for some reason this seemed to irritate her. She waved him away with a brusque, almost rude gesture and as she did, her chin came up. This girl came from the streets of New York and she didn't care who knew it. She's my daughter after all, Dan thought. That kind of fight was bred out of Vanessa generations ago.

He hurried across to join his daughter. When he saw she was drinking water he looked dismayed.

'Surely after all these years we can do better than fizzy water.'

He beckoned the waiter across. Then, without consulting the wine list or his daughter, he ordered a bottle of vintage Bollinger.

When the waiter had gone, Freddie turned to him. 'I wish you hadn't done that,' she said softly.

Dan was mystified. 'I thought all girls liked champagne.'

'That's what the waiter said when he came to fill my glass. I'd been drinking water, and he asked me if I was ready for a grown up drink, as if there was something sissy and pathetic about not getting sozzled in the middle of the day. It's my decision as to what I drink. If I was a man you wouldn't have gone ahead and ordered like that.' Freddie sighed.

Dan leaned back in his chair and studied her for the second time that day. 'I thought you were tough the last time we met,' he observed. 'But this is silly. I know I haven't been the best father in the world, but I still look out for you and I still care for you. You know that, so stop treating me like an enemy.'

Without warning the tears welled up in Freddie's eyes. 'How am I meant to treat you? You never call me. You never come around and take me out the way you used to when I was little.'

The champagne arrived with two glasses. Dan looked at his daughter.

'Shall I have the waiter take yours away, or will you join me after all?'

Freddie nodded her acceptance and Dan continued with what he was saying.

'I don't call you and take you out because you're not a baby any more. You're a grown-up woman, and whatever your mother says I don't force myself on grown-up women. If you'd wanted to see me after our last get together you would have got in touch. I remember doing exactly what you asked me to do but you didn't thank me. You didn't even indicate I'd pleased you in any way. So I left you alone. I figured you'd be around next time you needed something, and I was right, wasn't I? You didn't ask me to take you out for lunch for old times' sake?'

Freddie felt ashamed. She had been angry with her father for years now. So angry that it had become a habit. 'If I'd said thank you for Norman,' she ventured warily, 'would we have been friends? I mean, would you have seen me now and then, or would you have worried about upsetting your wife?'

Dan looked at her steadily.

'Of course I would have seen you,' he told her. 'My wife doesn't dictate my choice of friends, or daughters. But you still haven't answered my question. Why did you call me after all this time? What do you want?'

Freddie put her head in her hands.

'Oh, Pop,' she said. 'I wish I didn't have to do this. I wish I didn't have to come begging for favours every time I see you.'

Dan went out to her then, pulling her gently upright until she faced him, ruffling his hand through the springy blonde curls.

'I'd rather you came to me for a favour, than not at all,' he told her. 'I do love you, you know.'

'Then you'll help me?'

'I expect so,' he grinned. 'If you tell me what it's about.'

She reached for her glass of champagne and took a deep swig.

'It's about Mom,' she said nervously. 'She's in jail.'

There was a brief silence.

'Christ Almighty,' Dan breathed. 'What's she done?'

Freddie debated whether or not to tell her father

the truth. She could just say Vanessa had been caught with cocaine on her. Cocaine she had been carrying for a friend. Then she thought, who am I kidding? The moment he hires a smart lawyer, he's going to find out anyway.

She sat up straighter in her chair.

'Mom was working for an escort agency when she was arrested. Apparently she was carrying drugs as well as doing the other thing.'

Freddie looked very young as she said it. Very young and very brave and very scared. From nowhere Dan was overwhelmed by a wave of love for her. Another girl would have run to him in hysterics the minute it had happened, but not Freddie. She'd bottled it all up, kept all the grief to herself, then when she'd got it under control, she'd come to him to negotiate terms. At her age he would have done exactly the same.

'I take it the whole thing came as a surprise,' he said gently. 'You didn't know what your mother was doing.'

Freddie shook her head miserably.

'I suspected something was up. I thought maybe there was some man, but not this. Not an escort girl for pity's sake.'

The waiter came to take their orders and after they'd decided what they wanted Dan turned to Freddie again.

'Have you told anyone else about this business?' he asked.

Once more Freddie shook her head.

'I thought about calling Grandma in England, but she's very frail now. I guess you don't know but Grandpa died last year. If Grandma knew about Mom it would be like another death in the family. I couldn't do it to her.'

Dan sighed. This daughter of his had a lot to carry on those slender shoulders. He paused for a moment, considering the options.

'Are there any friends?' he asked. 'Anyone in the city your mother's close to?'

'There was someone.' Freddie wrinkled her brow. 'I think Mom must have called her from the police station because she came straight to me and told me what had happened. Then when I tried to speak to her again, she'd disappeared. She'd left her apartment and gone away.'

'Do you know who she was? Or where she worked?'

Freddie looked depressed.

'Not really, though I think she did the same thing as Mom. They were always going off together in the evening, and if they were talking and I came into the room, they'd both go quiet and change the subject. Talk about dumb. How could I *not* know what was going on?'

As Freddie spoke her hands fluttered across the tablecloth, straightening the plates, rearranging the cutlery. They reminded Dan of a pair of nervous butterflies. When he could no longer stand it, he reached out and took hold of them.

'Stop agonizing,' he told Freddie. 'What's done is done. We can't change that. What we have to do now is help Vanessa. We're all she's got now. She's depending on us.'

40

After he and Freddie parted Dan walked the twenty blocks back to his office. It was a good walk and took him through the theatre district and across Times Square. On other days he might have worried that the expensive cut of his suit would be a magnet for muggers, but today there were other things on his mind.

A picture of Vanessa the last day he had seen her came back to him. Elegant, beautiful, totally dumb. How could I have let myself get so involved, he asked himself? I bought off all the other girls who got pregnant, sent them to exclusive clinics to get abortions. This one I had to take under my wing.

Then he remembered the menage they had in the early days. They had been close then, bound together by secrets and the love they had for each other. Dan had never seen his two sons being born, but his daughter had had his whole attention from the moment she struggled into the world.

'She's so beautiful,' Vanessa had marvelled, flushed and exhausted from giving birth. 'What shall we call her?'

Dan hadn't hesitated. 'I always wanted a son called Frederick,' he told her. 'I had a favourite uncle by that name.'

Vanessa had laughed when he said that. 'We'll call her Fredericka then. Freddie for short.'

We were so happy, Dan thought. The happiest couple in New York. Who would have thought that my mistress would end up on the streets? And my daughter, my Freddie, would grow up resenting me?

Dan had managed to knock some of the anger out of her over lunch but she still didn't trust him. It would take him years to repair all her broken dreams, but he wanted to do that for her because she was his daughter, with his fight and his cold, clear way of looking at the world.

Dan vowed to find a way of getting Vanessa off the hook. But as he took the decision, his heart sank, for he knew that if he got involved with her current troubles, Ruth was bound to find out. There would be reporters down at the courts and if Vanessa got the expensive help Dan could provide, somebody would notice her. Once that happened they'd remember who she was, and then it wouldn't be too hard to find out who was footing her bills.

Ruth'll divorce me, Dan thought. If the papers publicly link me with Vanessa, my wife will take me for everything I've got – or half of everything. She'll put the boys against me, she'll even put my father against me. If I'm not careful I could wind up on the street, too.

Christ, he thought, there must be someone apart from me, who can save Vanessa's skin. Then he had an idea. He was striding past Macy's when it hit him. The walk had taken Dan past the main window and it crossed his mind to check a couple of the departments out and see how his merchandise was doing. Then he suddenly remembered. Of course, he breathed. Why the hell didn't it come to me before? Vanessa has a blood-sister living in England. Dan's mind went back over seventeen years to the one and only time he had met Liz. It had been a disaster, of course. It couldn't have been anything else. Not under the circumstances.

Dan had been living with Vanessa six months when Liz came into town. She'd visited once before, but he hadn't been there that time and now Vanessa wanted to put things right.

'I want Liz to see with her own eyes how happy we are,' Vanessa had said. 'Then maybe she'll approve of what I'm doing.'

Dan remembered the confusion he felt, and the fury.

'She's not your mother,' he protested. 'From what you've told me, she's not even related to you. She's just some woman you shared an apartment with. Why should it matter what she thinks?'

But Vanessa wouldn't be swayed. This Liz, whoever she was, was the only important friend she had ever really had. The only friend since school, that was.

'She rescued me from an impossible situation, with an impossible man. If it hadn't been for Liz, I wouldn't be here with you today. Now she's in New York, I can't just ignore her.'

'I'm not asking you to cut her,' Dan yelled, exasperated, 'I'm just asking why you think it's so important that she meets me. You doubtless told her I'm married, so I'm not surprised she doesn't approve. Having dinner together isn't going to make things any better.'

Vanessa had burst into tears then. It was a ploy she generally fell back on when she couldn't win an argument. In the end Dan had agreed to take the two girls out to dinner. With any luck the English girl would be jet-lagged, so they wouldn't have to spend too long together.

Dan was known in the restaurant he'd chosen. It was the first place his father had taken him to when he was twenty-one and old enough to visit something more sophisticated than a chop house.

When he walked in the door of the restaurant on

East 50th Mr Soltner himself hurried forward to greet him.

'Who are the two beauties?' he enquired looking at Vanessa and Liz. Dan introduced them, making sure that Vanessa was presented as his top model, the girl who was to launch the new collection. This didn't go down well with Liz.

'Why didn't you say she was your girlfriend?' she asked snappishly. 'You are living together, aren't you?'

I'm also married and I'm also taking care of the bill tonight, Dan was tempted to say, but he didn't. He bit his tongue and suffered in silence.

The English girl had got on his nerves from the minute he set eyes on her. She was a looker, all right. You couldn't deny that. But she was too skinny for him, too intense and too clever by half. For the hundredth time he wondered what Vanessa had in common with her. How on earth could she understand someone so tough, so calculating when she herself had none of those qualities?

Dan sighed and looked at his watch. It was seven thirty. The evening stretched ahead of him, a minefield full of surprises and hidden traps. He walked up to the zinc-topped bar and ordered champagne for the three of them, hoping that a little wine would improve Liz's mood. It did nothing of the kind. It seemed as if Liz was looking for a fight, for nothing seemed to please her at all. The pint-sized bar room which Dan had always found so charming, she thought was poky. She dismissed the marble café tables and the posters of Paris round the walls as pretentious.

'Where I come from,' she said, 'we don't try to imitate a French atmosphere. We go there instead.'

Dan couldn't let that one go.

'It's not exactly difficult for you,' he observed, 'is

it? All you do is hop on a plane and you're there in an hour. You could hardly do the same thing from New York.'

Liz arched her eyebrows, instantly making him feel inferior.

'You mean you don't take your favourite models for little dinners in Paris now and then? I would have thought a man in your position would have been on to that in a flash.'

Then Vanessa had cut in. 'For heaven's sake stop it,' she begged. 'Can't you see you're making me unhappy.'

But once she had started nothing short of an earthquake was going to prevent Liz from speaking her mind. She turned to her friend and studied her pensively.

'I wish I could make you understand,' she said. 'You think you're unhappy because I don't admire Dan the way you do. Well that's nothing compared to how unhappy you're going to be if you insist on staying here. Can't you see what's happening to you? This man is turning you into a kept woman. One of those old-fashioned mistresses who eventually gets shoved into a corner. If this great new collection of his really takes off, you don't think he'll go on using you to promote it, do you? In a year or so, he'll bring in another model to show the clothes, or sell the perfume, or whatever. He has to. If you get too necessary to his business, you might just start calling the shots. You might just insist he divorces his wife. And that wouldn't suit his book at all.'

Dan stood up looking tense. 'I don't have to stay around and listen to this,' he said. 'Why don't you two go ahead and have dinner. Talk over old times, I'm sure you've got a lot of catching up to do.'

He turned to Vanessa. 'I'm going back to the

apartment. If you feel like seeing me again, that's where you'll find me.'

Then he swung round and headed for the door to the street.

He was busy hailing a cab when he heard her footsteps behind him. Her pregnancy was just beginning to show and she couldn't run very fast, but she was doing her best to catch up with him and he felt his heart go out to her.

'You changed your mind about dinner,' he said.

She nodded, tears in her eyes.

'There didn't seem any point if you weren't going to be there. After all, it's not as if she's my mother. Like you said, Liz is just some woman I used to share an apartment with.'

Liz called the next day to apologize.

'I meant every word I said,' she told Vanessa, 'but I shouldn't have gone on like that in front of Dan. It was unforgivable and I'm sorry. Blame it on the jet-lag.'

Vanessa accepted what Liz had said. They even had lunch together before Liz left town, but Dan knew things had changed between them. As long as the affair went on they would never really be friends again. Good riddance, he thought savagely. Who needs the rude bitch?

Now he did need her. He needed her bad. For she was the only other human being in the world apart from Freddie who gave a goddam for Vanessa. I've got to find Liz, he thought desperately. Wherever she is, I have to tell her what's happened. If she listens to me for one second, if she'll just give me the time of day, I'll go on my knees to get her here. I'll even pay her fare.

41

Liz fastened her seat belt and snuggled deeper into her mink coat. The air conditioning in first class nowadays was too fierce for comfort. She sighed. It had to be all the Japanese travelling across the Atlantic on corporate business. They needed the cabin to be cold and bracing so they could concentrate on their portable computers.

Bugger business, Liz thought, signalling to the stewardess for a final glass of champagne. Just living is taxing enough, without considering the demands of an office.

She thought about her husband and the routine she had erected around him. Since he had taken over the *Chronicle* things had changed. Their social calendar was more demanding. Now that David could influence public opinion, they were asked everywhere. Before, the gatherings they went to were strictly social: fundraisers, hunt balls, visits to the opera. There were political dinners of course, but David was never taken seriously on these occasions. With Lord Dearing's retirement all that had changed. David was the one who was sought out now and because of it, Liz finally had power. She didn't have to sneak stories into gossip columns to get attention any more. All she had to do was invite the people she wanted to impress to dinner or drinks. As long as her husband was present, they came running. She found she had a second career on her hands organizing David's diary, and it was fun.

Now when they went to the opera, they were entertained to dinner in the private dining-room at Covent Garden.

Quite often they would go to Chequers at weekends, and at Ascot the company box was Liz's to command. If she didn't like a certain cabinet minister, or a popular entertainer had irritated her, then they didn't get an invitation on Ladies' Day.

Liz was aware that a whole sub-group in London made a study of her moods and tastes. If she favoured dressing at Alaia one season, then none of the women who wanted to keep in with her would touch the designer. If it was known she was on a particular diet, every London hostess made it her business to find out exactly what she could and couldn't eat and would alter their menus accordingly. Liz was pandered to, imitated, and everyone listened to what she had to say.

There was only one fly in her ointment. She still didn't see enough of David. The promise he had made to her in Zurich was a hollow one. He didn't put Liz or their daughter before the paper at all. It still consumed him, eating up all his spare time and emotion. Nowadays when Liz saw him, she had to share her husband with all the other guests at the soirée they were attending. Sometimes she wondered if David would even notice if she wasn't there, but she lived with the situation. She had to. It was either put up with things the way they were or lose him to a younger prettier woman who didn't nag.

The idea of it made Liz grind her teeth. She thought about Doctor Lejeune and thanked God she had found him in time.

Without the surgery she would be starting to look her age. The surgery, the hair tint every week at Daniel Galvin, and of course her personal trainer. Liz looked down at the seatbelt resting just above her perfectly sculpted thighs. There's no way, she thought, I could keep in shape without an hour with the weights every morning.

She started to worry. She had planned to be in New York for a few days. Long enough to hire a good attorney and get Vanessa out of jail. But could she fit in a work-out at the same time? Would the hotel have someone on their staff who could take her through her routine?

With an effort she put the matter on hold. Her figure wouldn't fall apart if she took a few days off. Right now she had more important things to occupy her mind.

Freddie waited in the arrivals hall at Kennedy and felt nervous. In half an hour she would come face to face with her mother's saviour. The rich friend from England who was going to move heaven and earth to put things back the way they were.

Fat hope, Freddie thought moodily. Even if Liz Dearing can get Mom out of jail, what happens then? She goes back on the game and they throw her in the slammer a second time. A wave of depression swept over her as her father's words came back to her.

'Stop worrying about the future,' he had told her. 'Soon you'll be away in college. Then your mother will have to start looking out for herself.'

How typical of my father, Freddie thought. He salves his conscience by putting the problem on to someone else. Then he walks away from the whole thing. Well I can't do that.

She was so engrossed in her own problems that she didn't notice the time. If the arrival of the London flight hadn't been announced on the tannoy she might have stood dreaming all afternoon. Instead she pulled herself together and headed off to find Liz. Dan had told her what to expect. A thin, dark woman, about her mother's age. Expensively dressed and probably wearing lots of jewellery. She craned her neck to get a better view of the passengers coming off the flight but she could see no-one of that description. There were a lot of businessmen carrying overnight bags, a couple of blue-rinsed matrons, some students a year or so older than she was and a blonde film star type in a mink coat. Freddie shook her head. Maybe Liz had been held up. It sometimes happened on those long flights.

She stood around until the rest of the passengers disembarked, but still there was no sign of her mother's friend. She was about to give up and head back to the city when the blonde she had seen earlier came up to her.

'You wouldn't be Freddie, would you?'

She did a double take.

'Yes,' Freddie said.

'Ah, I'm meant to be meeting you.' The blonde put out her hand. 'I'm Liz Dearing,' she said. 'Your mother's friend. Dan told me you'd be here.'

Freddie took a step backwards. The woman had startled her and now she realized why. She had a picture in her mind of dark hair and maturity. This was the shoulder she was going to cry on. Now she knew she had been mistaken. Liz Dearing looked incapable of comforting anyone. She was right. Before she could tell her anything about Vanessa, before she could even open her mouth, the woman was giving her orders.

She was dispatched to find a porter and organize a taxi. In that order. They were going to the Waldorf Astoria. Liz, it appeared, had no interest in coming back to the apartment, and no interest in what

Freddie's plans were. As far as she was concerned, Freddie was there for her convenience.

Freddie did as she was told, but as she waited for Liz in the taxi queue, she felt herself getting angry. She had hoped to like Liz. Any old friend who could jump on a plane and come to her mother's rescue came high in her estimation.

So why was she gripped by the desire to shake her? Hold your horses, Freddie told herself. Liz has just come off a long flight. Maybe she's not feeling her best. When she's unpacked and had a lie down, she'll be different. She wasn't, though she did look different, Freddie had to admit that. When she went to meet her in the evening, Liz had changed out of her travelling clothes into a short, tight dress.

She really does look like a film star, Freddie thought marvelling. She reminds me of Catherine Deneuve.

Liz had had a successful day. She had managed to get hold of the New York attorney her husband's family used.

'He's going down to Riker's Island first thing in the morning,' she told Freddie. 'Once he's had a chance to talk to Vanessa we'll have a clearer idea of what to do next.'

Freddie started to feel better. Perhaps Liz wasn't such a brassy blonde after all. Perhaps she just looked like one.

Liz had arranged to have dinner in the hotel restaurant because she was too tired to venture out. Freddie was invited to join her. So was Freddie's father. A small irreverent thought flicked across Freddie's mind. This woman was behaving a bit like royalty visiting her less fortunate cousins. She even sounded like she imagined the Queen would. Very hoity toity and paying special attention to every word, as if she learned how to speak in school.

Freddie wondered if her father liked Liz.

Then she thought, no, he can't do. Not if he liked my mother.

If Dan didn't approve of Liz, he didn't show it. In fact, Freddie thought, she had never seen her father make more effort to be charming. Every time Liz got out a cigarette, Dan's lighter was ready in his hand. He seemed to know everything about the paper Liz's husband owned, he even managed to dredge up a few acquaintances they had in common. By the time they got to the coffee and liqueurs they'd hardly talked about Vanessa at all.

Freddie felt it was high time she put this right. She started to ask about the attorney Liz had hired and what her mother's chances were of getting off. She expected Liz to say Vanessa was home free, but she didn't. Instead she looked worried.

'Ben Chasen is the best there is,' Liz told her, 'but even he can't work miracles. It's the drugs thing that worries him. It's not easy to prove complete innocence if there are drugs involved, and from what he tells me they found drugs on Vanessa.'

Dan picked up his brandy balloon and stared into its depths.

'She hadn't done anything like this before. It was the first time. Her first offence.'

Liz nodded.

'I know. That goes in her favour. If anyone can make it work for her, Ben can.'

Dan called for the bill.

'I have to meet someone at Studio 54,' he said. 'If you're not doing anything, would you like to come and have a drink?'

The question was addressed to Liz and Freddie laughed to herself. Dad is being polite, she thought. He knows she's too tired to go out of the hotel, so he can look as if he's making a fuss of her without any chance she'll take him up on it.

Freddie was stirring sugar into her coffee when Liz said something that made her pay attention.

'I'd love to come and have a drink,' she replied warmly. 'I haven't been in a nightclub in ages.'

Freddie couldn't believe she was hearing it, but Liz was already putting her cigarettes back in her bag and signalling for her coat. She looked at her father, handsome and attentive, the lion's mane of his hair glowing in the overhead light. Poor darling, Freddie thought, I bet he wished he'd kept quiet about Studio 54.

Liz was glad to see the back of the child. Ever since she'd set eyes on her at the airport, her nerves had been on edge. There was something critical and disapproving about Freddie, as if her eyes could see right through her to the cellulite on her thighs, the scars the surgeon had left behind her ears.

She's only a little girl, Liz told herself. Nothing to get worried about. Now the father. That's another story.

Liz hadn't been looking forward to seeing Dan again. Eighteen years ago she had dismissed him as a married lecher, a user of women. She had told him as much to his face and he had walked out on her.

After that she'd added another condemnation to her list. He's a rude bastard as well, she thought. Then out of the blue he had called her. Only this time he wasn't rude at all. He was utterly charming because he wanted something.

Liz came over of course. How could she refuse? Vanessa was her oldest friend. But she still had a bone to pick. A score to settle. So when she realized she was going to be stuck in New York on her own, she summoned him. Now the boot was on the other foot she could tell Dan Levin exactly what she thought of him. She could spell it out in huge letters and this time there was no way he could walk out.

She hadn't torn him off a strip after all. He didn't give me a chance, Liz thought. All that business lighting my cigarettes and talking about my husband caught me off guard. I'll put things right when we get to the club.

She didn't of course. Once they'd fought their way through the bouncers at the entrance to the club she lost her concentration. Liz hadn't been there for years and it was darker than she remembered. The cigarette smoke was thicker, and there were more people. Dan managed to find them a table and she started to relax again. Then a bottle of champagne arrived without Dan having to do a thing and Liz began to feel good.

He hasn't lost his touch, she thought. He still knows how to make a woman feel special. Then Liz chided herself. What am I thinking of? She decided to put him on the spot.

'Where is your friend?' she asked. 'The one you said you were here to meet.'

Dan had the grace to look embarrassed.

'There wasn't any friend,' he confessed. 'I invented him.'

So he hadn't changed after all. Liz arched her brows.

'Still up to your old tricks then?'

Rather than replying Dan took hold of her and pulled her to her feet.

'Come and dance,' he said shortly. 'You told me you liked nightclubs.'

The floor was tiny and even darker than the bar. Liz had no choice but to fit herself into Dan's arms and follow the music. As she did, something inside her came alight. This can't be happening to me, she thought. Not tonight. Not with Dan Levin. He started to smile and Liz noticed the network of tiny lines around his eyes.

'Let go,' he told her gently. 'The whole thing is much more fun if you go with it.'

He reminded her of Vic. There was the same smoothness, the same arrogant assumption that just because he wanted her she would roll over on her back.

'Did I tell you you were a rude bastard?' Liz said. Now the smile became a laugh.

'No,' Dan chuckled, 'but I like it.'

Liz realized she shouldn't have had so much to drink with dinner.

Drink and jet-lag never did go together. No wonder she felt dizzy.

When the music stopped Liz let him help her back to the table and just before they got there she stumbled. Her heel gave way and she fell against Dan. If he hadn't put his hands around her waist she would have wound up on the floor. As it was she wound up in his bed.

It was his touch that did it. One moment Liz was all stirred up inside, but keeping it under control. The next, she was begging Dan to take her back to the Waldorf. And he obliged. Smoothly, charmingly as if he had known this was going to happen all along.

Looking back on it, Liz wished she had put up more resistance. She had a suite at the Waldorf after all. She might have offered him a drink in her drawing-room for heaven's sake. Yet she didn't want any more to drink, she didn't want a cigarette and she didn't want any more conversation. So when he walked through into the bedroom she followed him without protest.

When they got through the door she made one last attempt to save her face.

'I'm not one of your floozies,' she said, 'so don't think you can do anything you like with me.'

Dan looked as if he had heard a very good joke.

'I'll only do what you ask me to do,' he said. Then he spun her round and undid the back of her dress. The designer had made it to come off in one piece, and it fell in folds to the floor.

I should pick it up, Liz thought desperately. It cost too much money to leave like that. But Dan didn't give her the chance. His hands were already on her stockings, rolling them down her legs. Unclipping, unfastening everything that held her into place until she stood naked in front of him.

He lifted her up then and carried her across to the bed. Then he started taking his own things off.

He was a huge man. Taut and strongly muscled. He reminded Liz of a jungle beast, and in that moment she knew he had lied to her. Dan Levin wouldn't do what she asked him at all. He would make love to her in any way he wanted to. He would please her, she knew that, but he would please himself first and she realized she didn't care. At first he touched her very gently, running his hands over the surface of her as if he was trying to imprint her body on his memory. Then he put his mouth where his hands had been and Liz felt herself respond. I'm at his mercy, she thought. No man ever did this to me before.

Dan pulled away from her and Liz watched fascinated as he parted her legs and raised himself above her. Then he was inside her and in that moment Liz knew why Vanessa had given up her life to follow this man. He made love the way Menuhin played the violin and Renoir painted. She felt sensations she had never known existed, and she wanted the night to go on forever.

Dan left her at five o'clock that morning.

As Liz saw him put on his suit in the hotel bedroom, she knew she had been used. She knew she was like all the other girls who had rolled on their backs for him. And she knew something else as well. She knew that if he called her again, she would come running.

42

Ben Chasen had nothing good to tell Liz about her old friend. From what he could see, she was as guilty as hell.

'The police caught her with half her clothes off,' he related, 'so she can't exactly say she didn't know what was going on. Then there's the drugs thing. When they asked her if she charged extra for providing drugs, the stupid woman admitted she did. The only thing we've got going in our favour is that there wasn't a tape running while she said it.'

Liz paced up and down the hotel suite. There has to be a way out of this, she thought. I'm paying top dollar for this attorney.

'Is there any way you can cut a deal with the police?' she asked him. 'I know you've got contacts.'

Chasen sighed. He was afraid it might come to this.

'Look, I've already had a word with the relevant parties, and it's no dice. I can't keep her out of the slammer. There might not be a tape, but they did find cocaine in her bag and there's no way of disguising that kind of evidence.'

'I believe you,' said Liz softly. 'But there must be something you can do.'

Chasen looked at the woman in front of him. He'd been dealing with this kind of rich bitch for years now and they didn't get any easier. He was tempted to tell her to go to hell, then he thought about the retainer her husband paid his firm every year. After that, he knew he didn't have any option. Like it or not he would have to clean up her mess.

'By any rights,' he told her, 'your little hooker friend should go down for fifteen years. Maybe more depending on the judge.'

He sat down heavily on one of the spindly chairs the hotel provided, and mopped his brow.

'What I can do for you is to reduce the sentence. Don't ask me how I'm going to do it, but with the wind blowing in the right direction, she could be looking at two, maybe three years maximum.'

Liz regarded him sceptically.

'That's your best shot?'

Chasen looked weary.

'That's my only shot.'

For a moment Liz hovered on the edge of indecision. She could fire Chasen and shop around. There had to be someone smarter than him in town, or someone more crooked.

She took a decision.

'Do what you have to do,' she instructed him.

Chasen rose to go, but before he reached the door, Liz stopped him.

'There is just one other thing.'

'What's that?'

'I want to go and see my friend before she goes to court. I need some time alone with her. Can you arrange that?'

The attorney nodded. He'd have to get round one of the prison officials, but that wasn't a problem. The rest of the wheeling and dealing he wasn't so sure about.

It was an ugly building. Squat and institutional looking. If Liz wanted to fool herself, she might have imagined it was a high school. Then the car drew up to the front door and she stopped pretending. The grille on the door left her in little doubt where she was. This was the Singer Centre. The place her oldest friend was being held on charges of drug trafficking and prostitution.

Liz got out and told the driver to wait for her, then she squared her shoulders and headed for the dusty, rose-coloured building. The sooner she got this over with the better.

In the lobby she announced herself to the duty officer who checked her name against a list. When he was satisfied she was who she said she was, a woman prison official came to escort her through the electronic gates separating the prison from the outside world.

The moment they clanged shut Liz knew she had left reality behind her. Where she lived there was space and stillness. Here people shouted and argued and jostled each other. It was like being in an animal pen. Everyone was in everyone else's way. The prisoners who crowded the hallway where she stood seemed incapable of passing each other without colliding, and with each collision came a stream of expletives. Liz looked at the angry faces around her and shrank into herself. What if Vanessa was this way too? What if this place had turned her into an animal?

Feeling self-conscious in her summer shift and sling-backs Liz followed the prison officer down the corridor. Soon they came to an enclosure guarded by another set of electronic bars. The grid must have had a mechanism hidden inside it, for it slid aside as they approached to reveal a large bare room furnished with moulded plastic chairs and circular tables made of the same material.

Liz looked at the room remembering the last place she had met Vanessa. She had just moved in with

Norman then and the three of them had had dinner in the Four Seasons. Vanessa had looked fragile that night. Fragile and expensive. The restaurant, with its starched white linen and ankle deep carpets, had made a perfect setting for her.

The prison room came into focus again and Liz saw how dirty the walls were, how rank it smelled. Without meaning to, she shuddered and the warder looked at her in understanding.

'It has to be this way,' she said. 'Our lady guests make it this way. If we gave them proper chairs and tables they'd tear the legs off and turn them into weapons.'

Liz turned to say something, but the words froze in her throat. A woman had come into the room from another entrance. A woman who recognized her and greeted her by name.

She was wearing a shapeless prison suit and her hair, which had been bleached and showed darker roots, was pulled back into a tail. If Liz hadn't been expecting Vanessa she might not have known who it was.

The delicate, ladylike prettiness of ten years ago had been swept away – her features had coarsened somehow. Her eyes, which had always reflected her moods, were dead now. Something had depleted her. Either the men she had lived with or the men she had slept with had taken something away. For what remained of Vanessa was used up and tired.

Liz thought she was going to burst into tears, but she stopped herself. That kind of messy emotion was no good to either of them. With an effort she went towards Vanessa and attempted an embrace. Vanessa accepted it awkwardly, then she sat down.

'How long have we got?' she asked the prison officer. The woman made to leave.

'Half an hour, so make the most of it.'

The grid clanged behind her. Then there were just the two of them. Vanessa broke the silence.

'It must be a shock to you. Seeing me like this.'

Liz considered lying. It's not so bad, she could say. A visit to the beauty parlour will soon set you to rights. Then she decided against it. They'd known each other too long for that.

'How did it happen?' she asked. 'Why did you let it happen?'

Vanessa looked tired.

'I was an optimist,' she answered. 'I truly believed nobody, no man that is, would ever let me down.'

She looked bitter now. 'I was also convinced I would never get any older. So when both things started to happen I closed my eyes and refused to accept it. Have you any idea how many years you can go on doing that?'

She shook her head. 'I'm rambling now and you don't have time to listen to my babble. Tell me, Liz, have you talked to your smart attorney yet?'

Liz nodded.

'What did he say? Is he going to get me out of here?'

Once more Liz thought about lying and rejected it.

'No he isn't,' she told Vanessa frankly.

Vanessa looked as if somebody had hit her.

'It can't be true,' she said weakly. 'You can't just leave me here to die.'

Liz thought back to the day when they first met. Vanessa had been in trouble then too. She was pregnant by some ghastly man she didn't even know, and Liz had got her out of it. In a way, it put the seal on their relationship. Vanessa got herself into scrapes and Liz spent her time getting her out of them. Only this time it wasn't so easy.

'You were found with drugs on you. Cocaine and marijuana and God knows what else. Nobody could get you out of here after that.'

Now Vanessa started to cry. She put her head in her hands and gave herself up to her grief, and as she did she seemed to fall apart. Liz felt herself starting to get short of breath. I've got to put a stop to this, she thought. I've got to make some sense of the situation.

She pulled Vanessa up into a sitting position. Then when she had a clear view of her, she hit her round the face. It was a sharp blow with no sting in it and it pulled her up short.

Now Liz had Vanessa's attention, she started to talk.

'I came here to help you,' she said. 'But I won't accomplish anything by listening to you sob your heart out.'

She rummaged around in her handbag until she found a package of tissues. She handed them to Vanessa and watched while she wiped her eyes and blew her nose.

'That's better,' she said. 'Now we can talk about the good news.'

Vanessa attempted a smile.

'Don't tell me,' she said. 'They've reduced my sentence to three weeks with twenty years' community service.'

'Not exactly, though you're getting close.' A flicker of interest showed in Vanessa's eyes.

'So your attorney is cutting some kind of deal.'

Liz nodded. 'The way things were, you would have been lucky to have been out of here inside twenty odd years, but Ben Chasen has managed to lean on some of his influential friends and now it looks like you might get off with two years. Three, maximum.'

Vanessa sighed as if someone had put a pin in her and let the tension out along with the air.

'It's still horrible,' she told Liz, 'but I think I can live with it. Just. It's not going to be easy, though.'

'I've got something else to tell you that might make it easier. I've decided to take Freddie under my wing. I know she's going to college in a year, but a year is a long time to leave a teenager alone in New York.'

Vanessa made a face. 'I'm grateful to you – but my daughter won't be. If she leaves the city now she won't be able to complete her studies.'

Now Liz wrestled with her conscience. She didn't like Freddie and if she could rid herself of her she would have gladly done so. All she had to do was make arrangements for her to stay in some hostel. Then she could take her exams and go to college and to hell with her. But Liz couldn't do that. She'd seen with her own eyes what living alone in New York had done to Vanessa. She couldn't save her friend now – it was too late – but she could save her daughter.

'There are plenty of colleges in England,' she said briskly. 'If she's set her heart on further education, I'm sure I can fix that up. I'm not without influence.'

Some of the colour came back to Vanessa's face.

'Will you really do all that for Freddie?' she said. 'It's very good of you.'

Despite herself, Liz grinned. She had heard Vanessa say that sort of thing before long ago when she'd given her tickets for Wimbledon or lent her a favourite dress. 'It's very good of you.' The phrase was pure Sloane Square, and in an obscure way it cheered her to hear it. Life could do its worst to Vanessa, but there were some things that couldn't be destroyed.

There was a sound behind her, a scraping of iron mesh, and she turned to see the warden come back into the enclosure.

'It looks as if our time's up,' Liz said as cheerfully as she could.

She took hold of her friend and held her in the briefest of hugs. 'Try not to worry too much, darling. I'll take care of Freddie until you come out. Until then, keep your chin up.'

Vanessa watched Liz as she was led out of the room. She was dressed in the latest fashion, her make-up was perfect. She'd even put on scent that day. Ten days ago, she thought, I looked like that too. Now I'll never look like that again. After three years of this place, nothing and nobody will ever put me back together again.

The cell she shared with three others filled her senses now. There was a lavatory without a seat in the corner of it. High up the opposite side was a small barred window. All around her there was dirt and darkness and the sour smell of women caged up for too long. As she turned to go back there she knew she had been sentenced to death.

43

London, 1986

The house in Cheyne Walk reminded Freddie of the flat she had lived in with her father but on a grander scale. It was the staircase that made the difference. Broad and sweeping, it led upwards to bedrooms, music rooms, libraries and a secret hidden conservatory which housed a tame Amazon parrot.

The bird belonged to Barbara, Liz's daughter, and in the first few weeks when Freddie was finding her feet, he provided consolation. His name was Oscar, and he had the uncanny habit of imitating the telephone. Sometimes when she was down the hall she would rush to where the ringing was coming from only to find the bird sitting on top of its cage looking pleased.

It was Oscar who provided the bridge between Freddie and the Dearing family. She had come to London in the depths of despair. Her mother had been sent to Riker's Island for three years, and if that wasn't bad enough, her pushy English friend Liz had stepped in and wiped out her chance of a college education. Freddie had set her heart on one of the Ivy League places. Smith or Radcliffe or Bryn Mawr. She had had a good chance of getting accepted until the disaster with her mother. Now all she had to look forward to was a dreary grind at the American College in London.

David Dearing had been very decent about getting her in. Apparently finding a place there hadn't been easy. She knew she should feel grateful, but she wasn't.

She was mad as hell. What right did these people have to uproot her and take her away from everything and everyone she had known? If she'd stayed in New York, she could have visited her mother every week. She could have gone on with her studies. She might even have managed to see her father. But nobody trusted her to look after herself. That was the worst thing of all. Nobody believed she could do the one thing she had been doing all her life.

Freddie thought of all the years she had spent humouring her mother's boyfriends. All the years she had kept a roof over their heads by playing backgammon with Norman and talking fine art and baseball with Ted. She wasn't just good at looking out for herself. She looked out for her mother as well. She told Liz all this when she announced her plans to move her to England, but she might as well have been talking to herself. Liz had taken her decision and her mother, the betrayer, had gone along with it. All that remained for her to do was to pack her things. They had even notified her headmistress that she wouldn't be coming back.

Freddie thought of going to her father but Liz had beaten her there as well. They had had dinner the night after she had visited her mother in prison. She would never know what Liz had said, but by the time she spoke to him his mind was made up.

'You'll be better off with the Dearings,' he told her. 'They're rich people, so you'll be well looked after and Liz has your interests at heart. She may seem a bit tough, but underneath all that she's a very warm person.'

How do you know that? Freddie wondered. She didn't seem such a warm person the night the three of us had dinner. Aloud she said,

'But Dad I'll be so lonely. All my friends are here. Don't make me go to England, I beg of you.'

Her entreaties fell on deaf ears.

'It won't be so terrible, darling,' he said. 'I'll come and visit from time to time just to make sure you're okay. I love London and you're the best excuse I know for taking an interest in our English operation.'

And that was that. Freddie was seventeen years old and she had to do what she was told. What she didn't have to do though, was put a good face on it. She sulked in the first class cabin all the way over the Atlantic. She wouldn't eat the airline lunch. She even refused the champagne. By the time they touched down at Heathrow, she and Liz were hardly speaking.

Things got worse when they arrived. Liz's husband was going to be out that night at a dinner in the city, which left Freddie with Liz and her fat lump of a daughter.

Freddie hated Barbara Dearing from the first moment she set eyes on her. She was so big and noisy and horsey. She even insisted on wearing riding breeches around the house, which was pretty unfortunate considering the size of her hips.

Over dinner, Freddie noticed that Liz didn't exactly see eye to eye with Barbara either. They kept arguing about a diet she was meant to be on. Liz wanted Barbara to stick to seven hundred calories a day, which sounded pretty extreme, and Barbara wasn't having it.

'If I lived on lettuce leaves,' Barbara pointed out, 'I wouldn't have any energy at all. I don't think my new boss would be all that impressed if I started passing out in the office.'

Barbara had just started as a trainee reporter on a Fleet Street news agency – another thing her mother didn't approve of. It seemed she wanted her daughter to do something ladylike like interior decoration or working in an art gallery. But Barbara wasn't having that. It was the family tradition for the Dearings to be in newspapers. She wasn't a boy, but she didn't see why that should stand in her way. There were plenty of distinguished women journalists and she wanted to be one of them.

If Freddie hadn't hated Barbara so much, she would have agreed with her. Why should she be stuck arranging flowers just because it was expected of her? As it was, Freddie kept her opinions to herself and picked at her dinner. The Dearings were a snooty English family who had taken her in as an act of charity. They were bestowing this great favour on her, not because they cared for her – they knew she didn't want to be here – but to satisfy themselves, so that Liz could dine out at the Ritz and tell all her rich friends what a wonderful thing she had done and Dan could look at Liz with new eyes and start calling her a warm person.

Well, Freddie wasn't going to join in that game. She would keep herself to herself and endure the time she had to spend in this house. The only other living creature she allowed herself any intimacy with was the parrot. For a bird, he was very affectionate.

Freddie found this out gradually. Oscar lived in a high, domed cage at the far end of the conservatory. The table and chairs were grouped together at one end, and Oscar reigned in solitary splendour amongst a clump of orange trees.

Freddie supposed nobody liked him very much and it gave her a fellow feeling for the bird.

'We're both exiles,' she told him mournfully one evening when she had come in from school. The family made it their custom to gather in the drawing-room for drinks before dinner. David, usually late from the office and full of it, would sit with his wife and daughter and gossip about the antics of their various friends. It was an easy, cosy time of the day and on the one or two occasions Freddie joined them, she felt like an outsider.

In the end she opted for the parrot. He was easier to understand and required less effort. The moment she came into the conservatory, she knew he was pleased to see her, for he stood to attention on his perch and called out 'hello'. Then when Freddie approached, he poked his head through the bars demanding to be stroked. In a day or so, she started letting him out. The parrot loved this and would flutter round the room perching on the edge of chairs and sinking his beak into the wooden backs.

Freddie worried about this. She knew enough to realize that the furniture in here might have some value. David Dearing, she imagined, could be highly irritated to discover his priceless antiques had been rendered worthless by a pet parrot. She started to encourage Oscar to roost on her, where she could keep an eye on him, and so they became friends. They developed a routine. Freddie would come home from school, get changed and rush into the conservatory. The second she was in there, she would open the cage and Oscar would fly straight to her shoulder. Then they would start to talk.

Oscar would run through his repertoire, which consisted of 'Hello, goodbye', 'Who's a good boy' and 'Anyone for Tennis'. After, that he would whistle two bars of 'Pop goes the Weasel' and start to nibble Freddie's ear. Then it was her turn. She would tell the bird everything she had done that day and he would interrupt her from time to time with a special parrot gibberish of his own. When he got bored with her shoulder, he would climb down her arm and sit on her hand where he could see her. Then Freddie really got down to business. All the trauma and disappointment of the past few months of her life came pouring out of her. She told Oscar about her mother and the shock she had when she found out she was being sent away to prison. She didn't get round to telling Oscar why this was for a week or so. But when she finally did, there was no stopping her. When she came to the end of it the bird looked at her, put his head on one side and said 'Hello'.

'So that's all you have to say about it,' Freddie said sulkily. 'If you must know, I think that's a pretty poor comment.'

'Actually,' said a voice behind her, 'he wasn't talking to you at all. He was saying hello to me. I came up to find out why you didn't want any dinner tonight.'

Freddie swung round to find David standing by the parrot's cage. Before she could say anything, he gave a whistle and the bird flew off her hand and on to David's shoulder where it nestled into the crook of his neck.

'You're not the only one Oscar listens to, you know.'

Freddie felt very silly. She had hardly spoken two sentences to this man since she had arrived in England yet here she was pouring out the story of her life to a bird. He must think she was nuts.

'How long have you been here?' she asked.

'Long enough to find out why you sent the whole family to Coventry. I didn't realize quite how terrible it was for you in New York. I assumed your father must have broken the news about your mother. I never dreamed it was the other way round.'

David looked at her with genuine sympathy.

'It must have been very lonely for you carrying all

the responsibility for your mother on your own. How did you do it?'

Freddie's hackles started to come up. She'd had enough charity from this family to last her a lifetime. All she needed on top of it all was this man's pity.

'I've always been responsible for Mom,' she replied. 'I know you see me as a pathetic little waif, but I'm not like that at all. If it hadn't been for me, Mom would have gone to pieces.'

She half expected David to slap her down, but he didn't. Instead, with infinite gentleness, he reached up and put the parrot back in his cage. Then he put his arm round her and led her over to the sitting area.

'Suppose you tell me about it,' he said.

Freddie hesitated. 'You came to fetch me for dinner,' she said. 'What will the others think if I go on keeping them waiting?'

David grinned, and for an instant he looked barely grown-up. 'They'll be furious,' he told her. 'I dare say my wife's started in on the claret by now, and Barbara will be working her way through the breadsticks. Tell you what, why don't we leave them to it? I'll get the butler to feed them both downstairs and send something up for us on a tray. It's quiet up here and I think it's time you talked to somebody.'

If Freddie had been in New York she would have probably told David to get lost. She was used to fighting her own battles and keeping her own counsel. But she was far from home now, and out on a limb. There didn't seem to be any more she could lose.

She started to tell David about the day she heard about her mother's arrest, but he stopped her.

'I want to hear it from the beginning,' he said. 'Right from the moment when your parents split up. How old were you then?'

Freddie went back in time to when she was a little

girl and her father told her she was going to live with Uncle Norman. The nightmare had started for her then. Until that moment there had been someone to run to, someone to look after her. Now there was no-one. Her mother did her best of course, but she was so helpless. There was so little of her to go round.

As the years passed her mother waned, but it didn't matter for Freddie was getting stronger as she grew. When the crisis came with Uncle Norman she was able to go to her father and demand help.

When Ted's drinking became a problem it was Freddie who shielded her mother from the worst of it.

'But what did it do to you?' David interrupted. 'A lot of girls in your place would have felt bitter.'

Freddie shrugged. 'It wasn't like that. In the beginning I thought Uncle Norman was a bit of an ogre, but when I got to know him, he wasn't that bad. He taught me backgammon and how to understand Wall Street. He was lousy to Mom, of course, but a lot of that went on behind my back. So I didn't get the chance to really hate him.'

She paused. 'Ted was a different story. He wasn't nasty at all. He was just weak.'

David regarded the girl with a sort of wonder. She was sitting hunched up in the padded armchair, dressed in the shapeless blue serge she had arrived in. To look at she was a schoolgirl, the terror of St Trinian's, only now he had started listening to her he knew her appearance was a lie. This was a woman he had under his roof. A woman in girl's clothing, and for a moment he felt helpless.

What am I going to do with her, he asked himself. I can't go on leaving her on her own, but I can't be her friend either. She needs someone of her own generation for that. He thought about his daughter,

Barbara. It was the obvious solution, yet the two hadn't taken to each other.

'It's a pity about Barbara,' he said aloud. 'She could have done with someone like you to talk to.'

Freddie made a face. 'She doesn't look as if she needs anybody.'

'So that's what you think,' he said slowly. 'You've got less judgement than I thought. My daughter may look as if she's got everything, and she has. The problem is she hasn't got the faintest idea what to do with it. She might as well have nothing at all.'

'How can I help her?'

The servant arrived with supper and while he arranged the beef, the vegetables, the wine and the cheese on the table in front of them, David thought for a moment.

'You've never had anything very much, have you?' he said.

Freddie shook her head.

'So if somebody suddenly gave you carte blanche, could you handle it?'

Freddie looked suspicious. 'What do you mean by carte blanche?'

David took his time pouring out the wine before he went on.

'I suppose I'm talking about the season,' he said. 'This town can be a lot of fun for a girl if she's got the right connections and a little money to spend on herself. It should be a lot of fun for Barbara, but it isn't. So I'm making you an offer.'

She looked at him from under her lashes.

'You want me to be Barbara's walker.'

David resisted the impulse to hit her.

'No, I don't want you to be Barbara's walker. I want you to be her friend – if you're capable of it. If you can't be genuine, consider this conversation closed. My daughter doesn't need anybody's charity.'

How strange life is, Freddie thought. All these weeks I thought I was being patronized, when really the boot was on the other foot.

'I'm sorry,' she sighed, 'I didn't mean to be rude but I do find Barbara off-putting.'

'You mean because she's noisy and jolly hockey-sticks?'

She considered.

'I guess so.'

'Have you ever wondered why she behaves like that? Well, I'll tell you. Barbara's a big girl. If she wasn't so big, she'd be attractive, but she doesn't give herself a chance to be. I suspect she's afraid of competing with her mother. Anyway, she makes up for her lack of looks by being hearty and this puts people off even more, which is a shame. Underneath all that bluster is a very sweet, rather frightened girl.'

Freddie felt her heart sink. Wherever she went, there would always be somebody waiting to be looked after. First she had her mother. Now there was Barbara.

She thought about turning David down. Then she remembered about the London season. There would be dances and race meetings and picnics by the river. If she was lucky she might meet someone special, maybe there would be more than one. Just thinking about it cheered her up. She took a sip of the heavy, expensive claret David had poured for her.

'I'll try to do my best for your daughter,' she said.

44

They called Barbara 'Boobs' at the news agency where she worked. It was because she was always making mistakes, and because she had an enormous bust.

In the rarefied atmosphere that Liz created in Cheyne Walk, Barbara was a lump. Down among the reporters she was a big, sexy girl. This became apparent to her the moment she started work. The boys who worked with her all competed to buy her drinks in the pub and the news editor, who was a couple of years older than the rest, took her to one side and gave her a warning.

'A lot of girls like you get ahead on their sex appeal. I think you can do better than that, and I want you to prove it by working your socks off.'

He gave her the toughest assignments on the desk. If there was a fight on a council estate or a wrongful eviction Barbara was sent to cover it. She worked lunchtimes, she worked nights. She worked all the hours that God made. When she finally proved herself as a reporter, her boss rewarded her by taking her out and buying her a curry. After that he seduced her.

'I couldn't resist,' he apologized afterwards. 'You are such a turn-on, it's a wonder I kept my hands off you as long as I did.'

Barbara didn't mind in the slightest. She loved going to bed with her news editor. He was the first man who made her feel female. With him and the other boys who worked at the agency she wasn't the horsey no-hoper her mother thought she was.

In Fleet Street she was a success. Professionally and sexually.

She kept all this to herself when she came home. There was no point in alerting her parents. It was hard enough getting their permission to train as a journalist. She didn't want to spoil it all by boasting about her social life. She knew Liz had ambitions to launch her on the deb circuit and so far she had managed to head her off. If she admitted she actually liked boys, she actually had sex with them, then her mother was bound to insist she make friends from her own social level. Whatever that was.

So Barbara played herself down. She would have got away with it, if it hadn't been for Freddie. Now the American girl was on the scene it gave her parents the perfect excuse to put them both through the season.

'Freddie will give you confidence,' her father explained to her. 'When you go to a ball, you won't have to walk into the room alone.'

There were times, Barbara thought, when her father could be very irritating. She loved walking into rooms on her own. She knew that in the right sort of clothes, tight dresses that showed her cleavage, she attracted a lot of attention. There was no way she wanted to share that attention with Freddie. Or anyone else.

Now she didn't have any choice. Freddie was there. She was stuck with her. She was also stuck with the London Season. There was nothing for it but to make the best of it.

The first hurdle was the shopping trip Liz had planned for all three of them. They needed dresses to dance in, dresses to have tea in, something to wear for Ascot and Henley and Wimbledon. That was just to begin with.

Barbara had a very clear idea of how she wanted to look. So did Liz. The problem was the two notions didn't coincide. Barbara solved it by getting Freddie on her side. She invited her to have lunch in Langan's.

The invitation caught Freddie off-balance. She had done her best to show some interest in the burden she was being made to carry around, but she had had little success. Every time she tried to get Barbara to one side for a chat, she was always involved in something. The dog needed walking. She had to transcribe an interview she was working on. She had a driving lesson.

When Barbara asked her to lunch, Freddie was ready to throw in the towel. How could she be friends with somebody who quite obviously didn't care whether she lived or died. Only now she seemed to have changed her mind. She suspected her father must have had a word with her.

The invitation was for the following day and Freddie braced herself. She had nothing in common with Barbara. She didn't ride, she didn't particularly like animals, and she didn't understand the country. Yet somehow she had to get through to this girl. She was still puzzling over the problem when she arrived at Langan's. She had read in the gossip columns that this was a fashionable watering hole, and she wasn't disappointed. The moment she walked through the door she was engulfed by a throng of people. They all seemed to be talking at the top of their voices. Freddie started to worry for her lunchtime companion. It was clear to her that Liz must have organized this restaurant. It was just the kind of place she liked to be seen in.

She left her coat with the girl at the door and found a waiter.

'I'm meeting Barbara Dearing,' she told him. 'Has she arrived yet?'

The waiter seemed to recognize the name and broke into a smile.

'She's in the bar,' he said. 'At her usual table.'

He must have got it wrong, Freddie thought.

Horsey Barbara wouldn't have a table in a place like this. Once more she detected the hand of Liz organizing things in advance. Why can't she leave the girl alone, Freddie thought. She'd probably have been far happier at the Army and Navy.

She threaded her way through to the bar area at the back of the restaurant. It was full of beautiful people. The girls all looked like actresses or pop stars, in slinky black suits covered in gold jewellery. Some of them, the ones who wanted to look casual, had opted for leather which they wore like a second skin. For a moment, Freddie thought she was back in New York. Ted had taken her mother to places like this when he was in the money. Freddie pulled herself together. There was no Ted any more. No mother either. All she had now was the Dearing family. The dreary rich Dearings and their dreary rich daughter.

She peered through the cigarette smoke in an effort to find Barbara but she was nowhere to be seen. Then she heard her name being called and she turned to find herself standing in front of Barbara's table. At first she couldn't believe what she saw. For Barbara didn't look like Barbara at all. For a start she had hair. Yards and yards of hair the colour of horse chestnuts. She had always worn it in tight braids before and now she had let it go it transformed her.

She was wearing make-up too, and instead of her customary scruffy jodhpurs she was sporting a short leather skirt and a stretchy top that fitted where it touched.

Freddie took hold of the chair beside her and sat down. Hard. Then she called the waiter and ordered herself a glass of Perrier water. She looked at Barbara.

'Who did this to you?' she asked. 'Was it your mother?'

The other girl smiled.

'If my mother could see me now, she'd have a blue fit. Nobody did this to me, you idiot. It's all my own work. This is how I like to look.'

Freddie shook her head. This was all wrong. This wasn't how the scene was meant to be played at all. She tried again.

'You can tell me the truth,' she said. 'I know this isn't you. Did you do it because your mother booked a table here?'

Barbara took a sip of champagne from the conical glass in front of her.

'If we're going to get along,' she said slowly, 'there are a couple of things I think you should know. The most important of which is that my mother has nothing whatever to do with today. I invited you here of my own free will. I know my father had a cosy little talk to you about getting close to me, but that's nothing to do with anything. Neither of my parents has the slightest idea of who I am. Or what I get up to.'

Freddie felt the situation slipping away from her. Nobody was what they appeared to be any more. Her mother wasn't the innocent she had once supposed, and now Miss Horse wasn't Miss Horse at all.

She was Dolly Parton in disguise.

'Why did you ask me here?' Freddie said weakly.

'To put you in the picture. You and I are going to be spending a lot of time together this summer. We'll be going to the same country house parties. Who knows, we might even share the odd boyfriend. So you're going to find out sooner or later what I'm really like, and I'd rather you found out from me.'

Freddie started to relax. She hadn't been prepared for this surprise, but now it had happened it wasn't as bad as she thought. This new Barbara might turn out to be fun.

The waiter approached with two menus scribbled on outsized cards. Barbara ordered two starters and another glass of champagne. Freddie did the same but stuck to Perrier water. Instinct told her to keep her head clear.

They were given a table in the front of the restaurant by the window. To one side of them sat Michael Caine and a party. On the other she recognized Marie Helvin and a girlfriend. In her head she gave Barbara ten out of ten. From the way she dealt with the staff, she was familiar with this place. Not just familiar, she was an important customer. Freddie needed to know how she did it. Over lunch Barbara told her. She started with the day the news editor seduced her and went on from there. From the way it sounded, Barbara had done a whole lot of growing up in a very short time.

'I was the original Alice in Wonderland,' she confessed. 'And I have my mother to blame for it. She had all these big ambitions for me. I was to be an English lady and marry a duke with a country estate. Actually she would have liked me to marry Prince Charles, but by the time I came on the market he was already spoken for. Anyway,' she went on, 'the whole thing was doomed from the word go. I just didn't look the part and the more my mother tried to change me, the worse it got. You know I actually put on weight, just to spite her. By the time I left school we were hardly speaking.'

The individual spinach soufflés arrived, plump and

fragrant. Barbara tucked into hers with the relish of somebody who would never go on a diet.

'The thing that saved my sanity,' she told Freddie, 'was finding a job in journalism. It was the first place I fitted in. The guys at my agency like me for me. They like my size and my brain and they don't give a damn about how much money my father has.'

Freddie regarded her thoughtfully. How could I have been so stupid, she thought. Liz would never dress her daughter like this. She would never encourage her to drink champagne in Langan's either. This new Barbara was a creation of the business she was in. The newspaper business. She realized with a start it was the same business David Dearing inhabited.

'Does your father have any idea what you've become?'

Barbara shook her head.

'Not the foggiest. And I'll thank you not to tell him. As far as Daddy is concerned I'm his shy little pigeon. It makes him happy to think of me like that. I wouldn't want to disillusion him.'

Freddie thought about David and the way he had let her pour her heart out in the conservatory. He was a good man. One of the first good men she had known. It bothered her that she should be a party to this deception.

'Won't he find out eventually?' she asked. 'You'll be eighteen any minute. You can't go on pretending to be a horse.'

Barbara looked stubborn.

'As long as I can get away with it, I will.' For a second she was anxious.

'You're not going to let me down, are you?'

The American girl sighed. Barbara wasn't her kind of girl. Not by a long chalk. If they had been at high school together she wouldn't have chosen her for a friend, but she didn't have choices any more. Liz Dearing and her mother had seen to that. All she could do now was make the best of the situation she had been thrown into. Right now, Barbara seemed the only option.

'Stop worrying,' she said, 'I won't give you any problems.'

At the beginning of May, Freddie received a letter from her father. '*I hear from Liz*,' Dan wrote, '*that you will be doing the London Season. I can't tell you how excited I am for you. You will see things and do things you never imagined existed when you lived in New York. I know being sent to England made you unhappy but this Summer should put a stop to all that. There will be new friends and a fresh start for you now.*

'*Just to help you keep your end up*,' he went on, '*I am enclosing a cheque to cover your dress bills and any additional expenses. If it isn't enough, wire me and I'll send whatever extra you need.*

PS: I hope to be coming to England for Ascot. I plan to stay at the Dorchester, so if I can tear you away from the social whirl, maybe we can spend some time together.'

The cheque that came with the letter was made out for twenty thousand pounds. When she saw it, Freddie thought Dan had made a mistake. Nobody could spend that kind of money on a few dresses. That sum alone could put her through college with change at the end of it.

She took Barbara into her confidence about the money, and the younger girl surprised her.

'I don't think it's all that much,' she said. 'A simple ball dress will set you back about a thousand – and you need at least four of those. Then there's Ascot and Glyndebourne, Henley and Wimbledon and all the cocktail parties and lunches in between. If I was you I'd wire him back straight away and ask for another ten.'

Freddie thought Barbara had gone mad.

'I don't believe you,' she said. 'You're making it up.'

Barbara grinned and put her arm round her.

'Mummy's taking me shopping tomorrow,' she said. 'Why don't you come along? Then you'll see if I'm making it up or not.'

The following day they went to Murray Arbeid, Caroline Charles and Browns in South Molton Street. On the way they stopped off at Maude Frizon to look at shoes and Hermès and Chanel to choose handbags. After that, Freddie did as she was told and sent the wire. She didn't ask for ten thousand, though. She demanded twenty. Forty thousand pounds was far in excess of her needs. With a little creative thinking she knew she could look quite stunning for a fraction of that amount, but she asked for the money because she wanted to see how far she could go.

In her heart she knew she was an embarrassment to her father. An illegitimate leftover from a past affair. I bet he wishes I'd just disappear and never be heard of again, she told herself. Well he's fresh out of luck. I've fallen in with the monied classes over here, and Pop's money has to compete with the Dearings' money. Well, serve him right, she thought. It's about time he put himself out for me.

The extra twenty thousand Freddie asked for came by return of post. She put it into the new bank account she had opened for herself and began to feel rich. The money didn't make her any happier. Only love could do that for her, but she knew better than to ask her father for something he couldn't give.

45

The Season started with Glyndebourne. The opera, held in a country house on the Sussex Downs, marked the beginning of the summer's jamboree. All the Dearings' friends polished the silver, locked away all the portable valuables and opened their houses to their children and their children's friends.

'It's a vast marriage market,' Barbara explained. 'Forget the rubbish about entering into society. We'll do our duty and listen to the opera and watch the races. But what it's really about is meeting the right boy.'

Freddie was visibly enthused by the prospect. 'You mean we go to a different party every night so we can meet dates? It sounds wonderful.'

Barbara regarded her new friend with despair. She knew she had been born and bred in Manhattan. She also knew she had had a pretty ropey past.

'Not everyone you meet is going to be Prince Charming,' she sighed. 'So don't hold your breath.'

Liz had booked tickets early for Glyndebourne. She wanted her daughter to be launched at the opera because of the setting.

Since the 1930s the grand old house outside Lewes had played host to the sons and daughters of the rich.

But the house and the opera, although necessary ingredients for the occasion, weren't really what it was all about. The secret of Glyndebourne's magic was its grounds. Acre upon acre of manicured lawns, beds bursting with roses, archways leading to secret sanctuaries – all of this stretched out beyond the converted country house. In the centre of the gardens ran a stream and it was here that the opera-goers made for in the interval, armed with picnics and bottles of champagne.

'Glyndebourne's intervals average around ninety minutes,' Barbara informed Freddie in the back of the Rolls going down to Sussex. 'It's up to us to make the most of the time.'

Although it was only tea-time, the whole family was wearing black tie. It was a cool night and Liz had thrown a long mink coat over her evening dress. The girls, who didn't know the terrain, braved it in bare shoulders. David looked at them both and worried. The sky looked decidedly stormy outside, if it rained they would have to make a run for the house and he doubted whether either of them would survive the journey. His daughter's dress was so low cut, she looked as if she might pop out of it if she attempted anything but a leisurely amble. And Freddie? Freddie looked as if she would blow away at the first puff of wind.

The American girl had surprised David that night. He knew she was older than she looked. Brighter too. But he found it hard to accept her as a grown woman in the pleated skirts and jeans she wore about the house. Tonight was different. From the moment she had walked into his drawing room he had been astonished by her.

Liz had told him her father had provided a wardrobe, but David had no idea what Freddie was going to look like in it. Then, two hours ago she and Barbara had come down the staircase and into the hall.

The first thing David noticed was Freddie's neck and the way it set off her shoulders. She had taken her hair back from her face, and the effect was to make her look regal. Freddie wasn't a schoolgirl any more: she was on the verge of womanhood. David didn't know why, but the sight of her moved him. It also made him feel guilty for he should have reacted to Barbara. Evening dress had transformed her, too, but it was an expected transformation. She had always been big, and now she looked big and sexy.

She'll find a man, David thought. She couldn't fail to, looking like that. And she'll lead whoever it is one hell of a dance. But Freddie he wasn't so sure of. She'd attract her share of suitors, but how would she handle them? The thought of the oafish sons of his friends trying to get one over on her appalled him. She's too innocent for them, he thought. She's not tough enough to tell them to go to hell.

For a moment, David remembered the conversation they had had in the conservatory the night he caught Freddie confiding in the family parrot. She had told him then that she had looked out for her mother all the years of her childhood. She must have been lying, he thought. In that dress she doesn't look as if she could take responsibility for a kitten, let alone a grown woman.

They arrived at the opera house and joined a mile long queue for the car park. David looked at his watch and prepared himself for the next few hours. Glyndebourne was always the same.

You hung about for hours to see whatever opera you had managed to get tickets for. If you were lucky it didn't rain. Then, at the end of it, you sat in the car for another two hours until you got home. He wondered why he did it every year. It was a day out of his life that could have been better spent running the *Chronicle*.

Out of the corner of his eye he saw his father's

Bentley pulling into the car park. David had arranged to join up with his parents and share a picnic and without thinking he went over the latest circulation figures in his mind. Lord Dearing still retained a fascination with the paper. Tonight, when everyone else was busy socializing, they could have a good long talk about it.

David didn't waste any time. All the way down to the gardens he went over the plans for a new property supplement. It had been his idea: a response to the new boom in housing. And only when they got to the water's edge and the chauffeur brought out the champagne, did he feel the first few spots of rain. He turned to his wife.

'Do you think this is a good idea?' he asked. 'Perhaps we should try for a place in the restaurant.'

Liz gritted her teeth. 'Everyone we want to see is going to be down here. The Harmsworths, Patrick Lichfield. I even heard Scott Harding was coming tonight.'

So that's what's on her mind, David thought. Scott Harding, the Canadian golden boy. She's stalking him for Barbara.

'What makes you so sure about Scott?' he asked.

Liz looked smug. 'I spoke to his mother three weeks ago. Apparently he's over here on an assignment for *The New York Times*. From what she says it should keep him here all summer, so we should be seeing something of him.'

As Liz prattled on, David wondered about Scott. He had been doing business with the boy's father for years now. Chad Harding supplied most of his paper and when Scott was looking around for something to do, David offered to advise him. Then he met the boy and realized he didn't need advice at all. What he was looking for were contacts. He'd set his heart on being a journalist while he was still at college, and from the looks of him he seemed destined to succeed.

There was an energy about Scott that David had responded to and he offered him one or two assignments on the *Chronicle* to start him off. Since then, his career had moved ahead in leaps and bounds. Now *The New York Times* had sent him to London. He made a mental note to ask him what it was all about when he ran into him.

The rain had managed to hold off and the servants started setting up the picnic, unfolding tables and laying out the white linen. David checked on the rest of his party and saw they all seemed to be getting stuck into the champagne. Barbara was even stringing bottles together to dunk in the stream, though he couldn't for the life of him think why. It was so cold tonight, the wine didn't need any extra chilling.

At a hidden signal everyone started to troop towards the main house. The performance was due to start and David hoped his party would survive it. Tonight the opera was 'Simon Boccanegra', one of Verdi's lesser known works. He had heard it once, years ago at the London Coliseum and he had hated it then. It lacked the bounce and melody he so enjoyed in Verdi's other operas and he had no idea why it had been included on the programme.

Half an hour into the opera, Freddie was wondering the same thing, though her view was less informed than David's. Norman had liked the opera and she grew up listening to his tapes.

The experience had tuned her ear to the music. She could understand the easy stuff – 'Rigoletto,' 'Madame Butterfly,' 'Tosca'. But she couldn't make head or tail of 'Simon Boccanegra'. She let her mind wander to the picnic in the interval. There was poached salmon in the hamper, and piles of strawberries. They would sip champagne and Pimm's sitting on the rug by the water's edge. Freddie visualized the scene: the grass was wet and fresh smelling, tiny insects buzzed among the roses, everyone was looking wonderful in their best party dresses.

She was unaware of just when she stopped listening to the music or when the stage in front of her dissolved into a blur, but the next thing she knew was her head was resting on David's shoulder and the curtain was coming down.

'Wake up,' he whispered. 'Everyone's staring at us.'

Freddie jerked upright in her seat, blushing to the roots.

'How long have I been like that?' she asked.

Her host looked amused. 'About an hour, I'd say. You dozed off shortly after the Overture. I can't say I blame you.'

Freddie was covered with shame. This was her first excursion into the English social scene. Her debut. And she had blown it. The entire audience must have seen her snoring away during the performance. She'd never live it down.

She followed the rest of the family as they left their seats clutching their programmes. Barbara smiled at her sympathetically.

'I thought it was bloody boring, too,' she whispered. Liz was less generous.

'You might have tried to put a good face on it,' she hissed. 'It was only an hour for God's sake.'

Freddie was thoroughly miserable now. A wind was getting up and for the first time that night, she felt chilly. It had been cold all along, but she had been so excited she hadn't felt it. Now the magic had gone and she felt all alone in her misery.

Barbara came to her rescue. They had reached their

picnic and a group of young men had come over to join them for a drink. Freddie felt herself being pulled into the circle and soon she stopped caring about what had happened in the opera house.

Barbara seemed to know everyone there. She'd grown up with a lot of them sharing the same schools, the same pony clubs, the same dancing classes. Nobody wasted time reminiscing. The main topics of conversation were what parties were on next week, and who was going to the summer exhibition at the Royal Academy.

Freddie started to relax. Everyone was very easy with one another. The New York kids that she knew were always competing, as if they already knew that life was a jungle, and only the strongest and the pushiest would walk away with the prizes. Here, by the river, nobody needed to fight. Everyone's father had money or a title or both.

She glanced up to see one of the boys was holding a fresh bottle of champagne and was filling up the glasses. When he got to her, he paused and looked at her thoughtfully.

'I don't think you should have any more,' he said. 'You don't want to risk nodding off again in the last act.'

He was very tall and sporty-looking. All the other boys here were laid back and languid. This one looked as if he played tennis and worked out every day.

'You're American, aren't you?' Freddie asked.

He shook his head.

'Canadian actually. My folks come from Toronto, though I went to school in New Jersey.'

It turned out that this was Scott and he wasn't really part of the Season at all.

'I'm over here to do some work for *The New York Times*. They want an in-depth analysis of Thatcher's

Britain and I thought the social season was as good a place to start as any.'

Scott wanted to know how Freddie had fetched up here, and she told him she was staying with the Dearing family.

'Liz Dearing and my mother are old friends,' she explained.

He looked quizzical.

'Mrs Dearing has quite a network. She goes back a long way with my mother too.'

For a moment Freddie felt panicky. It's not going to take him long to find me out, she thought. Scott or any other boy I meet this summer. All they have to do is have a word with Liz and I'm sunk.

He must have read her mind for he looked concerned.

'Was it something I just said?' he asked. 'You look as if the world was about to end.'

'It is,' she said quietly, 'but it's nothing to do with you.'

At that moment, Barbara bounded up slightly drunk and more than pleased to see Scott.

'How are you, old bean?' she asked, planting a kiss on his cheek. Then she saw Freddie and smiled broadly.

'I see you two have met.'

A wave of dizziness came over Freddie. I must have had too much champagne, she thought. If I go on standing here, I'll start to make a fool of myself.

'I have to go,' she said quickly, too quickly. 'I promised your father I'd tell him something.'

Barbara watched her as Freddie threaded her way through the crowd.

'What's the matter with her?' she asked. 'You didn't make a pass or anything, did you?'

Scott Harding took a sip of his drink and frowned

into the gathering dusk. The shadows on his face put Barbara in mind of a young Michael Douglas.

'No, I didn't make a pass at Freddie,' he replied. Then his face broke into a grin. 'I'm saving that one up for Ascot.'

46

Liz was pleased with the way the evening had gone at Glyndebourne. Apart from Freddie's regrettable lapse, everything was the way she had planned it. Barbara and Scott had made contact again.

She sat in front of her kidney-shaped dressing-table and started putting cold cream on her make-up. My daughter looked good tonight, she thought. She's a little heavy but she's got my skin and her father's features. There's a lot of sex there, too. Most of the young men there looked as if they couldn't wait to get her into bed. She paused while the cream sunk into her skin. But after the bed thing, she wondered, would they take her seriously? Would a young man – a young man like Scott – want to marry Barbara?

She started rubbing at the cream now with damp cotton wool, smearing the eye-black and the paint across her face. Of course Scott will want to marry my daughter, she told herself. They have everything to give each other.

Liz did a fast inventory of the Harding empire. They had paper mills and great tracts of forest in Canada. That was their connection with the Hardings. The Dearings had newspapers. The Hardings had paper. They needed each other. With Scott and Barbara safely married, they would have one another for all time.

David walked into the room with a whisky in his hand.

'You look very intense,' he observed. 'What were you thinking of?'

Liz came straight to the point.

'I was thinking about Scott Harding,' she said. 'What's he been up to in the past year or so? He travels around so much these days, I seem to have lost track of him.'

David took a sip of his drink and wondered what to tell her. If he painted too rosy a picture she'd be making wedding plans and he didn't want her to do that. Scott was a grown man. He knew his own mind. His wife could make a fool of Barbara by throwing her at his head.

But what could he say? For the life of him he couldn't find a black mark against Scott. Everything he'd done, right from the moment he'd started him off on the *Chronicle*, had been touched with success.

Like a lot of young men who graduated from Yale, Scott had had an interest in politics, but he wasn't content to sit in Washington and take it all from the American point of view. His horizons were broader and he proved it at the first available opportunity.

At the beginning of the 1980s Gorbachev was beginning to make his presence felt in Russia and David remembered Scott coming to him and asking if the *Chronicle* would send him to Moscow. He turned the young man down of course. His foreign editor ran a tight ship and certainly wouldn't appreciate his proprietor foisting an untried Canadian on him. So Scott got to Moscow under his own steam. While he was there, he filed a series of reports on the new communist leadership which *Newsweek* snapped up and used as a cover story.

After Moscow, he journeyed to the Gulf and did a series on the oil sheiks which was syndicated across America. David had cursed his short sightedness, for

Scott had the knack of seeing a situation from the other man's point of view. The stuff coming out of the Gulf could have been written by a man who had grown up in the desert.

None of his foreign staff could have come anywhere near it. But by that time Scott was lost to him. The big guns – *Time*, *Newsweek*, *The Washington Post* – had first call on him. The money they paid saw to that.

Yet David didn't resent it because he wasn't brash. He marvelled at that. Scott had one of the top family names in Canada. He was a success in his own right, and he was damned good-looking. David wouldn't have blamed him if he had tried to throw his weight about, but he didn't. The only fault he had, if it was a fault, was that the boy didn't suffer fools. If he thought someone had made a stupid remark, he said so, and girls weren't exempt from his criticism. Half the debutantes in New York had had their hearts broken by his crushing scorn. All of a sudden, David had an idea. If he told Liz the boy was insufferably arrogant, she would be thrown off the scent. He smiled.

'I know what you're planning,' he told Liz. 'You want to marry Barbara off to Scott, don't you?'

Liz stood up and shrugged off the lace peignoir. They had been married nearly twenty years and she still came to bed naked. David looked at her with a mixture of fondness and desire.

'There's no point in hiding it from me,' he went on. 'I can read you like a book.'

'What if I do want that for our daughter? It's not such a dreadful ambition, is it?'

David sighed and drained the last of his whisky.

'I'd agree with you if I didn't know Scott better. He's not for Barbara. The man's an intellectual snob. He despises anyone who isn't as well informed as he is and he likes a debate. I can't see

Barbara arguing the finer points of the economic situation with him. She's turning out to be a good little journalist, but she's no giant in the brains department. Scott would be bored with her in two seconds.'

There was a silence while Liz turned this over in her mind.

Finally she said, 'I think you're wrong about Scott. He may be very bright, but men like that get all the conversation they need from other men. They confide in their colleagues or the men they go shooting with. When they choose a wife they want her for entirely different reasons.'

She came over to him, removing the glass from his hand and pulling him towards the bed.

'I think it's about time I reminded you of that.'

The next day Freddie received two dozen red roses from Scott. She was so embarrassed by the gift that she took the flowers into the conservatory and hid them behind the parrot.

Barbara was appalled. 'What are you doing?' she demanded. 'If Scott Harding sent me roses I'd put them in the drawing-room for the world to see.'

'It's different for you,' Freddie said. 'Your mother didn't get put in the slammer for pushing drugs.'

So that's why she walked away from him, Barbara thought. She's worried about her background. For a second she was tempted to tell her to forget Scott. With Freddie out of the running everyone else would have a chance. Then she thought, no. I can't do that. It simply wouldn't be fair. She tried to talk some sense into Freddie.

'Scott doesn't want to take you out for your mother, for Christ's sake. He wants to know you for you. Nobody cares that much about pedigrees any more.

Americans don't anyway. Why don't you give him a chance?'

But Freddie wouldn't be persuaded. Scott rang twice that day; once to ask her to the ballet. Then when said she was busy, he called back to invite her to dinner. She said no to that as well. When Barbara tried to reason with her, she locked herself in her room and refused to come out until the English girl changed the subject.

But Scott Harding wouldn't go away. He started turning up at the house on the pretext of wanting to see David. At first everyone was fooled. The newspaper series he was writing was an analysis of Thatcher's Britain and David was close to the Prime Minister. It was only natural he would want his input. But after a while it became apparent that researching his series was not the reason Scott haunted the house in Cheyne Walk.

Liz was the first person to cotton on. On his second visit, the family was having a drink in the drawing room, and Scott asked where Freddie had got to.

'I heard she was staying here,' he said, 'but I never see her when I'm here.'

'She goes out a lot,' Liz said vaguely. 'She's still in school, you know.'

She smelt a rat when Scott wanted to know which college Freddie went to.

'Why are you so interested?' she asked. 'You don't want to take her out or something, do you?'

Scott gave Liz his best smile. The one he kept in reserve for difficult women on the wrong side of forty.

'I certainly don't want to take Freddie out,' he told Liz. 'What I have in mind is keeping her in.'

In the end it was Barbara who solved things. She arranged to meet Scott in Jules's Bar, and when she reached the cocktail lounge in Jermyn Street she didn't waste time on niceties. Scott liked her, she knew that, but he didn't fancy her, so she dispensed with small talk.

'I came here to put you straight about Freddie,' she told him.

The young man ordered a round of drinks and watched Barbara trying to arrange herself on one of the ridiculously high, small bar stools.

'I'm glad somebody's decided to talk about her,' he said doing his best not to look at the expanse of thigh that Barbara was showing. 'Anybody would think the girl had some sort of problem with men. Every time I try to pin her down she bolts.'

'Freddie doesn't have a problem with men,' said Barbara. 'She has a problem with her family.'

She proceeded to tell him what she knew about her new friend. Freddie had told her a lot of it. The rest she gleaned from her mother. When she had finished, Scott was grinning broadly.

'She thinks she's not good enough for me,' he said. 'Is that it?'

'Of course that's it,' Barbara said crossly. 'Freddie doesn't think she's good enough for anybody. Though I don't see why you're looking so happy about it.' Scott patted her knee, suddenly not minding about the oversized thighs.

'I'm looking happy,' he told her, 'because I know Freddie doesn't hate me now. Before, I thought she found me offensive. I had no idea she was worried about her mother.'

Barbara looked at Scott over the rim of her glass.

'Don't count your chickens,' she said. 'Freddie might think you're nice, but you've still got to find a way of persuading her that it doesn't matter about her background.'

Scott signalled to the barman for another round of drinks. So Freddie is ready to fall in love, he thought. He heaved a sigh of relief. It was going to be easier than he thought. He needed her to love him. He was depending on it. He couldn't possibly marry a girl who was incapable of a grand passion.

47

Scott made his move at Lucinda McNaill's coming out ball. The McNaills, who owned vast tracts of land in Ireland, had decided to hold the dance at Claridges in London.

The smart set were perfectly willing to go down to the country for a ball, but the family doubted if everyone would take two days out to trek to Ireland and back. With so many parties to go to, nobody could afford to leave town for longer than a night.

Barbara and Freddie were no exception. They were booked up for weeks ahead. Sometimes they went to three parties a night and contrary to their fears and expectations, they enjoyed them.

'I'm so glad Lucinda's bash is at Claridges,' Barbara said. 'It will be the high point of the week, particularly since the Princess of Wales is going to be there.'

That really impressed Freddie. Since she had come to London, she had danced with dukes and flirted with heirs to several fortunes, but never in her life had she been presented to royalty.

'What do I do?' she asked in a panic. 'If somebody takes me over to meet the Princess. Will she expect me to curtsey?'

'You bet you'll have to curtsey,' Barbara said. 'I'll show you.'

For the rest of the afternoon, Barbara rehearsed Freddie in the protocol of meeting the Princess. Then, when she was satisfied that the American knew what to do, she let her go to her room to change into her ballgown.

They had both spent all morning at the hairdresser's, getting the right look. Barbara had her hair piled up into a chignon in order to wear the family tiara. Freddie had chosen the same simple style she wore to Glyndebourne, an upsweep held in place with two jewelled combs. It suited the dress she had chosen from Belleville Sassoon.

It was a very romantic outfit with vast sweeping skirts and a tight strapless top that emphasized her waist. It made her feel like Scarlett O'Hara.

'All you need,' said Barbara, 'is a beautiful necklace or a pair of dangly earrings and you'll be perfect.'

Freddie looked worried. 'I didn't think to buy any.'

'Good thing,' Barbara told her. 'Even your father's donation wouldn't run to what I have in mind. Anyway you don't buy jewellery, not the real thing. You inherit it. Mummy got stacks from my grandmother. Come on, let's see if we can get her to lend you some.'

Freddie was carried along by Barbara's enthusiasm. Normally she wouldn't have dreamed of asking Liz for anything, but there was something festive about tonight. Everyone, even David, was getting excited about the dance. They were going together as a family. Liz will want me to look nice, Freddie told herself. A poor relation wouldn't do her any credit at all.

But she was wrong. Liz wasn't interested in parting with any of her baubles.

'It's the insurance,' she explained. 'I'm not covered for a third party. If anything falls off in Claridges, it's gone for ever.'

Barbara was unconvinced. 'Mummy,' she protested, 'you lent me your diamond necklace only last week and you didn't say anything about insurance then. Anyway Freddie wouldn't lose anything. I can vouch for her.'

Liz looked at her daughter, all dressed up in her party dress. Barbara was attractive, she had to acknowledge that. In the simple little Hartnell dress she almost looked svelte.

Then her eyes crossed the room to Freddie and she knew she had been deluding herself. Next to the American girl, her daughter looked exactly what she was: a big hearty country girl on the hunt for a husband. At Claridges there would be hundreds like her.

Liz sighed inwardly. Doesn't Barbara have enough competition, she thought, without adding to her problems. In that dress, Freddie looks good enough to eat. Give her jewellery as well and she'll turn into a princess.

She made her mind up. There was every chance that Scott would be there tonight. The boy already had eyes for Freddie. There was no point in serving her up on a silver plate.

'Freddie can't have any jewellery,' she said firmly. 'She's not used to it. She wouldn't know how to respect it. It's different for you, Barbara, you were brought up knowing about that sort of thing.'

It was like a slap in the face. One moment Liz was her usual unhelpful self, simply bossy and critical. The next, she had turned into a bitch. David, who had come into the room minutes earlier, came to Freddie's rescue.

'You look beautiful just the way you are,' he consoled her. 'At your age, you don't need expensive stones. Your skin has its own glow.'

Freddie was grateful for that, and for the way David looked at her with such obvious admiration. Liz had made her feel like a poor little match girl picked up off the streets. At least David restored some sense of self-worth.

Freddie let him lead her out of Liz's room and into the drawing-room. Downstairs a cold supper had been set up for the family. There was smoked salmon, Russian caviar and several different salads. Yet Freddie couldn't eat anything.

Liz's hostility over the jewellery had confirmed everything she had suspected. The woman hated her. She had brought her to London as a favour to her mother and nothing more. As far as she was concerned she would put up with her under her roof. She would go through the motions of friendship, but underneath she was probably counting the days until Vanessa came out of jail and she could go back to New York.

Any other girl might have thrown a tantrum and refused to go out, but Freddie wasn't any other girl. She was used to living with her enemies. When Norman had threatened her mother's safety, she had placated him. When Ted had been slow to pay the rent, she had been the one to prise the money out of him. Never once did she complain. Never did she call either of them cheap, even though she ached to. She had used her charm instead, and it had proved a potent weapon. She set her face. She would use the same weapon on Liz.

Whatever this proxy mother of hers did, she was going to be sweet. For every one of Liz's scowls there would be ten smiles, ten ingratiating simpers. It wouldn't fool her, of course. The woman wasn't born yesterday. But it would confuse her, for she wouldn't be able to guess what Freddie was thinking.

Freddie's appetite began to return and she helped herself to a heap of sticky black caviar. For good measure, she piled hard boiled egg, raw onions and thin brown toast on to her plate. As she did so, she saw Liz come into the room. She was looking vampish in black and the girl noticed she was covered in diamonds. Freddie hurried over to where she stood. 'I'm sorry about the jewellery,' she said. 'It was pushy of me to think I could borrow it.'

Liz raised her eyebrows. So the child had come to her senses after all.

'It wasn't pushy, Freddie,' she said gently. 'I would never accuse you of that. It was simply unrealistic, and I'm glad you see that.'

Freddie turned her face away. You bet it was unrealistic, she thought. I should have known not to expect anything of you.

The McNaill family had gone to town on their daughter's coming out dance. The ballroom at Claridges had been transformed to look like a garden in the South of France. Every wall had been covered by a trellis over which were twined fresh pink and white roses. The theme of the ball was pink and white, and acres of bushes had been harvested to produce this effect. All the tables had cascading arrangements at their centres, and in the four corners of the room, four artificial rose trees had been specially constructed. They had been made to support the pièce de resistance: four pairs of white doves. Freddie imagined they must have been drugged for they perched decoratively round the room with hardly a squawk between them.

They had arrived at Claridges slightly late and the dance was in full swing when they came into the rose-scented room. Every debutante in London seemed to be there, and when Freddie recovered from the sight of the white doves, something else struck her. She was the only one with a bare neck. All the other girls were dolled up in grandmother's pearls, great-grandmother's tiara or daddy's diamonds. For a moment, her confidence started to ebb, then she remembered the way David had looked at her when he came into the bedroom. He said I glowed, she thought. He's given me something to live up to.

She stood very straight and keeping her head high she marched across the room. Scott Harding was standing at the bar watching her progress. The only other girl who walks like that, he thought, is the Princess herself. She looks as if she owns the place. He put his glass down and went towards her.

'Freddie,' he said. 'You're just the girl I'm looking for. Will you have the next dance?'

Freddie seemed to falter and go into herself. 'I can't,' she said nervously.

'Why can't you?'

The truth danced inside her head. Because you're too attractive. Because I'm half in love with you already. Because if I give into this feeling, I'll be done for.

She attempted a smile. 'I promised this one to David,' she said. Just as she said it, she saw David deep in conversation with an elderly man in white tie and a baronet's badge. She rushed over to him.

'I'm so glad I found you,' she said. 'I've been looking everywhere.'

Out of the corner of her eye she saw Scott looking at them.

'Dance with me,' she muttered under her breath. 'I'm trying to get away from someone and you're my only hope.'

David put his arm around her waist and led her onto the floor.

'I'm not sure I like being used as a blunt instrument

to beat off your suitors, but an old man like me can't be choosy.'

Freddie smiled up at him, relaxed and comfortable now that the danger had been averted.

'You're not such an old man,' she said. 'If I was a different sort of girl, I'd be tempted to flirt with you.'

David looked at her seriously then, and Freddie wished she hadn't played the coquette. David Dearing wasn't just any man to be made eyes at and manipulated. He was her ally in this confusing new world. Apart from Barbara he was probably her only friend.

'Don't patronize me,' David said sharply. 'If I was a different kind of man you could be in for a surprise.'

She was suddenly very conscious of how closely she was dancing to him. The smell of him was on her breath. Expensive aftershave mixed with something else, and for no apparent reason she felt frightened. She looked over his shoulder and saw Scott standing behind them.

'Can I cut in,' he said. 'She did promise me the next one.'

David smiled broadly.

'Scott,' he said. 'I didn't know you were here tonight. Of course you can cut in.'

Without ceremony David handed Freddie over to the young man, and she was surprised to find she felt relieved. Scott was her own fighting weight. He made her nervous as hell, but she knew she could handle him.

'Why have you been running away from me?' he asked without preamble. 'I've been trying to get hold of you for weeks now.'

Freddie braced herself. She was going to have to tell this man where he stood, and the sooner the better.

'I don't want to get involved,' she said, 'and I suspect you do.'

Scott looked at her sideways.

'What gives you that idea?'

'The flowers. The phone-calls. If you were after a casual friendship you wouldn't be quite so . . . so urgent.'

The band started to play the theme from *Dr Zhivago* and Freddie felt herself floating in his arms. I'm enjoying this too much, she thought. Why don't I just walk away?

But she couldn't. Somewhere in the middle of the waltz she had lost her concentration and imperceptibly she felt Scott take over.

'I'm glad you got the message,' he said pleasantly. 'I wouldn't want there to be any misunderstandings between us.'

Freddie looked up at him.

'What do you mean?'

'I mean I want to make it very clear, right from the start, that I'm one hundred per cent serious about you. More than that, I think I'm falling in love with you.'

'Don't do that.' The words were out of her mouth before Freddie could stop them.

'Why not,' Scott said. 'Are you worried your mother's little stretch in prison might put me off? Well let me tell you, there's not a chance. I don't give a damn who your mother is, or what she's done. I'm not some deb's delight, running around the dances collecting pedigrees.'

She stopped in her tracks. Right in the middle of the ballroom at Claridges, Freddie stood stock still and let the rest of the world revolve around her.

'How do you know about my mother?' she said.

Scott took her by the arm and hustled her away from the rest of the dancers. He didn't stop until he'd managed to find an alcove in the corner of the room. Then he deposited her on to a tiny gilt chair and pulled up another for himself.

'I know about your mother,' he said patiently, 'because I took the trouble to find out about you. When you started to avoid me, I suspected something was wrong. Girls don't usually run away from me. Especially when they hardly know me.'

'You have quite a good opinion of yourself, don't you?'

Scott tipped back the flimsy wooden chair.

'Yes, actually. I know who I am and what I want. Right now I know *who* I want.'

Freddie felt herself smile. It was an involuntary thing. One moment she was an ice maiden putting up every resistance, the next she started to melt.

'I . . . I can't promise you anything,' she said.

'I'm not asking for promises,' he told her. 'I'm asking you to come out and have dinner with me. Are you prepared to commit yourself that far?'

Freddie suddenly felt rather foolish.

What am I running away from, she asked herself. Scott Harding is perfectly straightforward. He's nice, he's Canadian and he doesn't frighten me one little bit.

For a moment, she remembered the dance she had had with David that night and the feeling she had of not being able to cope. I wonder what got into me, she thought.

48

Why am I so nice, thought Liz. I run half way across the world to help out a friend I lost touch with years ago. Then I offer to take in her daughter. As if I didn't have my hands full enough already.

She was in the middle of preparing for Barbara's coming-out party. The unanimous decision was to have it at the house in the country and Liz was at the caterers' in Market Harborough trying to make sense of the menu. It should have been child's play. The food for these kinds of parties followed a formula. Smoked salmon, Coronation chicken, asparagus, assorted salads and strawberries. The firm in Market Harborough had been doing it for years. They even threw in breakfast free of charge for the determined late-nighters.

So why was she finding it so difficult? It's Freddie, she thought. The child's been on my mind since that silly business with the jewellery. She knew she had been right to withhold it. Freddie even came and apologized for asking, but nobody else had given her any peace. David thought she had been unnecessarily tough and Barbara – Barbara went on endlessly about what she had done.

'I know insurance is a worry for you Mummy, but why did you have to be so nasty to her? I saw her face when you said she didn't understand good things. She was really hurt.'

Well, serves her right, thought Liz. She deserves to be hurt. Who does she think she is, walking off with Scott Harding. Stealing him from under our noses. She must have known right from the start Scott was going to inherit a fortune. I bet she looked up his father in Forbes.

Her train of thought was interrupted by the caterer, who was making lists. She had reached the vegetables and needed advice.

'Do you want to provide baked potatoes or boiled?' Liz hesitated for a fraction of a second, her mind still miles away.

'I understand Madam,' the woman said misinterpreting. 'You want me to do both.'

'No I don't,' Liz snapped. 'I'm doing a ball, not a coronation. We'll have boiled.'

'What about the salads? Or do you want salads? Maybe vegetables would be cheaper?'

The woman was all of a dither and Liz knew she was the cause of it. Barbara's coming out was the most extravagant the county had experienced for many seasons. Armies of cleaners had been recruited to polish the house from top to bottom. Extra cooks and maids and bottle-washers had been laid on for the night, and even the local garden centre had drained its entire stock in order to cover the place in extra greenery. That was quite apart from the florist's contribution which would come later.

For the next half hour Liz did her best to concentrate on the food for the evening, but try as she might the image of Freddie kept coming back to her. She looked so damned beautiful the night of Lucinda McNaill's ball. Even without jewellery she put everyone else there in the shade. She even made me feel past it, Liz mused, and that doesn't happen very often.

It was all David's fault of course. Telling her she had a special glow. Even if it hadn't been there before, he managed to put it there. All hundred watts of it. No wonder Scott had been dazzled. Scott and her husband and every other man in the room.

Liz felt a pang of unreasoning hatred for the girl. She's had it too easy, she thought. Well, life isn't like that. Freddie can't just walk into our lives, scoop up the finest catch of the Season, and live happily ever after. She doesn't deserve it, and she certainly didn't earn it.

No, Liz thought, the person who deserves Scott Harding is Barbara. She can bring more to the marriage than sex appeal and a pretty face. She has her father's empire and her family name. In the long run those are the assets that will endure. When Freddie's beauty is just a memory, Barbara's inheritance will wax strong. But how can I make that clear to Scott, Liz thought. From the way things were going it looked as if he was on the point of proposing to the American waif. For the past few weeks they had never been out of each other's company and the house was full of his flowers. If she didn't do something soon, everything would be lost.

When she got back to the house there was a message for her. A Mr Levin had called from the Dorchester. Would she call him back as soon as she could?

Liz's first reaction was to go to the drinks cabinet and pour herself a strong whisky. She hadn't spoken to Dan since she had left New York. Once or twice she had thought of calling him on some pretext, but she never did. What had happened between them had been ecstasy. Magic almost. It was a dangerous magic though, for it rendered her helpless. She knew if she saw him again, even once, she'd fall into bed with him all over again and she didn't want to risk another affair. She had survived Vic Chirgotis by plotting and planning and having her face lifted, but it had been a near thing.

Liz shuddered, remembering, but the whisky brought back other memories too. Her hotel bedroom. The way Dan had undressed her. The skill of his love-making. She was seized with an uncontrollable need to bring back that night. But she fought it. Instead of dialling London, she took refuge in another whisky. A bigger whisky.

She was half way through it when the phone rang. She picked it up. It's probably Barbara, she thought, or the woman from the caterers'. When she heard Dan's voice she knew she had been deluding herself. Liz knew enough about men to realize he'd call back.

'What a nice surprise,' she said, 'I wondered what you were up to.'

Dan didn't waste any time on small talk. He was in London for Ascot and to see his daughter.

He was also there to see her. Would she be free one evening?

A hundred different excuses came into Liz's mind. She was a married woman. New York had been a mistake. But nothing, not even a protest, made it to her lips.

'I'd love to see you one evening,' she told Dan, her words slurring slightly.

'Good,' he said. 'What about tonight?'

49

The sun shone brightly for the last day of Ascot. In a way it was a blessing, for all week the weather had been grey and miserable with the odd shower. The bookies on the rails between the Royal Enclosure and Tattersalls defended themselves with brightly coloured umbrellas, but no matter how cheerful they pretended to be, their mood didn't catch on with the punters. Not the smart punters anyway.

They had all put on their hired top hats and best silk dresses to show off in front of the royals and the elements were getting to them. Most of the women wore that pinched unhappy look that comes from spending too much money in Harrods and getting wet through for their trouble. None of this misery seemed to reach Liz, who floated through Ascot week with a silly smile on her face and a kind word for everybody. Including Freddie.

Freddie wondered what had got into her. It can't be the company she's been keeping, that's for sure, she thought.

All week Liz had been the mistress of ceremonies in the *Chronicle*'s box. This meant being charming to a stream of circulation managers, newspaper executives and the odd columnist and racing correspondent. Freddie thought they were all deadly dull and kept as far away as she could from David's business entertaining. Even when it was raining, it was more fun to stand in the champagne bar at the back of the Royal Enclosure than it was to pile into the cramped little room over the racecourse.

Her father took her to task over this.

'You might try gracing David with your presence for five minutes,' he told her. 'He's relying on you for a bit of light relief.'

For a bit of decoration more like, Freddie thought. The place is crawling with grey old men on the make.

The first day she was there, she met her father for lunch in the box. After that she decided she had done her bit. Freddie's problem was that she wasn't a racing fan. She liked the smell of the horses in the paddock, and she had a whale of a time going through the *Sporting Life* and putting money on the most unlikely names, but she didn't actually enjoy watching the horses gallop round the course. She hated being squashed in front of the box while everyone pushed and shoved to get a better view.

'It's not that I don't care who won,' she explained to Barbara, 'it's that I can't really tell what's happening when I'm in that stuffy little room.'

The other girl smiled.

'Don't let Daddy hear you talk like that about his precious box,' she said. 'It's been in the family for years and it costs an absolute fortune to run.'

'I don't care,' Freddie pouted. 'I'd rather be here any day.'

They were standing in the car park on the last sunny day of Ascot flitting from lunch party to lunch party. The Duke of Devonshire, true to form, had reserved three spaces next to the paddock and was entertaining seventy people to poached salmon and strawberries. The two girls hadn't exactly been asked to join, but Barbara remembered her mother saying she might look in if she could get away.

So she assumed one member of the family was expected.

Not that it mattered. She knew most of the guests anyway and now the week was drawing to an end nobody was standing on ceremony. She was wondering whether or not to chance her luck and ask for some salmon when she saw Boots Winchester. He was slightly the worse for wear, staggering, rather than walking, across the turf and she groaned inwardly. He's seen us, Barbara thought. Now there's no escape.

She and Boots had never seen eye to eye. At children's parties he had bullied everyone, and when he grew old enough to be invited to drinks his behaviour hadn't changed. He was arrogant and pushy.

Barbara looked up to see him standing next to her. 'Hi, Boots,' she said distractedly. 'Having a nice time?'

He ignored the question.

'Who's the dishy girl you came with?'

When Barbara didn't reply, he leaned closer.

'Come on, Ba,' he said. 'Be a sport, introduce me.'

Barbara glimpsed Freddie hovering in the background looking nervous. 'You're wasting your time,' she said firmly. 'The dishy girl is taken. Scott Harding staked his claim weeks ago.'

Boots seemed to find this amusing.

'Scott can go stuff himself,' he grinned, 'I'm still going to say hello.'

Before she could prevent him, the tall beefy man pushed his way through the crowd to where Freddie was. Barbara thought about intercepting him, then she saw Freddie smile politely and attempt to hold a conversation. She's doing fine, Barbara thought. The Season's turning her into a real trouper. She turned her attention to Scott, who was coming into the car park with her mother in tow. Where on earth did she get that outfit, she thought. It was meant for somebody half her age.

Liz had decided to wear her skirts short for Ascot that year. She had instructed her dressmaker to take two inches off everything she had delivered. The result was that she resembled a little chorus girl. The whole thing looked even more startling because of the hat she was wearing. It was a Herbert Johnson creation, broad brimmed and covered in full-blown roses.

With an effort Barbara kept a straight face. 'Mother,' she said with as much sincerity as she could muster, 'you look astonishing.'

Liz grinned. 'Thank you darling. Scott was saying much the same thing just before.'

She caught Scott's eye and he gave her a broad wink.

For a second Barbara felt profoundly irritated. Mother, she thought, why can't you be your age?

A waiter came round with a tray of champagne cocktails and Scott scooped up three and passed them round.

'Is that Boots Winchester Freddie's talking to over there?' he asked curiously. 'I didn't know she knew him.'

'She doesn't,' Barbara said, 'but he seemed very keen to meet her.' Then she saw Scott's face and she regretted telling him, for the Canadian looked stricken.

'Come on,' he said. 'It's time we broke up this little tête-à-tête.'

A puff of wind blowing in from the paddock tipped Barbara's hat askew and she smelt the air around her. New mown grass and horse dung, she thought. The scent of the races. How I love it. As she trailed behind her mother and Scott, her eyes took in the scene around her. Everyone had had their cars polished for today. Gleaming Mercedes stood bumper to bumper with Rollses and Bentleys and Aston Martins. All around stood foldaway tables covered in white linen and antique silver.

Barbara had been here three years running, she had drunk champagne all around the the course, yet the car park was her most favourite place. For her it epitomized Ascot. Only the English, she thought, would dress up to the nines for a picnic out of a car boot.

Boots looked shifty as the three of them approached.

'I was just explaining the finer points of the Tote to your girlfriend,' he told Scott. 'Hope you don't mind.'

The Canadian shrugged and did his best to look casual.

'Why should I mind?' he said. 'I don't own Freddie.'

'That's not what she told me. I'm having the damnedest time trying to talk the girl into drinks with Lord Paget after all this is over.'

Scott fought down the urge to strike Boots. He was muscling in on his territory and he knew it. Then he looked over to Freddie and saw how animated she looked. She's enjoying this, he thought. She probably thinks I'm going to challenge this drunken idiot to a duel. He fought down his anger.

'Have you met Lord Paget?' he asked Freddie.

She shook her head.

'In that case,' he went on, 'you really ought to drop by and make his acquaintance. He's charming. A true British eccentric.'

Freddie started to say something, but Scott had had enough. Turning on his heel, he pushed his way through the throng and out of the car park. Freddie made to follow him, but Liz restrained her.

'Let him go,' she told her. 'If you start explaining things now you'll only make him crosser. In half an hour he'll have calmed down. If I were you, I'd leave it till then.'

Freddie faltered. 'Are you sure?'

Liz's smile was bright and full of false charm.

'I'm positive,' she said.

Boots, Barbara noticed, had stopped drinking and had switched to Perrier water. The effect it had on him was nothing short of miraculous. Before he was a blustering bully. Now he was light and amusing and full of delicious gossip. He seemed to know about everyone there that afternoon. Who was sleeping with who. Who had lost more on the horses than they could comfortably afford. He even had the names of everyone who had gatecrashed the Duke's party. Barbara sent up a prayer of thanks that her mother had turned up after all. Without her she would have been as suspect as all the other uninvited guests.

After a bit, Boots suggested they all went up and watched the racing. He really was an expert on the Tote and he knew all about form and the merits of the different trainers.

'I have a system all worked out,' he told them. 'If you stick with it, I promise you'll make some money this afternoon.'

Freddie looked doubtful. 'I really should go and find Scott,' she said. 'He'll wonder what I'm doing all this time.'

Boots laughed. 'Then let him wonder. The bugger had no right to go walking out on you like that. It wasn't as if you were doing anything wrong after all.'

For once Barbara agreed with him.

'Keep him guessing,' she said. 'It will do him good. It's high time a woman stood up to Scott.'

Freddie allowed herself to be led back to the Royal Enclosure. I'll stay with them for twenty minutes, she promised herself. Then whatever anyone says, I'm off. This silly fight has gone on long enough.

On the way back to the course, Boots bought a copy of *Sporting Life*. Then as the women scanned the stands, waving to the people they knew, he studied the pages. There were five races left. For each, the paper had made its selection and as usual the estimates were conservative. The favourite was always tipped as were the horses from world famous stables. There were no wild guesses on rank outsiders. Whoever was running the *Sporting Life* had the interests of the punters at heart. If any of the smart set lost their shirts, it wouldn't be the fault of the racing paper.

Boots made his decisions, then called to his companions. It took ten minutes to talk through the next race. Liz was the most experienced when it came to it. She loved racing and had evolved her own system which was roughly similar to Boots's. Both of them knew the owners, both of them listened to gossip and their decisions were based on what they judged to be true. Barbara opted to follow the *Sporting Life*, because it was easy.

The odd one out was Freddie. She wasn't interested in informed gossip or informed tipsters. When she gambled, she did so out of blind instinct. If she liked a name, she went for it, regardless of form. The name she put her stake on in the race to come was Butterfly's Wing.

'You've got to be joking,' Boots told her. 'The mare is a rank outsider. She's never done anything in her life. Why don't you go with the favourite. At least you'll be guaranteed a place.'

But Freddie wouldn't be persuaded.

'I want five pounds on Butterfly's Wing,' she said

firmly. 'And I'll put it on the nose. I just know she'll win.'

'Don't you think you're being a little foolish?' asked Liz.

Freddie stuck her chin out. 'No,' she said. 'I don't.'

Before anyone could stop her, she marched into the stands and up the stairs to the Tote. Liz looked after her despairingly. She's too headstrong, she thought. If she'd stayed a minute longer she needn't have gone to the trouble of hiking up all those stone steps.

Everyone put their bets on. Liz chanced two hundred pounds on the Aga Khan's horse, Barbara followed the tipster's choice in the racing paper and Boots did the same as Liz. Five minutes later Freddie joined them. She looked oddly intense, as if she had put all her savings on Butterfly's Wing instead of the stake she had bought. Liz shrugged. She's probably fretting about Scott, she thought. Serves her right, she doesn't deserve him.

The race started and as usual Freddie paid no attention at all. She didn't understand what was going on. She didn't even know which colours her horse was carrying. The only thing she cared about at all was the result. She noticed the crowd seemed more excited than usual. She leaned towards Barbara.

'Is anything wrong?' she asked. 'Everyone seems to be talking at once.'

Barbara sighed. 'For heaven's sake concentrate,' she hissed, 'Butterfly's Wing is in the lead.'

The rest of the race went by in a blur. Everyone around her was pushing and shoving, trying to get a better view. Freddie felt someone tread on her toe, but it didn't matter. All her attention was focused on the course in front of her. Butterfly's Wing was pulling away, increasing her lead, and the crowd went wild with excitement. Freddie lost sight of the race then.

The heads in front of her seemed to fuse into one dark mass and she didn't know what the hell was going on. Then the tannoy crackled into life filling her ears with metallic sound.

'It's Butterfly's Wing,' it boomed, 'Butterfly's Wing wins by two lengths.'

Freddie couldn't believe it. All she had was a wild instinct for an improbable name. And now she was rich. As well as her five pounds she had added the one hundred pounds her father had handed her earlier.

She was seized by a sudden curiosity. Turning to Boots she said, 'What were the odds on the winner?'

He looked at her in disbelief. 'You mean you don't know?'

Freddie shook her head, and he started to laugh.

'You're more of a noodle than I thought you were. Your nag came home at twenty to one, so whatever you put on it you can afford to buy all of us a bottle of champagne.'

Freddie felt her laughter bubble up, the celebration soaring in her blood.

'I can afford more than a bottle,' she told him. 'I can lay on a whole bloody crate. I've just won over two thousand pounds.'

She took the stone steps two at a time with Barbara and Boots in hot pursuit, and when she got to the Tote and handed in her slip, the bookie delivered her winnings in four neat piles of notes. She had never seen so much cash. Her father's cheques went straight into her bank account so she had no idea of what it meant to have money. Now she did, the feeling went straight to her head.

The sheer exuberance of the girl made Liz feel slightly uneasy. She's capable of almost anything now, she thought. I should get her back to her father.

She looked at her watch. It was nearly tea time. Dan would still be in the box.

'Why don't you come back up with me?' she said briskly. 'Then you can sit down for a few minutes.'

But Freddie was having none of it.

'I don't want to sit down with a lot of boring old men,' she said. 'I want to celebrate.'

Just for a second she paused and in that moment she realized she'd gone too far.

'That was rude of me,' she said to Liz. 'Forget I said it.'

But she was too late. The look in Liz's eyes told her everything. She was a pushy little American, unworthy of being taken to Ascot. Unworthy of her charity. She made one last attempt to save the situation.

'I'm going to buy everyone Krug in the champagne bar,' she declared. 'You will join me, Liz, won't you? Just for one glass.'

But Liz shook her head. 'I'm late already. I'll catch up with you all afterwards.'

She pushed the cartwheel of roses more firmly onto her head and made to leave.

'Have fun,' she said.

There was a holiday feeling to the bar in the back of the Royal Enclosure. A clutch of tiny circular tables were scattered over the lawn outside and at every table a group of brightly dressed revellers celebrated their winnings. Even the punters who had lost their shirts were celebrating, because there was always the next race. It was this that was beginning to consume Freddie's attention.

'Maybe I should look at the form this time,' she said. 'I don't think I've been taking it seriously enough.'

They had been joined by a group of Boots's friends

and everybody who had heard the story of her win laughed her down.

A tall man in a morning coat handed her his racing form.

'If I were you I'd close your eyes and stick a pin in it. The technique seems to work for you.'

'It wasn't like that,' she wailed. 'I had a feeling, a kind of instinct about Butterfly's Wing.'

There was more ribald laughter and finally Freddie put her foot down. She went over to Boots and insisted on being taken to the paddock.

I'll show them, she thought. If I can get a feeling just by seeing a name, imagine what seeing the horses will do for me.

Boots did as she asked, leading her over to the Grandstand and down some steps into an underground tunnel.

'This is a very famous route,' he informed her. 'I took you round this way because I wanted you to see it.'

She looked around her. It seemed a perfectly ordinary tunnel to her. A bit like a cut-through on the underground.

'What's so special about it?'

Boots put his arm round her.

'Its reputation,' he said. 'It's known as adulterer's walk. There was a time when divorcees weren't allowed into the Royal Enclosure and they had to use this way to get to the paddock. Whenever I come down here, I still get a feeling I'm doing something I shouldn't.'

She looked at him.

'Do you have that feeling now?'

He gave her shoulders a squeeze. 'Don't ask silly questions.'

Freddie started to feel guilty. It was past four and

she still hadn't caught up with Scott. I shouldn't be doing this, she thought. Drinking champagne and flirting in the sun. Then she looked at Boots and the way his eyes crinkled up at the corners when he smiled. He was a first class shit if ever she saw one, but so attractive and such fun.

The hell with it, she decided. This is my first time at Ascot and if I can't be silly for one afternoon, then when can I be?

They came up into the paddock in time to see the parade of horses for the fourth race. Standing in the front with the owners Freddie got her first close-up of what she was putting her money on. She was dazzled. As a child in New York, she had never had a pony. Her nearest contact with any horse had been glimpses of the riders in Central Park. But this was different. Now she was within spitting distance of some of the most beautiful animals she had seen in her life. They were so graceful, like ballet dancers, quivering and trembling with nervous energy. She was tempted to reach out and touch the polished flanks, but she didn't dare. So she stood and watched in a kind of trance.

Boots cut into her thoughts.

'Which one do you fancy?' he asked.

Her mind went a blank. Earlier on in the racecourse she had been so sure of herself. Convinced she had some god-given instinct for winners. Now confronted with the runners, she realized she had simply been lucky. She smiled up at the raffish-looking man standing beside her.

'I fancy all of them,' she admitted. 'I've no idea what to do next.'

'At least she's honest,' he chuckled. 'I'll tell you what. Why don't you let me choose for you this time? I don't pretend to have any unusual instincts, but I do know my horseflesh. Will you trust me?'

Freddie nodded, and Boots brought out his racing form and a pen. After looking at the field he started to go through his options making notes in the margin as he did so. Finally he handed the list across to Freddie.

'I've marked the three I fancy. You can pick any one of them, but do something for me. Promise you won't stake everything you've got on one horse. Nobody gets the same luck twice running.'

Freddie picked out Boots's second choice, Fearless Fighter, because she thought any horse with a name like that had to have guts. Then, as she was closing the booklet, her eyes fastened on another runner. It was called Vanessa's Chance. Vanessa, she thought. That's my mother's name. I have to put something on it. And once more the feeling she had over Butterfly's Wing came back to her. She knew without a shadow of a doubt that Vanessa's Chance was the only horse in the race.

When they got to the Tote, she put fifty pounds on Fearless Fighter. Then she put another fifty on Vanessa's Chance. Then she changed her mind and upped her last bet to two hundred.

'What did you go and do that for?' Boots said. 'Vanessa's Chance hasn't got a hope.'

Freddie looked at him. 'We'll see,' she said.

On the way back to the Course Boots ran into a friend from the Jockey Club. He was a fat, rather pompous man who owned a bank and when Freddie admitted how much she had put on the race, he threw his head back and roared with laughter.

'I must make sure you have a ringside seat,' he told her.

He settled them both in the front of the Jockey Club stand which was just next door to the Royal Box. If Freddie stood on tip-toe, she could see both the

Queen and the Queen Mother sitting right in front of the glass enclosure. The Queen Mother was wearing a toque made of overlapping lilac petals and Freddie thought of Liz's overblown rose creation. Why do Englishwomen, she wondered, go right over the top for Royal Ascot? They all look perfectly normal the rest of the year.

Boots interrupted her reverie.

'I see you've lost interest in the racing today,' he observed.

Freddie heard the tannoy announcing the off and she pulled herself together.

'No I haven't,' she said.

This time she had made a point of remembering her colours. Fearless Fighter was wearing red and green. Vanessa's Chance, purple and amber. Her eyes noted them both standing at the starter's post.

Then they were off. At first all the horses looked the same to Freddie. A rush of spindly legs with the stick-like figures of the jockeys perched on their backs, but as they came to the bend they started to separate out. Freddie craned her neck, trying to make out the colours of the liveries. Fearless Fighter was in the first four, but she couldn't locate Vanessa's Chance.

She shaded her eyes in an effort to see better, and as she did she felt a tap on her shoulder.

'Here,' said Boots. 'These will help.' He had handed her a pair of racing binoculars and she used them gratefully. Now she had a clear view, she had her first sight of Vanessa's Chance. She was trailing at the back. Damn, she thought. I can't be wrong. It isn't possible.

She switched her attention to Fearless Fighter. He was holding his own, moving up from fourth position to third. The horses swung into their second circuit and Freddie was aware that something had changed.

There was a buzz in the stands around her and she noticed the Queen was standing up. Then the name came pounding over the tannoy. Vanessa's Chance. Something was happening to her horse.

She raised the racing glasses to her eyes in time to see the purple and amber colours of Vanessa's Chance coming up on the inside. The horse was half way up the field and gaining fast. I was right, she thought. I do know how to pick a winner.

She was glued to the course. Vanessa's Chance was lying in fourth place now. Then as they came into the home straight the filly flashed past Fearless Fighter still lying third, caught up with Blue Stag, the second horse, and began to draw level with the front runner. Then it happened. Vanessa's Chance faltered. Just once. For an instant. But it was enough to send the horse veering off-balance. In the last seconds of the race, within sight of the winning post, Vanessa's Chance faltered, stumbled and finally fell. There was a groan from the stands. Then the winners came over on the tannoy. First was Belmez, the horse that Boots backed.

Second, Blue Stag and third, Fearless Fighter.

Freddie felt her heart sink. Her luck had finally run out. She saw Boots looking at her and started to feel foolish.

'Cheer up,' he said. 'You didn't lose everything. Anyway there's another race to go yet.'

But the magic had gone out of the afternoon. Some of the crowd were already heading for their cars in an attempt to miss the traffic jam out of Ascot and Freddie wondered what had become of the rest of her party. Most of all she wanted to know what had become of Scott.

They had planned to spend the evening together. There was a film they both wanted to see at the

Chelsea Odeon. If they were back early, Scott had said, they could change and go for a meal in Fulham afterwards.

Where can he have got to, Freddie thought. There had been no sign of him all afternoon. It occurred to her that he might have been visiting friends in one of the boxes. He might even be in the *Chronicle*'s box. She turned to Boots.

'It's time I thought about going home.'

He raised an eyebrow. 'So soon? You were just beginning to enjoy yourself.'

A string of excuses came to mind, but she decided to be straight with him.

'I have to find Scott,' she told him. 'I can't go on putting it off.'

'But Scott left hours ago.'

Freddie looked at him in disbelief.

'You're making it up.'

'No, I'm not. He told me he was off when you were up at the Tote putting your shirt on Butterfly's Wing. I meant to tell you when you came back, but the race had started and I didn't get the chance.'

Freddie was furious.

'Why didn't anyone else say anything? Barbara would have noticed Scott leaving.'

Boots folded his arms across his chest and prayed for patience.

'Barbara didn't see Scott leaving. She was over at the bookie's with Liz. The only reason I ran into him was because I was standing on the course. I'd organized all my bets beforehand.'

The breeze, which had tilted a few brims that afternoon, started to get up in earnest. It was coming from the north and blew the remaining heat out of the day. Now the racecourse which had been so festive half an hour ago started to look grey and sullen.

'Did Scott say why he was leaving?' Freddie asked. 'We were meant to be meeting later.'

Boots rubbed the side of his face and looked embarrassed.

'That's not what he told me. He said something about driving north to see some cousin or other.'

He reached inside his jacket for a pack of cigarettes. Then he took one out, lit it and thought for a second.

'Look,' he said. 'I could have got the whole thing completely wrong. For all I know Scott is sitting in his hotel in London waiting for you to get back. He's probably called your flat and left a message on the answering machine.'

'I don't have a flat. I'm staying with the Dearings.'

Boots smiled.

'Better still. If Scott's been in touch, the servants will know. Why don't you call and find out? I've got a phone in my car.'

Freddie should have gone back to the box and made her call from there, but something stopped her. It was the prospect that Scott really had walked out on her. If he had gone to see a cousin, then there would be no message at Cheyne Walk and she would have to share that fact with everyone from her father to Liz. She couldn't bear it. Better to find out now, she told herself. At least Boots won't go blabbing her embarrassment to the entire family.

She let him lead her away from the course and into the farthest section of the car park where he had left his shiny red Mercedes. Then, while Boots waited outside, she sat in the front seat and made her call. The phone answered on the second ring, the butler instantly recognizing her voice.

'I was expecting a call,' she told him. 'From Scott Harding. Has he phoned?'

The manservant kept his voice neutral. Nobody had called for her. Did she want to leave a message?

Freddie debated her options. There was no message she could leave that didn't sound petulant, that didn't give the wrong impression.

'I won't bother now,' she said at last. 'I'll phone again later. If Scott does get in touch would you tell him that?'

She slammed the phone back in its holder and got out of the car. Boots was by her side instantly.

'How did it go?' he asked. 'Is it good news?'

Freddie pulled a face.

'It's bloody awful news. There's no word.' She sighed. 'I guess you were right. Scott's gone and pushed off somewhere.'

Boots did his best to look sympathetic. Sympathetic and harmless. It was a face he put on when he was hunting. It always works, he thought. Tell any dolly here that her boyfriend had run out on her and ten to one she'd swallow it whole. For the life of him he'd never understand why girls were so insecure. If she'd only given him a bit more time, he reasoned, Scott would have contacted her eventually but she's too frightened for that. Too anxious.

He looked at the American girl almost greedily. She was wearing one of those thin silk dresses the designer shops ran up for Ascot. She shouldn't stand against the light like that, Boots thought. She doesn't know it, but she's showing me everything she's got. A feeling of pure contentment came over him. What a feast little Freddie was going to provide tonight.

'I've got an idea,' he told her. 'Instead of going back to the *Chronicle* box, why don't you drive back to London with me? I promised I'd look in at a couple of drinks parties on the way. It might just take your mind off things.'

Freddie was tempted. It was still early enough to do the parties and be home in time for dinner if Scott did turn up.

'Okay,' she said. 'It sounds like a nice idea.'

The phone rang at seven fifteen in the Dearings' house on Cheyne Walk. Liz, who was sitting right beside it, picked it up automatically.

'Dan,' she said. 'I was waiting for you to call.'

There was a silence on the other end of the line, and a quite different voice said:

'This isn't Dan. It's Scott. Is that you, Liz?'

Liz breathed in deeply, the way she had been taught in relaxation classes. Then she said, 'Scott, how lovely to hear your voice. I take it you want to talk to Freddie. Well, I'm afraid she isn't here. Were you expecting her?'

Scott sounded agitated, almost angry at her news.

'Of course I was expecting her,' he said. 'We were meant to be having dinner tonight. Where is she?'

For the past week Liz's attention had been entirely focused on Dan Levin. Now the Freddie question intruded on her consciousness. For weeks she'd been looking for a way to cool down this big romance of Freddie's. Perhaps the chance was coming sooner than she thought.

Liz searched her mind for the last time she set eyes on the American girl. She had been with Barbara when she left her. Barbara and that friend, Boots Winchester. Her daughter came into the drawing-room and she put her hand over the phone.

'Darling, when you left Freddie, what was she up to?'

Barbara helped herself to a glass of wine and sat down.

'She was going off to the paddock to look at the horses, I think. Why?'

Liz looked vague. 'No reason, I just wondered if anyone was looking after her. Or if she was on her own.'

'Of course she wasn't on her own,' Barbara replied. 'Boots was in attendance, the lecherous bugger. He looked like he was making plans to eat her. It's a good thing Scott whisked her off at the end of the day or he might have done.'

Everything clicked into place. So neatly, so perfectly that if Liz had planned for it to happen it would never have gone that way. Something, some divine intervention had separated Scott and Freddie. And now Freddie was delayed. Her imagination did the rest. Liz lifted the phone to her ear again.

'Darling,' she said, 'are you still there? Good, Barbara just came into the room and I had to stop and have a word with her. It seems you're out of luck if you want dinner with Freddie. The last time I saw her she was rushing off with some young man called Boots. She said she wouldn't be in till very late – maybe not at all, but then you know her better than I do.'

When she put the phone down she saw her daughter look curiously at her.

'Who was that you were talking to?' she asked.

Liz looked her daughter straight in the eye.

'Scott Harding,' she said crisply. 'It looks like he missed the boat with your little American friend.'

50

She could still feel his hands on her body. Rough, intrusive, impertinent hands. Hands that expected everything except what she had delivered. I didn't grow up in New York, Freddie thought, without knowing how to defend myself.

Boots had attacked her five miles outside Ascot. On the pretext of visiting a friend, he had driven down a winding country road that seemed to go nowhere. All around them were ploughed fields and woodland.

'I thought we were meant to be going to a party,' Freddie said. 'There isn't a house around here for miles.'

Boots slowed down then and pulled over to the side of the road.

'Everything in good time,' he told her. 'First let's get to know each other.'

Freddie knew she was on a loser then. Boots was out for what he could get, and if he couldn't talk his way into her pants, her instinct told her, he wouldn't draw the line at using force. I should have seen through him, she thought. I should have known all that charm and attentiveness was a sham. Men like him don't waste their time for nothing.

She put her misgivings behind her and concentrated on the present. Boots was about to pounce. Somehow she had to deflect him. She put her hand on the door handle and pushed. The door opened. For a moment Boots looked surprised.

'So she likes her sex alfresco,' he observed. 'Well, why not? It's a nice night.'

Before Freddie realized what was happening Boots was round her side pulling her out of the car. She didn't put up a struggle. Experience taught her to conserve her energy. The only advantage she had was surprise. She would use it when the time was right.

Boots took her lack of resistance as a kind of consent. The bank where they had pulled in led down to a wooded copse and he drew her towards it.

'We can be private there,' he said.

Freddie stopped walking then. Once they were out of sight of the road, she knew she was well and truly lost.

For a moment, Boots looked concerned.

'You haven't changed your mind, have you?'

'I never made up my mind.'

The concern turned to anger. One moment Boots was the confident Lothario. The next, he was the playground bully.

'Don't tease,' he said roughly. 'It's too late for that.'

He came at Freddie then, grabbing her by the shoulders and pushing her over. Still she didn't fight back. They were lying side by side now on the damp grass and Boots moved across until he loomed over her. Then, slowly, he started undoing the front of her dress. There was a smugness about him, a deliberate cruelty that put Freddie in mind of someone pulling the wings off a butterfly.

As the dress fell away, he started to take her bra off. Still she didn't move. For what she had in mind, she wanted Boots good and ready.

The sight of her naked breasts slowed him down. His hands stopped in their journey downwards, hovered undecided until finally he couldn't resist. He heaved himself onto his haunches and started to close in on her. Freddie jerked her knee up sharply. The moment of impact seemed to knock the breath out of Boots, for he let go of her and keeled on to his side roaring out in pain. She was on her feet then, pulling her dress together. Then she made for the car.

The key was still in the ignition and she climbed in and started the engine. Out of the corner of her eye she saw Boots crawling up the bank, then she took hold of the wheel and put her foot down. Freddie didn't take her eyes off the road until she saw a signpost for London. Then she relaxed and prayed nobody stopped her. She wasn't licensed to drive in this country.

When Freddie got back the house was empty. Then she checked the time. It was nearly eight o'clock. Everyone must have gone out for dinner, she thought. She wondered if Scott had called and she thought about going to find the butler, when Barbara appeared.

'What on earth are you doing in?' Freddie asked.

The other girl returned the question. 'What on earth are you doing back? I thought you were out on the town with Boots Winchester.'

'Who told you that?'

'Mummy. She said she saw you going off with him at the races.'

Freddie shrugged and felt vaguely annoyed. What business was it of Liz's who she was with.

'Well your mother got it wrong,' she said crossly. 'I never planned to do the town with Boots, as she puts it. I'm meant to be having dinner with Scott. Did he call, by the way?'

Barbara looked embarrassed. If she told Freddie the truth she would have to go into what Liz had said to Scott and she didn't feel strong enough for that. Instead she settled for a white lie.

'I've no idea who called,' she said. 'I've only just got in myself. But why don't you ask Williams. He's bound to have taken a message.'

The butler had no record of any call for her and in the end, Freddie stumped up to her room, determined not to give in and call Scott herself. She sat on her bed, fidgeting and fretful. Then she decided to have a hot bath. After what she had been through, only total immersion was sufficient.

Scott didn't call the next day, or the day after that, and Freddie started to get worried.

She knew Scott was serious about her. She also knew he was capable of the kind of jealousy that bordered on the irrational. Just seeing her with Boots at the races was enough to make him walk out, but it shouldn't have stopped him from calling for two days. There had been spats over other men who had chatted her up, but after a few hours Scott had always seen reason. He knew how she felt about him. He also knew she was a virgin, so he never stayed jealous. There wasn't any point. He knew she wouldn't give herself casually to just anyone.

Freddie made her mind up not to panic and call him. Barbara's ball was coming up after the weekend. He was bound to be in touch over that. He had to be.

On Thursday there was a call for her. It was her father. He had tickets for 'The Merchant of Venice' on Saturday night. Would she like to go with him? Without thinking, Freddie said yes. If Scott called she could always meet him after the play.

Dan came to collect her at tea time on Saturday.

'You're early,' she said. 'I didn't think the curtain went up till seven thirty.'

'It doesn't,' Dan told her, 'but it will take us till

then to drive to the theatre. Stratford-on-Avon is a long way from London.'

The penny dropped. Freddie wasn't going to see a play in the West End at all.

She looked at her father with alarm.

'You're not planning to stay over or anything are you?'

Dan looked disappointed.

'Not if you don't want to. I didn't know you needed to be back in London so fast.'

For a moment Freddie felt defeated. Scott still hadn't called, and the weekend stretched out in front of her, lonely and empty. She had turned down every invitation in order to sit by the phone.

'Have you made hotel reservations in Stratford?' she asked.

Dan nodded.

'I thought we might spend some time together. You've been so busy with all your parties, I've hardly seen you since I got here.'

Dan was quite right, of course. Her father had trekked halfway across the world to see her and she'd virtually ignored him. She thought about the cheque he'd sent to cover her dress bill and she felt guilty.

'There isn't all that much for me to do in London, Pop. Not this weekend. If it's still okay, I'd love to stay over in Stratford.'

They put up at the Shakespeare, right on the edge of the river. It was the kind of hotel made specially for American tourists. On the outside it was pure sixteenth century, all white plasterwork and half timbers, but inside there was nothing olde worlde about it at all. They could have been in the Hilton from the look of the patterned carpets and the shiny fittings. Freddie suppressed a smile. Trust my father, she thought. I'm sure there are hundreds of sweet little places we could have stayed. Genuine places run by local people, but there's no way he'd have done that. If he couldn't have access to a fax and twenty-four-hour room service, he'd probably have a nervous breakdown.

Dan had reserved a suite with two bedrooms leading off a palatial drawing-room. In deference to Stratford's history, the hotel had furnished the main room with antiques and lush-looking Persian carpets. But the bedrooms belonged to the 1980s. There was an adjustable television set over each big double bed, with a second set in the bathroom. Both rooms had a bar, a battery of telephones and on the desk in the corner there was even a word processor. Freddie wondered if everyone who came down here needed to keep a constant watch on their businesses. Then she saw the tariff on the back of the door and reckoned they probably did.

Freddie took a lot of trouble with her appearance that night selecting a slinky, silk jersey dress by Jean Muir. When she put it on, Freddie wondered if she had done the right thing. The dress was too old for her. It gave her curves she didn't possess and a sophistication that looked all wrong. She was about to take it off when she heard her father in the next room.

'Hurry up,' he called. 'We're going to be late for curtain up.'

Freddie shrugged and grabbed her bag. So I look like an old time vamp, she thought. It doesn't matter. I'm only with my father and he couldn't care less what impression I give.

They made it to the theatre with seconds to spare. There wasn't even time to have a drink or buy a programme.

'Never mind,' Dan told her. 'We'll do all that in the interval.'

By the first interval, Freddie had fallen in love with the drama. In the beginning the language had been tough to follow, but after half an hour her ear had tuned in and now she couldn't wait to see how the play unfolded.

'You mean you didn't do this at school?' her father chided. 'After all the money I paid for your education.'

They were pushing their way towards the bar and Freddie was already thirsting for something to drink. It was hot that night and she could feel the thin silk dress clinging to the backs of her legs.

She turned to her father.

'I didn't know you paid for me to go to school. I thought Norman took care of all that.'

'He did at the beginning, but when he got difficult I took over the responsibility. I'm quite rich you know. It wasn't a problem.'

Freddie looked at Dan with affection. He was very debonair that night. His hair was longer than usual and it suited him. There was a new suit as well. Something Liz had organized for him in Savile Row.

'I'm glad I'm not a problem,' she said. 'I used to worry about it once. I hate to think I might be a drain on you.'

Dan put his arm round her.

'You're not a drain,' he said. 'As a matter of fact money is something we should talk about. You'll soon be nineteen and I can't go on sending you a cheque every time you need a new dress. So I have something a bit more permanent in mind. What would you say if I told you I was going to give you a proper allowance?'

Freddie was over the moon. All her life she had asked this man to notice her. To love her, the way she loved him. Now for the first time she realized he did after all.

She put her arms round his neck and gave him a hug.

'Pop,' she said. 'You're the best.'

Over his shoulder, over a sea of heads, Freddie could just make out the bar. Whichever of them queued for the drinks was in for a long sticky wait. She decided right then it was going to be her. Dan protested, but she stood her ground.

'After what you just promised me, it's the least I can do.'

Before he could say anything else Freddie was off, pushing her way through the throng of theatre-goers until she was in sight of the barman. Her father, she knew, would want a whisky and soda. She decided on a Perrier and lime juice. It was too hot to think of anything stronger.

After several attempts Freddie caught the barman's eye, but her way was barred by the people crushing round her.

'Do you mind moving,' Freddie called out crossly. 'I'm in rather a hurry.'

A man turned round and she nearly lost her footing. For standing just in front of her was Scott Harding. He was the first to react.

'Fancy seeing you here,' he said calmly. 'I'd no idea Shakespeare was your thing.'

There was an edge to his voice and Freddie knew instantly he was still upset with her. Damn your jealousy, she thought. Damn you for not phoning me.

'Shakespeare isn't my thing,' she said stiffly. 'It's my father's thing. He brought me here tonight.'

Scott was smiling now, she noticed, but it didn't make him look any more friendly.

'So that's who you're with. What happened to Boots Winchester?'

Freddie was aware of the heat and the crowd pressing in on her.

'Nothing. It's not the way you think,' she said quickly. 'I never saw Boots again after the races.'

'That's not what I heard.' Scott's voice was angry now and Freddie wondered what on earth was wrong. Why was he talking to her this way.

'What did you hear?' she demanded. 'What lies have people been spreading behind my back?'

'I'd be careful before you start handing out accusations. Liz Dearing's very fond of you. She's got no reason in the world to lie about where you were that night.'

Now Freddie knew she was lost. Liz was treacherous. She realized that the night of the big ball when she refused point blank to let her borrow any jewellery.

'I'm not accusing anyone of anything,' she replied as calmly as she could. 'But after what happened with Boots, there's no way I'd want to spend any time with him.'

Scott's expression didn't change.

'What did happen between you two?'

Freddie wondered whether or not to tell him the full story. An interval at the theatre was no place for this kind of confidence and her father was waiting. But she loved Scott and he hadn't called for a week, and the thought of losing him forever filled her with terror.

'He tried to rape me,' she said as quietly as she could. She looked up at Scott, expecting some kind of understanding. None came.

'Boots tells it differently,' he said, coldly. 'In his version, you couldn't wait to get your clothes off. It seems you're very passionate when you make up your mind.'

Freddie's head started to swim.

'Do you really believe that?'

'Give me one good reason why I shouldn't? I saw you leading him on that afternoon. Flirting away like some cheap little tart. You completely forgot you were with me, didn't you? You even forgot we had a date later on.'

Fury welled up inside Freddie. Her enemies were ganging up on her and Scott, the man who was meant to care for her, was taking their side.

'I wasn't the one who forgot about our date,' she shouted. 'You did that. You even pushed off without saying goodbye. What the hell did you expect me to do?'

For a moment he looked uncertain. Then he set his jaw.

'What I expected,' he told her, 'is purely academic now.'

He turned round, picked up a bottle of champagne and some glasses and made to leave.

'Forgive me,' he said, 'but there are some people waiting for this. I really must go and find them.'

Without another word he turned and walked away from her.

If Freddie hadn't been so angry, she might have cried. Instead she turned back to the bar and placed her order. She'd changed her mind about the water. She was going to have a whisky now, like her father. After Scott's betrayal she decided she needed it.

51

Freddie told her father all about it over dinner. Right from her first meeting with Scott to their final encounter in the theatre bar. And Dan was surprisingly sympathetic.

He couldn't believe that any man was capable of behaving as badly as Scott had at Ascot and he told her so.

'If I was dating a girl and some other man pushed in on me, I'd do something about it. I wouldn't just stand there and let it happen.'

Freddie pulled a face. 'He didn't just stand there,' she told him. 'He stormed off in a huff.'

They had got to the coffee and brandy stage and Dan called the waiter over and asked for a cigar. Then he turned to Freddie.

'Did you give this boyfriend of yours any reason to be so jealous?' he asked.

'No,' she replied. 'I'm not like my mother.'

Dan looked at her sharply.

'Would you mind explaining that last remark?'

Freddie remembered the fights Vanessa had had with the men in her life. First with her father, then with Norman. She had been too young to understand why her mother and the men she loved always seemed to be at each others' throats, but as she grew up she realized all the wrangles centred around one issue. Sex.

Freddie said as much to Dan. Then she said, 'I wasn't prepared to put myself on the line like that.

I wanted Scott to value me, so I didn't let him make love to me.'

Dan looked at this girl he had fathered with a mixture of sorrow and exasperation. How do I tell her, he wondered, that life isn't like that at all. That if she goes on viewing it that way, she'll end up an embittered old maid.

He took hold of his cigar and chewed the end off. Then he lit it, thinking all the while. Finally he said,

'I think I should get a couple of things straight with you. First, your mother isn't the woman of the night you think she is. When I met her she was one of the warmest, brightest, most desirable girls in New York and I was one of half a dozen men who were at her feet. When I finally took her to my bed, I didn't look down on her for what we did together. I loved her for it, and I stayed with her for it for a damn long time. We eventually parted for all sorts of reasons I'm not prepared to go into. But sex wasn't one of them.'

Freddie regarded him across the table.

'Are you saying I was wrong not to go to bed with Scott?'

'Damn right I am. Why the hell do you think he acted the way he did? He must have been out of his mind with frustration.'

Freddie started to feel uncomfortable.

'I thought you were on my side.'

'I am on your side, darling. I want all the things you want for yourself. But you're not going to get them, and you're certainly not going to get Scott, if you go on behaving like a first class tease. If you want to know what I really think, I reckon that you got that guy of yours so crazy with jealousy he was prepared to believe any baloney he heard about you. Now if you and he had been having a cosy affair, he wouldn't have listened to Boots Winchester, because he would have known the incident he described simply couldn't have happened. No woman in the world looks around when she's happy and satisfied with what she's got.'

Freddie regarded her father with a certain wonder. He was full of surprises tonight. First he offered her an allowance she really didn't need, then he urged her to divest herself of her virginity. She had to hand it to him, he had style – though it wasn't the kind of style you expect to find in a parent.

'So what do I do next?' she asked him. 'Come on, you seem to know all the answers.'

Dan reached out and took her hand, and as he did she noticed he looked rather sad.

'I wish life was that simple,' he said. 'But the truth of it is there isn't a pat solution for your problem. You had a good thing going with Scott, but you blew it, and there isn't a damn thing you can do. If anyone does anything now, it's got to be him. All you can do is wait.'

Freddie didn't sleep much that night. Now she realized she had lost Scott – really lost him – she mourned his passing. I'll never feel his body next to mine, she thought. Some other girl will print herself on him now. Someone who deserves him less. Someone who probably doesn't even care.

The finality of it made her feel empty and with the emptiness came tears. Freddie wept noisily and bitterly until the dawn came up and when she was drained of emotion she dozed fitfully.

When she got back to London, Barbara took over. The minute she set eyes on Freddie she realized something had gone seriously wrong. She also realized that whatever had happened, her mother's story about Boots couldn't have helped.

'We've got to talk,' she said. 'Now.' They went up

to the conservatory where Barbara opened a bottle of wine. Then, without preamble, she levelled about what Liz had told Scott.

The American girl didn't seem unduly surprised.

'I know about Liz,' she said. 'I heard all about it at the theatre.'

She told Barbara what had happened that night.

'Scott was very thorough,' she said. 'He talked to your mother, he talked to Boots. The only person he didn't bother to talk to was me.'

'But you were the only one who knew what was going on. What on earth was the matter with him?'

Freddie remembered what her father had said.

'He was jealous,' she said simply. 'He wanted to go to bed with me and I was too frightened to let him. So he suspected anyone and everyone of stealing a march.'

Barbara looked at Freddie. She wasn't wearing any make-up that day. Not even mascara. Her red-gold hair was ragged and wild, yet she still looked good enough to eat.

What was Scott thinking of, she wondered. Any other man would have laughed her out of her inhibitions. She thought about the man she worked with, the one who was her lover, and she felt sorry for Freddie.

'I've come to a decision,' she announced. 'I'm going to break the rule of a lifetime and interfere in someone else's love life. If I don't neither of you will ever see each other again.'

Freddie looked at Barbara with a mixture of fondness and exasperation.

'You've already done that once. How many more times are you going to stick your neck out?'

'Until you two get into bed. Or get married. Or both – only don't tell my mother.'

'Why not?'

For a moment Barbara looked worried, then she said, 'Mummy has this fantasy about me and Scott. She thinks just because our two families do business, Scott and I should end up together. It's all nonsense of course. People aren't like that. I've got no intention of marrying anybody for years and when I do, it's going to be somebody I choose. Not somebody chosen by my parents. Anyway Scott doesn't want me. He wants you.'

Now Freddie felt completely wretched.

'No he doesn't,' she said. 'I'm the last person on his mind.'

The English girl reached in front of her for the telephone.

'We'll see about that.'

There was no answer from Scott's apartment and it puzzled Barbara. Normally when Scott was out, he left his answering machine on. He must have forgotten, she thought. I'll try again later. There was no answer all evening, and finally she gave up.

'He's probably gone away for the weekend,' she assured Freddie. 'He's bound to be in his office tomorrow morning. If he isn't, at least they'll tell me where I can find him.'

Scott wasn't there the next day and the *New York Times* was cagey about his whereabouts. The girl on the desk asked if Barbara wanted to leave a message and against all her instincts, she left her name and number.

'When he gets in, tell him to call me,' she said.

He didn't of course and she had a hunch he was avoiding her. He knew she and Freddie were close. If he was serious about ditching her, she'd be the last person he'd call.

She decided to confront the problem. The journalist

in her knew there was only one way. The personal approach. Scott could avoid her all he liked on the telephone, but there was no way he could duck out if they were face to face.

She decided to call in at his flat on her way to work. When she was doing a day shift, she usually started early, around seven to catch the evening edition. No matter what Scott was up to, he had to be home around six thirty. He wasn't.

In the end Barbara called her office and told them she would be late. Then she went home and made herself breakfast. Around eight she returned to Scott's apartment. He still wasn't there. Maybe he's gone straight to his office from wherever he spent the night, she thought.

She took a taxi to the city and arrived at the *New York Times* bureau before nine. None of the secretaries was there yet, but the duty editor was sorting through the mail.

He looked up when he saw Barbara standing there.

'Can I help you?' he asked.

'I'm looking for Scott Harding,' she told him. 'Do you have any idea when he'll be in?'

The man looked momentarily confused.

'He won't be in,' he replied. 'Not in this office at any rate. Scott went back to New York a couple of days ago. I can pass on a message if you like.'

Barbara shook her head.

'It doesn't matter. I take it he isn't coming back.'

The newsman looked impatient.

'Not that I know of. Are you sure you don't want to leave a message?'

Barbara gave him her best smile.

'I'm perfectly sure,' she said.

All day long she debated what to tell Freddie.

There was something final, almost brutal, about Scott's departure. He hadn't even left a note. Damn the man, she thought, and damn his pride. If he'd thought for five minutes before flying back to New York – if he'd made a few enquiries – he might have found out he'd been mistaken about Freddie.

She thought about the American girl and how alive she'd been for the past few weeks. Before Scott, she'd been lost and somehow ill at ease. He had changed all that, by giving her some faith in herself. Barbara sighed. Fat lot of good it did her, she thought. The minute Freddie comes out of her shell, the handsome prince tramples all over her and flounces off in a huff. And I'm the one who has to break the news . . .

52

David was standing in the features department of the *Chronicle* on Friday afternoon. All around him busy executives were putting the final touches to the weekend supplement and for the first time that day he relaxed. The lead story was in the bag – the diary page was sewn up, and all his columnists had delivered.

David leaned against the main desk and thought ahead to the evening. He and Liz were going to see the new Alan Bennett at the Lyric. Afterwards, they were joining Freddie and her father for dinner at Harry's Bar. A feeling of pleasure suffused David. It was a good way to end the week. An undemanding way. A family way.

The features editor interrupted his reverie. The dummy was ready for him to see now.

David straightened up and made his way to the end of the office. There was a drawing board there and pinned to its surface the roughly sketched pages of tomorrow's supplement. He flicked over each page looking for the ads. As much as anything, the pull-out section was an advertising vehicle. Without that input there was no point to it. He did a rough count then nodded. The input was there. Now for the editorial, he thought.

That week the paper was devoting the weekend section to parties. In particular the best parties of the summer, or so the headline proclaimed. Once more he nodded. It was July and they were in the middle of a heatwave. People were in the mood for champagne breakfasts and punts on the river.

He looked up at the black-haired young man who designed the paper.

'I take it we have some good pictures to illustrate the party feature?'

The features editor answered for him.

'We commissioned Brian Aris to do something special for us.' He led the way over to a long table in the corner.

'This is our final selection,' he said. 'I think you'll like what we've got.'

David sighed. I should leave this to my executives, he thought. After all, they're qualified to judge what the readers will go for. But even as he acknowledged this truth, he knew he would never leave the details to anyone else. Now his father had gone, the *Chronicle* was his newspaper. Right down to the paperclips. It was a part of him now, it kept him awake at nights. It ate into his private life, but he could no more deny it, than he could deny himself.

David started to sift through the glossy ten-by-eights and as he did he felt glad they had hired a name photographer. Staff men were fine for news shots, but this kind of moody, magazine stuff was best captured by someone like Aris.

The photographer had an eye for a pretty girl, he noticed.

Both the Ascot and the Henley Regatta shots featured English womanhood in all its glory. There were blondes with naked shoulders eating strawberries, brunettes with their hair swept into extravagant hats, redheads with porcelain complexions. All of them laughing and flirting and having the time of their lives.

One of the pictures caught his eye. It was a portrait

of a middle-aged couple in the Royal Enclosure at Ascot. Normally he couldn't have looked at it for longer than a moment, but there was something compelling about it. The man was obviously rich. The cut of his suit and the depth of his tan told him that. And the woman adored him. More than that. She lusted for him. If she could make love to him right there in the paddock, she would do it, he thought.

The face was blurred, yet there was something familiar about it. Then he stopped in his tracks. Of course the face was familiar. He'd known that particular profile for nearly twenty years. It was Liz. Christ, he thought, it can't be. She can't be up to her old tricks.

A long time ago David's father had taught him that a gentleman should never show his feelings. You could be in agony, either mental or physical, yet the expression must always remain bland. Now, in the middle of the features department, on a Friday afternoon David's father didn't fail him.

He picked out the picture of Liz and Dan at Ascot and tossed it over to the designer.

'Destroy it,' he said tersely. 'The negative too, while you're about it. The *Chronicle* isn't interested in people of that age. Not in a weekend supplement. Not when we're trying to attract the under thirties.'

Then he turned on his heel and left the office. The meeting was at an end.

There was something about David that bothered Dan. From the moment he and Liz arrived at Harry's Bar, things had got off on the wrong foot. First it was the drinks. Liz and David ordered Bellini's – peach juice and champagne – Harry's Bar specials, only David didn't think they were so special.

'They've got the mixture wrong,' he complained. 'There's too much sugar.'

At his instigation they both had to send their Bellini's back and somehow it deflated Liz. She was dying for a drink and once she tasted hers she wanted to finish it. David wouldn't hear of it.

'What's the matter?' she asked. 'Did something go wrong at the office?'

Her husband grunted, and looked uncomfortable.

'I had a difficult time with the supplement,' he said finally. Then he changed the subject.

It went on like that all evening. David found fault with everything. The fried aubergines Liz ordered were soggy, their table in the front of the restaurant was too noisy, the service was wanting.

What's going on with him, Dan thought, looking round the pastel-coloured restaurant. It can't be Harry's Bar, that's for sure. There's nothing wrong with the place. The glitterati were still coming here in droves, he observed. On one table he spotted James Coburn who was in town for a film premiere. Next to him was the big-bosomed female editor of one of the Sunday supplements dining with a cabinet minister. Further down the room he saw Princess Margaret with her regular escort.

Nobody in the opulent, over-decorated room was particularly young, but they were wearing their money and success where everyone could see it. It gave them a certain, indefinable glamour.

Dan turned his attention back to his group. The place hasn't changed, he thought. So what's eating David? For a moment he wondered if he was playing the jealous husband, then he cancelled the thought. There was no way David could possibly know about him and Liz. They had both been too careful for that.

He looked at Liz advising his daughter on where to get her hair done and for a second he wished she belonged to him as well. If the three of us were together, he thought, we'd be the best-looking family in town. He smiled inwardly. I'd better not tell her that, he thought. She just might like the idea. Then where would I be?

Dan had called Liz the moment he got into town. He hadn't meant to. His plan had been to visit his wholesaler behind Oxford Street, then take a tour of the main outlets for his English line.

Liz was on the agenda of course. So was Freddie. But he had decided to put them both on ice until he had made a start on his business. Only it didn't work out that way. When he got into his hotel room he found a selection of magazines on the coffee table. Force of habit made him pick up the *Vogue*, and that's where he saw her. On the party page right in the front.

Liz was attending a reception, and the moment Dan saw her the memories came flooding back. He was in her bed in the Plaza again. Christ she had been hungry that night. Starved to death. He had wondered then about the state of her marriage.

In the morning he had thought of asking her to stay in New York for a few more days, but he didn't. It was too risky and there was too much going on in his life. The new model girl he was trying out would never forgive him.

Now he didn't have to consider the girl. He didn't have to worry about his wife either. He was in London for a month and he could do what he wanted. Suddenly he knew what that was. To hell with the business, he thought. It does perfectly well when I'm in New York. It can do well for a bit longer.

He made a date with Liz for that night, then he

took a shower and called his daughter. He might be neglecting his business, but nobody could say he ducked all his responsibilities.

He met Liz in the bar at seven. And the instant he saw her he knew he had been right.

The lady was neglected. Whoever she was married to didn't dig her any more. Either that or she was a sex maniac. For the messages coming from her were unmistakable.

He ordered them both a drink then, as they made small talk, he let his eyes roam over her. Liz was wearing a dark mink coat over a slim white jersey dress. Experience told Dan this wasn't the product of a British designer. It was too subtle for that. She got it in Paris, he thought. Either at Balmain or Dior, and the couturier fitted it on her.

Liz probably had the diamonds made to go with the dress, as well. There were two clips on either side of the neckline, made of intricately woven stones. The diamonds at her ears and wrists were of the same cut and he smiled inwardly. Her old man might not provide much for her in bed, but he more than compensated in all the other departments.

Dan wondered how much time she had. Would she drink and run back home, or was her leash longer than that?

'If you feel like it,' he said, testing the water, 'I thought we might have dinner at the Gavroche.'

Liz had looked genuinely amused. 'You don't have to court me,' she told him. 'I'm not one of your little girls.'

He was caught momentarily off balance.

'What is it you want from me?'

'I would have thought that was obvious.'

There was a short silence. He wasn't used to a woman talking to him like that. He knew they did nowadays, but he went out of his way to avoid that kind of encounter. In the battle between man and woman he liked to take the lead. He thought about cutting Liz down to size, when she did something unexpected. She got up.

She didn't make a big deal of it. She simply put down her glass, shrugged her coat around her and made to leave.

'Where do you think you're going?' he asked sharply.

'I don't know, but I'm not staying here any longer.'

Dan was intrigued.

'Why this sudden change of heart?'

'My heart didn't change,' Liz said calmly. 'Yours did. I told you why I was here and you hesitated.' She frowned slightly. 'I didn't like that.'

Before Dan could reply Liz was on her way out of the bar. He thought about running after her, then he trashed the idea. He wasn't a toy boy or a walker. He didn't jump every time some woman clicked her fingers.

Moodily he finished his drink. Then he signed the bill and took the elevator back to his suite. I'll ask Freddie what she's up to tonight, he decided. Maybe she'll take me to one of her parties. The thought depressed him. Wherever she went the place was bound to be full of little girls. Pretty, pouting available little girls. A couple of nights ago he would have jumped at the chance, but now he had lost his taste for that sort of thing. It's Liz's fault, he thought bitterly. The bitch has turned me onto something different.

As he came through the door he smelt her perfume. She was wearing Lauren, heavy and sexy and full of carnations. What on earth, he thought. Then he saw her mink. It was draped over one of the sofas. So she changed her mind, after all.

He went up to the abandoned fur and as he did he saw it wasn't the only thing she had left behind. All the way through to the bedroom there was a trail of her clothes: her shoes, the Paris dress, even the diamonds lay scattered in her wake. Dan felt a moment of pure, unadulterated, delicious excitement. Then he pushed open the door and walked in on her.

She was waiting for him on the bed and he noticed she hadn't taken everything off. She was wearing a basque with old-fashioned suspenders and the effect was both shocking and erotic. For it focused the attention on her bare breasts and the fact that she wasn't wearing any pants. The hell with manners Dan thought. The hell with decency. I have to have her like that.

He took his jacket off and loosened his tie and as he did she sat up.

'So you like it?' she said.

There was something about her heavy breasts spilling over the boned corset that reminded Dan of the Moulin Rouge.

'You look like a chorus girl,' he told her. 'Is that how you want to be treated?' Liz didn't say anything, so he walked over to the bed then and pulled her round until her feet were resting on the floor. Then he leaned over and started playing with her breasts. While he was doing it he talked to her. As if they were back in the bar at the Dorchester and she was a passing acquaintance. She noticed he made no attempt to get undressed, and she started to feel cheap.

'I'm not a whore, you know,' she told him, and Dan smiled.

'That's what you think,' he said and he pushed her backwards onto the counterpane.

Liz saw him undoing his trousers and shame came washing over her. Then, in the wake of shame, came a new emotion. A furnace of an emotion that rendered her helpless. She needed to be conquered by this man. She wanted him to pillage her. To lay waste to her. And she wanted it now.

It was as if Dan read her mind, for he parted her legs and pushed himself into her. And she came alive.

When Dan made love to her in New York, Liz had thought there was no man like him. Now she was convinced of it. Before she abandoned herself completely, a warning signal came into her mind. What I'm doing now could cost me everything I've got. My home. My marriage. My standing in society.

It didn't make any difference. For the first time in her life, Liz simply didn't care.

After that they met every day. Sometimes it was lunch that they never got round to eating, or tea that they didn't drink. And occasionally when both their schedules were full, they met en famille. Dan would come to the house on the pretext of seeing Freddie, and Liz would just happen to be there.

If David was there too, Dan would play the responsible father doing his parental duty, and nobody suspected a thing. David even suggested Dan accompany them to Ascot. Then they knew they had got away with it.

Dan remembered the way Liz had flirted at the races, eyeing him and clinging on to his arm like a newly-wed.

'Shouldn't you cool it while David's around,' he had warned her. 'What if he notices?'

Liz had laughed at him for that.

'My husband stopped noticing me years ago,' she told him.

He had believed her then. But tonight, in Harry's Bar, he wasn't so sure. Liz was wearing a satin slip of a dress from one of the new British designers and David made a great show of admiring it. If he had known differently he would have thought the man was showing affection to his pampered darling of a wife. But he did know differently. This wasn't David's form. He was an Englishman first and foremost and they didn't go in for that kind of public display. What's he playing at, Dan wondered.

The menus came round again, and then the sweet trolley was wheeled over. Freddie made a huge fuss when she saw it, agonizing over whether to have crême brûlée or strawberries. She finally appealed to Dan for help and he laughed at her.

'Have both,' he said.

Freddie rolled her eyes.

'But that's greedy.'

'So be greedy. I like to see you indulge yourself. It makes me feel I'm spoiling you.'

The waiter served two portions and put the food in front of Freddie. Then it was Liz's turn. Force of habit made her shake her head, but David intercepted her.

'Have something,' he urged. 'To please me.'

Liz looked at him as if he had gone mad. David wasn't that interested in food. He certainly never cared what she ate.

'But I don't want anything,' she told him.

But he couldn't leave it alone.

'You'll change your mind when it's in front of you.' Before she could say anything else he signalled to the waiter to give Liz a portion of the chocolate cake. It was a very rich confection, covered in whipped cream.

Gingerly, the waiter cut a slice and manoeuvred it onto a plate. Then he passed it across the table.

Nobody knew whether the waiter was being clumsy

or David brought his hand up too sharply, but somewhere in transit, the plate flipped over, sending its contents splattering into Liz's lap.

Liz let out a yelp of surprise and David responded by shaking his napkin over her which seemed to spread the cream in every direction. 'Your poor dress,' he apologized. 'I'm so sorry, darling.' Dan stared at the scene appalled. Poor bitch, he thought. That husband of yours has been trying to make a fool of you all evening and now he seems to have got his way.

A hush fell over the restaurant while the other diners stopped their conversations and tried to get a better look at what was going on. Then the maître d' came to the rescue. Wielding a tiny silver trowel, he scooped the offending cake off Liz's lap and into a bowl. Then he threw a fresh linen napkin over her. But the damage was done. The conversation went back to normal but Liz didn't. It was clear to everyone at her table that she was seething with rage and indignation. It was only a matter of minutes before she said she had a headache and asked to be taken home.

As they left the dining club, Dan decided he needed a change of air.

'Come on, Freddie,' he said turning to his daughter. 'I'll take you to Annabel's. You could do with a bit of exercise after all that food.'

A cab sailed by with its light on and he hailed it. Then he waved goodbye to David and Liz and dragged Freddie in after him.

'I think those two need to be on their own for a bit,' he observed. 'The lovely Liz looks as if she needs to get a couple of things off her chest.'

Liz stared moodily out of the window while the Rolls purred its way round Berkeley Square. Normally, she and David chatted after a dinner party, but now she had nothing to say to him. Finally, when the car nosed its way into the park, David broke the silence.

'I get the distinct feeling I upset you tonight,' he said quietly.

Liz's eyes widened and glistened brightly in the half darkness.

'Whatever gave you that idea?'

'Don't play games with me,' he told her. 'You know exactly what I'm talking about.'

Now she let her anger show. 'Don't tell me not to play games. What have you been doing all evening?'

David laughed and the sound grated on her for she knew he wasn't amused. Something's wrong, she thought. Something's up. Then because she had things to hide, she shivered slightly.

'You can't be cold,' he said. 'It's eighty degrees out there.'

He took his jacket off.

'Here,' he said. 'Wear this. We can't have you catching cold.'

Now Liz was really rattled. David simply didn't behave like this. He never admired her clothes – in private or public – and he didn't go in for fussing over her either. It didn't mean he didn't care for her. He just wasn't brought up to show it.

She turned to her husband.

'Okay,' she said. 'Cut out the phoney sympathy. Something's bugging you. It's been on your mind all evening. Why don't you tell me what it is?'

He took out a cigarette and lit it, deliberately prolonging the moment.

'I was getting round to it,' he said, 'but I thought it could wait till we got home.'

She knew then he was on to her. She wondered how he'd found out. They had been so careful. Then she remembered her last affair and the way she had failed to cover her tracks. She felt beaten. Somebody told him, she thought. He's got some kind of proof. Otherwise why behave this way?

Normally Liz was impatient when they got to Chelsea. The car was always so slow getting through the back streets, but tonight they seemed to get back in no time. Before she had had time to work out any kind of strategy she was following her husband into the high-domed hall of the house on Cheyne Walk.

'I thought we might have a nightcap in the study before going upstairs,' he said.

So he did know, and he was going to be tough. Liz's instincts never failed her at times like this. She set her chin. If David wanted a fight, she'd give it to him.

He led the way into the study and the moment she was through the door Liz knew why he had chosen this place for a showdown. It was his territory. From the book-lined walls to the solid mahogany furniture, no woman's hand had been put to work in this room. The desk that dominated one end of it had belonged to David's grandfather. Paintings of his ancestors decorated the walls. There was even a pair of mounted stags' heads on either side of the grandfather clock.

Liz walked over to the silver tray where David kept his drinks. There was a heavy old cognac and the American bourbon he liked to drink. She settled for a brandy. There seemed no point in rubbing salt in the wound.

'What will you have?' she asked tonelessly.

David waved a hand. 'Whatever you're drinking.'

Liz splashed the spirit into a second balloon and brought it over to the leather buttoned chair where he was sitting. Then she perched herself on the edge of the desk.

'You had something to say to me,' she said.

The cognac was very special and Liz expected David to warm the glass, enjoy its perfume. Instead, he threw it back in one gulp. It seemed to give him the energy he needed, for he sat straighter in his chair and Liz felt her skin prickle.

'How long has it been going on with Dan Levin?' David asked brusquely. 'And don't bother to deny it, because I won't believe you.'

He looked Liz full in the face, daring her to contradict him. There was no change in her expression and he marvelled at her gall. All those years ago, he thought, when I first met you, you wouldn't have been quite so cool. He remembered the Liz he fell in love with. Passionate, loyal, rough round the edges. Then he regarded the woman she had become and he hardly recognized her. For over the years she seemed to have recreated herself. Expensive hairdressers, plastic surgeons, top couturiers had made her glossy. Glossy and false. He fought down the impulse to go across and shake her.

'Well,' he said. 'Say something. I'm waiting for your answer.'

Liz's voice, when she found it, seemed to be coming from a long way away.

'I'm not going to lie about Dan,' she told him. 'Six months ago when I ran into him in New York, I was lonely and at a loose end. He restored my faith in myself. He actually made me feel like a woman, which is something you haven't done in a long time.'

Her words had the impact of a blow. She can still hurt me, David thought. Whatever she's become, she can still draw blood. 'Liz,' he said softly. 'What did I do to you this time to drive you away from me?'

Liz had been prepared for David's rage. She had

even nerved herself for a battering. But this. This defeat she couldn't take.

'You didn't do anything,' she said wretchedly. 'Not a damn thing. You were always so busy with that paper of yours that I might not have existed.'

She put her drink down on the desk, then she got to her feet.

'I thought after that first time, when you returned from America, that things were going to be different. You even promised me they would be. I remember you telling me that with your father out of the way, the business wouldn't be so demanding. But it was all a lie, wasn't it? You had no intention of leaving that precious brainchild in Fleet Street – not for me, and not for your daughter either. We were just decoration. Icing on the cake. The real part of your life took place in the office. It always had done and I suspect it always will.'

David came over to where she stood.

'I'm sorry, Liz,' he said quietly. 'I didn't mean to do that to you.'

She made a face and for a second she looked like the old Liz again. Maybe she isn't a doll after all, he thought. Maybe it's all an expensive façade. He brought his hand up to ruffle her hair but she backed away from him.

'Don't,' she said sharply. 'It's too late for that.'

David went back to where he was sitting, and the next time he looked at her his face was devoid of expression.

'Do you want to divorce?' he asked.

Liz considered for a moment. 'Not particularly,' she told him. 'Unless you do.'

He went over to the desk and poured another brandy. Then he held the bottle up, gesturing towards her glass. She shook her head.

'Not for me.'

'You mean you can contemplate the death of our marriage stone cold sober.'

He sounded bitter when he said it and Liz was surprised. She'd stopped believing in David a long time ago. She didn't think he disliked her. It was merely that she felt her husband was indifferent to her.

'I didn't realize it bothered you so much,' she said. 'If I'd known you actually felt something . . .'

He cut in, then.

'Don't tell me you might have stayed out of Dan's bed, because that's not true.'

So this is how it ends, Liz thought. Squabbling over the same things that have always divided us: his business and my infidelities.

Just for an instant, she wondered if it could have been any different. If David had taken more time off from the *Chronicle*, if he had cared for her more, noticed her more, would she have looked at anyone else?

Images of Dan and Vic floated into her mind, and for the first time she realized both these lovers of hers bore a resemblance to her husband. They were dark, powerful-looking men. Tycoons in their own right. Yet neither of them held a candle to David. Beside the man she had married they were merely playboys.

She looked at David again, sure of the truth now. If things had been different, she thought, I would have stayed with you to the end.

He cut in on her thoughts.

'We'll have to do something about the house,' he told her. 'We can't go on living like this.'

Liz started to feel frightened.

'What's wrong with the way things are?'

There was a silence, then he said, 'You know what's wrong, Liz, so stop being a goose. We can't go on watching television together, or staying in for cosy little dinners.' He paused. 'We certainly can't go on sleeping in the same bed.'

Liz thought for a moment before she answered him, and when she did it took a considerable effort to keep her voice steady.

'The house is big enough for both of us if we change the rules.' She drew a deep breath then she went on. 'I don't want to rush into a divorce, David, and I don't think you do either. Your family wouldn't like it and it would destroy Barbara. She's just the wrong age for this kind of upset.'

David looked at her. 'Go on,' he said. 'I'm fascinated. Tell me exactly how you'd change the rules of this marriage.'

It was as if Liz was outside herself, observing her reactions like a detached stranger. Her hands were trembling, she noticed, and she was sweating slightly in the middle of her back.

Damn it, she thought, I still love him. No matter how far we get away from each other, the feeling's still there. She took a firm grip on herself.

'For a start,' she said, 'we don't have to go on sharing a bedroom. The house is so big that nobody would notice if we slept in separate rooms. As for the rest of it, we don't have to go on having cosy family dinners. You're a busy man, everyone knows that. If you start using your club more often I don't suppose too many people will be surprised.'

David looked at her. 'You can live with that?' he queried. 'Divide the territory up into his and hers and still be friends at the end of it.'

Liz shrugged. 'Why not,' she said. 'Other couples do.'

David passed a hand over his face and for the first time that night Liz saw how weary he was. I should go to him now, she thought. I should go to him and put my arms round him and beg for forgiveness. I should do it for both our sakes.

He was on his feet before she could move. On his feet and heading towards the door.

'I'll leave it to you to carve the house up,' he said. 'You seem to have the whole thing worked out.'

He put his hand on the door knob, then he hesitated and looked back at her.

'Don't worry about the bedroom arrangements,' he told her. 'I'll sleep in my dressing-room tonight.'

53

New York, 1988

Every morning Vanessa would be woken at dawn by a warder bringing breakfast – oats the consistency of cardboard, congealing on the plate, scalding coffee with powdered milk.

There was a taste to prison food that took her back to her infant school. It was a boiled taste, as if everything had been stewed in old cabbage leaves. In the beginning she couldn't get anything down. She'd put her fork into a fatty stew or a plate of rice, she'd get as far as lifting it to her mouth, then she'd gag. I'll die in here she told herself. They'll carry me out a victim of starvation. But it didn't happen, because her body took over. She began to get hungry and as the feeling grew, she stopped smelling the food. Then one day she ate all her breakfast oats without even thinking about it. After that she ate everything. There was no enjoyment to the sensation but there was no revulsion either. She was simply indifferent to it. Food was there to fuel her. To keep her going.

She felt the same way about all the indignities the prison heaped on her. She accepted them. She took them into herself. Then she blanked them out. It was the blanking out process that saved her.

When she had earned her living as a whore she had used drugs to separate her from her existence. In prison there were drugs to be had at a price, but it was too difficult. The cell was stripped once a week and they were all body searched. The prisoners who sold the drugs often wanted sexual favours as well as money and she drew the line at that. That was in her past. It was bad enough being locked away in prison, she didn't have to work there as well.

Vanessa developed mind control as a kind of defence. She could see what was going on around her: the cell that she shared with two other women, poky and dark like an animal's cage, the blackened floor in the shower room strewn with cigarette butts, the filthy latrines that she had to take it in turn to scrub. But none of these things got to her, because she didn't let them.

She would have remained numb for the whole of her three year incarceration – keeping herself to herself, walking around in a haze of indifference – if she hadn't put her back out. But it was the pain of this, the screaming, mind-wrenching agony, that finally brought her back to the real world.

Vanessa had no idea exactly how it happened. One moment she was bending over picking up a pile of laundry, the next she felt a searing pain at the base of her spine. It was so intense she gasped and cried out. Then she remained where she was. Doubled over.

Two of the prison warders ran over to her.

'What is it,' one of them demanded. 'What's all the fuss about?'

'It's my back,' Vanessa whispered in pain. 'I think I must have strained something.'

Thinking she was faking, they tried to get her to straighten up, but all she could do was scream in agony. In the end they half dragged her, half carried her into the hospital area. She was put into a cell much like the one she had before, except it was quieter. The two other women who shared the space helped her on to the bed, and there she lay until the doctor came along.

He was a tall man with a bloodless face, sandy hair and a self-righteous expression.

'What seems to be the problem?' he asked curtly.

Vanessa told him it was her back, and when he asked if he could take a look at it, she thought about refusing. Then she looked into his eyes and her knowledge of the streets told her she was facing a sadist. Without a word she rolled over on to her stomach and pushed up her dress. He found her pain spot right away, and she jumped.

'Don't do that,' she pleaded. 'It's agony.'

As soon as the words were out of her mouth she regretted them.

A man like this would get off on her suffering. It would encourage him. She was right. The doctor prodded her around some more and with every jab of his fingers she felt as if red hot knives were going through her. After he had finished with her back, he made her stand up.

'I want to see you walk,' he said.

Vanessa did as she was told, pacing unsteadily across the floor. His next instruction was less easy to obey.

'Bend over and touch your toes.'

She regarded him with disbelief.

'I can't,' she said. 'It's simply not possible.'

A smile enlivened the smug expression.

'Nothing is impossible,' he told her.

Slowly Vanessa leaned her body over into an arch, then the pain attacked again. Searing, white-hot agony stabbed at her, threatening to break her in two.

'I can't do it,' she told him. 'I can't move.'

The doctor took hold of her shoulders, jerking them towards him in one fast, vicious movement. Vanessa passed out then, blackness wiping away everything.

When she came to, she was lying on her bed.

One of the other prisoners was crouched by her side.

'Are you all right?' she enquired. 'I thought that bastard was going to kill you.'

Somewhere, through the waves of pain, Vanessa managed a smile.

'I thought so too,' she said. 'Has he gone?'

The woman nodded.

'For now, thank God. He said he'd be back later with some painkiller, though if I were you I wouldn't take anything he handed out. For all you know he could be giving you poison.'

Vanessa sighed.

'If it is, I don't think I care all that much. Right now death would be a blessed relief.'

She was kept in the hospital cell for three more days. The doctor supplied her with regular doses of a green liquid that made her feel dizzy and gave her a dull headache. But it cut out some of the pain, so she took it.

It was during the days of her back injury that Vanessa realized that something was wrong. Her mind had stopped protecting her. With the coming of physical pain, emotional anguish returned. Now when she saw the prison doctor, instead of blank indifference she felt fear. But it wasn't just the doctor who agitated her. She was back in touch with herself now and every indignity upset her. The callousness of the warders. The human detritus she saw smeared on the walls. The filthy food.

She became depressed and only the compassion of her cellmates stopped her from falling apart altogether. By the time she was able to stand up again, she felt genuine regret at having to leave.

Her regret increased when she was put back to work, for the warders had burdened her with her least favourite job. Scrubbing the trolley route. The muddy wheels of the food trolleys would come in from the yard, squelch across the floor, then complete their circuit by going back into the yard and picking up more dirt. Every time she cleaned one section of the corridor, a fresh trolley would come trundling in and undo all her work.

Vanessa thought about her back and wondered if she could get out of this job. There must be easier tasks she could do. But when she put this to the officer in charge of the wing, she knew she had no chance. She was told that if she refused the job, on whatever grounds, she would go down to the punishment block. So she got on with it.

She found that if she rested every fifteen minutes, she could just about get away with it. The warder on duty was a heavy smoker. She liked to go into the yard when she lit a cigarette, in the misguided belief that the nicotine would do her less damage if she consumed it in the fresh air. This suited Vanessa. With the warder out of the way, she could lie on her aching back long enough to get some kind of relief.

The system worked well enough until the weather turned bad. Cleaning the trolley route became a farce after that and Vanessa was moved to another job in the same wing. This entailed carrying all the huge rubbish bins from one part of the prison to another.

This one she knew she couldn't do. Her back could only just bear her own weight. An additional load would put her in the sick bay.

This time when she went back to the officer, she made herself as plain as she could. She couldn't lift anything. Rubbish bins, laundry baskets, even tea trays. The warder cut her short.

'Are you, or are you not, going back to work?'

She was a big woman with heavy shoulders and

ample hips, and she regarded Vanessa with a mixture of suspicion and scorn. I have to make her understand, Vanessa thought desperately. My back just won't take it. I'll be a cripple.

She started to explain but the woman didn't seem to hear her.

'I am ordering you to go to work,' she shouted.

Vanessa was near to tears. 'I just told you I can't do that. It's a physical impossibility.'

The woman was immovable. 'I am giving you a direct order to go to work.'

'And I'm telling you I can't.'

The warder's eyes grew hard now, reminding Vanessa of an unfriendly bull terrier.

'So you're refusing a direct order?'

She nodded and the officer took hold of her and marched her silently back to her cell. An hour later the warder was back, this time with four others. They were all of big build, and Vanessa wondered what the hell was going on.

She wasn't carrying a weapon. She didn't have a reputation for violence. She was weak as a kitten. What did they expect her to do?

The head woman ordered her to pack her things. Then she was frog-marched to the punishment block. They weren't done with her yet. When they got outside the cell she was told to get undressed and her clothes, even her underwear were thoroughly searched.

Vanessa shivered in the cold corridor for she knew what was going to happen to her. They're going to body search me, she thought. As many as can get away with it. She felt bitter. I bet it's one of the perks of the job.

It took half an hour for all of them to explore her flesh and when they finally pushed her into the cell she was bruised all over. Every inch of her skin, every fold of her, had been squeezed and pinched and prodded. Only this time the hurt went deeper than her skin because she couldn't get away from it any more. She couldn't detach herself.

By rights, the life that Vanessa had led should have hardened her, and for a while it did. When she arrived at Riker's Island she was a tough whore, without pride and beyond caring.

Now a change seemed to have come over her. It wasn't a sudden thing. She didn't wake up one day and see the truth in a flash of light. She simply stopped being resigned. Before, she didn't mind how people treated her. Now every intrusion, every invasion of her privacy filled her with anger and loathing. She wanted to kill the warders who had taken her casually outside the cell, and she knew now why they had searched her things before they plundered her. If she had had a weapon, a knife or even a table leg she would have used it on one of them.

She remembered feeling this way when she was a girl living in London. In those days she would go to the ends of the earth rather than compromise herself. I had an abortion, she remembered. A painful, terrible abortion that nearly killed me. But I went through with it, because I didn't want to settle for marrying a stranger.

When did I lose touch with myself, she wondered. When did I stop noticing the things people did to me? Her mind focused on Dan, who had changed the course of her life and for the first time she hated him. She didn't feel hurt, the way she had before. She felt fury and the need for revenge. With this new emotion, this anger, she was cleansed.

When her bruises had faded Vanessa started to look around her. She was in a small cell with a basin in one corner and an iron bedstead in the other. The pillow and the bedding were covered in graffiti, the walls were smeared with faeces, yet there were compensations. It was quiet. There were no stomach-tightening demands from officers. No inmates to puncture her privacy.

She was all alone with her thoughts and the few possessions she was allowed to keep. In her bag were a couple of books from the prison library. A Sony Walkman. Some writing paper.

She started to write to her mother. Her last contact with Sybil had been when she was living with Ted three years ago. For one of those years she had been a prostitute and during the other two a jailbird. Do I lie about it, Vanessa wondered. Do I write, '*Dear Mother, sorry I haven't been in touch, but my social life has been rather demanding of late.*'

The notion made her smile. The old Vanessa would have written that. The woman she once was would have hidden behind subterfuge and half truths because she cared so much about what people thought. Now Vanessa was beyond caring. Her only concern was that her mother would be hurt by what she had to tell her. Then she thought, she's a tough old bird, my mother. Tougher than me, by far. If I can survive living these last few years, my mother can survive hearing about them.

She picked up her pen and started to write.

54

London, 1988

Dan wanted to give a big party for Freddie's birthday. His idea was to hire a room in a flashy New York hotel, invite all his business contacts and keep on dancing till the early hours.

'If we hold it in Trump Tower,' he told Liz, 'we'll end up with press coverage as well.'

Liz liked the idea. A party in New York would put some distance between her and David. It would give her a valid excuse to see Dan, and an even better excuse to buy an entire new wardrobe.

'Have you told Freddie about all this?' she asked. At the mention of his daughter's name, Dan frowned.

'I'm having trouble with Freddie,' he confided. 'She finally found out you and I were an item.'

They were having dinner at the St James's Club at the end of April. Weeks earlier, Dan had shown his collection in New York and now he was taking time out with Liz. She was looking particularly fetching that night. She'd changed her hairstyle again and her hair colour. Now she was a dark Titian, and she wore her new glowing tresses in soft waves around her face. He marvelled at her. I've known this woman on and off for over twenty years, he thought, yet she never ages.

If anything she's better looking now than when I first saw her. He thought about his wife. Ruth had grown fat with the passing of the years. Fat and grouchy. She looked more like his mother than ever.

Liz interrupted Dan's reverie.

'It's high time Freddie did know about us,' she said sharply. 'Everyone else does.'

Dan sighed and signalled to the waiter for more wine. I'm going to have to do something about this situation, he thought, before it gets out of hand. He cast his mind back to the last time he saw Freddie. It was two days ago and he'd just got off the plane from New York. She'd come to meet him at the airport. At the time he had been puzzled. His daughter didn't normally put herself out like this. She liked to see him, of course – there was no question about her feeling for him. But coming all the way out to Heathrow? Something had to be up.

It was. The second he was through immigration she let him have it.

'How long have you been screwing Liz Dearing?' she demanded.

Dan had been tempted to tell her to keep her nose out of his business. It was nothing to do with his daughter who he went to bed with. Then he thought, she does live with Liz. In a way Liz is almost family, so he was softer with Freddie than he intended.

'Who told you about Liz?' he enquired.

There was a set to her shoulders he didn't like.

'A guy who works on the *Daily Mail*, a friend of Barbara's. Apparently the gossip columnist has known about it for ages, but the powers-that-be won't let him print it.'

Dan looked at his daughter sharply. She was telling this story with a bit too much relish for his liking.

'This is my private life you're talking about,' he said, 'not some hot gossip item. I'm not prepared to discuss it standing outside terminal three. If you want to talk about it, we'll do it someplace else.'

He looked at his watch and saw it was past seven.

'If you haven't got any plans, I could buy you dinner at the hotel.'

'Perfect,' Freddie said. 'I love the food at the Ritz.'

Dan watched her as she strode out in front of him and hailed a taxi. Freddie had certainly changed since she had first come to England. Two years ago she had been pretty in an American-girl way. You certainly wouldn't have passed her on the street. Today she was more than merely decorative. London had given her a gloss, a sophisticated edge. Her tumble of unruly dark blonde curls had been tamed into a silky, shoulder-length bob. She was wearing make-up now and the new season's clothes. Yet it was more than just her surface that impressed him. Freddie had learned to wear her sophistication, and be comfortable with it.

She's turned into a regular heart-breaker, Dan thought. I feel for any of my sex foolish enough to fall in love with her.

They got to the hotel before eight and Dan took Freddie straight into the restaurant.

The maître d' remembered him from his last visit and gave them a quiet table at the back overlooking the park. Dan was glad of that. The last thing he wanted tonight was to be recognized and interrupted. As they sat down, he beckoned over the wine waiter and ordered a bottle of champagne. Then when it arrived he relaxed. Now he was on his own territory with a glass of iced Krug in his hand, he was in control of the situation.

'You wanted to know about Liz,' he said conversationally.

'It would be helpful to know what's going on,' Freddie replied. 'It's not every day you find out your father's making out with your landlady.'

Dan felt a stab of irritation. 'Liz isn't your landlady,'

he said crossly, 'and I'm not making out with her. It's more involved than that.'

'You're not telling me you're serious, are you?'

'Why shouldn't I be? Liz is a remarkable woman.'

Freddie reached across the table to his pack of cigarettes, selected one and made a great performance of lighting it. The way she did it was very self-assured, very laid-back and that irritated Dan further.

'I didn't know you smoked,' he said.

Freddie smiled.

'I only do it when the going gets rough. And right now, I'd say it's very rough indeed.'

'Because Liz is my mistress? Or because I like it that way?'

Freddie took a deep drag of the cigarette.

'Both,' she replied. 'Have you ever stopped to think about anyone apart from yourself? Did it not occur to you that seducing Liz might hurt people? Me for example. Or David.'

She didn't look so laid-back now and it reassured him.

'David's a big boy and he can look after himself,' Dan told her. 'It's you I'm concerned about. Why are you hurt?'

'Because the whole thing's so damn tacky.' The words came bursting out of her. 'All my life I had to live with other people's messes. First you and Mom don't get married, like all my friends' parents. Then Mom moves in with Norman. Then you start dating a string of bimbos around town and I have to read about you in the gossip columns.' Freddie paused for breath. 'The only time I saw anyone behave decently at all was when I moved here. Before you came along Liz and David seemed to have a very good marriage. They liked each other. They talked. They weren't seen around with other people. After a bit I started to believe in what they had together. I even believed in marriage. Then you came riding into town and blew the whole thing apart.'

Dan looked at his daughter with a mixture of admiration and concern.

'I guess I had it coming,' he said. 'Life isn't all it appears you know, and it's not as black-and-white as you think it is. For a start, there's no such thing as a perfect marriage. There's a perfect honeymoon, but once that wears off, most people come to terms.'

The waiter came with the food Dan had ordered, but Freddie didn't feel like eating.

'You're telling me,' she said, 'that the entire world is full of married people who cheat on each other. Well, I refuse to accept that. I know there are decent people out there who love each other. Liz and David were those kind of people for God's sake.'

Dan thought about telling her the truth. He wasn't Liz's first affair. There had been the Greek before him. And David wasn't such a saint either. He'd probably got up to something in Aspen. But Dan stopped himself. She's still young, he thought. Let her have her dreams for a few more years.

'I'm truly sorry about Liz,' he told her. 'I know it's too close for comfort. And I know it's upset you, but sometimes things happen that are beyond our control.'

He looked at her Dover sole. It was the most expensive fish on the menu and she had ordered asparagus out of season to go with it.

'Try to eat something,' he begged. 'It's not good for you to drink on an empty stomach.'

To encourage her, he attempted to change the subject.

'It's your birthday any minute now,' he said. 'Are you planning a party?'

Freddie shook her head.

'Barbara and I thought we might invite a few friends over to the house.'

'I think I can do better for you than that.' He went on to tell her about his plan for a glittering evening in New York.

'You could ask all your smart English friends – the ones with money. I could field a couple of top Seventh Avenue manufacturers and some Wall Street types.'

Freddie made a face. 'Any minute now you'll be telling me you want Liz along.'

'I do want Liz along.' He stopped what he was saying, realizing too late that he had fallen into a trap she had set for him.

'You can have Liz along,' she told him, 'but don't expect me to put in an appearance. What you have in mind doesn't sound as if it's for my birthday at all. It doesn't even sound like it's for me. It's just an excuse for you to put on a vulgar display for all the people you want to impress.'

Freddie was on her feet now, pushing the table away from her.

'Pop,' she said. 'We're miles apart from each other. We don't even enjoy the same kind of parties any more.'

Before Dan could stop her she was on her way out of the restaurant.

Now, sitting with Liz, he could still see her strutting out of the room.

He came back to the present.

'Freddie's in a temper with me,' he told Liz. 'She doesn't like the fact that we're together and it's poisoned her whole attitude. In this mood she won't even discuss her birthday party.'

Liz looked at him.

'What are you going to do about it?' she asked, troubled.

He shrugged. 'Nothing for the moment. I'm not going to beg Freddie to let me spend half a million dollars on a party for her. If she doesn't want me to do it, that's her loss.'

He looked into Liz's pale, beautiful face and felt the first stirrings of desire. They had been together every night since he had arrived in London and he still couldn't get enough of her.

'There's one thing I can promise you,' he said. 'I'm not going to let my daughter interfere with what we have.'

55

The pool at the Sanctuary was empty when Freddie got there. The whole place was deserted save for the tame cockatoos which perched at discreet intervals amongst the jungle foliage.

At another time the hot house atmosphere of the health club-cum-beauty parlour would have soothed her. But today Freddie was beyond soothing. Men, she thought. Why is it that whenever my life looks set fair, some member of the opposite sex has to walk into it wearing heavy boots.

It had been three days since she had dinner with her father and she was still steamed up about it. If he had explained himself, she thought. If he had just given me one logical reason why he was messing around with Liz, I would have tried to forgive him. But he didn't. All he told me was that I didn't understand. He still sees me as a little girl, she fumed. A child to be placated and brushed aside.

A Chinese girl in a pink-checked overall came up to her.

'Miss Grenville,' she said. 'We're ready for you now.'

She followed the girl past the tethered pink parrots and down the pine walkway to a cubicle at the back of the swimming-pool. Inside the beautician had set up a reclining bed and a long table which had an array of jars and pots of perfumed oil. The aroma reached her as she walked into the room. Rose essence mixed with musk and something indefinable which seemed to penetrate deep inside her.

Freddie took off her wrap and lay face down on the bed. Then she closed her eyes as the aromatherapist began to massage the oil into her back.

At first the heavy odours relaxed her. Her sinews started to expand, the knots slowly undoing themselves. She felt pleasantly hazy as her mind reached out for sleep. Then the beautician started to talk.

'I expect you've been busy this week,' she said. 'You told me your father was coming into town.'

Freddie came awake with a start. Not now, she thought. Not when I was just beginning to forget about him.

She took a deep breath of the scented air and tried to climb back onto her pink cloud, but it was no good. Her brain was off again and running. Dan was back to torment her. Dan and Scott and all the others. The trouble with men, she thought, is that they promise one thing, then they go off and do exactly the opposite. Dan was going to look after me for the rest of my life, until he changed his mind and went back to Ruth and the family he had before. I should have let go of him then, she decided. I should have made my mind up to do without a father, but I thought I knew better. I really imagined that if I ran after him, I could make him love me.

The girl lowered the towel until it was below her buttocks. Then she started rubbing in a different kind of oil. It smelt of carnations and was designed to slow her down, but Freddie went on raging.

I was such a fool, she berated herself. Such a complete idiot to believe that Pop really kept coming over to London to see me. All he came here for was to screw Liz. I was incidental to his plan. But then wasn't I always? She sighed deeply and the girl, taking this as a signal, flipped her over on her back.

As her body changed position, so did her mind.

Now she brooded about the other disappointment in her life. Scott Harding. It had been over two years since she had seen him. He hadn't been in touch since he walked out on her at Stratford, but he still lived on inside her. A tantalizing piece of unfinished business. A lover who never loved her.

Freddie had made up for it, of course. More than made up for it. A smile flitted across her face as she recalled her first conquest. He was very aristocratic. If she had drawn a diagram of a well-born young scion, complete with title and family tree, she couldn't have done better than Charlie Bevan. He had it all. Looks, money and the kind of manners that can only be learned at the best public school.

Freddie had met him at Henley, and the minute she set eyes on him, she knew he was the candidate she was looking for. Even before he asked her out she was imagining how he would relieve her of her virginity. This time she didn't waste her opportunity. As soon as the drinks, the opera, the obligatory dinner were over, she made herself clear. She wanted to be seduced.

Charlie didn't fail her. They spent the night in his bachelor penthouse in Chelsea Harbour. It had just been done out by one of those trendy interior decorators and was all plate glass and black leather sofas. Freddie sat on the sofa and looked at the river view for exactly ten minutes. Then she took the candidate she had selected by the hand and led him through to the bedroom. After it was over she wondered what all the fuss was about. She didn't feel any different. Of course it had been exciting, but her heart didn't beat any faster when she looked at Charlie in the morning. Truth be told, she couldn't wait to get up and hurry back to the comfort of her own bathroom.

She saw Charlie several times after that, but she

never felt any closer to him than she had the night she first met him. He was simply a pleasant, perfectly mannered man friend who would one day inherit a title. None of this impressed her and when she met a yuppie banker who drove a black Porsche and carried a portable telephone, she ditched Charlie instantly.

The banker lasted a bit longer. Freddie finished with him after four months when she got weary of hearing about the stock market. After the banker there was a Parisian interior decorator, then a Hollywood film director. Each time she took a lover, Freddie felt exactly the same. She was attracted at the first meeting, allowed herself to be courted, and finally she fell into bed. After that she lost interest. She never really understood why this was.

None of her lovers was dull or boorish. Most of the girls she knew would have given their eye teeth to be seen out with them. Including Barbara.

'You're too hard on your boyfriends,' her friend observed. 'You don't treat them like people at all. If anything, you're nicer to my dog.'

There was nothing Freddie could say. She wasn't a man hater or a rampant feminist. She didn't mean to leave a trail of hurt feelings, but she didn't mean to fall in love either. She'd loved two men in her life, Dan and Scott, and it had done her no good at all.

Now all she wanted to do was have fun. If that meant trampling on a few egos she couldn't be held responsible.

The scented massage was coming to an end. She could tell by the way the girl's touch was becoming lighter, more feathery.

'I expect you want to sleep now,' the beautician told her. 'If you like I'll come back in half an hour.'

Freddie sat bolt upright, the towel slipping down to her waist.

'Whatever gave you that idea?' she smiled.

There was a letter waiting for Freddie when she got home. The postmark told her it came from Cheltenham, and that puzzled her. I don't know anyone who lives there, she thought.

She took the letter through to the drawing room where David was sitting nursing a whisky.

'Are you in tonight,' he asked, 'or am I dining alone?'

Freddie told him she was in and went and got herself a glass of white wine. Then she started to feel brighter. David was one of the few men who didn't bore her silly. He didn't lecture her like Uncle Norman or tell her lies like her father. He simply talked to her as if she was an equal.

She carried the letter and the drink over to the sofa and sat down.

'This came for me from Cheltenham,' she told him. 'It's probably an invitation to a horse show.'

She opened it and saw it wasn't. Someone had written to her. The lettering was spidery and old-fashioned, and she didn't recognize it.

'*Dear Freddie*', went the letter, '*your mother told me about you some years ago and since then I've been longing to meet you*'.

Freddie was hooked now. A link with her mother, any link was precious to her. Half way down the first page she saw that the communication was from her grandmother. She read on. Apparently Vanessa had written to her from prison, confessing what had happened in her life. The old woman had been shocked and Freddie wasn't surprised. She'd been shocked too.

She shrugged and turned the page, fully expecting to find herself and her mother shut out of the Grenville family forever. To her surprise she was wrong. Her grandmother had found it in her heart to understand and forgive. More than that, she had made plans for Vanessa to come home to England and live with her.

'Since your Grandfather died,' she wrote, 'I've been very lonely down here on my own. I need my family around me now.'

Even though your daughter is a convicted prostitute, Freddie thought, and your grand-daughter is illegitimate. She glanced up from the letter to find David looking at her.

'Who's it from?' he asked curiously. 'From your expression, it's obviously important.'

'My grandmother,' Freddie told him. 'The Honourable Sybil. It seems that she and Mom have been writing to one another and all is forgiven.'

David raised an eyebrow.

'Is that good news?'

'I suppose it is in a way. At least Mom's got somewhere to go when she gets out of Riker's Island, though I always thought she and I would get an apartment in New York and we'd live on my allowance.'

Freddie regarded the man sitting opposite her for signs of disapproval. She hadn't told anybody about her plans for the future before and she wasn't quite sure how he'd react.

'Do you want to go back to New York?' he asked. 'I thought you were happy staying here.'

'I am happy here,' she told him. 'Happier than I've ever been. But it can't go on indefinitely.'

Again she saw the raised eyebrow and the indefinable, almost continental shrug.

'Why can't it go on?' he asked. 'It's a big house. You don't get in anybody's way. Barbara wants you. She'd be lost if you went back to New York. You're a sister to her.'

Freddie sighed. Didn't David know what was going on in his own house?

'Barbara's going away in the New Year. Around the same time as Mom comes out of jail. I thought you knew about the job in San Francisco?'

'Yes, I did know about the job in San Francisco, but I'd put it out of my mind,' he responded. 'I hate the idea of her going. I hate the idea of you going as well. What am I going to do with myself all alone in this house?'

The words were out before she could stop them.

'You've got Liz,' Freddie said.

The blush started at the base of her neck, crept up to her chin then spread all over her face. She put her hands up to hide it.

'I'm sorry,' she said. 'That was tactless of me.'

David walked over to the silver tray and made himself another whisky. Then he settled himself back into the tall leather chair he always sat in.

'What was tactless?' he asked. 'The assumption that Liz and I are still together? Or the suggestion that my wife is pursuing her own interests?'

Freddie had no idea what to say. If this had been another man, one of her lovers, she would have pressed on regardless. But David couldn't be treated so lightly.

'Look,' she said. 'I really don't want to talk about this. I'm bound to say the wrong thing.'

David smiled. 'I'm sure you'll say the wrong thing,' he told her, 'but it's all right. You're part of the family now, you're allowed to speak your mind.'

Relief washed over Freddie. She'd been keeping the whole business with Liz and her father bottled up inside her. She hadn't been able to talk about it to Dan because he wouldn't let her. And she hadn't dared bring it out in the open with Barbara. She knew the other girl had heard the story too, but Liz was her mother after all. The whole subject was fraught with danger. Now David, the last person she'd imagined, wanted to talk about it. She took a deep breath.

'I think my father's out of his mind,' she said. 'I think Liz is too. If I was married to someone like you, I wouldn't start having affairs all over the place.'

'You don't know what being married to me is like,' David told her. 'Maybe I'm to blame for Liz's defection.'

His answer made Freddie curious. 'How are you to blame?' she asked.

He thought for a moment before replying. When he did he sounded sad.

'There weren't any other women, though in my position it would have been easy enough. What I did to Liz was worse than taking a mistress. I ignored her. I did so for years because I was fascinated with what I was doing. I thought nothing of standing her up for dinner if there was a crisis on at the *Chronicle*. And when I did get home, I was so busy worrying about the business I never really listened to what she had to say.'

'Was she interested in what you had to say? Did you talk about the paper when you were together?'

David shook his head.

'We did in the beginning, but only in the very broadest way. Liz wasn't all that fascinated in how the family earned its fortunes. It was enough for her that we had the money, and in the end I talked about the paper to my colleagues, or my father. Sometimes Barbara, when she began to take an interest in journalism.'

Freddie started to feel uneasy. David's taking too much on himself, she thought. It's almost as if he was the guilty party. Aloud she said, 'You don't sound very angry with Liz.'

'What do you want me to do?' he asked. 'Take Dan to my club and tell him to stay away from my wife, or would you like me to challenge him to a duel?' He smiled. 'Life isn't like that, Freddie. When you've put time and energy and emotion into a marriage, you don't devalue it by making ridiculous gestures. I did that once, by the way. A few years ago Liz disappointed me and I walked out on her. But I couldn't keep it up.'

Freddie was aware that David was unburdening himself now, but she made no attempt to halt the confession. After a minute or two he went on, 'A marriage is a bit like a business. I wouldn't close down a company just because my managing director started to make mistakes. You close down a company because it isn't viable any more, because it doesn't work.' He paused. 'When I think something needs to be done about Liz, I'll do it. In my own way and in my own time. Nobody, not Liz, not your father, not even the scandalmongers are going to push me into that decision.'

Freddie had never seen David this agitated before, because all the time she had known him he had been the head of the Dearing dynasty. He had played the part to perfection. Now this crisis had stripped away the façade and what she saw in front of her was a man at the end of his tether. She could identify with him now, and it gave them an empathy that had never existed before.

At his suggestion they went into the dining-room. The butler had done something with the dark wood table, contracted it somehow, so it no longer looked as if a family was sitting down to supper. There were fresh white flowers, Freddie noticed. Candles as well, and the formality of it all made her feel grown-up. He's treating me like a woman, she thought. Despite herself she felt flattered.

The food was different from the usual fare in Cheyne Walk. When Liz knew she was going to be in, she always made sure the cook had something healthy on the menu. A salad or a piece of fish. Something guaranteed not to put an ounce on her hips. When she was out, she left the kitchen staff to their own devices and tonight they seemed to have forgotten Liz's diet. They started with foie gras, which David told Freddie had been imported from the South of France. Then there was a haunch of beef in a pastry case, accompanied by a thick red wine from Provence and finally, Stilton and port.

Freddie realized he had chosen the meal himself, yet he made no mention of it. The entire subject of his marriage had been swept aside and she was glad of it. She knew they would talk about it again, but for the moment there were other things to discover about David Dearing.

He started to ask her about her childhood in New York and she found herself telling him about it, adding to what he already knew.

She talked about New York for nearly two hours concealing nothing. What David hadn't known was how she felt about the events that crowded her childhood. When she told him, he didn't seem surprised.

'It explains your attitude,' he observed. 'I didn't think anyone could behave as heartlessly with men as you do without a damn good reason.'

Before she could say anything, he changed the subject.

'What are you going to do about your grandmother?' he asked. 'Will you go and see her?'

Freddie shrugged.

'I suppose so. I need to know how serious she is about bringing Mom back to England. It could alter a lot of things.'

David looked serious for a moment. 'I meant what I said before,' he told her. 'You're welcome to stay on here if you want to.'

Freddie thought about the idea. She liked the way she lived now. It suited her. London suited her. It would be the easiest thing in the world to install Vanessa in Cheltenham and go on as if nothing had happened. Yet something told her it wouldn't be that simple. Surviving in New York had sharpened her senses. Freddie could spot trouble before it even happened and she knew without understanding why that something was going to change.

She surveyed the man sitting opposite her. He was older than her. Much older and his face was full of shadows. Yet she was drawn to him. How much longer, she thought, can I live under the same roof as you without wanting to climb into your bed?

56

New York, 1989

Some people fall in love just once in their lives. Freddie was Scott Harding's love object. From the moment he met her he knew she was the only woman he would ever take seriously. This didn't stop him from getting engaged to someone else, however.

In the autumn of 1986, when he returned to New York, he was introduced to Imogen Fellowes, the daughter of a prominent Boston banker. All his life, girls like Imogen had been paraded in front of him by every member of his family, and all his life he had run a mile. For Imogen had been trained for one thing and one thing only. To be married to a rich and successful man.

But there was something different about this girl. She wasn't the usual spoilt socialite. She had taken the trouble to get herself an education, and now she had one she didn't let it go to waste. Imogen didn't do anything as crass as getting a job. What she did do was devote herself to good works. She was on the boards of most of the major charities in New York. She visited hospitals, she organized lunches and dances. She cared.

This side of her personality was what impressed itself on Scott. After the Freddie debacle he was feeling vulnerable and bruised. He needed someone to build up his confidence again. And Imogen obliged. Right from the start she made no bones about the fact that she admired him. She seemed to have read everything he had ever written and when he produced anything new he fell into the habit of showing it to her before he submitted it.

He knew she would always tell him whatever he produced was wonderful. But that wasn't the point. He didn't want criticism. The tough guys at his office would dish out plenty of that. What Scott wanted was his ego massaged and this was Imogen's forte.

After a month or so he got into the habit of listening to her. Then he started to depend on her unstinting admiration. It was then that she made herself plain.

'We've known each other for half a year,' she told him. 'Is there any future in going on with this relationship?'

They were lovers by then. Not passionate lovers, but lovers all the same and Scott thought the relationship was enough for her.

'What do you want from me?' he asked her.

Imogen told him what she wanted was a proposal of marriage, and because Scott could see little alternative apart from breaking things off, he complied with her wishes.

They were formally engaged at a huge party given by Imogen's parents. Then Scott embarked on his first serious business venture. He took over a moribund group of magazines specializing in finance. Wall Street backed him because of his reputation as an award-winning journalist, and he paid them back in spades. By the middle of 1987, two of the journals in the group had turned round and were making a profit. During the following year, the rest of the group caught up and the city's leading accountancy and advertising trade papers started to look nervously over their shoulders. It seemed that Scott Harding had everything he ever wanted. A rich and worthy fiancée, a growing business, and a beautiful townhouse in the eighties.

It was then that his entire world suddenly meant nothing at all, for he was introduced to Dan Levin at a cocktail party.

'Aren't you the young man who walked out on my daughter a couple of years back?' Dan asked him.

Scott looked blank.

'Remind me,' he said.

Dan told him his daughter's name was Freddie, and as he said her name the champagne seemed to go flat.

'I didn't walk out on Freddie,' he said stiffly. 'She found herself another boyfriend. After that there seemed no reason to stay around.'

The older man considered this for a moment, then he took hold of Scott and steered him towards the bar. When they got there he ordered fresh drinks for them both. Then he looked serious.

'I don't know if this is going to do any good,' he said. 'It's all too long ago anyway, but for what it's worth I'm going to put you right about my daughter.'

He talked about Freddie and the way she was during her first summer season. When he had finished and gone on his way, Scott realized he had been a fool. A badly behaved fool.

I couldn't help myself, he thought. Freddie made me so crazy it was a wonder I didn't kill anyone who stood in my way.

As he thought about the girl he still loved, another image came into his mind. Imogen, the girl he was going to marry. He would never kill for Imogen, he thought sadly. Their relationship was too civilized, too feet-on-the-ground for anything as pagan as that.

For a moment he considered the life he would have with her. He would be successful in anything he tried. Her money would see to that. They would move in the glittering society she was so much a part of. Their children would be beautifully behaved and go to the very best schools. And she would never ever give him a moment's doubt. A moment's jealousy. Of everything, this fact depressed him the most. For he knew Imogen would never make him jealous, because he didn't love her enough for that.

He decided to pull back from her a little. From that evening, he began to be less available for her constant charity dinners. He didn't go with her every weekend to visit her parents in the Hamptons. He made time for himself now, for his work and for his own friends.

Of course Imogen was put out. She was too rich to understand that people, even fiancées, had their own lives. When Scott proposed, she assumed he would spend all his time circling around her. When he didn't, she became irritable.

'Why won't you come to the heart benefit?' she would demand. 'Why can't you lunch on Sunday?'

She thought he would placate her before jumping into line, and when he didn't, they started to have serious fights. Imogen didn't do anything as short-sighted as throw back the ring. Scott, she knew, would make an admirable husband just as soon as she trained him properly. But while that was going on, it didn't do any harm to let him kick his heels for a bit.

At that point in the proceedings Scott decided to look up Barbara. She was his one link with Freddie, the one way he could find his way back to her.

Barbara was in San Francisco he remembered, doing a big job on the *Herald*. She had written months ago asking him for a reference and after he supplied it she had thanked him profusely. Apparently what he had said about her had clinched things. His intervention had got her her first Woman's Editorship.

Scott cast his mind back to the way David had

helped him on the *Chronicle* when he was starting out. The memory made him smile. Our two families, he thought. Helping each other over the years. Smoothing the professional way. He stopped himself short. The favour he was about to ask Barbara had nothing to do with business. What he wanted from her was more important than a reference or an introduction to a contact. He wanted Freddie back, and after the way he behaved in London, he wondered if Barbara would co-operate.

He decided to play the whole thing carefully. When he called Barbara he invented a meeting he had to attend in San Francisco.

'I have to stay over for a night or so, and I wondered if you'd like to meet for dinner?'

Barbara sounded enthusiastic. Her new job was going well and she couldn't wait to tell him all about it. Scott wondered whether to mention Freddie on the phone. Then he thought, no. She'll see through me right away if I do that. She knows me too well already.

He took Barbara to one of the big flashy restaurants on the waterfront, and the minute they sat down in the bar he knew she was on to him.

'Out with it,' she said. 'You're after something, aren't you?'

Scott did his best to look charming. 'That's a rotten thing to say to an old friend. Whatever gave you that idea?'

Barbara sighed deeply and gestured around the room. It was designed to look like a cruise ship with fairy lights running along the length of the bar and a ship's lantern on each table. The whole thing was unbearably twee and designed for rich tourists.

'Normally when we go out for dinner,' she said patiently, 'we end up in a basement where they're playing loud rock music and serving steaks. So either you're trying to get me into bed, or that stuffy fiancée of yours is having a bad effect on you.'

Scott laughed then.

'Maybe I am trying to get you into bed. It's not such a bad idea.'

Barbara looked at him sideways, and he was reminded of a latter-day Monroe.

'Let's face it,' she said. 'If you felt that way about me we would have got it together years ago. No, there's something else on your mind.'

Scott felt a moment of pure regret. Either San Francisco or her new job had made Barbara blossom. She seemed to have put on even more weight than when he saw her last, yet it suited her. She was soft and lush like a peach and if it hadn't been for the way he felt about Freddie, he would have been tempted to do something about her.

But he did love Freddie, so he came clean and told her about his meeting with Dan in New York.

Barbara narrowed her eyes. 'Can I help it if you're a jerk,' she said. 'If you'd stayed around instead of running back to New York, I could have put you right. But you didn't think, did you? You didn't give Freddie a chance.' A waiter came over with their drinks and Scott sampled his before replying.

'You're cross with me, aren't you?' he said.

'Damn right, I'm cross with you. Have you any idea of how much you hurt Freddie? She'd had a terrible time before she got to England. Her entire confidence in the human race had been knocked away. Then you came along on a white charger and carried her off into the sunset. Except you didn't. So instead of one trauma she had two to recover from. It took her months to get back on her feet emotionally. There are times when I wonder if she ever has.'

Now Scott looked stricken.

'Poor kid,' he said. 'I should have known.'

Barbara cut in on him. 'Don't give me the hearts and flowers routine,' she said sharply. 'It's me you're talking to, not some lovestruck airhead. By the way, how is Imogen?'

Her sheer venom took Scott aback. Barbara was one of his dearest friends. He counted on her support. Now she was attacking him like a vampire.

'Imogen's fine,' he said stiffly. 'I'd rather you didn't refer to her as an airhead. She's a fine woman. One of the most committed caring woman I know.'

Barbara didn't change her expression. If anything she looked even foxier.

'If Imogen's so wonderful,' she said, 'what the hell are you doing digging up memories of Freddie? Can't you let the poor girl rest in peace.'

Scott shook his head.

'I wish I could,' he said, 'but I love her. I know what you're going to say. I'm an inconsiderate bastard and I should leave her alone. But I can't do that. It's so bad, I'm seriously considering jumping on the first plane to London tomorrow.'

'Where does that leave Imogen?'

Scott fought down a feeling of quiet despair.

Barbara wasn't going to help him. He should have known it all along. When the chips were down women tended to stick together. For all he knew Barbara would have Freddie on the phone right after dinner. She'd warn her off. Then she'd dial New York and warn Imogen off as well. He swallowed the rest of his drink.

'Come on,' he said. 'Let's go in and have dinner.'

Barbara didn't move from her seat.

'You still haven't told me what you're going to do about Imogen?'

Scott decided to let her have it.

'I'm going to tell Imogen goodbye,' he said. 'I know it's a rotten thing to do and you'll probably hate me even more than you do now, but I can't help it. I just don't love her.'

Barbara was grinning broadly now and he wondered what the hell had got into her.

'I'm glad you told me that,' she said. 'Now I can save you the bother of going all the way to London. Freddie's going to be in New York next week. It's when her mother comes out of jail. So all you have to do is call her at the number I'm going to give you.'

57

David had insisted that Freddie stay at the family's apartment on East 79th Street and the girl didn't argue. Seeing her mother again after such a long interval was going to be difficult enough. Why complicate it further by dragging her back to some soulless hotel room?

Now, as the taxi drew up outside the apartment building, Freddie was glad she'd let David talk her into it. There was an unmistakable whiff of money about the place. She wasn't even on the sidewalk before the man on the door was hurrying to collect her bags. The elevator, she thought, will have wood panels and there will be thick carpet all over the lobby floor like one of the top hotels. She was right, though there was one thing she hadn't thought of: the paintings. As she came into the building she was stopped by them. It was like walking into a museum or an art gallery. Every wall seemed to be covered by glowing Victorian landscapes.

'They must have cost somebody a fortune,' she breathed.

The man carrying her bags overheard her and laughed.

'Are you talking about the pictures, or the price the tenants have to pay to keep them safe?'

Freddie pressed the button for the elevator.

'Both,' she replied. Then she started to feel guilty. I take too much from the Dearings, she thought. Her mind went back a year to the time when she was finishing college. Like all the other girls she was looking for a job, and like all the other girls she wasn't having much luck. Not that she needed a job. The allowance her father gave her ensured she need never lift a finger again, but she wanted to work, to be self sufficient and independent. Her life had taught her that if she was going to survive she would have to make her own way.

There was only one problem: her studies qualified her for very little. She had a thorough knowledge of the arts, English literature, history, a smattering of politics and economics. At grand dinner parties she could more than hold her own. But you didn't earn your living going to dinner parties.

Freddie talked the problem over with David who offered to put her to work on the *Chronicle*, but she refused.

'I'm not like Barbara,' she told him. 'I can't write and I don't have an appetite for digging up facts. It wouldn't be fair to inflict me on your staff.'

In the end it was Liz who solved the problem. She took Freddie round to see Jeremy Flynn who owned an interior design consultancy at the tail end of the King's Road.

'Go carefully with Jeremy,' Liz had warned, 'he takes some getting used to.'

Jeremy Flynn was a tall homosexual of indeterminate age and exquisite elegance. Several years ago he had had his face lifted by one of the top men in Harley Street which made him look like Peter Pan. He knew this and played on it.

When Liz and Freddie arrived at his studio, he made a great performance about opening a bottle of vintage wine. Half way through lunch, Freddie began to wonder what she was doing there. It's all right for Liz, she thought. She's having a fine time bitching about all her old café society friends, but where do I fit in? To pass the time she began to wander around the room. On one of the drawing-boards was a detailed sketch of somebody's room. From the looks of it, whoever lived there had a lot of money to waste, for at the top of the page was a list of items. Chandeliers, Persian rugs, ormolu sconces . . . Freddie was half way down when Jeremy interrupted her.

'Don't waste your time looking at that,' he said.

She turned round. 'Why? It's quite something.'

He sighed and for a moment he dropped his pose. Instead of a languid queen, Freddie saw a weary businessman.

'It *is* quite something,' he agreed with her. 'It took me a long time to put together, but it won't end up looking like that at all. When my client has finished messing around with it, the whole thing will be a travesty. A vulgar mistake.'

Freddie was surprised.

'And you let this client push you around like that? Whatever for?'

He shrugged. 'About a hundred thousand. That's the money I'll make on the job by the time I've finished.'

'It's not worth it.' The words were out of Freddie's mouth before she could stop them, and she regretted them instantly. She knew nothing about this man and even less about his business. What right did she have poking her nose into it?

To her surprise he looked amused.

'Why do you think it isn't worth it?' he asked. 'I'd like to know.'

Freddie was tempted to gloss over the incident, then she thought, why not tell him? It wasn't as if her opinion mattered.

'If you do the job the way your client wants it,'

she said, 'everyone who sees it will know you were responsible, and your reputation will suffer. In my book that's not worth a hundred thousand.'

'How much do you think I should make her pay?'

She hesitated then she took a gamble.

'I wouldn't take her money at all,' she said. 'I'd fire her instead. In the long run it will be cheaper.'

For a second nobody said anything. One of the assistants who was busy with his sketchpad stopped what he was doing and looked up. Liz seemed to have developed a torn fingernail, and Jeremy reached over and made a grab for the wine bottle. When he had refilled his glass he broke the silence.

'If that's how you feel about it,' he grinned, 'you tell Mrs Thyarchos to take a walk. It will be interesting to see how she reacts to the news.'

'But I don't work here. It's nothing to do with me.'

Jeremy Flynn looked Freddie in the eye.

'Would you like to work here? Liz tells me you're in search of a career.'

So that was it. That was why she had been dragged over to Chelsea on the pretext of a drink with an old friend. She looked around her and everywhere her eye went she saw chaos. Jeremy and his assistants knew how to do their job, she had little doubt of that, but they needed organizing. Pulling together.

Freddie smiled inwardly. There would be spectacular fights. Nobody cleaned up their act without some show of resistance, but it would be fun and she might even learn something.

'How much were you thinking of paying me?' she asked.

The job changed her life. Before, Freddie had been a

social butterfly playing with her lovers and worrying about her wardrobe.

Now there was a purpose to her existence and she started to take herself seriously. When Barbara left for America, she moved into a flat of her own. It was in Sloane Street, not a million miles away from the Dearings, but it was her own space. Her own territory. It made her feel grown-up.

Then one day at the end of summer her grandmother called and told her the news. Vanessa was coming out of prison in September. It was as if three years had been wiped away and Freddie was a little girl again. A little girl with a mother who was always getting into trouble. A little girl staggering under the weight of a heavy responsibility.

She didn't back away from it. For along with the responsibility there was love and a mutual dependence built up over years. When she left her mother behind her in New York, Freddie had cried for her more often than she cared to remember. For a long time she lived for the letters that came for her every month and it was only recently with her new job and her new independence that she had found a strength of her own. She wondered if her mother would sap that strength, drain it out of her. It was then she decided on a plan of campaign.

Freddie wouldn't let her mother pull them back into the morass. She had made a fresh start in London and that was where they would build their future. There was enough room in her flat for Vanessa to stay if she didn't choose to spend her time in the country. Money was no problem either. Freddie's salary, along with her allowance, would support both of them.

58

What will Grandmother think, Freddie wondered. She was counting on Vanessa coming to her. She laughed at herself. How arrogant we both are, she thought. We think we know what's best but we haven't even considered what Mom wants. She sighed, it's probably time one of us asked.

In the end the task fell to her. Her grandmother couldn't be expected to make the journey to New York. She was too old for that. Anyway, Freddie knew the city. When Liz and David heard what she was doing, they insisted on going to New York with her.

'There could be complications,' Liz told her. 'You can't handle everything on your own.'

This last remark made Freddie dig her heels in. She wasn't a child anymore to be ordered about and pushed around. Those days were well and truly past. She turned down Liz's offer and was so firm about it that both she and David backed off.

The next day David called Freddie and offered her use of the apartment. He sounded so penitent that Freddie didn't have the heart to turn him down. Now she was here in New York sitting in this ritzy apartment wondering what the hell she'd got herself into.

David's day had gone badly. First thing that morning his managing director had come on the line and told him there was no way he could avoid a price rise.

When they'd been through the figures together he was forced to agree.

Starting the following week, the *Chronicle* would cost another five pence. There was one thought that consoled him. They were in the running for a major series. Sergei Kasov, a defecting star of the Bolshoi Ballet, was about to spill the beans in a big new book.

Murdoch, Maxwell and Dearing were all against each other in the race for serialization rights, aiming to buy well ahead of the UK publication and Dearing looked like coming out on top.

We need this one, he thought, as he waited for his editor to join him for their morning conference. If we stretch it over one full week, coinciding with the price rise, we shouldn't lose any readers. They'll be so anxious to read about Kasov behind the iron curtain they won't even notice the extra five pence.

He looked up as Donald Evans came through the door. In the years he had served Lord Dearing, Donald had always come to the morning meeting in his shirtsleeves. The change of proprietor hadn't affected his style. He still looked as if he had just got up from his desk in the middle of a crisis and it reassured David. The man was wedded to his job. He took it seriously. He just wished there were more like him.

Three minutes later he reconsidered. For the first thing Donald told him was they had lost the Kasov series.

'Maxwell's flying to New York after lunch to sign a contract,' the editor said ruefully. 'It looks like it's all over.'

David felt decidedly irritated.

'Who are the American publishers?' he enquired.

'Madisons, why do you ask?'

There was a silence while the senior man digested this piece of information. Finally David said, 'I know John Madison. My brother was in the same year with him at Harvard business school. We all used to go sailing together.'

Donald looked dejected. 'It's a bit late in the day to drag all that up.'

'I don't see why. You say Maxwell's going to America this afternoon. What's to stop me jumping on a plane now? New York's five hours ahead. If I make Concorde I can be at Madisons well before lunch.'

The editor gave David his full attention. It was a bold tactic and rather disreputable. Lord Dearing would never have considered it in a million years. No gentleman would have done, but then this new proprietor was from a different school.

'I'll get on to the airport straight away,' he said. 'I should be able to wangle you a seat.'

David grinned, and looked at his watch.

It was coming up for nine.

'John will still be in bed,' he said. 'I'll call him the minute I get into the car the other end.'

Madison gave him a tough time. Friendship might be one thing, he told David, but he had given his word to Maxwell as a businessman. If he pulled out now it would look bad.

David stood his ground. He hadn't come half way across the world on Concorde to be fobbed off with an excuse.

'You're behaving as if businessmen never had last minute changes of heart,' he argued. 'That's nonsense.'

John Madison looked nervous. He had arranged to have lunch with one of his biggest authors that day. The man was threatening to change publishers if he wasn't paid a lot more money and he didn't need the extra worry.

I should have put David off, he thought. I should have instructed my secretary to tell him I was in a meeting all day. He looked at David pacing around his office. He wouldn't have taken a blind bit of notice, he decided. That was always the trouble with the guy. He made a last attempt to get him out of his hair.

'Some dealers might go around behaving the way you do, but I don't have any truck with that sort of thing.'

David shot him an old-fashioned look. Now he had Madison exactly where he wanted him.

'So why are you doing business with Bob Maxwell? He's as gung-ho as I am. The difference is that you know me. We go back a long way together.'

It was really no contest. In half an hour John Madison had called in his lawyer. By mid-day David's signature was on a cheque for half a million dollars. After that John Madison offered everyone a drink and started to rearrange his life. He got his secretary to move his lunch to the next day. Now David was in town, they might as well catch up on old times.

An hour later he and David were having lunch in the swimming-pool room of the Four Seasons. Now the business was over, both men fell into the easy friendship they had had years ago. Lunch didn't finish until well past three and David toyed with the idea of going straight back to his apartment, and getting into a bath. Then he remembered Freddie. Wasn't the girl's mother coming out of prison today?

He cursed his bad luck. The last person Freddie wanted to see right now was him. She'd as good as told him that when he spoke to her in London. He sighed. This might be a bad time for Freddie, but it wasn't that convenient for him either. He hadn't packed to come to New York. There hadn't been time and he didn't need to. Everything he needed was in his apartment. He had to put up there, whatever her objections.

For a moment he laughed at himself. Here he was, a rich man, well into his middle age and he was worried about the temperament of a little girl. A little girl he was extending his hospitality to. He took a decision. He was a ten minute walk away from his New York bureau, and he needed to let the boys back at the *Chronicle* know about the Kasov series. Why not stroll round there, finish the business he had come here to do, then call Freddie. She'd had all day with her mother, they'd probably both appreciate being taken out somewhere for dinner.

There was more to do in his New York office than he first thought. The paperwork alone kept him busy until past six and he could see himself spending the rest of the week in the city. Things had mounted up since he had last visited.

He called the apartment at seven and got Freddie on the second ring. The minute she answered he knew something was wrong. She sounded tense. Desperate.

'What's the matter?' he asked. 'You sound terrible.'

'I'll tell you in a minute,' she said. 'Did you get my messages?'

Now he was truly foxed.

'What messages?'

'The messages I left at your office. I've been calling all day.'

For a moment David felt exasperated. Somebody might have told her where he was. Then he remembered he had instructed his secretary to keep quiet. There was no way he wanted anyone to get a whisper of what he was up to.

'I haven't been in my office,' he said shortly.

'I'm here in New York. Something urgent came up.'

There was a brief silence. 'Thank goodness for that,' she said.

He reached around in his pocket for a cigarette. 'Perhaps you'd better tell me what's going on.'

He thought he heard her catch her breath, then he dismissed the notion. Freddie wasn't the sort of girl that cried.

'Mom didn't show up today,' she said. 'I went to Riker's Island at nine this morning, but there was no sign of her.'

'Are you sure you got the time right?'

'Perfectly. There were two other prisoners leaving that day and they both came out at nine. I asked them if they knew about my mother but neither of them did. Then I went inside and asked the officers on duty, but they didn't know anything either. I hung around till lunchtime in case she'd been delayed. Then I came back here.' There was a pause. 'David,' she said, 'I don't know what to do anymore.'

He felt a wave of sympathy for her. Freddie had been through enough with her mother without this.

'I'll put in a call to my lawyer here,' he said, 'then I'll come straight back. One of us should be able to sort out this mess.'

A thought struck him. 'Have you spoken to Dan?'

'I tried, but he wasn't there either.'

David felt relieved. Right now he didn't want anyone else involved with Freddie. The girl had been his responsibility for over three years. He'd become used to dealing with her problems.

'Listen,' he told her, 'don't do anything else until you see me. I won't be long.'

He was already summoning his secretary before he put down the phone.

* * *

David reached the apartment just before eight and Freddie was there waiting for him. She was sitting perfectly still on a high-backed chair in the formal drawing-room, staring out of the window. He guessed she had been there for some time for none of the lights was on.

'Who on earth do you think you are?' he asked her. 'Miss Havisham?'

He flicked on the main switch and the lamps on all the side tables glowed into life. Now he could see her he realized she had been crying. He went over to where she sat and put his arms round her.

'Come on,' he said. 'It's not that bad.'

'It is that bad.' Her voice came muffled from the depths of his jacket. 'She was the only one who really cared for me. Really minded whether I lived or died.'

David let go of her and walked over to the drinks cabinet.

'I wouldn't normally suggest it, but a stiff drink might pull you together. I'm having one myself.'

Freddie nodded her assent, then suddenly she smiled.

'I'm behaving like a little girl,' she said. 'It must be the shock.'

David looked at her. I wish you looked like a little girl, he thought. It would make life easier.

She was wearing what she'd gone to meet her mother in earlier that day – stretch leggings and a tee shirt that had seen better days. But she was tall and strong and filled her clothes. So instead of looking like a waif, she looked like a slightly dishevelled, totally desirable woman.

David felt uncomfortable. It wasn't right to be alone with her like this. The memory of countless dinners in

Cheyne Walk came back to him. They had been alone then, but it had been different. There were servants in the house and the presence of his wife.

'Would you like to go out for dinner?' he asked calmly. 'There's a place I know near the Met. How long will it take you to get ready?'

Freddie told him half an hour and kept him waiting twice that time, but when she came back there was a distance between them again. It was as if her clothes and make-up formed an invisible barrier and David was glad of it. He didn't go in for taking advantage of other people's grief.

They got to the restaurant just as it was starting to fill up. When the curtain came down later in the opera house it would get noisy. Until then there was time to talk and David asked the waiter to show them to a quiet table. Freddie needed to know what he had found out about her mother's disappearance.

Before David had left his office he had spoken to Ben Chasen, the attorney who had handled Vanessa's case three years ago. Chasen had got on to the prison authorities and half an hour later he came back with some answers.

Freddie's mother hadn't shown up today because she hadn't been on Riker's Island for the past week. She had been released earlier.

'Did she know she was coming out ahead of schedule?' David asked.

Chasen said she did.

'Riker's Island don't go in for last minute changes of plan. My guess is that Vanessa lied about when she was due to be released. She probably didn't want to see her daughter, or anyone else she knew. This is not the first time an inmate has disappeared. Things happen in prison. People find themselves changed, and sometimes they don't want their loved ones to see those changes. Not at first anyway. Vanessa will turn up, by the way. They always do.'

David felt he had reached a dead end.

'Have you any idea when she'll get in touch?'

'That depends what resources she has,' replied the lawyer. 'If she's short of money, she could turn up tomorrow. Freddie must have written and told her where she was staying in New York.'

David felt a glimmer of hope. From what he knew Freddie's mother was flat broke. He thanked the lawyer and told him to keep an eye on the situation.

'Call me,' he instructed, 'if you hear anything else.'

Now all he had to do was break the news of Vanessa's disappearance to Freddie. He played for time by going through the wine list, and chose a Californian. It was light and non-committal. The way he felt.

When they had finished ordering dinner, David turned to Freddie and told her what Ben Chasen had said. At first she didn't believe him.

'If there was anything different about Mom, she would have written and told me,' Freddie protested. 'We didn't keep secrets from each other.'

David raised his eyebrows.

'You mean all the time she was hooking, she kept you in the picture about it?'

Freddie felt cross. 'That was different,' she said.

David leaned back as the waiter poured the fragrant, fruity wine into their glasses. Then he raised his in a kind of salute.

'I think it's time you grew up and stopped kidding yourself,' he told her. 'It's okay to kid other people, but never fall into the trap of lying to yourself. Your mother sounds to me like a rather private woman. I've never met her, but I would guess she kept a lot to herself.'

'You make it sound as if she didn't love me at all.'

David looked serious.

'From what I can tell, she loved you too much. Why do you think she risked her neck working as a hooker in New York? It would have been much easier for her to go with the flow and take on another rich boyfriend, but she didn't do that, did she? She went out on a limb and did what she did because she didn't want to inflict another of her lovers on you. She wanted you to grow up without that pressure.'

For a moment Freddie looked beaten. 'You make me feel as if all this is my fault.'

The sympathy David felt for her earlier came back. She seemed terribly young in the formal black dress she was wearing. Young and tough and somehow isolated.

A couple of hours ago in his apartment he had wanted to take her to bed. Now the feeling was with him again. Only this time it was stronger. I'm old enough to be her father, he thought. Old enough to know better.

Freddie must have known what was on his mind, for she leaned in close and he saw she was smiling.

'It's not such a terrible idea,' she said. 'I've always thought you were the most attractive man I knew.'

Her move made David cross. She had no right to talk to him like that. He wasn't one of the playboys she wound around her fingers.

'I don't go in for the kind of games you have in mind,' he said roughly. 'And even if I was tempted, I wouldn't play them with a little girl like you.'

Freddie pulled back then, her eyes huge and dark and hurt looking, but he wasn't letting her off the hook.

'I've changed my mind about staying in the apartment tonight,' he told her. 'It will be better for both of us if I put up at a hotel.'

Freddie tried to look brave, but the effort was beyond her. It was as if someone had cut the ground from under her feet and there was nowhere left for her to go.

'Don't leave me,' she whispered. 'Not tonight. You can go where you like tomorrow, but don't leave me now.'

David felt himself soften. Looking the way she did now, Freddie really wasn't such a threat. What can she do, he thought. It's not as if I'm frightened of being alone with her.

'It's been a long day,' he told her, 'and we've both let things get out of proportion.'

The coffee arrived and Freddie seemed to calm down. David didn't talk about going to a hotel again and after a few minutes he realized he didn't have to. Freddie had gone back to being a child again. She was sleepy and slightly fretful and talked a lot about her mother and what she would do when she found her. By the time he got her into the car she had run herself completely down. He reckoned she'd be out for the count before she'd had time to take her make-up off.

David didn't turn in immediately. The day had stirred up emotions and memories he wanted to forget and he went into the library and made himself a nightcap. The fire was still burning in the grate and he took his drink over to it and sat down.

As he looked into the flames he started to wonder about himself. I shouldn't be looking at Freddie, he thought. If Liz and I were still a couple, I wouldn't even consider the idea. He sighed. I can't go on this way, he thought. I'm not made of steel. David had no idea how long he had been sitting there, but when he looked up Freddie was in the room. He felt confused.

'I thought you'd be in bed,' he said. 'You looked all in.'

'I couldn't sleep,' Freddie told him. She was wearing a soft cashmere cardigan that buttoned down the front. Except she hadn't done the buttons up, and when she came across the room David realized she wasn't wearing anything underneath.

Damn Freddie, he thought. I should have known better than to believe that little girl lost act. She was standing next to him now and he could smell the faint floral scent of her perfume.

'Go to bed,' he said tightly. 'Can't you see the effect you're having on me.'

But Freddie paid no attention. Instead she sat down beside him and as she did the soft wool parted revealing her nakedness.

'Look at me,' she demanded. 'Can't you see I'm not such a little girl now?'

David felt his carefully maintained control beginning to slip.

'You'll be sorry in the morning,' he said. 'You may not think so now, but you will be.'

Freddie took his hand in hers and drew it down so that it covered one of her breasts. Then she moved up against him.

Something in David snapped. This was no ingenue sitting in his lap. No innocent virgin. This was a determined young woman who wanted to get laid whatever the cost. He decided not to disappoint her.

He took hold of Freddie's shoulders and started to kiss her. There was nothing tender about his embraces. She had stirred him up inside, pushed him right to the edge and now he couldn't guarantee the consequences.

His harshness didn't seem to frighten her, and to his surprise he discovered she had a passion of her own. A wildness he never knew existed. For a fraction of a second he was reminded of his first time with Liz. Then just as quickly her image was blotted out by this new woman.

He thought about taking her through to the bedroom but she didn't give him time. Instead he found himself half sitting on the sofa while she undressed him. He had the uncomfortable feeling that she had played this scene before and it irritated him. With more force than he intended he took hold of her hands and pushed her away. The gesture sent her sprawling over onto her back. She lost her cardigan then. The cashmere covering parted from her and she was revealed to him. He knew then he'd have to finish what he started.

There was a whiteness about Freddie's skin, a softness that was faintly shocking. David wanted to touch her all over, to take the plump, pointed breasts in his mouth. To run his tongue over her stomach and into the dark cleft between her legs.

Freddie must have seen the desire on his face for she didn't cry out in protest. She arched her back and moved her legs apart.

David took her then. It was as if he was possessed by a kind of frenzy, for once he had started making love to Freddie, he couldn't stop. He had expected a girl, somebody inexperienced who needed to be coaxed and shown the way. What he discovered, too late, was a woman with an appetite that matched his own.

When he finally took her to his bed it was past midnight. She was asleep the moment her head hit the pillow and he realized as he looked at her, how much the day had taken from her.

Later, when he opened his eyes again, he noticed

she hadn't moved at all that night. She had gone on clinging to him as if he was the only thing she could be sure of. He remembered what she had said before they made love, when they were still in the restaurant. 'You can do what you like tomorrow, but don't leave me now.' He smiled, thinking how determined she looked. As if she really meant it.

59

They stayed in New York for a week. During the days, David went to his office on Second Avenue and sorted through the tangle of his American companies. His brother ran most of the family printing and publishing interests on this side of the Atlantic, but David had bought into a cable network and a syndication outfit some years back when his father was still running the *Chronicle*. In those days it had been his escape route. If he had called it quits with Liz the first time they broke up, he would have set up a base in New York and run the companies full time.

Now they were just another outpost of his empire needing his attention when things got too much.

In the beginning, Freddie was thankful that David's business took up so much of his time. She needed space to sort out her feelings. She had suspected that she and David could end up together. It was something she had always known, right from that first moment when he had found her alone in his conservatory pouring her heart out to the family parrot. In those days her feeling for him was nothing more than a fantasy. A childish crush on a glamorous older man. Yet he was always somehow in the background. As she grew up she looked to him to confirm the fact of her womanhood.

With every new dress, every change of style it was David's approval she sought. Most of the time she was only dimly aware of what she was doing, until the night about a year ago when they were sitting having dinner at the house in Cheyne Walk. The night they had talked of Liz and Dan's affair. David had never confided in Freddie before, and she had suddenly become aware of him. This was a man she was with that night, not a surrogate parent. The knowledge filled her with a terrible foreboding.

Freddie could handle any number of little boys, but someone as grown-up as David, a serious, important, man – that was beyond her. So she had moved on. The little flat in Sloane Street removed her from his orbit once and for all. Now, quite by chance, they found each other in New York.

Freddie wondered whether she should have let him stay the night in a hotel, the way he had wanted. Then she thought back on the way he had made love to her and was glad she hadn't. She had grown up that night. Before then she had been an infant, going through the motions with other infants. Feeling nothing but emptiness when she woke in the morning. With David it hadn't been like that, because for the first time she hadn't been alone.

She supposed she was falling in love, for she could hide away from the world with this man. Lose herself in him so that nothing and no-one would make her unhappy again. No-one, except for her mother. Even David couldn't protect her from that.

Freddie worried about what she was going to do. She had been in New York for days now and there was no sign of Vanessa. David's lawyer had said to sit tight and wait until she made contact, but it seemed such a passive thing to do. Such a waste of her time. In the end, she embarked on a plan of her own.

Freddie made a list of all her mother's friends and contacts in the city. Then she called on them. She visited Norman and Ted, and when they could tell her nothing she paid a call on her father.

Dan was overjoyed to see her. Freddie had dropped by his office at the end of the afternoon and he insisted she have dinner with him that night.

'I'll take you to The Rainbow Room,' he promised her. 'It's the hottest place in town. You'll fall in love with it, I can guarantee that.'

Her heart sank. All she wanted to do that night was to be with David, but how could she tell her father that? In the end she compromised.

'I'm staying in David Dearing's apartment,' she ventured. 'I guess I should let him know I won't be in tonight.'

It was easier than she thought. Dan was surprised David was in town, but he seemed pleased someone was looking after her.

'It's a damn difficult time,' he said. 'I wish I could take the time to be with you myself. But you know how it is.'

I know how it is, Pop, Freddie thought. It's never been any different. When the going gets tough, all you ever do is pat my hand and spend some money and you think it solves everything. Well it doesn't.

Freddie called David and told him about her dinner arrangements.

'I can't get out of it,' she said, 'but I can be back early. Do you mind?'

'Not really. I have a late meeting in Wall Street. It wouldn't hurt to let it go over supper.'

As Freddie put the phone down she felt unaccountably anxious. She knew the banker David was seeing was a woman. He had told her so earlier on. Maybe she's one of his girlfriends, she thought. She remembered what he said. 'It wouldn't hurt to let it go over supper.' Who wouldn't it hurt, Freddie wondered. Her or me?

The Rainbow Room was a revelation. A vast

terraced dining-room on the sixty-fifth floor of the Rockefeller Center, it had been done up and decorated two years ago to the tune of twenty-five million dollars.

What the customers got for all this expense was an Art Deco extravaganza with aubergine silk walls and wrap-around views of the city. It was the period detail that knocked Freddie's eyes out. According to Dan, thirty artists had worked on the ballroom with its revolving floor and giant crystal chandelier.

As Freddie walked through to the restaurant she saw the tiered bandstand. I'm in another age, she thought. It's as if ghosts of the pre-war years have been jitter-bugging up here all along, and we've been invited here to join in. Dan had managed to get a table right on the edge of the dance floor and Freddie gazed mesmerized. She turned to her father.

'You decide what we're going to eat,' she told him. 'I'm happy just sitting here looking at the sights.'

New York was more colourful than Freddie remembered it. All the waiters tonight wore red tuxedos and twitched their hips in time to the band playing show music. It was the moving dance floor, though, that had her attention. Or rather the couples on it. They had all dressed in the mood of the Rainbow Room. Most of the men sported evening dress, and the women seemed to be covered in sequins or encased in showy lamé.

The arrival of dinner finally broke the spell. To start with, Dan had ordered the shellfish extravaganza. This was an ice platter heaped with mussels, oysters, clams, lobster, crab and a couple of things Freddie couldn't identify.

She piled into it. Since she had arrived in New York she had hardly eaten and she was determined to more than make up for her oversight. Dan had ordered steak tartare crowned with caviar to follow and only when Freddie had finished that too, did he get a word out of her.

'Tell me about your mother?' he asked. 'Has David had any luck tracking her down?'

Freddie told him what Ben Chasen had turned up. 'I don't have too much faith in his theories,' she said. 'So far Mom hasn't got in touch and I wonder if I'm doing the right thing waiting around for her in New York. For all I know she might not even be here anymore.'

Dan looked thoughtful. 'Where might she be, do you think?'

'Anywhere. She could turn up in England at my grandmother's house. But if somebody else supplies her with money, then anything's possible. There are lots of things Mom didn't tell me. I was hoping you could help me fill in a few gaps.'

For the next two hours they talked about Vanessa. Dan told her the names of all the people she was close to in New York. Stylists. Other model girls. He also supplied the whereabouts of her hairdresser and the places where she liked to shop.

'Somewhere in that maze there has to be a clue to where she is now,' he said. 'Do you want me to help you look for her?'

At a different time Freddie would have gladly accepted his offer, but now she had her own secrets to protect. It was too late to fit her father into her life.

She glanced at her watch.

'Pop, I have to go. Look, I'll think about your offer, but I'm probably better off nosing around on my own. I'll call you the moment I find something.'

If Dan was put out she was leaving early he didn't show it but offered instead to give her a lift to David's apartment. Freddie hesitated before accepting. She didn't want him inviting himself in for a nightcap. Then she realized that was unlikely. He was, after all, Liz's lover. She started to feel nervous about the situation. It was so sordid somehow. Like a TV soap opera. Then she pulled herself up. Here she was fantasizing about a great love affair with David when all she had had was a one night stand. When I get back, she thought, he could behave as if nothing had happened. He might even still be out with that woman banker of his.

She was wrong on both counts.

When she got in, David was in the study watching the late news on television. He turned the set off as she came through the door and held his arms out to her. She flew into them.

'I was so worried,' she said.

'What on earth for?'

It came pouring out. Her nerves about the Wall Street woman. Her fear that she didn't matter to him. That he might think she was just another passing bimbo.

David laughed when he heard it all.

'What is this?' he teased. 'A proposal of marriage?'

Freddie pulled away from him, and when she turned to him again she was serious.

'It's not a proposal of marriage,' she said, 'but it is a proposal. You see, I think I've fallen in love with you. I didn't want to – I'm not that keen on getting close to anyone right now – but that's not the point. I'm wild about you, David, and if you don't feel that way about me I have to know.'

David looked at her.

'What will you do if I don't?'

He had meant to keep it light, but when he saw the pain in her eyes he realized he had said the wrong thing.

He pulled her back into his arms and held her tight.

'Darling Freddie,' he said, 'I can't be as intense as you. I'm too old for that. But I do care about you and I do want to go on with whatever it is we started last night. Beyond that I can't make any promises.'

60

It was two days later that Scott rang. Freddie was on her own in the apartment when the call came and at first she didn't recognize his voice.

'Who is it?' she enquired.

There was a strained silence, while Scott wondered whether or not she was putting it on. Finally he said:

'It's Scott Harding.'

He was tempted to add, 'the man you were once in love with', but he thought that might be pushing it.

Freddie was taken off-guard.

'How on earth did you find me here?' she asked abruptly. 'This isn't exactly a social visit.'

Scott sounded apologetic. 'Barbara gave me the number. She told me about your mother coming out of prison and I wondered if I could do anything to help.'

'Come off it,' Freddie said tartly. 'The last time I saw you you were never going to speak to me again. Why this sudden change of heart?'

Scott hesitated for a second.

'I met your father a couple of weeks ago at a drinks party.'

Freddie felt the stirrings of curiosity.

'What did my father have to tell you?'

'The truth.' Freddie thought she heard embarrassment in Scott's voice. 'I was wrong about Boots Winchester . . . and a couple of other things as well.'

For reasons she couldn't quite fathom Freddie felt

sad. A year ago, she thought, even a week ago, I would have given anything to hear him say this. Now it doesn't matter any more.

'You don't have to apologize,' she told Scott. 'It was all a long time ago.'

'Then you'll have lunch with me.'

It was Freddie's turn to hesitate. She might be ready to forgive and forget, but having lunch was something else.

'Did I hear you say yes?'

She stifled a laugh. Scott had lost none of his pushiness.

'You didn't hear me say anything,' she replied firmly. 'I'm leaving town any minute now and I'm not sure I have time for lunch.'

'Well, make time. I want to see you.'

Freddie felt her stomach lurch, then she thought about David and felt guilty.

'I've only really got today left,' she said weakly.

'Nothing wrong with today,' Scott told her. 'I'll book a table at PJ Clarke's. See you there at one.'

He rang off before Freddie could say anything else, and she was astonished by his arrogance. Scott was behaving as if they could turn the clock back to when she was a naive little girl, willing to be swept off her feet by the first good-looking man who happened along. You've got a lot to learn, she thought. It could just be fun teaching you.

Nevertheless, she went to a certain amount of trouble to make herself look good.

She didn't want Scott back or anything. It was far too late for that. But she did want to show him exactly what it was he had thrown away.

She took out a Chanel suit she had bought in Bond Street. It was one of the new designs with a long, quilted jacket and a very short skirt. With it she wore flat suede pumps and thick tights, the same shade of fondant blue as the rest of the ensemble. As a final touch she added gold Chanel earrings the size of dinner plates and several strands of gilt and pearls.

Her hair, which she had washed that morning, swung smoothly down to her shoulders. I could pass muster on the cover of *Vogue*, she thought, satisfied. If Scott doesn't notice I've changed, then he's blind as well as stupid.

He was waiting for her at the bar when she arrived. Most of the tourists had left New York now that autumn had come and there was room to stand and have a drink. Freddie ordered a Bloody Mary, then gave Scott the once over.

He hadn't changed. His hair was blonder than ever and he still looked as if he played tennis every day. I must have been crazy not to have gone to bed with him all those years ago, she thought.

She stopped herself. This was no way to go on. She had a lover now. A serious lover who cared for her and protected her from the world. David wouldn't fly into a jealous rage if he thought she was having lunch with an old flame. He was too grown-up for that. All the same, she decided not to tell him about meeting Scott.

They made small talk for half an hour. Scott told Freddie about leaving his lucrative career as a freelance journalist and setting up his magazine group. Freddie countered by telling him all about her new job in London, and her new flat.

As they talked, she noticed the looks he was giving her. She was glad she had pulled out all the stops, she decided. In the old days she always felt slightly self-conscious when she was with Scott. As if she hadn't got herself quite right. Now she knew she was spot on. She had only seen him look this way at one other woman. Liz. When she was all done up in one of her designer outfits, Scott had the self-same expression in his eyes. Admiring and slightly awe-struck.

They were half way through the second round of drinks when Scott suggested they went to the table. He had reserved a spot in the back behind the bar and Freddie allowed him to steer her towards it. When they had ordered burgers and salads, the conversation changed abruptly.

'I've missed you,' he told her without preamble. 'I'd be lying if I said there hasn't been anyone since. There has been, but it wasn't the same.'

He was going to go on, but he stopped himself and she knew then that she couldn't go on playing with him.

It would have been irresistible to hear how he couldn't do without her, but she couldn't let him say it. Not now. Not with David in the picture.

'I guess I'm flattered,' she said awkwardly, 'but . . .'

'But you're having an affair with somebody else at the moment,' Scott finished for her.

Freddie was staggered.

'However did you know that?' she asked.

He smiled and leaned back in his chair. 'Easy,' he told her. 'It's written all over you. My guess is you're involved with some playboy type who showers you with expensive presents and takes you to all the rich man's hangouts.'

Freddie started to regret piling on the glitz the way she had done. It was way over the top.

'You're jumping to the wrong conclusions,' she said irritated. 'I've been wearing Chanel for years. My father buys it for me.'

'I wasn't talking about your clothes,' Scott told her.

'They've got nothing to do with anything. It's the way you are that's getting my attention.'

He paused for a second, then he went on.

'When a woman's being thoroughly spoiled by a man, she gives off a certain aura. A signal that tells all the other men to keep their distance because she's spoken for. I've had that feeling about you ever since you walked in the door.'

He smiled and Freddie realized the casual easy air he was affecting cost him a great deal.

'Tell me,' he said. 'Who's the lucky guy?'

It occurred to Freddie to lie. David was a married man, even though he and Liz had been living separate lives. Anyway it was none of Scott's business who she was sleeping with.

But she didn't lie. An old loyalty she had once had for this man stopped her. Things might be different now, but she could never be dishonest with Scott.

'The man I'm in love with,' she said, 'is David Dearing.'

She didn't add anything to her confession. She didn't justify or explain it to Scott because she simply couldn't do so. Instead, she sat looking at him in silence.

Scott began to giggle. His whole face creased up and fell into contortions, as if Freddie had just told him an irresistibly funny joke.

'You can't mean it,' he spluttered. 'Tell me you're having me on.'

Freddie gave him her coldest stare.

'Why should I be having you on?'

'Because David Dearing's old and tired and sad. Face it, Freddie, he's past it. You can't be involved with him.'

'David's not past it,' Freddie shouted. The chatter at the tables around them suddenly stopped. Freddie grabbed hold of the hamburger the waiter had left in front of her and sank her teeth into it. She took a long time with her lunch and eventually she lost her audience. When things had gone back to normal, Scott resumed their conversation.

This time he kept his voice down.

'Look, I'm sorry I said all those things about David. I didn't mean half of them, but I do think you're crazy getting involved. If Liz ever finds out she'll kill you. And don't tell me she doesn't care, because I know different. She gives David a lot of rope but if she even suspected that this was going on, she'd raise hell.'

Freddie started to feel nervous. The whole conversation was getting out of hand.

'I don't think Liz would raise hell,' she said slowly. 'She's got someone of her own.'

'You're not going to drag up that old thing with your father are you?'

Scott shot her a look of the deepest scorn and Freddie started to lose confidence. I'm out of my depth, she thought. I can't cope with any of it.

'Do you think I might have a cup of coffee?' she asked abruptly. 'Then I really must be on my way.'

'Yes, you can have some coffee. But I'm not going to let you leave this place until I've talked some sense into you.'

Freddie suddenly felt very tired. She had come here to bury a ghost and she had hoped that at the end of it she and Scott might part friends. Now she wasn't so sure.

'I don't think you understand,' she said. 'The thing with David isn't some cheap little fling. When I told you I was in love with him I meant it. Nothing you can say to me is going to make any difference to that.'

Scott looked sad.

'Then I really am too late.'

Freddie nodded.

'I'm sorry,' she said. 'I probably shouldn't have come.'

Once more, he affected an air of exaggerated ease. If Freddie hadn't known him better she would have been convinced he didn't give a damn.

'I'm not going to give this new liaison my blessing,' he said. 'You can't expect me to do that. But if you need a shoulder to cry on, you know where I am.'

He called the waiter over and settled the bill. Then he helped Freddie into her coat, and walked her through to the street.

'Goodbye,' he said warmly. 'It was nice to see you after so long.'

Freddie proffered her cheek for the expected social kiss and Scott ignored it. Instead he took her by the shoulders and kissed her full on the mouth. Freddie was so surprised she found herself responding. Then it was too late to draw back. In broad daylight on Fifty-fifth Street, Freddie and Scott went into the kind of clinch Scarlett and Rhett made famous in 'Gone with the Wind'. It was a long time afterwards before she forgot it.

61

Liz found out about Freddie and David just before Christmas. She was sitting in the hairdresser having her roots touched up when she heard. The bearer of the news was a rather raddled-looking woman who didn't know Liz at all. She didn't know David either, but it didn't stop her from talking about him at the top of her voice. About both of them to the man who was cutting her hair.

In the space of half an hour, Liz heard her relationship with Dan dismissed as a brief fling which amused her. Then she heard Freddie's name mentioned, and that stopped her in her tracks. She was so surprised she went over to the woman and cut in on her conversation.

'You can't really mean what you said about Freddie Grenville,' she insisted. 'My husband virtually brought her up.'

The woman, who clearly didn't recognize Liz, looked conspiratorial and lowered her voice.

'Shocking isn't it?' she said. 'If you ask me, I think she led him on.'

Now Liz was fascinated. 'What makes you think that?'

'The girl's reputation. Everyone knew she was a scalp-hunter well before she got her hooks into David. It doesn't seem to bother him, though. The old ram seems to be thoroughly enjoying himself.'

Liz had heard enough. The woman was clearly a dangerous gossip. I can't let her know I'm married to

David, she thought. I've got to get clear of this place before she decides to ring the tabloids.

She signalled frantically to her hairdresser who came to her rescue.

'Time we got you under the backwash,' he said, hurrying over. 'If you'd like to follow me, Mrs Dearing.'

Liz went rigid with horror. This is all I need, she thought. As soon as they got out of earshot, she demanded to be taken to a cubicle. If the gossip couldn't see her, she'd be spared any further conversation.

She was wrong, of course. As soon as her hair had been rinsed off and the drying process was under way, Liz's new acquaintance was back. She parted the curtains that concealed Liz from the rest of the salon and simply barged in on her.

'I should have known you were Liz Dearing,' she boomed. 'I didn't recognize you with your hair like that.'

Liz turned to her hairdresser and asked him to switch off the dryer. Then she spun round and faced her inquisitor.

'What are you doing in here?' she hissed. 'Can't you leave me alone?'

The woman looked startled. 'But we were having such a nice chat.'

Liz gave her her most withering glance. The one she reserved for servants who stepped out of line.

'I came and asked you a question,' she said. 'That hardly qualifies as a chat. And by the way, next time you sound off in public, make sure you get your facts right. At a rough count, I'd say you slandered my husband, myself and Mr Levin on half-a-dozen counts. Now get out of my cubicle, will you?'

The woman fled, leaving Liz in silence. When the

hairdresser had finished, she handed him a tip and asked him to bring her coat. She needed to go home, to see David and perhaps her lawyer.

There was no way David was going to get away with this. If he insisted on humiliating her, it was going to cost him a great deal of money.

If anything Liz's rage had increased by the time she got back to Cheyne Walk. How could he do this to me, she thought. It's not as if I begrudged him a fling. I made the rules quite clear. We could both live our own lives as long as we were discreet.

Liz remembered how circumspect she had been with Dan. She never stayed the night with him. They were never seen in public holding hands. To all intents and purposes Dan was an old friend of the family. If mischief-makers wanted to say otherwise, it was nothing to do with anything. Liz had kept her side of the bargain.

But David – what on earth did he think he was doing? Freddie was a little girl, for Christ's sake. His daughter's generation. What he was doing wasn't simply indiscreet, it was positively indecent.

A vision of Freddie, the last time Liz had seen her, popped into her mind. She had turned up at a lunch party she was giving for a charity. It must have been three weeks ago and Liz had thought then how pretty she looked. She was thinner than usual and there was a wildness about her eyes she hadn't noticed before. I bet she has a new boyfriend, Liz thought then. One that keeps her awake at nights.

I was right, then. She did have a new lover, Liz thought sourly. Freddie was helping herself to my husband. Another memory assailed her. This time it was a memory of herself when she was about Freddie's age. She had just started seeing David, meeting him secretly in bars and restaurants. She too had had to hide their relationship in the beginning and she realized why she was so angry.

Freddie was drawing her back in time. Re-living her youth for her. Recreating the passion she and David thought was theirs exclusively. She started to cry. Great racking sobs that started in her stomach and shuddered through her.

A little girl had taken her husband, her property, and was teaching him how to love all over again. She wept all afternoon, retreating to her bedroom where she shut the door and drew the blinds. So steeped in her own misery was she, that she didn't hear the front door bang or the voices of the servants in the hall. Only when she looked at the chiming clock on her dressing-table did she know that it was getting on for half past seven.

Liz wondered if David was home, then she discarded the notion. He'll be with Freddie, she thought. They'll be having a drink before going out to dinner. Or perhaps she's preparing something for the two of them in that little flat of hers. She's probably looking all girlish and fresh in jeans and sneakers. There won't be a scrap of make-up on her face and David will be dazzled that something quite so young, quite so perfect is his for the taking.

Liz glanced up and caught sight of herself in the mirror in front of her. Her mascara was smeared half way down her face and it was flushed and swollen. I look a hundred, she thought. No-one who saw me now could even like me, let alone love me. For some reason she didn't care, for suddenly, the way she looked seemed irrelevant. It didn't matter how many visits to the hairdresser she made. How much money she paid the plastic surgeon. At the end of the day she couldn't compete any more. Because she wasn't young.

David loved Freddie not just for the way she looked, but for the way she was. She hadn't lived long enough to betray her illusions or to make any real mistakes.

Because of that, there was nothing spoiled about her. Nothing sour. When David puts his arms round Freddie, Liz thought, it must be like holding a new kitten or gathering in an armful of fresh flowers.

Liz sighed and began working cold cream into her face before taking off what remained of her make-up. I'll have supper sent up on a tray, she decided. I can't face seeing anyone tonight.

There was a tap on her door and automatically she called out, 'come in'. It was probably her maid wondering if she wanted her evening aperitif. It wasn't her maid, it was David, and he was half way through the door before Liz realized her mistake.

'I heard you were in,' he said, 'so I came up to see what you were up to. If you're free, I thought we might have dinner.'

What perfect timing he has, Liz thought bitterly. We never spend the evening together nowadays. He's probably come to ask me for a divorce.

'I don't feel all that sociable,' she told him.

Liz noticed the concern in his face.

'Is something the matter? You look terrible.'

Liz passed a hand across her eyes.

'I found out about Freddie,' she said sharply.

David had the grace to look embarrassed.

'Who told you?'

'Some harpy I ran into at Daniel Galvin. Apparently you're the talk of the town. You and that little slut I've been keeping under my roof.' She paused. 'How could you, David? You could have chosen anyone in London. Anyone in the world. What made you go for Freddie?'

David sighed and walked over to the window.

'I didn't go for Freddie,' he replied. 'It wasn't as calculated as that. If it interests you at all, I did my best not to get involved.'

'I don't believe you.' Now Liz's anger started to take hold of her. 'You always had a weakness for innocent little faces.'

David turned to face her then and she saw the thunder in his eyes.

'I didn't start it,' he said. 'If this marriage is a shambles then you're the one who made it that way. You and your taste for a little bit on the side.'

Liz started to interrupt but he wouldn't let her.

'I know what you're going to say. I neglected you. I was too involved with my work. Well, maybe that was true, but that's no excuse to run off with the first greasy playboy that crosses your path.'

Liz put her head in her hands. Not now, she thought. Please not now. Aloud she said,

'We've been through all this before. Do you really think I like living this way?'

'I've no idea what you like any more, Liz. I haven't been near you in years.'

Liz looked at him in astonishment.

'Don't tell me you're missing your conjugal rights. I would have thought little Freddie kept you far too busy for that.'

She saw the smile creep across his face and she felt like hitting him.

'You sound jealous, my dear. I'm flattered.'

It was then that it happened. One moment Liz was arguing with her husband, the next she was going to murder him. Her rage was like a flash-fire burning through her. She seized a tall glass jar full of cotton wool and hurled it at him. It missed, so she grabbed a china ashtray and followed it with a silver hairbrush, a bottle of scent, everything she could lay her hands on. If David had stayed in the room, she would have throttled him with her bare hands. But he didn't. He got out fast.

This time Liz heard the front door slam behind him as he left the house. He's running to Freddie, she thought, and the knowledge soured her. You can run to your little girl all you like, she decided. But don't try to hide in her skirts. I haven't finished with you yet.

62

The night of the row, David moved into a suite at the Savoy. Now things were out in the open, he and Liz couldn't go on living under the same roof. He had no idea what Liz would do next, or when she would do it, but until the dust settled David felt safer on neutral territory.

For Freddie, the move came as a relief. She and David had been happy in New York because they didn't have any reason to hide. There was no-one there waiting round the next corner to catch them out and report everything back to Liz. But it had to end. David had to get back to the *Chronicle* and she couldn't justify waiting around in Manhattan any longer. None of the contacts her father had given her had come up with anything. As far as all of them were concerned, Vanessa had vanished off the face of the earth three years ago when she went into prison. Nobody had heard from her, nobody had visited her and, if the truth be known, nobody really cared anymore whether she was alive or dead. Her mother had been just another piece of beautiful decoration to be swallowed up in the maw of the city. After living in London for a few years, Freddie was appalled by the heartlessness of the people she grew up amongst, yet their indifference hardened her resolve.

If it takes the rest of my life she vowed, I *will* find my mother. And when I do, I'll make damn sure never to lose sight of her again.

Before she left the city, she registered Vanessa's

disappearance with the police. Her mother's name joined the list of thousands of missing persons and Freddie knew that's where it would probably stay. But she had to cover herself. While this went on, she had to tie up all the angles.

Coming back to London was like coming back to earth. Her grandmother knew nothing about Vanessa and was curiously unhelpful.

'Sit tight,' she told Freddie. 'She's bound to get in touch soon.'

Then, there was David to contend with. It wasn't that he was ashamed of her, but he was nervous about being open about their affair. If David went to a dance or a cocktail party, he usually went on his own and left early, meeting her somewhere afterwards. At grand dinners where an escort was called for, David took Liz. It was after one of those evenings that he and Freddie had their first serious row.

David had turned up at her flat after midnight and when she answered the door in her dressing-gown he seemed dismayed.

'Weren't you expecting me?' he asked.

'Of course I wasn't expecting you,' she told him crossly. 'You were spending the evening with your wife, weren't you?'

Now it was his turn to look impatient.

'I wasn't spending the evening with Liz. I was attending a boring dinner at the Guildhall. My wife was merely there to make up numbers. You can hardly call that an intimate tête à tête.'

Freddie didn't make any motion to invite him in and in the end he pushed past her, walking into her living-room where he helped himself to a drink. She closed her front door quietly and joined him.

'Will you be staying long?'

David looked at her sharply.

'What's the matter? Don't you want me here?'

There was something boyishly pathetic about this newspaper baron all done up in his dinner jacket looking for a place to stay. Freddie wanted to throw herself into his arms and tell him everything was all right, but she didn't do it. She had seen her mother play the accommodating mistress too many times in the past to want to fall into that trap. For her own sake, Freddie had to be tough.

'I'm not going to throw you out,' she told David, 'but I'm tired. I have to get up and go to work in the morning. Try to see it from where I stand.'

He scowled, and made to leave.

'I thought you'd get bored sooner or later,' he said. 'Forgive me if my timing was a little off centre.'

Freddie stopped him then, putting herself between him and the doorway so he couldn't go without pushing her over.

'I'm not bored,' she said. 'I love you and you know it. I just don't want to be used when it suits you.'

'I'm not using you,' David shouted. 'When did I ever use you? Right from the start I played fair. What do you want me to do?'

Now Freddie felt really weary. This was David talking to her. A man she'd known for years. A man she knew better than anyone else. Who did he think he was kidding?

'You know damn well what I want you to do. We've been through it often enough.'

David took hold of her then, gathering her in close so that she could feel his warmth through the starched front of his shirt. Despite all her intentions Freddie felt herself melt.

David seemed to sense this for he started to kiss the soft underside of her neck where he knew she was most sensitive. Now she was lost, but before she capitulated, she rallied one last time.

'Why don't you commit yourself?' she demanded. 'I'm not asking you to marry me. All I want is for you to leave that woman.'

'That woman,' he said softly, 'has been with me for over twenty years. You haven't been around longer than a few months. I think we should give it a bit more time.'

She let him take her to bed. It was what he came for and it was easier than going on arguing. But in the morning Freddie made her mind up. Either David took her seriously or she was going to call it quits. She wasn't cut out to be a mistress.

A few days later, Liz found out about her, and the problem which seemed insurmountable solved itself. Freddie would have preferred it if David had come to her, rather than put up at the Savoy, but she understood why he did it. He was a public figure after all. A rich man with an empire who ran expensive establishments all over the world. He couldn't very well move into her bachelor flat in Sloane Street. How would it look to the shareholders? How would it look to society? How would it look to his father and his family, come to that?

Two weeks later she found out how it looked. For that was when Liz presented David with divorce papers. In her petition she named Freddie as the reason for the break-down of her marriage.

David was up in arms.

'She can't do it,' he ranted. 'I won't allow it. My family would never survive the scandal.'

For some obscure reason Freddie felt let down. She had expected David to be exultant, as delighted and swept off his feet as she felt.

'What scandal are you talking about?' she asked.

'I'm your lover. I don't see why I should be ashamed of it.'

David told her she didn't understand.

'Look,' he explained patiently, 'you're not just any girl I met at a party. I virtually adopted you when you were seventeen. I housed you and brought you up as one of the family. Now my wife is saying I took advantage of the situation and your innocence, and made you my mistress. If this ever got out the tabloids would have a field day.'

Freddie set her jaw.

'I don't care what the papers say. I don't care what anyone says. I love you and that's the end of it.'

But it wasn't. The next day David received a call from his father. Lord Dearing had just come from having lunch with Liz and seemed in a great flap.

'Is it true you're having a fling with the little Grenville girl?' he asked. 'Liz has got herself in a terrible state about the whole thing.'

David sighed. So she had started to make trouble already. He really wasn't all that surprised. Liz wasn't the kind of woman to sit down and accept a situation like this.

'If I were you I wouldn't take everything Liz says as gospel,' he told his father. 'Why don't you come by for a drink later on and I'll tell you my side of the story.'

They arranged to meet in the American Bar at seven and David wondered what the hell he was going to say. His first instinct was to protect Freddie. She was the innocent in all this. A little girl who had lost her mother and turned to the first person she knew for comfort. He cursed his own weakness. I should have seen it coming and moved out into a hotel before she declared herself, he thought.

For now the affair had started there was no turning back.

Once or twice, when Freddie started to get intense, he was tempted to cool it. He didn't have the appetite for a grand passion. Yet every time he tried, something held him back.

It was the girl's helplessness. Since her mother had disappeared into thin air she had been lost, and David didn't have the heart to abandon her. Without me, he thought, she'll go off the rails completely. So he went along with her, until he was so tangled up that there was no escape. His life was complicated and compromised and just when he decided to lie back and enjoy it, his wife had found out and brought the wrath of God down on his head. The wrath of God, swiftly followed by his father's wrath.

David decided to tell his father the truth and let him make up his own mind. At his age he was beyond playing games.

He was the first one to arrive and he found a table several yards away from the padded banquettes favoured by the theatre goers. He was there to convince his father he hadn't lost his marbles and when Lord Dearing came bounding up the steps, he knew he had done the right thing. As soon as the older man saw him perched uncomfortably at the round wrought-iron table his face broke into a smile.

'Glad you picked somewhere private to talk,' he said. 'I knew I could count on you.'

He had a bottle of his father's favourite vintage Bollinger waiting on ice. When his glass was full, he got straight to the point.

'What has Liz been telling you?' he demanded.

Lord Dearing smiled.

'The usual woman's ranting. There was she playing the perfect upper-class wife, when some little American girl comes in and steals you from under her nose.'

David took a sip of champagne. Either she thinks I'm too much of a gentleman to tell my father the truth, he thought, or she imagines I'm a complete fool. Whatever it is, she's not getting away with it.

'I don't suppose she mentioned that she and I haven't had much of a marriage these past few years.'

He looked at his father's disbelieving face and knew he was right.

'The truth,' he went on, 'is that Liz and I agreed to go our separate ways some time ago. She'd been seeing someone else but she didn't want to rock the boat, so at her suggestion I moved into a bedroom down the hall. We look like the perfect couple, Father, but the whole thing's really a sham.'

Lord Dearing sighed heavily and David noticed what an old man he had become. The Reggie Dearing of old would have called him names or demanded a reconciliation. He would certainly have made a scene. All this man did was blow through his moustache and look resigned.

'Why do you put up with it?' he asked. 'Why don't you just throw Liz out and make a fresh start with somebody else. You're only in your forties, for heaven's sake. You've got plenty of time ahead of you.'

David stared into his glass. 'It's not as easy as that,' he said. 'When I married Liz back in the Sixties, I turned my back on every tradition I'd been brought up with. You and mother intended me to marry the right sort of girl. A deb with a suitably grand background and perfect breeding. Well, I didn't do that. I picked up a little girl from Southend who earned her living posing for *Vogue* magazine. She was even living in sin with a photographer.'

He paused and lit a cigarette, then he went on. 'It

wasn't easy turning Liz into a lady. I'm not saying she spoke with the wrong accent or anything like that. The girl had had the sense to acquire the right veneer, but she'd fought for her survival for so long, she thought like a jungle animal. It took years to knock it out of her and I did it because I thought it was worth the effort. You see when I finally decided to marry Liz, I did so because I valued her and I believed in her. Other people would call it love. But it was almost more than that. It was a meeting of equals.

'We've had our bad times, Liz and I. But we've come through them. Until recently, I never regretted the commitment I made to her. Even now, when we're hardly together any more, I still feel something for her. It's going to be tough to let it all go.'

All the time he spoke, his father looked at David closely. He noted the sadness in his eyes, the emotion in his voice and when he finally responded it was with caution.

'Perhaps you don't have to let it all go,' he ventured. 'All you have to do is bring Liz back to the straight and narrow.'

David laughed and poured out some more champagne.

'I fear it's too late for that. If I was going to change anything I should have done it years ago when I found out about her new boyfriend. No, it's gone too far now. Liz doesn't care for me any more.'

'And this little girl you're seeing does?'

David looked at his father in surprise. Perhaps he hadn't lost his grip after all.

'She says she does,' he said thoughtfully, 'and I want to believe her. There's a lot of good in her.

A lot of fire and a lot of guts. She'll make a fine woman.'

'Can you wait that long for her to grow up?'

David looked pensive.

'I don't know,' he said. 'I haven't made up my mind.'

63

In the end David went to see Liz. He didn't object to giving her a divorce, but there was one thing he wouldn't stand for: he wouldn't have Freddie's name dragged through the mud. Liz could have all the money she wanted. She could keep the house in London and the house in the country if she insisted, but David wanted Freddie kept out of it.

It was this he came to tell her when he drove down to the house near Market Harborough on Christmas Eve. Liz had decided to spend the holiday down there and he was surprised. He imagined she would have taken off for the Caribbean. After all, there was nothing to keep her in England any more. They were no longer a family – even Barbara, who had her hands full with her important new newspaper job, was going to be in San Francisco this year.

David wondered if Dan would be coming over for part of the annual break, then he realized that at times like this married men stayed close to home. Only married men like me have nowhere to go, he thought bitterly.

The thought of Christmas in Freddie's cramped little flat or worse still in the Savoy filled David with horror. In the end, he solved the problem by organizing a week in Paris. He and Freddie were flying out of Heathrow on the last plane that night. He had borrowed a grand apartment from an old schoolfriend. It was fully staffed and the live-in chef had been trained at Maxim's. The way David had planned it, he and Freddie would be celebrating Christmas day with caviar from Russia. There would be no Christmas pudding, no turkey, no crackers. Nothing to remind him of the way he spent Christmas all the days of his marriage to Liz.

He turned off the motorway and as he negotiated the winding country roads his mind went back to the way things had been. They had liked to spend Christmas in the country, driving down a day or so before so that Liz could mastermind the last details. She always dressed the tree in the hall herself, no matter how many servants they had. The Christmas cake was hers too, and so were the mince pies. David remembered how he used to tease Liz about it.

'It's your working-class past,' he would say. 'You'll never quite leave it behind.'

In those days Liz would pretend to be offended, denying she even knew of the existence of Southend-on-Sea. But she wasn't of course. Her origins were one of the many secrets they shared, like the road accident in Amsterdam that would have killed David if she hadn't been there to supervise his recovery. We had so much going for us, David thought. So much trust, so much laughter. Who would have thought I'd be driving down on Christmas Eve to talk about divorce?

As if it knew the way, the car nosed into their driveway, cutting through fields dark and muddy now with winter. From where David sat, he could see the house outlined against the sky. There was a fire burning inside and from the colour of the smoke he knew she was burning the wood from the orchard. The whole of the main room would smell of it, pungent and sweet. Suddenly, David looked forward to getting inside.

He was coming home, maybe for the last time, and

his feelings were muddled. Part of him wanted to stay there. The part that had loved Liz and the life they had made together. But there was another side to him now. An angry side. He had been betrayed by this woman he had trusted and because of it he no longer trusted himself. All he wanted to do now was to get the business over and done with.

He would make his final offer to Liz and he would tell her his terms. He had drawn up the papers already. All she had to do now was sign them, then he could get out of this house and out of her life. David thought about Freddie waiting for him in the first-class lounge at London Airport and the thought gave him the strength he needed. He pulled up outside the house and got out of the car slamming the door. Then he let himself in.

The first thing he saw was Liz's Christmas tree. She had decorated it the way she did every year, with little Victorian dolls and silver fairy lights. She did this on purpose, he thought savagely. Liz can't resist reminding me of all the things I am turning my back on.

He fumbled in his pocket for a pack of cigarettes, took one out and lit it. David expected Liz had done herself up to the nines and he winced at the thought. She won't get me with sex appeal this time, he decided. I'm finally immune to those charms.

Liz wasn't there when he went into the room, but she knew he was coming. A decanter and two sherry glasses were waiting in the corner.

David went over and helped himself to a drink, then he stationed himself in front of the fire. Twenty minutes later she appeared, and as always she surprised him. He had expected her to be laced into a Paris creation but she looked as if she hadn't bothered at all.

She was in riding breeches and a pair of battered leather boots. Over her shoulders she had thrown a cable-knit cardigan that reached half way to her knees, and her hair was still wet from the shower. She saw him looking at her and she laughed.

'I'm sorry I didn't make more of an effort,' she apologized, 'but it seemed pointless under the circumstances.'

David was taken aback. Liz never behaved like this. Not in all the years he had known her. Had she lost all her pride?

He went over to the decanter and poured her a sherry, but she shook her head.

'I need my head to be clear today,' she told him. 'I suspect things could get rough.'

David began to feel like a bastard, then he stopped himself. She's playing me, he thought. Trying to catch me off guard, but she can't take me in that easily. I've known her longer than she's known herself.

'You can stop playing the injured wife,' he said shortly. 'It doesn't wash with me. You would have done better if you'd walked in wearing full war paint. At least we both know all the moves in that game.'

Her head came up.

'Just what do you mean?'

'For Christ's sake, Liz.' Now David was really exasperated. 'Do you want me to spell it out?'

Liz stood looking at him with her arms folded across her chest, and David saw for the first time how very plain she really was. Without artifice, Liz was just a thin, middle-aged woman who looked as if she'd been through a trying time.

'I'm not trying to put one over on you,' she said quietly. 'Not this time. I think we're both beyond that. All I really want to do is sort this thing out and get on with Christmas. I'm spending it with your father by the way. That's the reason I'm down here.'

'Is that the reason you dressed the tree as well, or was that a private torture of your own?'

Liz pulled a face.

'I asked for that, though the torture wasn't aimed at you. That was a special one for me.'

David still didn't quite believe her.

'Why? Torture isn't exactly your style.'

Liz pushed a hand through her hair, loosening it from her collar and David saw that she had been letting it grow longer.

'Perhaps it's becoming my style. Even I can have regrets, you know.'

'It's a bit late for regrets,' David said harshly. 'You made your choice two years ago when you told me I didn't measure up any more. Now I've made mine and you're just going to have to live with it.'

Liz went very pale and David realized how brutal he had been, but he couldn't stop himself now.

'I'll give you your divorce, Liz, and anything else you want, but you've got to keep Freddie's name out of it. It's my only condition.'

'So you are in love with her.'

Her voice was low and faint and for a moment David thought she was going to cry. Then she rallied.

'Sorry,' she said. 'I shouldn't have asked that. It's none of my business any more.'

David felt his stomach turn. He had hardened his heart to Liz, yet even now looking like a hundred and drowning in self-pity, she could still reach him. He wondered why he was doing this. Why didn't I just leave it to the lawyers to argue it out? Aloud he said:

'No, it isn't your business Liz, but for the record it

isn't the way it was with us. There's no way I'd make that kind of fool of myself the second time around.'

'Then you're less of a man than I thought you were.'

David looked at her wondering if he had heard right.

'Don't tell me you want me to love the girl?'

Liz laughed then. A hard, bitter little laugh that sent chills through him.

'Of course I don't want that. If I had my way I wouldn't have you loving anyone else but me, but I haven't got my way anymore. I've lost you and life has to go on. You have to go on. You have to build a future and though I hate it, you have to love someone else too. If you don't do that, you'll shrivel up and die. I care for you too much to see that happen to you.'

David put his drink down and stared at her.

'Did you mean what you just said?'

Liz sighed. 'Of course. I wouldn't have said it otherwise.'

David felt slightly light-headed, as if he had taken a whiff of pure oxygen. Liz cared for him enough to see him happy with somebody else.

'Did you always feel that way about me? I mean, when you took it into your head to betray me with Dan, did you care for me then?'

Liz started pacing up and down the floor in front of the fire, wrinkling her brow as if she was trying to make sense of her feelings.

'I always cared for you David,' she said at last. 'The others were there to fill up the space you left when you couldn't be with me. You knew that, surely. I never stopped telling you.'

'Then why did you turn me out of our bedroom?' David looked exasperated.

Liz came up to him now and stood in front of him.

'I didn't turn you out. You turned yourself out.'

He realized she was right. The night he had confronted her with Dan, he hadn't done very much listening. All he heard was his own voice, damning and accusing.

'If you remember,' Liz said quietly, 'you mentioned divorce. If I hadn't stopped you we wouldn't be here having this conversation now.'

Everything began to come clear. Liz hadn't wanted these last few years at all. She'd only gone for the compromise to stop them falling apart completely.

David took hold of her shoulders and was surprised how frail she felt.

'If I had asked you then,' he queried, 'would you have got rid of Dan?'

Liz looked sad. 'You didn't ask me,' she replied.

David gripped her harder now, the rage mounting inside him. Even if he killed her he had to know.

'Would you have thrown him out?' he repeated.

Liz saw the urgency in his eyes and something seemed to relax inside her.

'Of course I would have done,' she said. 'I only ever wanted you.'

David drew her close then, and her nearness and the familiar smell of her comforted him. This was his woman, his only love. There had really never been anyone else.

He started to kiss her. Tentatively at first. Then the old feeling, the fire they had always generated, rose up between them. His kisses were hungrier now, more demanding and he felt her pulling back from him.

'Come to bed,' she whispered. 'We can be private there.'

It was like coming home. Every curve of her, every side of her was familiar to him. Familiar yet strange, for each time David touched her the excitement was new. He would never conquer Liz, he knew that now. Like a cat there would always be a part of her that remained a mystery.

Only this time he didn't care any more, for he knew now he possessed more of her than any other man ever would. Liz loved him. Earlier she had declared that with her heart, and now with her body she declared it again.

They made love for what seemed like hours and after it was over, Liz lay very still in David's arms with her eyes closed. He looked at her with a certain wonder. How could I have thought you were middle aged and finished, he chided himself. You're as beautiful as when we first met.

Her eyes came open then, and in that moment he knew he would never leave her.

'Dan will have to go,' he told her softly. 'I meant what I said just now.'

Liz started to laugh.

'So you finally decided to lay down the law.'

'I should have done it years ago,' he told her. 'I should have tried listening to you as well. Except it wouldn't have done any good.'

He looked rueful. 'I had to learn the hard way. I had to find out that it wasn't so damn fascinating running a newspaper when there's no-one to come home to at night.'

For a moment he looked worried. 'You're still going to be there aren't you? You're not going to change your mind and go through with the divorce?'

Liz snuggled closer into the hollow of his body and now he really was reminded of a cat.

'Of course I'm not going to,' she told him gently. 'But you'll have to do something about that little girlfriend of yours. If there's even a smell of her, I'll scratch your eyes out.'

At the mention of Freddie, David suddenly realized he was in trouble. He was meant to be taking her to Paris in a couple of hours. What on earth was he going to tell her?

Liz saw the agonized expression on David's face and sat bolt upright.

'What's the matter?' she asked. 'She's not going to turn up or anything, is she?'

David grinned.

'No, poor lamb. But it's nearly as bad. I'm meant to be picking her up at Heathrow at six. I'd planned a romantic Christmas in Paris.'

'Poor Freddie,' said Liz. 'What a disappointment for her.'

David turned her over and started to tickle her under her ribs until she was helpless with laughter.

'Say you're sorry for that. Go on say it.'

'No,' she screamed. 'Never.'

He went on with the tickling until she conceded defeat.

'Okay, I'm sorry,' she spluttered. 'But you've got to do something with Freddie. I'm not having her here for Christmas.'

David got out of bed and headed for the bathroom. Once he was under the shower, he'd get a chance to think straight. It didn't help. However hard he tried there was no easy way out of this one. He sighed. Was there ever an easy way to say goodbye to a girl?

He was still turning over the options when he got dressed. He had to meet Freddie at Heathrow, he knew that. But what the hell was he going to say? There's been a change of plan. Liz and I are together again.

It seemed the only thing he could say, but it was so brutal. Hadn't the kid suffered enough, he asked himself. David wondered if he should lie to her and as he played the alternative scenarios in his mind Liz came into the room. She was carrying a tray piled with tea and toast, and when she saw David she put it down and came over to where he was standing.

'I thought you'd like something before you set off,' she said. 'We somehow managed to miss lunch.'

He smiled at her gratefully and helped himself. 'I still don't know what I'm going to say to her,' David admitted.

Liz shrugged. 'Something will come to you in the car, I expect.' She bit into a piece of toast. 'I'm sorry,' she said. 'That was callous. Freddie is awfully young you know, and girls are much tougher than you think. By the New Year she'll be over the worst of the shock, and if Vanessa deigns to show up she could get through it even sooner. Is there any news of her by the way?'

David shook his head.

'Not a thing. I've got lawyers looking for her on both sides of the Atlantic, but nothing seems to surface.'

'Do you think she's dead?'

David rubbed his chin reflectively.

'I bloody well hope not. Haven't we all got enough problems as it is?'

He looked at his watch.

'Darling, I've got to get going, otherwise I'll never be there in time. I shouldn't think I'll be gone for very long. Once Freddie knows the score, she'll be off like a rocket. I reckon I'll be back here by supper time.'

Liz nodded and handed David his coat.

'I expect you'll be later, but I'll be here. Don't worry about that. From now on I'll wait for you however late you are.'

David had been on the motorway for ten minutes

when the drizzle set in. It was a fine, dirty drizzle almost like fog, and cut the visibility down to two inches in front of his nose. He turned on his lights and they helped a little. Good, he thought. Anything to stop me slowing down again. Even if I keep on going at this speed I'll still be twenty minutes late.

He cursed his bad luck. There had been heavy traffic on the side roads when he left the house, then he got stuck behind a tractor. When he finally got on to the motorway the rain started. David sighed. It was one of those days he decided, and it was going to get worse.

He thought about Freddie and how excited she had been when he told her about Paris. She was like a child being told she could stay up after her bedtime and now he was going to spoil it for her. It's a lousy way to start Christmas, he thought. She'll probably never be able to go on holiday again at this time of the year without remembering what I did to her.

A heavy goods lorry behind him was trying to overtake. David grimaced. The man was either a maniac or very bored with driving on this motorway. Anyone could see this was no night for going over the speed limit.

He signalled to the lorry that he was pulling over to the slow lane. Let the lunatic rehearse for the Grand Prix if he wanted. He was in enough trouble as it was.

It was raining very hard now. So hard the road in front of him blurred. David lit a cigarette, searching for a break in the traffic. Then he saw it and started to turn. No-one could have anticipated the skid. One moment he was driving along at fifty, holding the road comfortably. The next, everything was wildly out of control.

He gripped hold of the wheel trying to pull the

Mercedes back into line, but it didn't respond. The last thing he saw was the bumper of the car in front of him. Then he saw nothing at all.

The pile-up affected four cars in the slow-moving lane, but David's was the only write-off. When the police came to clear away the wreckage they had to cut him out of the car. They needn't have bothered. His neck was broken and he hadn't been breathing for some time. He had died on impact.

64

David's funeral was held two days before the end of the decade in a quiet country church outside Northampton. Lord Dearing arranged it out of town to avoid the media, but the press came anyway. From his own paper, from the competition and from all the television networks the news men came to pay homage.

David Dearing was one of the best and the bravest newspaper proprietors of his generation. There was no way his passing would go unnoticed.

Lord Dearing must have realized this, for at the last moment he organized loudspeakers along the outside of the grey stone Norman church so that everyone might hear the service. Freddie wondered if she could get away with listening to it outside. There was a place for her on one of the front pews next to her father, but she didn't want to take it. That meant sitting behind Liz and she wanted to avoid being anywhere near the woman.

If it hadn't been for Liz, David might be alive now instead of lying in that cold coffin.

The sight of it being carried into the church had brought tears to her eyes. She had expected it to be covered with wreaths and flowers, but the Dearings were too grand for that kind of sentiment. Instead, just one token rested on top. A simple display of white orchids and lilies. Liz's last goodbye to the husband she was leaving anyway. The irony of it intensified Freddie's misery. David had only gone to see her to finalize their divorce and Liz had said something so wounding, so deeply vindictive that the man she loved was in no fit state to drive a car. Bitch, she said under her breath. I suppose you're happy now.

Liz looked neither to the left nor right of her as she walked into the church. The hat she was wearing made it easy for her. The broad, sweeping brim and the heavy black veil almost completely cut her off from the crowd and she was glad of it. Apart from her daughter and her father-in-law, she had nothing to say to anyone there. She supposed she would have to face Dan who had flown in the moment he had heard of the tragedy, and there were things she should tell Freddie, but she relished neither confrontation. All she wanted to do now was to bury the man she had loved and go on her way.

She thought back to the phone call a week ago from the local constabulary.

'I'm afraid there's been an accident,' said the policeman. He didn't need to say anymore. She knew what was coming.

Another woman would have collapsed, or wept, or screamed hysterically. Liz did none of those things.

She had lived among the moneyed classes too long for such behaviour. I will mourn my husband, she promised herself, possibly I'll mourn him for the rest of my life, but now I have too many other things to do.

She told her father-in-law as soon as she had identified the body. Then she went about making arrangements for the funeral. Getting in touch with everyone who mattered – Barbara in San Francisco, Dan in New York, Freddie in London.

The young girl took it badly, as Liz knew she would, but she had too many problems of her own to get involved with another woman's grief. She simply told her that the funeral would be next week in Northampton, then she rang off. Under the circumstances she had done more than enough. Now, as she peeped from under her hat at the bowed heads all around her, she wondered if Freddie was among them. While the local vicar droned on Liz did a fast inventory of the church. Next to her were her father and mother-in-law, their faces pinched and withdrawn, containing their misery the way she knew they would. On her other side was Barbara who wasn't being brave at all. Ever since they left the house that morning she had been crying continuously and Liz didn't have the heart to stop her. After all, she adored her father. All the same, Liz felt sorry for Scott Harding who had come with Barbara. He looked strained and withdrawn, and Liz guessed he was feeling pretty bloody.

Liz stared in front of her. The church was filled with tributes from friends, family, colleagues. The air was heavy with their scent, but Liz hardly noticed. Her eyes fastened on the shiny walnut box containing the last of her husband. When she had been told about the accident her mind didn't quite accept it. There was a part of her that still expected to see him walking in the door telling her it had all been a mistake. Now she knew there was no mistake. David was dead, gone, finished.

The finality of it numbed her, just as it numbed Lord Dearing. The only people who gave vent to their feelings were those who didn't really know David. Barbara, his child, too busy with her own life. Freddie, his mistress, too young to understand him. Liz's attention was taken by a loud sobbing at the back of the church. Liz turned to see who it was and to her horror she discovered it was Dan. He was standing on his own, weeping unashamedly into a large silk handkerchief. She wondered what on earth he was upset about. He didn't even like her husband. Then she thought, of course, the ridiculous man feels guilty.

It's not your fault, she wanted to shout at him. You didn't kill David. A lorry did that. In the end you didn't even take me away from him. She sighed. What was the point? What good would it do to tell him that now?

With an effort, Liz focused on the prayer book in her hands. Lord Dearing was reading the lesson, a passage from Revelation, flowery and over-stated. A calculated crowd pleaser if ever Liz heard one.

Finally, the service wound to an end, and six pall-bearers lifted the heavy coffin and carried it out of the church. Liz got to her feet and followed them with slow measured steps, the way she had been taught. Darling David, she thought, this is our last walk together on earth. Despite all the manners she had learned over the years, Liz finally broke down. Tears gathered in the corners of her eyes and coursed down her face. In that moment of true emotion, she realized that she didn't give a damn after all. Holding her head high, she lifted her veil so that everyone could see her face. Let them know how I loved David, she thought. I don't ever want there to be any doubt about it.

She was out in the churchyard now, in full view of the crowd when she saw her coming towards her. Freddie, she thought. So you turned up after all.

The girl seemed ill at ease at first, yet when she came right up to her, Liz realized Freddie wasn't feeling self-conscious at all. She was seething with fury.

'I want to know what you said to him?' she demanded. 'You owe me that at least.'

For a moment, Liz was caught off-balance. Then she realized what Freddie was getting at. When she had last seen David, they were divorcing. Liz willed herself to be calm.

'I didn't say anything you need to get worked up about,' she said. 'We parted on good terms.'

The reply didn't seem to satisfy Freddie, for the girl went on standing there.

Finally she said, 'You're lying to me, Liz. David was a good driver. He would never have got involved in that accident if he hadn't been thoroughly upset.'

Liz wondered whether to tell her the truth. Freddie was way out of line coming up to her like that and virtually accusing her of David's murder. This was a family funeral, not a rough-house. She should have known better.

She regarded the pale, distraught girl in front of her. The black suit she wore seemed to have taken all the colour out of her. Her hair looked a little like straw and there were dark circles under her eyes. You should have put on some make-up, Liz thought. And you might have done something about a hat. If you were my daughter I would have insisted on it.

It was then she realized there was no way she was going to tell her how it ended with David. Freddie was a little girl. A child almost. It was none of her business that she and David had made their peace. It was none of anyone's business.

Liz put her hand out and brushed a stray wisp of hair out of Freddie's eyes.

'Go home,' she told her. 'You're making a fool of yourself and David wouldn't have wanted that.'

She thought Freddie was going to attack her, then something very strange happened. A tall, gaunt woman with iron-grey hair came striding over to them.

Without any ceremony at all she took hold of Freddie's arm and marched her away. It was only five minutes later, Liz realized she knew who Freddie's saviour was. I should have recognized her, she thought, but she's so changed now nobody would know who she was.

She turned around to see if she could get another look at her oldest friend. But Vanessa had disappeared into the crowd along with her daughter.

65

'Really Mom,' Freddie said. 'I still can't understand why you didn't get in touch the minute you got out of prison. Haven't you any idea how worried I was?'

She and Vanessa were sitting having tea in a rented cottage deep in the wilds of East Anglia. It was a lonely place, cosy and comfortable enough on the inside, but all around them as far as the eye could see there was desolate marshland. How could anyone want to live in a place like this, wondered Freddie. What was mother thinking of?

Freddie had been visiting Vanessa for nearly six months now, leaving her job in London every Friday night and coming back after the weekends. Every time she went there, she tried harder to understand her mother, but her progress was slow and painful, for somewhere along the way the two women had lost the ability to communicate. As a child Freddie could demand instant forgiveness, instant explanations, instant affection. Now she was grown-up it was different.

There was an invisible barrier between her mother and herself now, and every time she tried to breach it she came up against the same problem. She had no idea what Vanessa was trying to tell her. Sometimes she felt as if her mother was talking in a foreign language and she didn't have the vocabulary to understand it.

For the umpteenth time, she begged to be told about Riker's Island and for the umpteenth time,

Vanessa did her best to lay the whole thing out for her.

As she struggled through the story, the older woman looked at her daughter and started to feel sad. I should have known this would happen, she thought. I should have known it when I was in prison reading the letters she sent me. How could Freddie understand what it feels like to scrub out a long corridor when your back feels it's going to break? How could she know about prison food? Or prison brutality? When that was happening to me, she was going to cocktail parties and worrying about falling in love.

Vanessa sighed, remembering how beaten she felt when the time approached for her to go back into the world. There was no money, no man, nowhere to live. All she had was a daughter who was caught up in the kind of social whirl she no longer fitted into.

In the end, it was Freddie's grandmother who came to Vanessa's rescue. There was a great deal of family money that had somehow never come Vanessa's way because she had always been too proud to show she needed it. Now her need was all too obvious and her mother insisted that Vanessa claimed her inheritance. At her suggestion the money was transferred to her bank account in New York. All she had to do was go and get it.

Vanessa had spent the last few weeks on Riker's Island wondering what she was going to do with her new found riches. She was independent now. She could do as she pleased, except nothing pleased her any more. Her looks were gone along with her illusions, and there was nothing she wanted any more.

'What do I do now?' she wrote to Sybil.

Her mother's reply was simple as it was cynical.

'Do nothing,' she instructed. 'It was what you were brought up for!'

The notion amused Vanessa. Why not, she thought. I've striven all my life to make something of myself, and all the time I really didn't have to. What was the point of being a rebel when there was always Daddy's money at the end of the rainbow?

She decided she would come back to England. Her inheritance would buy her a little house somewhere. What it wouldn't buy her was a fresh start and that was her problem. The years in prison had isolated her. Given her a horror of people. Now what she wanted was to be left alone to read, to walk, to listen to music. She still had a lingering fondness for her mother as she had for Freddie, but she didn't want to be with them all the time.

In the end, Vanessa put the problem on ice. She lied to everyone about when she was leaving Riker's Island. Then when she came out, she simply dropped out of sight until her mind was made up. If Freddie had looked a little harder for her mother she might have discovered her in the heart of Manhattan. For Vanessa booked herself into the Waldorf when she came back into the world. After the deprivations of the last few years she needed to experience unadulterated luxury. She wanted room service and central heating and marble bathrooms, and the hotel catered to all her demands. She spent three months and several thousand pounds of her father's money indulging herself. When she was ready to face the world again, she got on a plane and flew to England.

What Vanessa hadn't bargained on were people's reactions to her.

Her mother was appalled at the change in her appearance, for when she walked away from being a whore, she walked away from selling herself to anyone. For Vanessa, appearance counted for nothing now. She wore her hair short and straight and let it go its natural grey. She had always been spare and now she did not bother to disguise it. So she looked like a governess. She didn't care. She was beyond being judged by anyone except her daughter.

It was a few weeks before she plucked up courage to approach Freddie and it might have been a few months if David hadn't died, but the event focused her mind. Liz and David had taken her daughter in. In a way they had become surrogate parents. Now one of them was gone, it was time to resume her role in Freddie's life.

And here she was now doing just that. Trying to explain herself to a girl who would never understand half of what she was saying and making a miserable mess of it. She was in the middle of telling Freddie about the problem she had with the prison doctor when she pulled herself up short. I'm not going on with this, she decided. There's no need for Freddie to shoulder the burden of my memories. She's never going to tread the same path as I did, so what good will understanding any of it do her?

She arranged a smile on her face, then she turned to Freddie.

'We've spent quite long enough talking about me,' she told her. 'It's your turn now. You never did tell me what made you decide to have an affair with David Dearing and I'd like to know.'

But Freddie was not forthcoming.

She'd told her mother all she needed to straight after the funeral, and now she didn't want to say anything more.

Vanessa looked at the daughter she had produced with a certain wonder. No wonder David got involved with her, she thought. There's no man on earth who could resist her. She examined Freddie with the eye of a photographer. Her neck was long and would look well with low necklines. She had a decent bosom. Better than Vanessa's had been. And those legs. Freddie could wear shorts, leggings, baggy culottes, and she would always look as if she was ten feet tall. For a moment Vanessa felt sorry that this lovely child had thrown herself away on her best friend's husband. A man old enough to be her father. Then she laughed at herself. Motherhood's made me soft, she thought. From all accounts, David Dearing was glamorous and experienced and ready for an adventure. It probably completed my daughter's education better than any finishing school.

Vanessa thought about Liz then and felt genuinely sorry for her. It couldn't have been fun at all standing by while it all went on. Vanessa remembered what Freddie had told her about Dan and Liz getting together, and she felt suddenly weary and past it. All these glittering people jumping into bed with each other, breaking each other's hearts, losing their way. They were all part of a life she had left behind.

Let Freddie go on with the dance if it amused her. As far as Vanessa was concerned the music had stopped.

'I'm considering buying this little house,' she told her daughter. 'It isn't exactly social round here, so I'm in no danger of being bothered by any neighbours. In fact,' she went on, 'I can go quietly to seed here and nobody will take a blind bit of notice.'

She saw the consternation in Freddie's eyes and started to laugh.

'Stop worrying, darling,' she said. 'I'm not asking you to come and live here too. You can visit sometimes, but that's as far as it goes. The days when you needed someone to look after you are over now.'

Freddie didn't sleep much that night. Her mind was

too full. Every time she dozed off, the events of the last few months came back to haunt her. In her dreams she saw David: charming, mercurial, impossible to pin down. The man she had loved and finally lost before she could convince him to love her back. She saw Liz too. Liz, who for some reason was laughing at her.

Why does she do that, Freddie wondered, waking up for the tenth time. What does Liz know that I don't? But the answer eluded her. Liz knew all sorts of secrets she would never be privy to, and the knowledge tortured her. Damn the woman, Freddie raged. She knows my father better than I ever will. She more or less grew up with my mother. Is there anyone in this world she doesn't have prior knowledge of?

Freddie was bad tempered when she woke up and she took it out on the kitchen, clattering and banging the crockery so loudly that her mother asked her what was bothering her.

'You know damn well what's bothering me,' she shouted. 'David's dead and I'm on my own.'

Vanessa appeared in the kitchen doorway looking less than sympathetic.

'There's no point in crying over spilt milk,' she said tartly. 'Or sulking over it either. It's not going to change anything.'

The two women ate breakfast in virtual silence. Vanessa was tempted to apologize, then she saw her daughter tucking into cereal, followed by eggs on toast and she decided against it. Freddie was displaying too good an appetite to be genuinely heartbroken.

At midday, when Vanessa was thinking of taking a walk into the village, there was a ring on the front doorbell. She wasn't expecting anyone, and anyway, no one knew she lived here. She went to the door, expecting to find the milkman or the grocer, but the young man standing there didn't look like a local. He was wearing blue jeans, though the silver buckle on the belt holding them up must have set him back over a thousand dollars. He didn't get his tan from an English summer either. Then he spoke, and Vanessa had all her answers. The guy was obviously an American, she thought. A pretty classy American from the sound of him. He wanted to see Freddie.

'Who shall I say is calling?' Vanessa asked.

'Scott Harding,' replied the young man. 'Tell her I've come to offer my shoulder. To cry on,' he added somewhat unnecessarily.

Vanessa turned back to fetch Freddie when she saw her daughter was already in the hall. The way she was looking at her visitor spoke volumes. Vanessa sighed. I don't suppose I'll be listening to her moaning about David Dearing for too much longer.

Through the door she could see a low black Porsche parked outside clearly belonging to Scott. She decided to take matters into her own hands.

'Why don't you two drive down to the village?' she suggested. 'There's a pub there that serves decent lunches.' The young man needed no further encouragement. He took hold of Freddie's arm and virtually propelled her out of the door.

'See you in a while,' was all he said.

Freddie had never been more surprised in her life. After the last lunch she had with Scott in New York, she fully expected him to pour scorn on her dilemma. He hadn't approved of David, and he hadn't liked what was going on between them. How could he possibly understand what she was suffering now?

But he did understand, and for the first time since the tragedy Freddie started to feel less alone.

Until she saw Scott, she had been totally adrift in

a sea of uncaring adults. Everyone she had spoken to had been sorry for her, but they had been sorrier for Liz. Even her mother had taken the other woman's side and it had hurt Freddie. It was as if her love for David had been an illusion. Something that hadn't happened. Then Scott came back into her life and reminded her that she was valuable after all.

The pub her mother had told them about was the genuine article. An old-fashioned English local that hadn't been taken over by one of the big breweries. It still had all its original wooden beams and a ramshackle disorganized bar with alcoves and corners where two people could sit and have a private conversation.

When they arrived the place was deserted, and Scott bagged a table as far away from the bar as they could get. Then, without consulting Freddie, he organized home-made sausages, a huge pile of salad and a very cold bottle of white wine. He sat down and ordered her to tell him about David.

If he had done the same thing in New York, Freddie would probably have told him to mind his own business, but Scott wasn't behaving the way he did in New York. He was still pushy, he still wouldn't take no for an answer, but he wasn't criticizing her any more. Freddie felt she could be candid with him now and she finally relaxed and let go of all the confusion and hurt the last few months had brought her.

Scott let her talk for nearly two hours, interrupting her only to ask questions. At the end of it, Freddie felt as if she had been set free. During her affair with David she had confided in no-one and she realized now that all the secrecy had intensified her emotions. If she and David had been ordinary lovers, she might have behaved quite differently.

'I felt I needed to marry David,' she told Scott, 'in

order to stake my claim. As long as Liz had him, I counted for nothing.'

Scott grinned. 'It sounds to me as if it was Liz pushing you into this commitment, not David at all.'

At the mention of Liz's name, Freddie felt angry again. Then she thought, what the hell, Liz is all alone now. At least I have Scott to lean on.

She made a wry face. 'I don't think any of that really matters any more,' she said. 'It's all over for us now.'

She expected Scott to look pleased, but instead he seemed anguished.

'I know about things ending,' he told her softly. 'I was going to get married a few months ago, only it didn't work out.'

Just for a second Freddie stopped thinking about David entirely. Scott going to get married? The notion seemed ridiculous, unthinkable almost.

'Who was she?' she asked. 'Would I know her?'

It suddenly seemed terribly important that she knew exactly what Scott had got himself involved in.

'Her name's Imogen Fellowes,' Scott said shortly. 'Her father owns a bank in New York.'

Freddie started to feel small. 'I suppose she's beautiful as well as having a rich father.'

'Not as beautiful as you.'

Freddie took a sip of her white wine. 'You don't have to placate me, you know. Just because David's dead and I don't have anyone.'

For a moment, Scott didn't say anything and Freddie felt herself speed up inside.

'What I feel about you,' Scott said slowly, 'has got nothing whatever to do with David.'

He reached over and took Freddie's hand.

'Look, this is the worst possible time to tell you this,

but I've no idea when I'm going to see you next and I have to get it out in the open.

'I love you, Freddie. I've probably always loved you, though when I had you, I was too bone-headed to realize it. I only really found out the way I felt when I lost you, and then it was too late.'

Freddie stared at Scott, willing herself to stay calm.

'What about Imogen Fellowes?' she asked.

Scott tightened his grip on her hand as if he were drowning and she was the only chance he had of survival.

'Imogen helped me forget about you for a time,' he said. 'I'd be lying if I admitted otherwise. Then I happened to run into your father who told me how you really felt about me and after that I couldn't marry another girl. Not even Imogen, so I broke things off.'

'You did that for me?'

Scott nodded, and Freddie fought back an irresistible urge to hurl herself into his arms. For something stopped her. A memory that wouldn't quite go away. The shadow of a man she thought she had loved.

Scott seemed to realize what Freddie was going through, for he let go of her hands and pushed his chair back.

'I'm sorry,' he said shortly. 'I didn't mean to lay all that on you. You have enough to deal with right now.'

Freddie looked across to where he sat and instead of the self-confident golden boy that was Scott, she saw another quite different man. He was vulnerable, as needy as she was herself, and now he had laid himself open, it knocked the gloss off him. So this is who you really are, she thought. Ordinary, a bit insecure, a little gauche. David would have never let me see him like this. As Freddie realized that, she realized something else. David had never really loved her.

She had known it all along of course, she just hadn't wanted to admit it.

David had liked her. He had had an affection for her and a lust for her, but he had never given anything up for her. He had never stripped himself bare of all pride, all pretence the way Scott was doing now.

What an idiot I've been, Freddie thought. A complete nickel-plated noodle.

She got to her feet and went over to where Scott sat. Bending down she put her arms round his neck. Then she kissed him.

The hell with explanations, she thought. We can figure out what all this means later.